Trespassing Boundaries

TRESPASSING BOUNDARIES

VIRGINIA WOOLF'S SHORT FICTION

Edited by

KATHRYN N. BENZEL

and

RUTH HOBERMAN

palgrave
macmillan

TRESPASSING BOUNDARIES

© Kathryn N. Benzel and Ruth Hoberman 2004

First published 2004 by
PALGRAVE MACMILLAN™
175 Fifth Avenue, New York, N.Y. 10010 and
Houndmills, Basingstoke, Hampshire RG21 6XS
Companies and representatives throughout the world

PALGRAVE MACMILLAN is the global academic imprint of the Palgrave Macmillan division of St. Martin's Press, LLC and of Palgrave Macmillan Ltd. Macmillan® is a registered trademark in the United States, United Kingdom and other countries. Palgrave is a registered trademark in the European Union and other countries.

ISBN 1–4039–6483–1 hardback

Library of Congress Cataloging-in-Publication Data
    Trespassing boundaries : Virginia Woolf's short fiction / edited by Kathryn N. Benzel and Ruth Hoberman
        p. cm.
    Includes bibliographical references and index.
    ISBN 1–4039–6483–1 (alk. paper)
        1. Woolf, Virginia, 1882–1941—Criticism and interpretation.
    2. Women and literature—England—History—20th century.
    3. Short story. I. Benzel, Kathryn N. II. Hoberman, Ruth.

PR6045.072Z8855 2004
823'.912—dc22   2004040504

A catalogue record for this book is available from the British Library.

Design by Newgen Imaging Systems (P) Ltd., Chennai, India.

First edition: October 2004
10 9 8 7 6 5 4 3 2 1

Printed in the United States of America.

To
Blake and Madeline

Contents

Acknowledgments

We would like to thank the contributors of *Trespassing Boundaries* for their patience and persistence, as we have prepared this collection amid our additional professional and personal responsibilities. For financial support of this long-term project, we thank Dean Ken Nikels and the University of Nebraska-Kearney Research Services Council and Eastern Illinois University's College of Art and Humanities. We also want to thank those who helped prepare the final manuscript for publication: Darcy Schultz, Phillip Ernstmeyer, Justin Sevenker, and Anna Thompson at the University of Nebraska at Kearney; and Ginny DiBianco at Eastern Illinois University.

We thank Joanne Trautmann Banks for permission to reprint her previously published essay in its revised form and Palgrave for permission to reprint a portion of Anna Snaith's essay.

Notes on the Contributors

Joanne Trautmann Banks is editor of *Congenial Spirits: The Selected Letters of Virginia Woolf* (Harcourt 1989) and coeditor with Nigel Nicolson of *The Letters of Virginia Woolf*, six volumes (Harcourt Brace Jovanovich 1975–80).

Kathryn N. Benzel is Professor in English at the University of Nebraska-Kearney where she teaches courses in modernism, literary criticism, the novel, and narrative theory. She has published and presented papers on Virginia Woolf, the Bloomsbury Group, women and the arts, and illustrated texts. Currently she is working on a book on the visual and verbal in Woolf's poetics of reading.

Julia Briggs is Professor of Literature at De Montfort University, Leicester, and an Emeritus Fellow of Hertford College, Oxford. She acted as general editor for the Penguin reprints of Woolf's works, and has written on many aspects of Woolf including her essays, short fiction, and novels. Penguin will publish her study of Woolf, *The Writer at Work*, in Spring 2005.

Krystyna Colburn is a common reader who reads Virginia Woolf for pleasure. She is an annual participant in the Annual International Conference on Virginia Woolf, coordinating its famous "Silent Auction" of Woolf, Bloomsbury, twentieth-century materials. As an active feminist she has organized a feminist lecture series in Boston for over ten years.

Beth Rigel Daugherty teaches at Otterbein College in Westerville, Ohio. She has published essays on the *Common Readers*, "Mr. Bennett and Mrs. Brown," and "How Should One Read a Book?" and is the coeditor of *Approaches to Teaching Woolf's "To the Lighthouse."* Her current project is a book on Woolf's apprenticeship.

Susan Dick has edited the original holograph draft of *To the Lighthouse* and *The Complete Shorter Fiction of Virginia Woolf*. She is a member of the Editorial Committee of the Shakespeare Head Press edition of Virginia Woolf and has edited *To the Lighthouse* and coedited (with Mary S. Millar)

Between the Acts for the series. She is Professor of English at Queen's University, Kingston, Ontario.

Ruth Hoberman is Professor of English at Eastern Illinois University, where she specializes in twentieth-century British literature. She is the author of *Modernizing Lives: Experiments in English Biography 1918–1939* (SIU Press 1987) and *Gendering Classicism: The Ancient World in Twentieth Century Women's Historical Fiction* (SUNY Press 1997). Her current interests include the depiction of museums and shops in early-twentieth-century literature.

Michelle Levy is Assistant Professor of English at Simon Fraser University in Vancouver, British Columbia, Canada. Her most recent project examines the wide range of literary collaboration that flourished in Romantic-era families. She is the author of forthcoming articles on Coleridge, Mary Shelley, and William and Dorothy Wordsworth.

Nena Skrbic completed her Ph.D. on the short fiction of Virginia Woolf at the University of Hull, UK. She was a member of the Editorial Committee of the *Virginia Woolf Bulletin*, UK, and is author of *Wild Outbursts of Freedom: Reading the Short Fiction of Virginia Woolf* (Greenwood Press 2004). Currently she is a tutor of English language and literature at Thomas Danby College of Further Education, Leeds, UK.

Anna Snaith is Lecturer in English at King's College London. She is the author of *Virginia Woolf: Public and Private Negotiations* (Macmillan 2000) and editor of the "Three Guineas Letters to Virginia Woolf" (*Woolf Studies Annual* 6). She is currently working on a book entitled *Colonial Modernism: Women Writing London 1880–1945*.

Alice Staveley is a Fellow in the Humanities at Stanford University. She has published articles identifying the photographs in *Three Guineas*, and on Woolf's *Monday or Tuesday* short fictions, and has coauthored (with Nicola Luckhurst) a study of Woolf's European reception history for *Palgrave Advances in Virginia Woolf Studies*. Her current research includes an article on the Hogarth Press's feminist marketing of *Three Guineas*, and a book-length exploration of Woolf's role as self-publisher and her emergent modernism.

Abbreviations

AHH	*A Haunted House*
AROO	*A Room of One's Own*
BP	*Books and Portraits*
BTA	*Between the Acts*
CE	*Collected Essays (4 vols.* Ed. L. Woolf*)*
CR 1	*The Common Reader*
CR 2	*The Common Reader, Second Series*
CSF	*Complete Shorter Fiction*
D	*The Diary of Virginia Woolf (5 vols.)*
DM	*The Death of the Moth and Other Essays*
E	*The Essays of Virginia Woolf (6 vols.* Ed. A. McNeillie*)*
F	*Flush*
GR	*Granite & Rainbow: Essays*
JR	*Jacob's Room*
L	*The Letters of Virginia Woolf (6 vols.)*
MEL	*Melymbrosia*
MOB	*Moments of Being*
MHP	*Monks House Papers*
MT	*Monday or Tuesday*
MD	*Mrs. Dalloway*
ND	*Night and Day*
O	*Orlando*
PA	*A Passionate Apprentice*
RF	*Roger Fry: A Biography*
TG	*Three Guineas*
TTL	*To the Lighthouse*
TTL Holograph	*Holograph Version of To the Lighthouse*
TW	*The Waves*
TY	*The Years*
VO	*The Voyage Out*

Foreword

Susan Dick

Long viewed as an annex to her novels, Virginia Woolf's shorter fiction has begun to receive critical attention in its own right. *Trespassing Boundaries*, the first collection of essays to be published that is devoted solely to Woolf's shorter fiction, illustrates how fruitful such attention can be, for it demonstrates that, like her novels, Woolf's shorter fictions are rich in meaning and may be discussed from a variety of perspectives. In her wide-ranging overview, for example, Joanne Trautmann Banks explores the ways they express many of Woolf's thematic and stylistic preoccupations. Other essays focus more tightly on particular aspects of a few stories: Michelle Levy and Ruth Hoberman, for instance, examine from different points of view some of the ways Woolf explores the relationship between the human and external worlds. My perspective in this Foreword reflects the process of editing Woolf's shorter fiction. The brief history of the writing and publication of these works that follows will, it is hoped, provide a useful backdrop for the original and insightful essays in this collection.

Virginia Woolf was thirty-five years old when "The Mark on the Wall" appeared in July 1917, as the first publication of the Hogarth Press.[1] Although she had already published *The Voyage Out* (1915) and was a busy and accomplished reviewer, she had attempted to publish only one work of short fiction before "The Mark on the Wall." In 1908, she began writing reviews for *Cornhill Magazine* and in 1909, submitted "Memoirs of a Novelist" to the editor, Reginald Smith, as the first in a series of fictional portraits. When Smith turned it down, she stopped reviewing for *Cornhill* (*E1* xiv–v). Like "Memoirs of a Novelist," the other short fiction she wrote before "The Mark on the Wall" is closely associated stylistically with her early reviews and resembles in both style and subject matter other apprentice works, in particular, as Anna Snaith demonstrates in her essay on the early stories, her experiments with biography.[2] By contrast, "The Mark on the Wall," one of the "treats" she allowed herself while writing her long conventional second novel *Night and Day* (1919), reflects her desire to find a radical new narrative method, one that would express through both its form and its content the multifaceted ways we experience reality (*L4* 231). "How readily our thoughts swarm upon a new object," she wrote as she began to recreate her wide-ranging and associative, often fanciful and comic, speculations about the origin of the mark on her wall (*CSF* 83). Responding in 1917 to David Garnett, who had praised "The Mark on the Wall," she said, "In a way its easier to do a short thing, all in one flight than a novel. Novels are frightfully clumsy and overpowering of course; still if one could only get hold of them it would be superb." She added, "I daresay one ought to invent a completely new form" (*L2* 167).

Reginald Smith's rejection of "Memoirs of a Novelist" highlights the important role the Hogarth Press played in Woolf's career, especially in the early years. She told David Garnett in the same 1917 letter, "its [. . .] the greatest mercy to be able to do what one likes—no editors, or publishers, and only people to read who more or less like that sort of thing." The Hogarth Press not only enabled her to publish her experimental work herself; it also gave her the opportunity to work with her sister, Vanessa Bell, whose wood-cut illustrations for "Kew Gardens" (1919), the second short fiction Woolf published, marked the beginning of their lifelong collaboration. Ironically, the success of these works, as well as Woolf's skill as a reviewer, soon led to her being asked by editors to submit short pieces. "An Unwritten Novel" (which she later called "the great discovery" [*L4* 231]), appeared in July 1920 in *London Mercury*, a monthly founded in 1919 by J. C. Squire, who invited her to write for it. She was also asked by J. M. Murry, the husband of Katherine Mansfield, whose story "Prelude" the Hogarth Press had published in 1918, to write for the *Athenaeum*, the critical weekly whose editorship he had assumed in 1919 (*E3* 519; *D2* 36). She published seventeen reviews there in 1919–20, as well as her story "Solid Objects" (October 1920). The publication of *Night and Day* and her decision in September 1920 to stop writing reviews for the *TLS* and the *Athenaeum* (*D2* 65–66) gave Woolf more time to devote to her short fiction. The result was *Monday or Tuesday* (1921), the only collection of shorter fiction she published.

Monday or Tuesday contains eight works: three of the four she had already published ("The Mark on the Wall," "Kew Gardens," and "An Unwritten Novel") and five others ("A Haunted House," "A Society," "Monday or Tuesday," "The String Quartet," "Blue & Green"). Vanessa Bell designed the book jacket and also contributed four wood-cuts, which illustrate "A Haunted House," "A Society," "An Unwritten Novel," and "The String Quartet." Woolf worried that her friends and the reviewers would not see that she was "after something interesting" in the collection (*D2* 106). And while not wholly favorable, the reviews made her "feel important (& its that that one wants)," she noted (*D2* 108). Sales were good and to her relief her friends praised her. Lytton Strachey and T. S. Eliot both especially liked "The String Quartet," and Roger Fry, whose influence on the collection Kathryn Benzel explores, told her she was "on the track of real discoveries" (*D2* 109, 125).

As Alice Staveley's examination of feminist narratology shows, that track had already led to *Jacob's Room* (1922), which Woolf was writing when *Monday or Tuesday* came out. It led next to *Mrs. Dalloway* (1925), which like its predecessor grew directly from Woolf's experiments with short fiction. As she was finishing *Jacob's Room* she began to plan her next book, a " 'short book,' " she wrote, " 'consisting of six or seven chapters each complete separately, yet there must be some sort of fusion' " (*CSF* 3). She sent T. S. Eliot the first chapter, "Mrs Dalloway in Bond Street," in June 1923, saying "Mrs Dalloway doesn't seem to me to be complete as she is—but judge for yourself" (*L3* 45). Eliot had published one of the most interesting of Woolf's stories of this period, "In the Orchard," in his quarterly *Criterion* in April 1923, but he evidently shared her assessment of "Mrs Dalloway in Bond Street" for he turned it down. (It appeared in July in the American periodical *Dial*, for which Eliot wrote a regular London letter.) The story probably seemed incomplete to Woolf because by the time she sent it to Eliot her plan for the book had undergone a major change: the linked chapters had been replaced by a complex chapterless design. As a result, the second story-chapter in the original plan, "The Prime Minister," remained unfinished (*CSF* 316–23).

Although Mrs. Dalloway's party is nearly over by the time the book ends, Woolf was reluctant to leave it. After completing the novel, she wrote eight stories, each of which focuses on one or two guests at the party. In these stories, the subject of Beth Rigel Daugherty's essay, the relationship between Woolf's short fiction and her longer altered pieces becomes clear. Instead of the novels growing out of the stories, as was the case with *Jacob's Room* and *Mrs. Dalloway*, the stories now continued a momentum begun by the novels. Further, while the stories of 1917–23 reflect first of all Woolf's desire to find a radical new fictional form, those that follow *Mrs. Dalloway* and *To the Lighthouse* (1927) are shaped by a strong interest in portraying the inner lives of her characters. While writing *Mrs. Dalloway* she had discovered what she called "my tunnelling process, by which I tell the past by instalments, as I have need of it" (*D2* 272), and this way of presenting her characters' memories became central to her exploration of "states of consciousness." "But my present reflection is that people have any number of states of consciousness," she wrote in April 1925, "& I should like to investigate the party consciousness, the frock consciousness &c" (*D3* 12). Mabel Waring's "frock consciousness" is the subject of "The New Dress," the only Dalloway story Woolf published. It appeared in May 1927 in the

American journal *Forum*, whose editor H. G. Leach had suggested she send
him a story. Although he published it and paid her $250, he must have had
some reservations about it, for when he requested another story she
declined to send him one, saying, "The stories I have at present are much
in the same style as The New Dress and are open to the same objections"
(*L3* 193, 217). One wonders what questions he raised about "Moments of
Being: 'Slater's Pins Have No Points,' " which appeared in *Forum* in
January 1928. "Sixty pounds just received from America for my little
Sapphist story of which the Editor has not seen the point," Woolf told Vita
Sackville-West, "though he's been looking for it in the Adirondacks"
(*L3* 431).

This story marked another important stage in Woolf's work, her growing recognition of the central role in her writing of "scene making."[3]
"Moments of Being: 'Slater's Pins Have No Points' " grew out of her memory of a comment made by her Greek teacher Clara Pater. "As usual, side
stories are sprouting in great variety as I wind this up," she wrote in
September 1926, as she was completing *To the Lighthouse*, "a book of characters; the whole string being pulled out from some simple sentence, like
Clara Pater's, 'Don't you find that Barker's pins have no points to them?' "
(*D3* 106). In the story, discussed by Krystyna Colburn within the context
of the lesbian intertext in Woolf's stories, Fanny Wilmot, surprised to hear
her music teacher Julia Craye make a similar observation about Slater's
pins, tries to imagine Miss Craye doing something so ordinary as buying
pins. While she searches for the lost pin, she tells herself what she imagines
to be Miss Craye's life story. Just as she finds the pin, she looks at Miss
Craye and sees a radiantly happy woman, not the lonely one she had imagined. As if to confirm this vision, Miss Craye suddenly kisses Fanny. She
then repeats her observation as Fanny pins the rose "back to her breast with
trembling fingers" and the story ends (*CFS* 220).

Woolf did not publish another story for nearly two years. She had written *Orlando* (1928) and started work on *The Waves* (1931) when "The
Lady in the Looking-Glass: A Reflection" appeared in *Harper's Magazine* in
December 1929. This story also originated in a remembered scene. After
visiting the painter Ethel Sands in Normandy in July 1927, Woolf wrote,
"How many little stories came into my head! For instance: Ethel Sands not
looking at her letters. What this implies. One might write a book of short
significant separate scenes. She did not open her letters" (*D3* 157). "The
Lady in the Looking-Glass" closes with Isabella Tyson, whom the narrator
has been contemplating as she watches her in a mirror, not opening her letters for "they were all bills" (*CSF* 225). Woolf would use this brief scene
again near the end of *Between the Acts* when the second post brings Isa
Oliver "only bills" (*BTA* 115).

Besides having dramatic potential for revealing hidden aspects of character, the short significant scene is an excellent vehicle for caricature, the method of giving "in a very few strokes the essentials of a person's character," as Woolf defined it (*D3* 300). Woolf's growing interest in caricature in the late 1920s and early 1930s marks another important stage in her writing. She used it brilliantly in *The Waves* where the six speakers, whose identities are blended by the uniform style in which they speak, repeat actions and phrases that make each a representative, or caricature, of a particular character type. Three months after publication of *The Waves*, Woolf wrote in her diary, "I could write a book of caricatures. Christabel's story of the Hall Caines suggested a caricature of Country house life, with the redbrown pheasants" (*D4* 57). A month later, in January 1932, she drew up a list of titles under the heading "Caricatures": "The Shooting Party./ 2.Scenes from English life/The pheasants/Scenes: Life on a Battleship" (*CSF* 306). She added "The Great Jeweller" to a similar list of "Caricatures" made in February. Early drafts of "The Shooting Party" are dated January 1932; drafts of "The Duchess and the Jeweller" as well as "Scenes from the Life of a British Naval Officer" were probably also written at this time. While the latter sketch remained unpublished, Woolf revised the first two in 1937, when her American literary agent, Jacques Chambrun, requested some stories. Both were published in *Harper's Bazaar* in 1938 (*CSF* 308–09).

Woolf wrote at least seventeen complete stories and sketches between September 1926, when she completed *To the Lighthouse*, and her death in March 1941, but published only five, the four already discussed plus "Lappin and Lapinova," which also appeared in *Harper's Bazaar* (1939). "And then oh the bore of writing out a story to make money," she wrote while "rehashing Lappin & Lapinova, a story written . . . 20 years ago or more" (*D5* 189, 188). Although she complained of writing for money and referred to the other two *Harper's Bazaar* stories as "pot boiling stories for America" (*L6* 252), the multiple typescripts of these stories, and of others left unpublished, indicate that she put them through the rigorous process of revision she applied to all her work. Much to her annoyance, two, perhaps three, other late stories were inexplicably rejected by *Harper's Bazaar*. Through her agent, *Harper's* requested a "dog story." She wrote "Gipsy, the Mongrel" and was paid £170 for it, but it was never printed (*D5* 272). *Harper's* also rejected "The Legacy," which she sent in response to an "urgent request" for an article or story (*D5* 329). And while there is no record of her having submitted "The Searchlight" for publication, it appears to have been prepared for submission and may have been the story *Harper's* judged "too sophisticated" when the editor asked for a dog story instead (*D5* 241).

Throughout the 1930s and into 1940–41, Woolf continued to write short fiction that was not tailored to meet the demands of any agent or journal. "The difficulty wh. now faces me," she wrote in 1937, "is how to find a public, a way of publishing, all the new ideas that are in me? I've written this morning 3 descriptions for Nessa's pictures: they can be printed by us no doubt, & somehow put in circulation." She continued, "But then theres in my drawer several I think rather good sketches; & a chapter on biography" (*D5* 57). The stories she revised for *Harper's* were probably among these sketches. She and her sister were apparently discussing "a book of illustrated incidents," entitled "Faces & Voices," in which she would write descriptions for twelve lithographs by Vanessa Bell. A group of untitled portraits found among her papers may be related to this project (*D5* 57–61; *CSF* 242–46). In 1940, she began to contemplate publishing another short book "of stories," as she noted in April, adding "I would like to recapture my own fling" (*D5* 277). This book became the posthumous *A Haunted House and Other Short Stories*, edited and published by Leonard Woolf (January 1944). Following her wishes, he included six of the eight stories from *Monday or Tuesday* (she had intended, he wrote in his Foreword, to omit "A Society" and probably "Blue & Green," as well), seven that had been published in journals, and five that had not been published before. The latter are three of the Dalloway stories, plus "The Searchlight" and "The Legacy," both of which had been prepared for publication.

Leonard Woolf's understandable reluctance to include more previously unpublished stories meant that for years much of Woolf's shorter fiction formed part of that vast collection of unpublished material that has been slowly revealed as her diaries, letters, memoirs, manuscript drafts, uncollected essays, sketches, and stories have been edited and published. We can hope that she would have been pleased that all her shorter fiction has now found, as the essays in *Trespassing Boundaries* show, the understanding readers she continually sought.

NOTES

1. The thirty-four page pamphlet *Two Stories* contained "Three Jews" by Leonard Woolf, "The Mark on the Wall," and four woodcuts by Dora Carrington (Kirkpatrick 13–14).
2. Early sketches can be found in *MOB*, *PA*, and *Carlyle's House and Other Sketches*.
3. "But whatever the reason may be," Woolf wrote in "A Sketch of the Past," "I find that scene making is my natural way of marking the past. A scene always comes to the top; arranged, representative" (MOB 145).

Introduction

Kathryn N. Benzel and
Ruth Hoberman

But let us bear in mind a piece of advice that an eminent Victorian who was also an eminent pedestrian once gave to walkers: "Whenever you see a board up with 'Trespassers will be prosecuted,' trespass at once." Let us trespass at once. Literature is no one's private ground; literature is common ground. It is not cut up into nations; there are no wars there. Let us trespass freely and fearlessly and find our own way for ourselves.

—*"The Leaning Tower"*

Defying anyone who—like the Oxbridge beadle of *A Room of One's Own*—would bid us get off the grass, we and our contributors have taken Woolf's advice seriously. From a variety of critical perspectives, we have sought to understand the ways in which Woolf herself trespassed, defying boundaries between reader and text, boundaries among readers (scholarly vs. "common," for example), and between kinds of texts ("highbrow" vs. "lowbrow," or short story vs. novel). The act of trespassing, we argue, is central to Woolf's view of how literature works, and particularly relevant to an understanding of her short fiction.

In the process we have, indeed, tended to "find our own way for ourselves," for criticism of Woolf's short fiction is surprisingly sparse. Few of Woolf's stories appeared in book form during her lifetime; only *Kew Gardens* and *Monday or Tuesday* were published as books and thus reviewed by contemporaries. The earliest commentators—T. S. Eliot, E. M. Forster, and Katherine Mansfield among them—emphasized Woolf's experimentalism and lyricism. After her death, critics tended to read the stories in terms of some essential Woolfian characteristic, finding there the same epistemological concerns, epiphanic moments, or androgynous unities they detected in the novels.[1] As Beth Rigel Daugherty points out in her essay in this volume, Avrom Fleishman, in his 1980 essay "Forms of the Woolfian Short Story," was the first to insist that Woolf's use of the short story "deserves a study of its own" (44), but until now, Dean Baldwin's 1989 *Virginia Woolf: A Study of the Short Fiction* has been the only book-length response to Fleishman's challenge.

In his 1980 essay, Fleishman divides Woolf's stories into two categories—linear and circular—and assigns each to a stage in Woolf's career. The linear stories, written in 1925 or before, depict a series of items or definitions, he argues, with the final term supplying the key to the whole. The circular stories, mainly written after 1925, end with words that echo their opening, evoking moments of insight that are complicated by their depiction in dialectic, ultimately ambiguous terms (69). Baldwin, in his 1989 book, also groups the stories in terms of chronological periods, though he lists three categories: an experimental period (1917–21), during which Woolf's main interest was in knowledge and perception; a Mrs. Dalloway's party period (1923–29), during which she focused on characterization; and finally, an oddly conventional period (1938–41), during which she foregrounded plot (4). Reading the stories biographically—in relation both to Woolf's life and to her developing identity as a writer—Baldwin links Woolf's persistent interest in epistemology and characterization to her famous essays "Modern Fiction" and "Mr. Bennett and Mrs. Brown," showing how the essays' theoretical concerns surface in the stories as well.

Besides these attempts to categorize the stories, there have been various essays on individual stories, which—like Baldwin's and Fleishman's work—have tended to place Woolf's stories within rather traditional conceptualizations of high modernism.[2] They assume that the critic's goal is to detect the underlying unity in the apparently inchoate short-story, or its integral relationship to the body of Woolf's work. While this past work has been extremely useful in helping readers recognize the intricacy and power of Woolf's short fiction, the stories have not yet received the complex, contextualized readings they deserve.[3]

The publication of Susan Dick's *The Complete Shorter Fiction of Virginia Woolf* (1985; second edition 1989), however, has brought new attention to Woolf's achievement as a short story writer and to the important role short-story writing played in her career. Long seen as occasional experiments or playful releases from the serious work of novel writing, Woolf's short stories can now be read in their own right: as ambitious and self-conscious attempts to challenge generic boundaries, undercutting traditional distinctions between short fiction and the novel, between experimental and popular fiction, between fiction and nonfiction, and, most of all, between text and reader. Our collection of essays is an attempt to come to terms with Dick's edition: its inclusiveness (the volume contains previously unpublished stories as well as generic borderline cases); its interest in revisions and

publication venues (as chronicled in its copious notes); its resolutely tenta-
tive naming of its own genre as "shorter fiction" rather than the more
assertive "short stories."

In retrospect, it seems astonishing that Woolf's short stories have been
read so rarely within the context of modernist writers' intense interest in the
genre. Woolf was herself immersed in the literary culture of the time,
through her father's career as editor and biographer, and through her own
and her friends' involvement in publishing, editing, and reviewing.
Especially important to this literary culture were the magazine and small
press, with their inevitable quota of short stories. Her father, Leslie
Stephen, edited the *Cornhill* magazine (albeit before her birth); Woolf herself reviewed for it until 1909, when, Susan Dick tells us, its editor
Reginald Smith rejected her story "Memoirs of a Novelist." During the
time that John Middleton Murry—spouse of her rival and friend Katherine
Mansfield—edited the *Athenaeum*, Woolf reviewed for it, read Mansfield's
stories in it, and published her own "Solid Objects" there. Virginia and
Leonard Woolf's Hogarth Press, with its laboriously handset type, encouraged the writing not only of experimental, but also of *short* fiction by Woolf
herself and by her friends. Hogarth's first publication, *Two Stories* (1917),
included Virginia Woolf's "The Mark on the Wall" and Leonard Woolf's
"Three Jews." It was followed soon after not only by "Kew Gardens" but
also by Mansfield's 1918 "Prelude." Mansfield, who defined herself solely
as a short story writer, was the woman whose literary conversation Woolf
most valued and whose writing she most envied. "Have you at all come
round to her stories?" Woolf asked Roger Fry in August 1920; "I suppose
I'm too jealous to wish you to, yet I'm sure they have merit all the same"
(*L2* 438).

Woolf's early career, in fact, coincided with a wave of experimentalism
in British short fiction. Brander Matthews's 1901 *The Philosophy of the
Short-Story* looked backwards to Poe's "unity of effect" for its definition of
what Matthews calls—insistent on distinguishing it as a narrowly defined
genre—the Short-story, but in fact, during the 1880s and 1890s, short fiction, under pressure from symbolism and prose poetry, was mutating in
various directions. In analyzing stories of this period, Eileen Baldeshwiler
describes a split between "lyrical" stories, focusing on internal change, and
"epical" stories, focusing on external action (231). Clare Hanson contrasts
"impressionist" and "imperialist" short fiction, usefully pointing out the
role of coterie magazines, with their differing aims and audiences, in reinforcing the contrast (11). *Yellowbook* and the *Savoy*, for example, encouraged the writing of self-consciously aesthetic, experimental stories. This
experimentalism appealed to "new woman" writers in particular; women
like George Egerton, Olive Schreiner, Dorothy Richardson, and Victoria

Cross found in the writing of fragments, dream visions, and episodic plunges into a single character's consciousness a way of conveying the inexpressible intensities of women's experience.

But there was also cross-fertilization between "lyrical" and "epical" types, as Suzanne Ferguson points out. What Ferguson calls the "aesthetic" story of the 1890s borrowed from ghost stories their psychological intensity and symbolism, and from detective stories, their concision, gaps, and "moment of illumination near the end" ("Rise" 188–89). Also linking "high" and "low" art forms, Elizabeth Bowen pairs the short-story, as an emergent genre, with cinema: "neither is sponsored by a tradition; both are, accordingly, free; both, still, are self-conscious, show a self-imposed discipline and regard for form; both have, to work on, immense matter—the disoriented romanticism of the age" (256). Certainly by 1906, when Woolf began writing short stories, the genre was both prestigious and vibrant.

But it was Chekhov, of course, as Nena Skrbic points out in this volume, who played the most obvious role in revolutionizing the short story, and Mansfield was his champion.[4] Mansfield wrote often about his influence on her and, with her friend S. S. Koteliansky, translated Chekhov's letters, which were published in the *Athenaeum* in 1919. During the years between the Hogarth Press's 1918 publication of "Prelude" and Mansfield's 1923 death, she and Woolf shared a peculiarly strained, yet intense conversation about writing, with the figure of Chekhov always hovering in the background. In May 1919 Mansfield wrote to Woolf, citing one of Chekhov's letters: "[W]hat the writer does is not so much to *solve* the question but to *put* the question. There must be the question put. [. . .] Come & talk it over with me" (quoted in Smith 64). In November of 1920, Leonard Woolf and Koteliansky translated Chekhov's notebooks together, publishing their work at the Hogarth Press in the summer of 1921.[5] When Mansfield, in 1920, invited Woolf to write stories for the *Athenaeum*, Woolf reports in her diary that she replied, "But I don't know that I can write stories"; Mansfield, however, responded that "Kew Gardens" was "the right 'gesture'; a turning point" (*D2* 44). And in fact Woolf's "Solid Objects" appeared in the *Athenaeum* in 1920.

Woolf herself reviewed several volumes of Chekhov stories in the *Times Literary Supplement*, in 1918–19. As she described Chekhov's method she was also laying out the conversation about the genre she was herself in the process of entering. In a 1919 review of a Chekhov volume, for example, she writes, "We are by this time alive to the fact that inconclusive stories are legitimate; that is to say, though they leave us feeling melancholy and perhaps uncertain, yet somehow or other they provide a resting point for the mind—a solid object casting its shade of reflection and speculation" (*BP* 123). Chekhov's stories "have the air of having come together by chance" she writes, yet finally cohere in their relation to something "more important and far more remote than personal success or happiness" (125)—a something she specifies in later writing about Russian literature as the "soul." In "The Russian Point of View" (1925), Woolf again articulates what's peculiar about Chekhov: "Our first impressions," she writes, "are not of simplicity but of bewilderment. What is the point of it, and why does he make a story out of this? we ask as we read story after story" (*CR1* 180). The proper response to these "inconclusive" stories, however, is not readerly frustration but readerly involvement:

> Where the tune is unfamiliar and the end a note of interrogation or merely the information that they went on talking, as it is in Tchekov, we need a very daring and alert sense of literature to make us hear the tune, and in particular those last notes which complete the harmony. (180)

The result, however, when we read properly, is powerful: "as we read these little stories about nothing at all, the horizon widens; the soul gains an astonishing sense of freedom" (182).

In "An Essay in Criticism" (about Ernest Hemingway's *Men Without Women*), Woolf labels this technique the "Tchekov method." The method she goes on to describe emphasizes Chekhov's refusal to provide closure and his emphasis on the reader's role in constructing the story's meaning: "everything is cloudy and vague, loosely trailing rather than tightly furled. The stories move slowly out of sight like clouds in the summer air, leaving a wake of meaning in our minds which gradually fades away" (*E4* 454). In "Modern Fiction," Woolf elaborates:

> No one but a modern, no one perhaps but a Russian, would have felt the interest of the situation which Tchekov has made into the short story which he calls "Gusev." [. . .] The emphasis is laid upon such unexpected places that at first it seems as if there were no emphasis at all; and then, as the eyes accustom themselves to twilight and discern the shapes of things in a room we see how complete the story is, how profound, and how truly in obedience to his vision Tchekov has chosen this, that, and the other, and placed them together to compose something new. (*E4* 162–63)

Particularly significant to the discussions in this collection, she concludes her remarks with a tongue-in-cheek comment about the generic transgressiveness of Chekhov's stories: "But it is impossible to say 'this is comic,' or 'that is tragic,' nor are we certain, since short stories, we have been taught, should be brief and conclusive, whether this, which is vague and inconclusive, should be called a short story at all" (*E4* 163). Here we see Woolf's challenge to the traditional assumption (since Poe at least) that a good short story provides a sense of unity and closure.

Woolf thus not only wrote stories herself, throughout her life, but also talked about them and reviewed them thoughtfully. She wrote her short fiction, in other words, within a generic framework that had a history and aesthetic of its own, a framework of which she was well aware, and one which—at this point in its history—asked the reader to take a particularly vital role in the construction of meaning. The essays in our collection seek to read Woolf's stories within the context of their chosen genre rather than as second best, as poor reflections of or preparation for her novels. In doing so, our authors reveal a diversity in Woolf's short fiction, which takes full advantage of the instability and open-endedness of the short story form at the time she was writing.

So varied in length, subject, and structure are Woolf's stories, in fact, that it is not always clear they should even be called "stories." Collectively, the essays in our volume suggest that as a genre, the short story served as the ultimate expression not of some Woolfian or generic "essence" but of her effort to destabilize, to render intangible, to "equivocate," to use Pamela Caughie's term (8). Woolf, according to Caughie, unwilling to replace old shibboleths with new, is content to undermine traditional terms (male/female; appearance/reality; false/true) without replacing them (5–6). Following Caughie's lead, we have been interested not in what Woolf's stories *say* about life, literature, gender, or sexuality, but in what they *do*: how they rouse the reader to participate in the making of textual meaning. Caughie cites Woolf's story "An Unwritten Novel" as one example of how Woolf "explores and discloses the ways in which the reader makes [. . .] connections" (92). We seek to read all the stories as "unwritten," as dissolving rather than constructing, so that the pieces may be assembled— with appropriate tentativeness—in the reader's own mind.

Woolf discusses this process by which readers make meaning out of texts in her literary criticism. "Do not dictate to your author," Woolf writes in "How Should One Read a Book?"; "try to become him. Be his fellow-worker and accomplice" (*CR2* 235). And in "Byron & Mr Briggs," Woolf writes of the reading process, "all this is nothing but a random game," that yields "more vividly and startlingly [. . .] a sense of something very real [. . .] of people" (*E3* 485). To read Woolf's short fiction, then, is not to read conventional narrative plot and characterization, but to experience the often uneasy alliance of form and content in a brief and fleeting moment. The short story's brevity is uniquely suited to the representation of such experience in these volatile and often self-contradictory terms. As Woolf continually violates her reader's formal expectations in order to facilitate the reader's "flash of understanding," she borrows from and juxtaposes such apparently incompatible genres as philosophic essay, novel, art criticism, ghost stories, biography, children's literature, and caricature. In the process, she questions the possibility of any single, inclusive definition for the short story.

This debate about definitions of the short story has garnered considerable attention for the past twenty-five years at least. Questions about its generic characteristics in contrast to the novel (how short must a short story be to differ from a novel?) and questions about "storyness" (how much must happen for it to differ from a prose poem?) have been at the center of these discussions.[6] Seeking to name characteristics unique to the short story, critics have proposed cohesiveness (Poe and Matthews), an emphasized conclusion (Ejxenbaum, see May, *New* xvii), and tension between story and theme (May, *New* xix). Wendell Harris argues that a *British* short story did not even exist until the 1890s, when writers like Kipling and Stevenson rejected the novel's tendency to depict individuals over long stretches of time amid a "broad human panorama" (187; 182). Echoing Frank O'Connor's famous formulation that short stories give voice to the lonely, isolated individual, Harris argues that the genre tends to depict the "outsider" or the "moment whose intensity makes it seem outside the ordinary stream of time," and that British—unlike American—writers became interested in depicting such isolated people and moments only in the late nineteenth century (188).

Harris's argument suggests a natural affinity among Woolf's feminism (which leads her to identify with outsiders), her modernism (which leads her to depict epiphany-like "moments of being"), and the short story form. Suzanne Ferguson, however, noting just such a linkage between modernism and the short story, comes to a conclusion different from Harris's: in the 1890s, she argues, far from coming into its own, the short story became indistinguishable in its aims from the modern novel and thus all but disappeared as a definable genre. She points out that both story and novel share a new emphasis on point of view, on inner experience, on style, and on figurative language, and that both reject the traditional, chronological plot ("Defining" 219). If Ferguson is right, there is no purpose served by examining Woolf's short fiction in isolation from her novels. But even Ferguson admits that the short story's relative shortness, when combined with modernist "impressionism," has a unique impact on its readers. The "deletion of expected elements of the plot," she writes, "[. . .] is the hallmark of the late nineteenth and early twentieth-century short story" (221). Given that, as most critics including Ferguson agree, readers look with particular intensity for the theme in short fiction, such deletions, along with the "foregrounding of style" (226) and the fact that the stories so often emphasize the privacy and inaccessibility of insight (228), make the experience of reading the modern short story uniquely intense and contradictory.

Unlike the novel, which, because of its length and inclusiveness, may be read as a "slice of life," as an experience in its own right, or too complex to be reducible to a single theme, the short story seems to invite thematic interpretation. What it includes is so obviously *selected*, the reader responds with a peculiarly intense effort to understand the principle underlying the author's choices. Yet, as Ferguson points out, the complexity, elisions, and even themes of the modernist short story make it resistant to interpretation. This tension between story and meaning, as well as generic uncertainties (What is a short story? What kind of story it should tell? What distinguishes it from prose poem or novella?) inevitably color the experience of reading a modern short story. Woolf herself, in a passage we already quoted, equated the reading of Chekhov with just such instabilities: "But it is impossible to say 'this is comic,' or 'that is tragic,' nor are we certain, since short stories, we have been taught, should be brief and conclusive, whether this, which is vague and inconclusive, should be called a short story at all" (*E4* 163). Finally, we want to suggest, Woolf mobilizes rather than settles these questions, using her readers' clashing formal expectations to involve them in the interpretive process.

Trespassing Boundaries opens with Susan Dick's foreword, which chronicles the crucial role the writing of short fiction played in Woolf's literary career. The remainder of the volume falls into two sections. Part I, The Modernist Context, addresses two concerns: how Woolf's experimentalism both borrows and differs from that of her contemporaries, and how her short fiction responds to the particular technological, socioeconomic and historical changes associated with modernity. Part II, Crossing Generic Boundaries, examines Woolf's stories as they intersect with specific genres: the novel, biography, and the visual arts.

The first essay of Part I, "Through a Glass, Longingly," by Joanne Trautmann Banks, excerpted from a longer essay originally published in 1985, provides a beautifully written and helpful reading of a number of Woolf's best-known stories, analyzing them in terms of Frank O'Connor's "significant moment": a point in time from which "past, present, and future are glimpsed at once." This definition suits Woolf's interest in "moments of being"—brief glimpses of a deeper reality beneath the cotton wool of daily life. Stories such as "The Searchlight," "Monday or Tuesday," "The Introduction," and "A Haunted House" depict the mind's oscillation between inner and outer worlds, offering at their climax an instantaneous "illusion of perpetual being." But while traditional readings of Woolf stop here, underlining the stories' cohesiveness around a Joycean epiphany or experience of wholeness, Banks argues the stories cease on a note of yearning. Her essay concludes that the very brevity and concentration of the short story form enhances Woolf's revelation of transcendence and its intimate connections with loss. The only previously published essay of our collection, we include it because of its elegant articulation of how the modernist moment and the short story form coalesce.

Nena Skrbic follows with a careful analysis of Woolf's debt to Chekhov and other Russian writers. Arguing that Woolf's deepest interest in Russian writing coincided with her most productive story-writing period, 1917–25, Skrbic relates Woolf's stories "Happiness," "The Lady in the Looking-Glass," and "Uncle Vanya" to work by Chekhov, Turgenev, and Brussof. The Russian writers, she suggests, tend to communicate not through a palpable authorial presence, but by giving the reader a sense of direct contact with both the minds of their characters and their physical surroundings. The stories that result leave the reader with a sense of inconclusiveness that mimics the characters' own confusions and uncertainties. Both the Russians and Woolf suggest, finally, that whatever might either answer the needs of their characters or grant the reader full understanding is outside the story, even outside language. Skrbic's readings thus offer one explanation for the sense of yearning Banks detects hovering about Woolf's epiphanic moments: Woolf, like Chekhov, depicts her characters' inner lives confronting an environment that is vivid but stubbornly unresponsive to their desire for meaning—an unresponsiveness underlined by her own authorial reticence.

Alice Staveley's "Conversations at Kew: Reading Woolf's Feminist Narratology" complements both Banks and Skrbic, by insisting that we read the stories for their social criticism as well as for their structure and subtlety. Staveley argues that reading Woolf's short fiction in terms of its modernist traits tends to emphasizes lyricism at the expense of social commentary. Reading "Kew Gardens" from the standpoint of a feminist narratology, she argues that its fragmentary, apparently random conversations are in fact crucial to an understanding of the story. While many critics have asserted that the stories Woolf wrote between 1917 and 1921 played a crucial role in her move toward the experimentalism of *Jacob's Room* (1922), few have looked closely at individual stories to see how exactly they do this. In "Kew Gardens," Staveley argues, "Woolf devises a new narrative form based on conversation as creative critique." She analyzes these conversations to show how they link domestic and public oppressions in ways that anticipate such later work as *To the Lighthouse* and *Three Guineas*. Alluding obliquely to class, gender, and war, these conversations undercut the story's lyricism in ways its many formalist critics have chosen to ignore. Only Mansfield, in a 1919 review, Staveley points out, noted that the gardens' beauty is "disturbing," their world uncertainly poised and charged with a "secret life"—terms that hint at the story's subversive relation to standard accounts of both gardens and war.

The final two essays in Part I deal with issues now seen to be crucial to Woolf's work: its treatment of sexuality and of consumer culture. Looking back on Woolf's most famous contemporaries—Lawrence, Mansfield, Joyce, Eliot, and Forster—it seems clear that they were engaged in an ongoing conversation about sexuality. Krystyna Colburn's "The Lesbian Intertext of Virginia Woolf's Short Fiction" argues that Woolf's stories celebrate women's relationships with each other while critiquing what Adrienne Rich has so aptly named "compulsory heterosexuality." Woolf, of course, famously referred to "Moments of Being: 'Slater's Pins Have No Points' " as a "nice little story about Sapphism," but Colburn traces the Sapphic thread throughout Woolf's short stories, from the earliest in 1906 to those written just before her death. Woolf's treatment of the kiss, of flower and jewel imagery, and of the "apparitional lesbian" (to use Terry Castle's term), encodes lesbian themes, according to Colburn. As she revised her stories for publication, however, Woolf often obscured their lesbian content. With its peculiarly intense relation to its reader, the short story genre both resists (with its fear of detection) and invites (with its invitation to interpolate) lesbian readings; Colburn demonstrates how the lesbian reader can find her own desires mirrored by reading for silences, symbols, sounds, and erasures.

Ruth Hoberman also emphasizes the role of the reader in "Collecting, Shopping, and Reading: Virginia Woolf's Stories about Objects." Hoberman discusses Woolf's depictions of collectors and shoppers in four short stories—"Solid Objects," "Mrs Dalloway in Bond Street," "The Lady in the Looking-Glass," and "The Duchess and the Jeweller." In the process, she explores two versions of modernist art: one that turns its back on the marketplace and conceptualizes art as the sum of heroically collected and preserved fragments of life; another that defines itself in and through the marketplace, its meanings multiple, negotiated, and coproduced by its consumers. Hoberman concludes that Woolf's sense of artistry is bound up in both the production and the marketing of literature for readers. The short story, whether it is self-published or sold to a magazine, brings writer and reader into a particularly intense relationship, one in which the act of reading is itself an act of consumption.

With Part II, the essays shift their focus to the intersection of Woolf's short fiction with specific genres or media: the novel, biography, historiography, and painting. The first essay of Part II, Beth Rigel Daugherty's " 'a corridor leading from *Mrs. Dalloway* to a new book': Transforming Stories, Bending Genres" examines the eight short stories written just before and after *Mrs. Dalloway* in order to articulate the peculiarly interactive process by which Woolf's stories both derived from and fed into her fiction. These stories, Daugherty suggests, are neither preludes nor afterthoughts to the novels, but "corridors" between them: a crucial means of moving between forms to find the appropriate shape for her ideas. "I am less & less sure that they *are* stories, or what they are," Daugherty writes, quoting Woolf. Ultimately, Daugherty argues, Woolf's use of repeated and transformed images in the novels and short fiction enacts a challenge to "genre, boundaries, and hierarchies" rather than imitating any generic, formalistic features of the novel.

"'A view of one's own': Writing Women's Lives and the Early Short Stories," by Anna Snaith, relates Woolf's early short fiction to her equally early interest in biography and historiography, particularly her effort to locate an alternative tradition of women's history and life-writing, one that melds private and public, biography and autobiography, fiction and non-fiction. Snaith argues that Woolf's early stories—such as "Phyllis and Rosamond," "The Journal of Mistress Joan Martyn" and "Memoirs of a Novelist"—should be read not as juvenilia but as originating texts for Woolf's complex ideas about women's history and auto/biography. Snaith concludes that their generic hybridity and self-consciousness allowed Woolf to redefine women and their significance in society.

In "Virginia Woolf's Shorter Fictional Explorations of the External World: 'closely united . . . immensely divided'," Michelle Levy joins Daugherty in complicating our sense of how Woolf's short stories relate to her novels, arguing that in her effort to depict the nonhuman, Woolf turned repeatedly to short fiction, even within the novels themselves. The "Time Passes" section from *To the Lighthouse*, the lyric interludes in *The Waves*, and all of *Flush* (generally read as a novel, but here treated as short fiction) share with a number of the more conventional stories an effort to get at nonhuman modes of existence without the intervention of a human consciousness. Levy argues that only the short story allowed Woolf the innovative use of perspective necessary to put the nonhuman world at the center of her narrative. "Human beings," Woolf writes in *A Room of One's Own*, are constructed "in relation to reality; and the sky, too, and the trees or whatever it may be in themselves" (*AROO* 114). In her readings of "The Mark on the Wall," "Kew Gardens," "In the Orchard," and "Nurse Lugton's Curtain"—as well as longer works—Levy suggests that Woolf develops an anti-anthropocentric discourse, dissolving human/nonhuman boundaries, and privileges the perspective of objects and animals. The short fiction form—whether within novels or independent of them—by liberating Woolf from more conventional types of plot and characterization, allows her to align herself with this perspective, with minimal distortion from human consciousness.

Kathryn N. Benzel's "Verbal Painting in 'Blue & Green' and 'Monday or Tuesday'" draws on Woolf's art criticism and connections with

Bloomsbury artists to investigate her 1921 short story collection *Monday or Tuesday*. These eight stories reveal Woolf's use of story telling in a non-novelistic way to represent the human consciousness at work, and in doing this, Woolf confronts and explores the difficulty of such representation in literature. In "Blue & Green" and "Monday or Tuesday" Woolf's "verbal painting," her use of color, line, and shape, is seen as a means of rendering "life or spirit, truth or reality, [. . .] the essential thing" ("Modern Fiction," *E4* 160) into an aesthetic quality with Post-Impressionist associations. Benzel contends these stories are examples of Woolf's attempt to bring together the visual and verbal arts into a coherent aesthetic theory and to represent an interdisciplinary focus of the arts in her contemporary context.

Finally, Julia Briggs looks at three sets of stories written by Woolf relatively late in her career: a group that deals with framed reflections ("The Lady in the Looking-Glass," "Three Pictures," and "Fascination of the Pool"); a group that caricatures the British Establishment ("Life on a Battleship," "The Duchess and the Jeweller," and "The Shooting Party"); and a pair that uses images of looking and focusing to explore the making of art ("The Searchlight" and "The Symbol"). Collectively, the stories reveal Woolf's persistent fascination with the "sudden intensities" of the short story form, even as she borrowed imagery and techniques from painting, photography, and caricature in her effort to keep those experiments "new."

Because our contributors approach Woolf's short fiction from a range of critical perspectives, the same stories may appear to radically different effect in different essays. Colburn reads "Mrs Dalloway in Bond Street," for example, as a scene of lesbian seduction; Hoberman reads it as a celebration of shopping. Levy reads "Kew Gardens" for its depiction of the natural world; Staveley for its human conversations and their implied critique of gender and class boundaries. Banks's "Monday or Tuesday" captures a moment of perceptual intensity; Benzel's invites a particular kind of participation from its reader. Snaith's "Memoirs of a Novelist" critiques traditional biography while Colburn's cloaks lesbian love. Skrbic, Briggs and Hoberman note that the mirror in "The Lady in the Looking-Glass" serves as a metaphor for art itself, but draw different conclusions: for Skrbic the mirror evokes a Chekhovian effort to find meaning in the face of disorder; for Briggs it suggests the loss of immediacy suffered by life when it becomes a "work of art," while for Hoberman it contrasts the emptiness at the heart of the "lady" with the narrator's capacity for "reflection." While trying to include essays that cover the widest possible range of stories, we have not hesitated to offer multiple readings of a few. When readers are invited to trespass, they are bound to take differing paths across the territory. What we all have in common, however, is an insistence on four assertions. First,

Woolf turned to the short story repeatedly not for release or practice, but because its generic volatility intrigued her. Second, the short story offered her a peculiarly intense relation to its readers (a relation meticulously analyzed by Benzel). Third, her short stories must be read in the context of Woolf's life and historical moment. And finally, the stories must be read in terms neither of form (the traditional, "new critical" tendency) nor content (as a reservoir of political messages), but in terms of what they do: the interactions they force between reader and text, the traditional categories and perceptual schemata they undercut, the boundaries they trespass.

NOTES

1. For epistemological readings see Jean Guiguet, David Daiches, Harvena Richter and Jean Alexander; readings focusing on the stories' depictions of "moments of being" include those of Avrom Fleishman, Joanne Trautmann Banks and Sandra Kemp. For readings in terms of androgynous unities, see Herbert Marder and Nancy Topping Bazin.
2. James Hafley, for example, published two essays on the stories as experiments in narrative voice. In "Pursuing 'It' Through 'Kew Gardens'" Edward Bishop argues that the story dramatizes the incongruity of words and things, though it ends with a sense of unity between people and the "phenomenal world" (271). Eileen Baldeshwiler links "Kew Gardens" to a typically modernist lyricism, while Victor de Araujo reads "A Haunted House" as depicting an ironic epiphany.
3. There are, of course, exceptions: Selma Meyerowitz provides a feminist reading of a number of stories in "What is to Console Us? The Politics of Deception in Woolf's Short Stories"; Janet Winston and Corinne E. Blackmer offer thought-provoking readings of a few stories in *Virginia Woolf: Lesbian Readings*; and recent proceedings from the International Virginia Woolf conference include a smattering of papers on the short fiction.
4. Susan Lohafer locates a shift in 1914, a year she calls a turning point for closure. From then on, the short story becomes an "exercise in sensibility and inference, rather than a gift of revelation" (109). On the relationship between Woolf and Mansfield as it pertains to Woolf's stories, see Trautmann and McLaughlin.
5. *The Note-books of Anton Tchekhov Together with Reminiscences of Tchekhov by Maxim Gorky* provided an important overview of Chekhov's themes and thoughts at a time when little of his work was available in English translation.
6. Two volumes of essays, Lohafer and Clarey's *Short Story Theory at the Crossroads* and May's *The New Short Story Theories*, take up these questions; see also May's *The Short Story*.

Part I

The Modernist Context

Chapter 1

Through a Glass, Longingly

Joanne Trautmann Banks

Virginia Woolf wrote novels, essays, biography, diaries, and letters. She also wrote at least forty-five short narratives. Amid the brilliant richness of the other work, however, the short pieces lie neglected. They are said, even by Woolf herself, to hint at the accomplishments of the novels.

Yet the short form is superbly suited to her famous vision. The title of one story, "Moments of Being," can serve as a metaphor for her particular knack of seeing into the center of those specks of time and space where reality becomes transparent. Reality is perceptible only in "scraps, orts, and fragments," says the scriptwriter, speaking for Woolf in her last novel, *Between the Acts* (188). She knows how to expand as well as condense time in order to uncover those suspended fragments. Moreover, she has a lyrical gift that fits the outburst of the short form. In fact, a typical story by Virginia Woolf could be a model of Frank O'Connor's definition of the genre as a "significant moment" from which "past, present, and future may be viewed simultaneously" (21–23).

The moment is her subject; the moment is her method. Perhaps there never was another short story writer for whom form and content were thus merged. An excellent example is "The Searchlight." Its opening captures a party of sophisticated people paused on a London balcony between dinner and theater. Casually drinking coffee, smoking, and chatting, they watch an air force searchlight probing the night skies. In one burst of light, Mrs. Ivimey "sees" something. She sees the setting and action of a story told her by her great-grandfather about his youth. It seems that he lived in a lonely tower on the Yorkshire moors. One day, using his telescope, he saw a kiss between a man and a girl. He saw love, and, leaving his tower, he ran miles across the moors to find that girl, whom he would later marry. That's all: "The light. [. . .] only falls here and there" (*CSF* 272). Present time restrictions intervene: "Right you are. Friday" (271). But with her story, Mrs. Ivimey has swept away one hundred years. She has had a glimpse of love observed, as with books and telescopes, as opposed to love embraced. Once again life has happened between the acts, between, in this case, dinner and the theater.

Like "The Searchlight," almost all the other Woolf stories have at their center a philosophical theme expressed in tones reserved by many writers for sensual experience. Woolf cares passionately about the precise nature of reality and the values of existence. She worries about philosophical dichotomies; the "knowing versus being" dilemma, for instance, is central to "The Searchlight." Woolf is likewise intrigued by the opposition of art and life, appearance and reality, subjectivity and objectivity, the self and the not-self, vision and fact. Even when she writes about social class division or, as she often does, the man–woman confrontation, her concerns are as much philosophical as political or psychological.

Above all, Woolf investigates the imagination as a tool for knowing, unifying, and finally transcending its environment through love. For her, short stories are also "religious." They constitute a search for lasting significance, albeit in natural and human phenomena. The sea, the landscape, animals, and especially the mysterious human figures themselves, beckon to her, then depart through mists. In "An Unwritten Novel" she writes: "If I fall on my knees, if I go through the ritual, the ancient antics, it's you, unknown figures, you I adore; if I open my arms, it's you I embrace, you I draw to me—adorable world!" (*CSF* 121).

Her work had these philosophical and religious emphases from the beginning. One of her first short stories, "Monday or Tuesday," manages in just three hundred words to present both details and panoramas of reality while simultaneously questioning its essential qualities. The story opens far from the human activity that is always for Woolf only one component of an overlapping universe. A heron, who can afford to be "lazy and indifferent" (*CSF* 137) because he knows his way instinctively, passes over the human sphere and under the sky. The personified sky is even more self-absorbed. Indifferent to lakes, mountains, and stars, the sky—though she "moves"—"remains" (137). Heron and sky, male and female, are contrasted with the active world of men, women, and children, of jarring omnibuses, reflections in London shop windows, and Miss Thingummy, who sits in her office drinking her tea. Could anything be more real than Miss Thingummy?

"And is truth then a list of observable details?" the narrative consciousness seems to be asking. So many details are simply reflections of something else. So many are transient and incomparable—"squandered in separate scales" (137). So much happens parenthetically. Though the questions are difficult, the searching long and laborious, still the mind behind this story is "for ever desiring truth" (137). Above it all, not needing to desire but simply to be, are the heron and the sky. The gap between the two worlds is traveled—"voyaging" (137) Woolf says, using her favored water metaphor—via the imagination. In the penultimate paragraph someone very like a conventional narrator takes shape home from all that activity, sitting by the fire, reading her way into the reality behind the flames, smoke and sparks—Platonic imagery for this platonic search. The view in the last lines drifts upward from the dross of everyday activity. Visions of mosques enter the consciousness, followed—higher up—by the Indian seas, then by blue space and the stars themselves. Is this perhaps truth at last? Or is it only psychic "closeness" (137) with the vast elements, which is all we have and all we need to have? As if in answer, the sky first covers the stars, those bright specks of near certainty, then uncovers them to our hungering gaze.

The human miracle of connectedness has happened amid the most ordinary facts of life. Realizations about the mind, the way it knows, and its involvement with the world outside itself, await us any Monday or Tuesday.

The abundance of her speculations sometimes threatens to dilute Woolf's considerable energies. A period of abstract questioning can drive her back to facts, to "Solid Objects" (another story title), to the Miss Thingummys. There she roots happily among direct experiences. But as soon as she describes the solid objects, she brings them sensuously to life. And once she has done that, she cannot help herself—she must daydream. So, like all us, Woolf oscillates between experience and interpretation.

She speaks of these matters directly in "The Mark on the Wall," as charming a piece of philosophy as has ever been written. Glancing up from her daily concerns one day, Woolf—for it is surely proper to identify the voice here as hers—notices a small black mark against a white wall. Is it a large nail mark? Thus begins a series of meanderings through, among other topics, the nature of fantasizing, selfhood as an infinite series of reflected phantom images, the male-induced fraudulence of social convention, and the vast ignorance behind what learned professors call factual knowledge. Life, she decides, is an accidental matter in spite of all our civilized attempts to control it. Very little sticks to us: "Why, if one wants to compare life to anything, one must liken it to being blown through the Tube at fifty miles an hour—landing at the other end without a single hairpin in one's hair! Shot out at the feet of God entirely naked!" (*CSF* 84). Therefore, it is useless to get up to see just what the mark on the wall really is. What it "really" is, is just another particle of so-called solid reality, which will not connect. Staying where she sits, this pensive Woolf wants "to sink deeper and deeper, away from the surface, with its hard separate facts" (85).

Just here she gets caught. To be sure, she opens up the world of speculation. But she does so by daring to deny the importance of long-established convention, such as which Anglican archbishop precedes which Anglican archbishop, thereby forcing Nature to protect herself. No one's thoughts must collide with Nature's reality. People must not be left dangerously adrift in solipsism. So in spite of her love of the daydream, Woolf finds she must learn what the mark on the wall is (it's a snail), and thereby hang onto something as definite and real as "a plank in the sea" (*CSF* 88). She seeks salvation by "worshipping solidity, worshipping reality, worshipping the impersonal world is a proof of some existence other than ours" (88).

When Woolf turns from the speculative story to a more recognizable version of the genre, she is nonetheless often working through the same issues. "The Introduction," for instance, dramatizes one of Woolf's lasting concerns, the endangered self. The theme is embodied in a shy, intellectually ambitious young woman who is introduced to an arrogant young man and learns that her role in civilization is merely to adorn him. One of several stories about people meeting and parting without significantly altering their isolation, "The Introduction" builds its feminist theme on the question of what is real. As Lily Everit drives to the party in a cab, she looks through the glass between her and the driver to see her own "white reflection in the driver's back inextricably mixed [. . .]" (*CSF* 184). Her personality, as in "The Mark on the Wall," is an infinitely possible rather than a definitely knowable thing. She responds to this situation, as other Woolf characters do, by calling life a series of dualisms between which one must steer the craft of one's self: "One divided life [. . .] into fact and into fiction, into rock and into wave" (184). At the beginning of the story, Lily's rock is her essay on Swift, for which she has just that morning received high praise from her professor. But in the hands of the unwittingly brutal Bob Brinsley, a gem of conventional English manhood, and harder, more assertively real, than her essay, she feels her own sense of reality melting away. Everything turns to water, "leaving her only the power to stand at bay" (185). Her hostess has flung her "into a whirlpool where either she would perish or be saved." In this whirlpool of the man–woman involvement, though there is "a kind of passion," there is no salvation. Lily has entered naked and vulnerable—like Eve, Woolf's languages urges us to remember—"in some shady garden" from which she is evicted, "a naked wretch," knowing at that moment of vision that "there are no sanctuaries" (188).

Even in the relatively plotted stories (which Woolf wrote for money, thinking plot was what most people wanted), she cannot turn her mind completely from metaphorical thinking. In "Lappin and Lapinova" she creates a plot that is saved from being cloying by the universality of its conceptual underpinnings. That the story is in addition romantic, sad, filled with longing, and tinged with comedy makes it among the most appealing of her short works of fiction. Rosalind and Ernest, a newly wedded young couple, are tucked into their own private, enchanting world. There she calls him King of the Rabbits, and she is his Queen Lapinova. With this construct, the honeymooning couple for some time control their outer worlds, for they can turn any disagreeable aspect of it into fictional shapes. An unpleasant sister-in-law is thought of as an ugly ferret in their woodsy kingdom. A bullying mother-in-law becomes the Squire. Rosalind and Ernest are very much in love. Their created world sustains them both, but it is essential for Rosalind. Without the collusion of her husband in the play, she is threatened with "being melted; dispersed; dissolved into nothingness" (*CSF* 265). At the end, that is just what happens. Rosalind is almost literally disenchanted by the now prosaic Ernest, who has given up the game and thereby forfeited her spirit to death, the secret opponent in all games. The author's terse conclusion is: "So that was the end of that marriage" (268). The statement is a variant of the Gogol phrase quoted by Frank O'Connor as a description of what any successful short story "means": "and from that day forth everything was as it were changed and appeared in a different light to him" (16). Everything appears in a different light to Rosalind because she can no longer use her imagination to achieve the delicate placement of art in life.

To the service of these themes, Woolf brought an astonishing array of technical skills. Some of the stories are, in the first place, so unusual as to merit, seventy-five years or so after they were written, the label "experimental." Stories like "Monday or Tuesday" and "Kew Gardens" have not so much a concealed narrator or shifting points of view as what has been called, with respect to the New Novel in France, "the experiencing mind" (Stevick xx). Frequently that mind makes the distance between observer and observed seem to disappear. Then there is the magic of what Woolf does with time. In the time it takes Fanny Wilmot in "Moments of Being" to search for a pin, she re-creates Julia Craye's lifetime and pinpoints her essence. Woolf also performs magic with space: in "The String Quartet" a piece by Mozart sends Woolf's readers racing around the sensual universe— to a pear tree on top of a mountain, to the silver fishes in the Rhone. Perhaps only with Proust is language equal to these same tasks. A further very contemporary touch in "The String Quartet" is the telescoped dialogue, which is like Harold Pinter's but without his overtones of absurdity, fear, and cruelty. Yet there are rich and ancient iambic rhythms to Woolf's language as well: "How lovely goodness is in those who, stepping lightly, go smiling through the world" (*CSF* 139). In fact, what marks Woolf's techniques throughout her fiction is this combination of the experimental and the traditional. In a story like "Monday or Tuesday," for instance, there are not true characters and only the haziest of actions. The setting floats; the conflict is intellectual. The piece is too philosophical to qualify as a traditional story, too personal and sensual to be called a traditional essay. And yet we can find our way back to Addison as one of its progenitors.

Much has been made of the visual elements in Woolf's style. She lived among painters and knew well the technique of Impressionistic pointillism. She adapted it perfectly to her philosophy that reality appears to us in light-illuminated moments rather than in big slabs of uninterrupted truth. Woolf is the prose painter in such pieces as "Blue and Green," where she demonstrates that color is not static; and the beautiful "Kew Gardens," the first paragraph of which is a profuse palette of primary colors and light.

In other stories Woolf is more photographer than painter, very much the great-niece of the famous Victorian photographer Julia Margaret Cameron. Brilliantly in "The Lady in the Looking-Glass," she contrasts immutable mirror images with the daily world, where change is constant. How can she fit a portrait of the unknowable Isabella, now moving about in the garden, into the fixed truth the mirror seems to offer? A Platonic exercise again. If the mirror seems at first dependent upon older photographic techniques, it becomes startlingly contemporary once Isabella moves into the reflection. At this point, the scene is reminiscent of the relatively static parts of Robert Altman's film *Images*, which uses mirrors to depict the multiple phantasmagoria of personality, and of Bergman's *Persona*. In "Kew Gardens" the point of view is as flexible as that of a film camera whose lens is resting in a flower bed. Sometimes it rises just above the bed to watch people as they pass, the audio turned up for a time, then turned down, as in another Altman film, *McCabe and Mrs. Miller*. Sometimes it zooms in for a close-up. A snail fills the frame. The way in which heat and color move through the air is as much like time-lapse photography as like cinema. Then the camera pulls back to reveal the larger design: couples are promenading along the grass paths, the glinting glass of the palm house is seen in the distance, an airplane is heard in the summer sky. (Woolf is very fond, too, of using the camera perspective for sweeping panoramas, as in the opening of "Monday or Tuesday.") A little like Alain Resnais's *Last Year at Marienbad*, and yet mysteriously evocative in its own way, "Kew Gardens" remains an avant-garde piece.

When we have spoken of the rhythms of her language and the bond between her outer and inner eyes, we have not yet explained the beauty of Woolf's style. Her prose moves as often through sensuous images, one leading directly to another, as it does through the linear method dictated by discursive reasoning and normal chronology. She writes a lyrical short story, not a mimetic one. She needs the freedom of prose to explore the corners of her mind, but the resources of poetry to record her discoveries. She writes telescopically. She condenses and intensifies. So elliptical are some of her stories that one must explicate them as one would a poem by her friend T. S. Eliot. Her sentences, her paragraphs, are long and elegant, yet not "feminine," as she feared, but sinewy, their anatomical strength achieved through the exercise of rewriting.

Behind all Woolf's short fiction is a complex motivation. To speak of it is to add to our understanding of the genre. As must be clear to all who know the outline of Woolf's life, she was haunted by what psychologists call impacted grief and by a concomitant ambivalence about her own death. Between the ages of thirteen and twenty-five, she lost first her mother and father, and then their substitutes, her half-sister and adored brother. Art, along with its handmaiden the imagination, worked wonders with her pain, but just at the point of its greatest beauty, art also "unseals [. . .] sorrow" (*CSF* 140), as she expresses that phenomenon in "The String Quartet." It may be that the short story is particularly dissatisfying in this regard. In Woolf's hands it creates an illusion of perpetual being that operates as an antidote to grief. Then the moment ceases, leaving as a residue joy, but also yearning. Along the continuum between time and eternity, the novel can mark more moments; so it was as a novelist that Woolf found her deepest pleasure. Eventually, of course, all fictions failed to sustain her, and she committed suicide by walking into a river. It was an interesting choice in that water always has dichotomous potentials in Woolf's stories. Water either unifies conflicting elements or it dissolves the self utterly (see, for example, the discussion of "The Introduction," above). Unification and dissolution: these, it seems are the two aspects of death for Woolf.

They are invoked again in "A Haunted House," where they are shown to be not two aspects of death, as logic would have it, but one very nearly mystical whole. Mysterious, elliptical, and bursting the confines of time, the story names the ultimate separation: "So fine, so rare, coolly sunk beneath the surface the beam I sought always burnt behind the glass. Death was the glass; death was between us" (*CSF* 122). Death comes between the narrator and the couple who died in her house hundreds of years before. Death—both the fact and the fear or it—comes between any potential "us." It is the frightening reflection in the glass. Of the ghostly couple who haunt the house, the wife died first, we learn. The bereaved husband first went north, east, and south—his wife, in the language of folklore, having gone west, one assumes. Finally he returned to their house, where the narrator encounters them, joyfully reunited in each other. The reunion occurs in a structure that seems to be at once a house and a comforting maternal body. For the most part, the "pulse of the house" beats regularly (122). It says, "Safe, safe, safe [. . .] the treasure buried" (122). In this state the house merges with human factors, both dead and alive. It dissolves also into natural factors—the wood thrush and the rose, the wind and the trees. Death seems to be defeated. In the midst of all this activity, however, the narrator hears the pulse stop short. Until she can find the buried treasure, whatever it is, she is at death's mercy. Happily, the ghostly couple, gazing down at the sleeping narrator and her beloved, see that they have fallen asleep with "love upon their lips" (123). The pulse of the house now beats strongly, bearing its message of perpetual security. Now the beam, in effect, breaks through the glass of death and transports the narrator, who knows with certainty that the long-sought hidden treasure is "the light in the heart" (123). The treasure is love, and all are saved.

On this occasion Woolf stops short of saying, metaphorically, that the searchlight's illuminations are without exception sporadic and that the exigencies of life and loss inevitably intervene. However, the readers of her brief fiction can't be fooled. She has taught us that these ecstatic glimpses of seamless reality cannot long be pinned down by language, even so remarkable a language as hers. Thus the implied ending of every story by Virginia Woolf is a steep precipice into a kind of grief. That she climbed out of it again and again until her energies ebbed is a mark of her great love for literature and for life.

Chapter 2

"Excursions into the literature of a foreign country": Crossing Cultural Boundaries in the Short Fiction

Nena Skrbic

Because Virginia Woolf was not a great theoretician of the short-story form, we do not have a critical vocabulary to describe her short fiction. However, a study of her practitioner criticism (which reveals a strong curiosity and enthusiasm for the Russian short story) and an examination of the intertextual relations between Russian short fiction and her own does provide a way of finding alternative and enriching explanations for her own stories. The Russian influence is evident in Woolf's narrative method, in the human content and in the psychological backgrounds of her characters, and in her comments on the short-story form. Like the Russians, Woolf was guided to a greater degree by feeling and intuition than by representational principles or traditional story elements, and she saw in them a realization of some of her own ideas about how the short story might effectively delineate character through a detached tone, a sense of proportion, and a peculiarly formless kind of form. Woolf's stories "Happiness" (1925), "The Lady in the Looking-Glass" (1929), and "Uncle Vanya" (1937) provide intriguing contextualizations of her connections to the Russian short story. I compare these stories to Chekhov's "Happiness" and Valery Brussof's "In the Mirror" (both published in English in 1918) to demonstrate that what Woolf ultimately shares with the Russians is a delight in the short story as a vehicle of discontinuity and impermanence

26

and as a conduit for the modernists' depiction of the self as fragile and fragmental.

Late-nineteenth-century Russia was the site of immense political and social unrest. Throughout this period, inventive, challenging artistic ideas arose in response to industrial, cultural and social change. Stephen Graham's introduction to his English translation of Valery Brussof's *The Republic of the Southern Cross and Other Stories* (1918) highlights the key role played by the short story in questioning the artistic reality of nineteenth-century Russian realism:

> In Russia [. . .] the short story is considered of much more literary significance than it is here. It is the fashion to write short stories, and readers remember those they have read and refer to them, as we do to the distinctive and memorable poems on our intimate bookshelves. But, then, as a rule in Russia a short story must possess as its foundation some particular literary idea and conception. The story written for the sake of the story is unknown, and as a general rule the sort of love story and "love interest" so indispensable with us is not asked there. It often happens, therefore, that a volume of short tales makes a real and vital contribution to literature. (vii)

Graham points out that the short story is a respected, literarily "significant" form in Russia that was embraced far more willingly there than in England. The ubiquity of the short story in late-nineteenth-century Russia (as a result of the flowering of journals and magazines at this time) meant that the readership for the form was vast. In their revolutionary experiments with form, characterization, plot, and language in the late nineteenth century, short story writers such as Turgenev, Tolstoy, Dostoevsky, and Chekhov displayed a new conception of what stories could be. In their hands, the short story displays a profound skepticism toward the idea of a narrative event (or a story "written for the sake of the story") as well as toward the metaphysical and religious underpinnings of the previous generation of writers. Instead, writers like Chekhov produced works that naturalistically explored individual consciousness and sensibility. Focusing on the absolute isolation of the individual and the simplicity of the day to day, Chekhov's stories center on the moment when the protagonist discovers the conflict that exists between physical and psychological authenticity and the material world.

The unanswerability that lies at the heart of this conflict is reflected in the absence of authorial guidance or judgment. In Chekhov's words,

> It seems to me that the writer of fiction should not try to solve such questions as those of God, pessimism, etc. His business is but to describe those who have been speaking or thinking about God and pessimism, how, and

under what circumstances. The artist should be, not the judge of his characters and their conversations, but only an unbiased witness. (*Letters* 58)

This view of the author, which originates in Flaubert's view of the author as "God in his universe, everywhere present and nowhere visible" (Barnes 4), because it privileges a particular kind of artistic practice that allows us neither to record nor understand the writer's philosophical concerns, encourages readers to evaluate the contents for themselves. As a consequence, one feels very strongly when reading such literature its readers' overriding freedom. For Chekhov, what is perceptible (what the author describes) is incidental and only part of the story:

> In my opinion, descriptions of nature should be extremely brief and offered by the way, as it were [. . .] you will evoke a moonlit night by writing that on the mill dam the glass fragments of a broken bottle flashed like a bright little star, and that the black shadow of a dog or a wolf rolled along like a ball, and so on. (quoted in Stone 8)

What we have in Chekhov's example is a total immersion in the senses in which the moment is conveyed solely in terms of the momentary and fleeting play of light. As such, the main emphasis is on extreme brevity, on a medium flexible enough to present a brief, temporary and ephemeral unit of action rather than a developed situation that is integral to a continuous narrative. It is a method of authorship that—as Charles May explains in "Reality in the Modern Short Story"— "insists on compression" and paradoxically "reveals meanings by leaving things out." Such stories thematize the author's dilemma of "trying to say the unsayable" (369) and are largely dependent on the particular materiality of the short story medium over and above a traditionalist understanding of narrative.

The short story's connection to the unspeakable is exemplified in Chekhov's "Happiness" (published in English in 1918 in *The Witch and Other Stories*). It is a summer night on the steppe and two shepherds are lying on the ground as their sheep sleep. A man on a horse stops to ask them for a light for his pipe, but stays to chat about the recent death of Yefim Zhmenya, an old man who had sold his soul to the devil. One of the men observes that there are many treasures buried in the local hills. "Yes," says the old shepherd, "but no one knows where to dig for them." Next he tells them about a map to the treasure and indicates that he knows precisely where to dig. However, when the horseman asks him what he would do with the treasure if he were to find it, the old shepherd cannot answer. Faced with the reality of possessing the treasure, no one knows what he would do if he did find it:

> And the old man could not answer what he would do with the treasure if he found it. That question had presented itself to him that morning probably for the first time in his life, and judging from the expression of his face, indifferent and uncritical, it did not seem to him important and deserving of consideration. In Sanka's brain another puzzled question was stirring: why was it only old men searched for hidden treasure, and what was the use of earthly happiness to people who might die any day of old age? But Sanka could not put this perplexity into words, and the old man could scarcely have found an answer to it. ("Happiness")

The treasure evokes a number of different themes in the story: freedom, old age, the value of human life. However, it is an elusive metaphor that constitutes a specious emotional center for the characters and predominantly suggests unfulfilled possibilities. The past conditional "if" belongs especially to modernist writing, emblematizing the creative questioning at the heart of the modernist vocabulary. In his dynamic description of the landscape and the visible world Chekhov foregrounds the sense that what the characters are seeking is nearer to them than they think and in fact has been within them all along:

> An immense crimson sun came into view surrounded by a faint haze. Broad streaks of light, still cold, bathing in the dewy grass, lengthening out with a joyous air as though to prove they were not weary of their task, began spreading over the earth. The silvery wormwood, the blue flowers of the pig's onion, the yellow mustard, the corn-flowers—all burst into gay colours, taking the sunlight for their own smile. ("Happiness")

Observable here is a sense of emotional transparency and the lack of distance in Chekhov's representation of the scene. The out-sized, oddly foreshortened images establish a unique sense of scale while offering an immediate and arresting pleasure. In this way the formal properties of the short story are brought to bear directly on the content: the silvery wormwood, the blue flowers, the yellow mustard, the corn-flowers—all of these colors materialize the feeling of happiness, revealing the beauty in the common and ordinary via a visual shorthand that captures an awareness of the physical world and conveys his characters' inner states through an accrual of figurative images. The inconclusive and moody ending mirrors the impasse in which his characters find themselves, trapped between a powerful psychological need and an awareness of the tragic nature of their search:

> The old shepherd and Sanka stood with their crooks on opposite sides of the flock, stood without stirring, like fakirs at their prayers, absorbed in thought.

They did not heed each other; each of them was living in his own life. The sheep were pondering, too. ("Happiness")

The treasure evokes a psychological authenticity connected to aspects of ourselves that remain silent and hidden. The unrepresented internal dialogue only intensifies our sense of the tragic nature of the search, the story's irresolution hinting that an answer, if there is one, lies outside the bounds of the story. Chekhov's representational strategies therefore provide little reassurance. It is rather as if the story's conclusion is a treasure that readers have to find for themselves.

Woolf understood this spiritual despondency and quest for psychological authenticity well, and her take on the problem of human happiness, although less tainted by superstition and fear than it is for Chekhov's characters, is similarly represented in one of her own stories, also entitled "Happiness" (1925). Like Chekhov's story, "Happiness" seems like an exercise in finding out what the bare minimum requirements for a short story might be. Here Woolf is interested in depicting (through linked motifs and metaphors, and a nearly identical vocabulary) the sense of unarticulated frustration that Chekhov explores. The story describes the brief and spontaneous rush of emotion felt by Stuart Elton (a melancholy but defiant character) at Mrs. Dalloway's party and his desire to keep hold of the feeling through an emotional estrangement from the other partygoers. Woolf's characterization of Stuart Elton casts a light on the volatility of personal freedom. The symbol of "the complete rose" succinctly expresses this idea of an ordered inner life while the "falling petal" alludes to the precariousness of any metaphysical search: "It chimed oddly with what he had been thinking and that sense of the soft downward rush of life and its orderly readjustment, that sense of the falling petal and the complete rose" (*CSF* 178). Woolf's present continuous description of Elton's state of consciousness as "a current of clean fresh clear bright lucid tingling impinging sensation" (179) creates an especially vertiginous reading experience so that we are almost chasing the experience for ourselves. Both Chekhov and Woolf share a profound interest in how the free-associative train of individual consciousness collides with the temporariness of the short story frame.

This very Russian conflict between a "superior" spirituality (evoking the presence of a force of order and a shaping emotion) and a universal humanity is presented by the rational arguments of Mrs. Sutton that counter Elton's private musings:

Was it balancing one thing against another, she asked? Was it a sense of proportion, was it? Was what, he asked, knowing quite well what she meant,

but warding off this harum scarum ravaging woman with her hasty ways[,]
with her grievances and her vigour, skirmishing and scrimmaging[,] who
might knock over and destroy this very valuable possession, this sense of
being [. . .] (178–79)

What strikes me most about the story, however, is the precariousness of
individuality, expression, and beauty. Elton poses a subtle threat to
Mrs. Sutton's middle-class values of "balance" and "proportion." This is
highlighted in the story's disavowal of a tight resolution for an emotional
climax that imbues the romantic vision of personal freedom and self-awareness
with fragility and fails to provide closure, objectivity, or coherence. What
is being expressed in both Chekhov and Woolf is the fact that human
sensation—emotion in its purest form—seems to lack any sort of describ-
able specificity. "But was it 'happiness'? No. The big word did not seem to
fit it, did not seem to refer to this state of being" (178). The phrase "He
would not tell her; he must tell her," built around the conditional "would
not" and the imperative verb "must," renders explicit the precarious balance
between unspoken dialogue and the materiality of the spoken word, yet is
also paralyzing. At the same time, the mixed tenses in "was his had been his
was his must always be his," instead of offering the reader an explanatory,
satisfying resolution—a "moment of being" in which one's place in the
world and some sort of "spiritual order" are temporarily assured—
noncommittally skirt around it. The concluding line, "Yes; it was all right.
He had it still" (180), reveals only the precariousness of the protagonist's
attempt to retain things as fragile as memory and sensation. Both writers
use the miniaturist short story to exploit expectations that shape how we
see the world close-up. In both stories this striving after poetic truth
involves taking the reader's experience in a more conceptual direction by
offering us an experience that cannot be affirmed in words. Both stories
highlight the way in which the short story's brevity can express, via its
inconclusiveness, the unarticulatable and unanswerable aspects of experience. This sense of "deferred cognitive closure" (Lohafer and Clarey 113)
has three consequences. First, it foregrounds the storyteller's lack of omnis-
cience; second, it leaves us with a story that we can reformulate in our own
way; and third, by doing so, it makes the reader's own contribution central
to the process of interpretation.

For Woolf, the Russians offered a paradigm of aesthetic experience: a
way of seeing the world in terms of a universal, archetypal human expression that overrides materialist interests, values, and attitudes. The conceptual implications of this perspective are to do away with the "well
constructed and solid" novel form, to free up the imagination by replacing
the traditional boundaries of literature with an "obscure outline of form"

(*CE3* 32, 35) that might contain modern experience. Such a form, Woolf suggests in "The Modern Novel," is to be found in the Russian short story. Woolf's theorizing about the Russians is at its most powerful in her essay "Modern Novels" (1919), which not only foregrounds her feelings that the creative approach of the Edwardians would not work for her but also reveals the impact that the Russians had on her aesthetic and intellectual concerns. The essay contrasts the materialism of English novelists (represented by Wells, Bennett, and Galsworthy) with the spiritualism of the Russians: not spiritualism in the religious sense, but in the sense that suggests a deeply felt belief in and sensitivity to humanity:

> The most inconclusive remarks upon modern English fiction can hardly avoid some mention of the Russian influence, and if the Russians are mentioned one runs the risk of feeling that to write of any fiction save theirs is a waste of time. If we want understanding of the soul and heart where else shall we find it of comparable profundity? If we are sick of our own materialism the least considerable of their novelists has by right of birth a natural reverence for the human spirit. (*CE3* 35)

Instead of offering the reader an explanatory, satisfying account of the world—the words that would turn something unstable and short-lived into something durable—the Russian short story is noncommittal and, as in Chekhov's short story "Gusev" (published in English in 1918 in *The Witch and Other Stories*), "The emphasis is laid upon such unexpected places that at first it seems as if there were no emphasis at all" (*CE3* 35).

"Gusev" is set in a ship's infirmary where five soldiers and sailors are returning to Russia after serving in the Far East. But the sense of homecoming is marred by the two central characters, the dying Gusev and Pavel Ivanych, who are beyond medical help. As Gusev sifts through memories of his family's farm, he hankers after something unattainable and indefinable:

> [. . .] a vague longing starts to trouble him. He drinks some water—that's not what he wants; he stretches towards the porthole and breathes in the hot moist air—that's not it; he tries to think of his homeland and the frost—that's not it either. Finally he feels that just one more minute in that sickbay and he'll be bound to choke to death. (246)

Pavel refuses to believe that he can die like the other patients and ridicules Gusev. But both characters die. The story closes with a vivid description of Gusev's body being buried at sea:

> Surveying this magnificent, magical sky, the ocean frowns at first, but before long it too takes on gentle, joyous, ardent hues which are difficult to name in the language of man. (248–50)

As in "Happiness," the plot is displaced by internal dialogue and by an all-encompassing sense of the unspoken. For Woolf, "Gusev" is successful because it is capable of being read "as a whole." Its extreme brevity is the key to understanding it, a point made also by Allan Pasco about the short story: "The short story, in particular, has a noticeable affinity for the epigrammatic, the formulistic, the epitome, the essential truth or idea or image which rises above time and negates whatever chronological progression the work possesses" (126). Taking full advantage of the short story's brevity, writers like Chekhov seduce the reader by withholding the conclusion to the narrative. But more important than this omission of closure is the context of intimacy and connectedness with the human personality that Chekhov and his fellow Russian short story writers create. Here Woolf saw in the Russians a reflection of some of her own ideas about how the short story might effectively delineate character. In "The Russian View" (1918), her review of *The Village Priest and Other Stories* by Elena Militsina and Mikhail Saltikov, Woolf writes:

> An able English writer treating the theme which Elena Militsina has treated in *The Village Priest*, would have shown his knowledge of different social classes, his intellectual grasp of the religious problem. His story would have been well constructed and made to appear probable. All this seems irrelevant to the Russian writer. She asks herself only about the souls of the priest, and tries to imagine what was in the hearts of the peasants when they prayed or came to die. As for the story, there is none. (*CE2* 341–42)

Woolf's definition of the Russian short story gestures at a storytelling based not on circumscribed ideas but on testing the creative potential that lies in the genre's brevity. Her main focus is on the Russians' formal inventiveness, their rejection of classical short story practice (in which the story is satisfyingly "well constructed and made to appear probable") in favor of "what was in the hearts of the peasants when they prayed or came to die." Woolf describes a working method stripped bare, allowing the very soul of the work to shine through its surface: "It is as if she had tried to light a lamp behind her characters," she writes of Militsina, "making them transparent rather than solid, letting the large and permanent things show through the details of dress and body" (*CE2* 342).

Along with Chekhov's brevity and the spiritual intimacy he sets up between reader and characters, Woolf was also drawn to his depiction of human meaning under threat. We have seen in the case of Chekhov how the inconclusive ending establishes a pervasive sense of human purposelessness, intensifying the characters' sense of disorientation and disquiet. In "A Glance at Turgenev" (1921), praising Turgenev for creating a somewhat similar atmosphere, Woolf uses the circle as a supreme symbol of wholeness and unity, a wholeness and unity constantly threatened by the chaos outside it:

> Like most Russian writers, he was melancholy. Beyond the circle of his scene seems to lie a great space, which flows in at the window, presses upon people, isolates them, makes them incapable of action, indifferent to effect, sincere, and open-minded. Some background of that sort is common to much of Russian literature. (*CE2* 316)

These observations on what is "[b]eyond the circle of his scene" find a counterpoint in Woolf's "The Lady in the Looking-glass," where there is a feeling that we are being denied a full experience since the mirror is interesting not for what it reflects, but for what it cuts out, leaving the greater proportion of the story (the question of who the "lady" is and what she could become) undisclosed.

Woolf evokes a similar contrast between the circle and what is outside it in praising Turgenev's "Three Meetings." In this story Turgenev, Woolf writes, "draws together the moon and the group round the samovar, the voice and the flowers and the warmth of the garden—he fuses them in one moment of great intensity, though all round are the silent spaces, and he turns away, in the end, with a little shrug of his shoulders" (*CE3* 316–17). Turgenev exploits the medium's brevity by leaving the reader to fill in the story's "silent spaces."

Another crucial contribution of Turgenev's is his emphasis on character at the expense of plot. Henry James, whose approach to characterization (and its relationship to structure) was significantly influenced by that of Turgenev, writes in his 1908 preface to *The Portrait of a Lady*:

> I have always fondly remembered a remark that I heard fall years ago from the lips of Ivan Turgénieff in regard to his own experience of the usual origin of the fictive picture. It began for him almost always with the vision of some person or persons, who hovered before him, soliciting him, as the active or passive figure, interesting him and appealing to him just as they were and by what they were. He saw them, in that fashion, as *disponibles*, saw them subject to the chances, the complications of existence, and saw them vividly, but then had to find for them the right relations, those that would most bring them out; to imagine, to invent and select and piece together the situations most useful and favorable to the sense of the creatures themselves, the complications they would be most likely to produce and to feel. [. . .] "To arrive at these things is to arrive at my 'story,'" he said, "and that's the way I look for it. The result is that I'm often accused of not having 'story' enough. I seem to myself to have as much as I need—to show my people, to exhibit their relations with each other; that is all my measure." (43)

What Henry James said of Turgenev's method of composition applies equally to Woolf, who worked on the Russian precept that the short story need not have a discernible plot. Both Woolf and Turgenev are more occupied with the observation of human beings than with recounting events.

The question of character delineation in the short story raised by Turgenev's methodology is of more striking formal significance in the work of the Russian science fiction writer Valery Brussof. In 1918, Brussof published a collection of stories entitled *The Republic of the Southern Cross and Other Stories*. Woolf read the collection for a review article that same year. The article is permeated with the same enthusiastic appreciation and curiosity that characterizes all her criticism of the Russians. However, her critical commentary is particularly intriguing because of her frustrated efforts to define Brussof's practice. Operating in the gray area between fantasy and reality, Brussof writes stories that defy understanding. "The Marble Bust," Woolf observes, documents "a dilemma which is always being dealt with by the mind: what is reality, and why are we so eager about things that are created for the most part chiefly by our own imaginations?" What makes Brussof's approach fascinating is its threshold quality: the sense that his stories "give shape" to the fact that "the things commonly held to be visionary may be real, while the reality may equally well be a phantom" (*CE2* 317). Intriguingly, the word "shape" implies structure and solidity, while Brussof's practice dissolves the boundaries between sanity and insanity, reality and dream, leaving the reader at an impasse. This threshold quality appealed very strongly to Woolf, and one of Brussof's stories, I believe, provided her with the idea behind "The Lady in the Looking-Glass" (1929). Woolf was intrigued by Brussof's investigations into border-line, socially invisible characters, especially by his account of a woman who "lives her true life in communication with her own reflection in the mirror" (*CE2* 318). "In the Mirror" documents a giddying, though silent, perceptual dilemma in which the failure to grasp fully what is seen in the reflection suggests a kind of *horror vacui*:

> What if the real I—is there? Then I myself who think this, I who write this, I—am a shadow, I—am a phantom, I—am a reflection. In me are only the poured forth remembrances, thoughts and feelings of that other, the real person. And, in reality, I am thrown into the depths of the mirror in nonentity, I am pining, exhausted, dying. (71)

Brussof uses the short story to examine the complex relationship between the ephemeral nature of the image and its documentation. He explores the instability of living excessively in the imagination by straddling the ghostly interface between the world outside the mirror and the reflected world.

The mirror is thus a metaphor for the short story, a notion that has a particular relevance to Woolf's "The Lady in the Looking-Glass." In this story, the short story and the reflection have similar time frames; that is, the unstable, short-lived mirror image figures as an interesting image of the short story itself, which, like the mirror, documents a random, real-time event. According to Marilyn Kurtz, through the image of mirrors and windows, Woolf captures the nature of modernism, the "sense of the fluid, the shifting, the fragmented in life" (2). Because the mirror holds nothing lasting in its frame—or does not hold it for very long—Woolf is interested in what happens beyond the limits, or in the silent spaces, around its frame. Brussof's use of the reflected image in the looking-glass as a metaphor for the imaginative and contemplative life in his story "In the Mirror" resembles Woolf's use of the looking-glass device in "The Lady in the Looking-Glass," in which the mirror frame suggests the unified subject caught in a formal structure. Although both writers recognize the security offered by the disciplined frame of the mirror, a frame offering a secure identity and face to present to the world, each story is shaped not by dialogue or positive human interaction, but, more suggestively, by a retreat into the self and a merging with the reflection. Both writers suggest that avoiding the frame of representation altogether leads to a multi-layered experience that cannot be captured in words, and is invisible to the rest of the world. Woolf writes:

> one was tired of the things that she talked about at dinner. It was her profounder state of being that one wanted to catch and turn to words, the state that is to the mind what breathing is to the body, what one calls happiness or unhappiness. (*CSF* 224)

Like Brussof, Woolf in "The Lady in the Looking-Glass" focuses on a moment of lucid, but painful, anagnorisis. Like Brussof, Woolf seeks out her characters' core emotions with a poignant sense of the unspoken and the unarticulated:

> At once the looking-glass began to pour over her a light that seemed to fix her; that seemed like some acid to bite off the unessential and superficial and to leave only the truth, [. . .] Here was the hard wall beneath. Here was the woman herself. She stood naked in that pitiless light. And there was nothing. Isabella was perfectly empty. (*CSF* 225)

This moment of lucidity, instead of providing some sort of poetic truth, offers the reader an experience that cannot be affirmed in words. The story's inconclusiveness reveals that although the mirror's frame may appear to be holding the narrative elements together, the sense of unity that it provides is superficial. Experience of the objective world has ceased to exist in this story and, like Brussof's beleaguered protagonist in "In the Mirror," we are going beyond surface identity altogether. The line of demarcation between "the real I" and the reflection, as in "The Lady in the Looking-Glass," is the threshold between being and non-being. In this way, the mirror reflection is used as an allegory of artistic practice: a way of toying with notions of representation and opening up the story to multiple interpretations. As Tracy Seeley explains, "No critic has yet hit on the formulation that the lady in the looking-glass is not Isabella at all, but the narrator, who glances in the looking-glass and finds her own sense of artistic agency vanish" (109). The looking-glass is a favorite device in Woolf's short fiction, and the mirror confrontation is an on-going battle in her work.

Given that the Russians have long disputed whether the Western public understands their culture, my placement of Woolf's stories in the context of Russian, rather than European, modernism may seem ironic. Woolf herself foregrounds the complexities of the Europe–Russia relationship in "Uncle Vanya" (1937), a very short sketch that, first of all, provides a useful taxonomy of Russian creative practice through the eyes and commentary of a Western theater-goer and second, suggests that Woolf was aware of her own, culturally limited perspective. Woolf wrote the story after seeing a performance of Chekhov's play of the same name (published in 1899 and translated into English in 1923). The story chronicles the firsthand observation of a British woman watching a performance of Chekhov's play, as she moves from apparent appreciation to a defensive rejection of the play's emotional intensity. The sketch takes the reader on a brief trip through her thoughts and sensibilities, the theatrical frame offering a window on the East at the same time that it clearly anchors the work in a privileged (Western) artistic context.

Chekhov, describing his own narrative method in terms that resonate with Woolf's story, argues that freedom of self-expression requires eliminating the author and working through the senses rather than through material description. This view of the author is central to a letter he wrote to Maxim Gorky, December 3, 1898, criticizing Gorky's heavy-handed narrative commentary:

> I shall begin by saying that you, in my opinion, have no self-restraint. You are like a spectator in a theatre who expresses his delight so unrestrainedly that it prevents himself and others from listening. This lack of self-restraint is especially evident in the descriptions of nature with which you interrupt the dialogue; as one reads these descriptions one wishes that they were more compact, shorter, say two or three lines or so. (Chekhov, *Letters* 84–85)

Chekhov uses the metaphor of theater-going to raise questions about artificiality and constructedness in fiction. Woolf's experiment with the theatrical frame in "Uncle Vanya" links her with Chekhov's theory in terms of its focus on the spectator's control as narrator. Her nagging rhetorical questions (which no one appears to be listening to) determinedly interrupt our reading, and their unanswerability stands in place of authorial guidance or judgment.

But the story is just as interesting for the theatrical window on the East that it provides. The spectator begins by recognizing that the play pierces the material surfaces that the British settle for: " 'Don't they see through everything—the Russians? all the little disguises we've put up? Flowers against decay; gold and velvet against poverty; the cherry trees, the apple trees—they see through them too,' she was thinking at the play" (*CSF* 247). The empathetic start to the story questions the Western angle, with the narrator quite clearly highlighting the absence of shared sensibilities between West and East: between the codes and conventions of unserviceable beauty on the one hand ("flowers," "gold and velvet") and social realism ("decay" and "poverty") on the other. This dichotomy invokes a parallel between two cultural spheres. The spectator's commentary revolves around this tension or psychological gap between the unfamiliar and the world we consider safe but dull:

> 'Now they've gone. Now we hear the bells of the horses tinkling away in the distance. And is that also true of us?' she said, leaning her chin on her hand and looking at the girl on the stage, 'Do we hear the bells tinkling away down the road?' she asked, and thought of the taxis and omnibuses in Sloane Street, for they lived in one of the big houses in Cadogan Square. (247)

The theater-goer, caught in a moment of personal reverie amid the hustle and bustle of daily life, can somehow step out of time and the limits of individuality for a glimpse into the essential nature of things. The theatrical framing ensures that the spectator is free of the need to accept this reality: " 'As for us,' she said, as her husband helped her on with her cloak, 'We've not even loaded the pistol. We're not even tired.' And they stood still for a moment in the gangway, while they played 'God Save the King' " (247). Although, initially, the central figure toys with identification with the intensity and suffering of the characters on stage, the truly Russian subject matter is ultimately rejected and labeled as "morbid." One comes away with an impression of a Western observer who is clearly apart from and somewhat dismissive of the culture she has just observed. The implication is that Woolf could not fully accept their reality. It is a marginal position that Woolf clarifies in "The Russian Point of View" (1925): "Doubtful as we frequently are whether either the French or the Americans, who have so much in common with us, can yet understand English literature, we must admit graver doubts whether, for all their enthusiasm, the English can understand Russian literature" (*CE4* 181).

Despite their cultural differences, Woolf's stories and criticism reveal the extent to which her own practice drew from the work of the Russians as she grappled with the particular challenges posed by the short story genre. It is not coincidental, therefore, that much of Woolf's commentary on the Russians derives from her most fertile short story writing period, 1917 to 1925, a time when she was also formulating her most crucial ideas on form and modern fiction. During this period, Woolf's knowledge of the Russians forced her to reexamine her own vision and style. In 1917, Woolf made a public bid for freedom with "The Mark on the Wall," her very first published short story. She wrote "Kew Gardens" in 1918, a story that— alongside "The Mark on the Wall"—represents Woolf's early attempts to move beyond traditional storytelling formulae. Throughout the 1920s, the short story would be crucial to her. In 1921 she published her most stylistically inventive short works in *Monday or Tuesday*, her first and only collection of short fiction. After the publication of *Monday or Tuesday*, Woolf felt "a sense of freedom" (*D2* 166) for the first time. This connivance of the short story with emotional truth forms the core of her admiration of the Russians and defines her later work. In a way that mirrors the work of the Russians—and Chekhov, in particular—Woolf's short fiction links the short story's brief duration to the immediacy of perception by removing nonessential material, focusing point of view, minimalizing physical description, and undercutting closure. Woolf's critique of the Russians suggests she embraced the short story as a form of practice that courts ambiguity through its brevity. She admired the Russians' ingenious use of narrative innuendo, their ability to evoke a total impression without saying too much. In this way, the short story is connected to aspects of ourselves that remain silent and hidden. The Russian influence persists throughout the remainder of Woolf's short fiction and is reflected in later stories like "Moments of Being" (1928), and in her fascination with border-line, socially invisible characters in the *Mrs. Dalloway's Party* stories. Ultimately, for Woolf and the Russians, story writing was more about a way of thinking—about the emotional register of the images used—than about a way of telling a story.

Chapter 3

Conversations at Kew: Reading Woolf's Feminist Narratology

Alice Staveley

When Virginia Woolf finished writing *Jacob's Room* (1922), her breakthrough modernist novel, she made a declaration of independence few feminist critics would need to have deconstructed: "There's no doubt in my mind that I have found out how to begin (at 40) to say something in my own voice; & that interests me so that I feel I can go ahead without praise" (*D1* 186). Woolf's liberating reclamation of her "own voice" coincides with a major transformation of her narrative style; it echoes what Susan Lanser, citing Luce Irigaray, describes as the familiar appropriation of a word which "for the collectively and personally silenced [. . .] has become a trope of identity and power [. . .]. [T]o find a voice (*voix*) is to find a way (*voie*)" (3).

It is a commonplace of Woolf criticism to argue that Woolf found her "way" out of the traditional narrative style of her second novel, *Night and Day* (1919), and into the "high" modernism of *Jacob's Room*, by experimenting with the genre of short fiction. Between 1917 and 1921, she wrote a series of short prose fictions that explored the depths of consciousness and flights of imaginative fancy for which her novels would later become famous. In 1921, she published a selection of these stories, *Monday or Tuesday*, under the imprint of the Hogarth Press, the private publishing house she and her husband had co-founded in 1917. Yet, the history of critical response to these stories has proven surprisingly resistant to the applications of feminist criticism, particularly in light of recent studies that have revealed its indispensable role in unlocking the methodological innovations of *Jacob's Room*.[1] For the prevalence of critical opinion arguing for some *a priori* connection between the stories and the novel, there is a striking disconnection between these recent studies of narrative voice in *Jacob's Room* and the voices of the stories that allegedly laid the path.

The explanation has to do, in part, with uneven developments, to borrow Mary Poovey's phrase, in the dissemination of critical strategies across a writer's canon, considering the attendant variables of time, place, and history. I have invoked Susan Lanser's words, however, because of her pioneering efforts to find a place for the methods and vision of feminist criticism within the more traditional, structuralist field of narrative poetics, or narratology. It is, above all, narratology's emphasis on close reading that should promise to illuminate the complex brevity of Woolf's shorter fictions. For many years, however, these two disciplines were seen as virtually separate species. Narratology claimed a place for itself among the arbiters of objective meaning and universal truth, while feminism argued the case for activist, subjective truth and material historical meaning.[2] Lanser seeks to bridge the divide, proposing that a doubleness inhering in the term "voice" opens a route to reconciliation. In the narratological sense, "voice" deals with "specific *forms* of textual practice and avoids the essentializing tendencies of its more casual feminist usages," while as a political term it "rescues textual study from a formalist isolation that often treats literary events as if they were inconsequential to human history" (Lanser 5; my italics). Lanser's ability to square the circle of narrative poetics and feminist politics—to integrate formalism with strategic forms—helped to legitimate feminist narratology as a disciplinary field throughout the 1990s. So successful was the enterprise that Robyn Warhol has recently declared that feminist narratology at the turn of the millennium "may now be taken for granted as one among many possible approaches within narrative theory," a distinct change from the early days when "a feminist had to feel guilty about being a narratologist" (342).

What follows in this essay is a close reading of the unquestionably formalist "Kew Gardens" (1919), the most significant short fiction Woolf composed prior to embarking on *Jacob's Room*, which repositions its central importance to Woolf's innovation of narrative form in the spirit of its feminist politics: to situate Woolf's narratological feminism as the crucible in which her formal(ist) experiments with genre were forged, and to locate its genesis in her inventive depictions of the multivalent, conversational voices that drift, apparently waywardly, though "Kew Gardens." These four disparate dialogues hold the key, I argue, to Woolf's own shifting narratological allegiances, to the way she was beginning to reconceive the relationship between feminist critique and modernist experimentation, en route to expiating the "guilt" (in Warhol's words) that she was, at heart, both a formalist *and* a feminist. Moreover, I interrogate the history of the story's critical reception as it reflects the competing agendas within the narrative itself, showing how Woolf's formal narrative strategies uncannily anticipate the story's long progress toward finding (and creating) a readership willing to hear its simultaneous feminist and modernist voices.

"Kew Gardens" was no aleatory discovery. Written in the summer of 1917, a few months after the Woolfs had founded the Hogarth Press, establishing themselves as amateur but enthusiastic printers and self-publishers, the story debuted publicly in the spring of 1919. It appeared originally as a small, hand-printed booklet, bound in brightly hand-painted paper covers, complete with two woodcut illustrations by Woolf's sister, Vanessa Bell. It was, in one sense, a clear bibliographic touchstone for the materially liberating atmosphere Woolf had found not just as the composer, but also as the compositor of her own texts: "It [printing] is tremendous fun, and it makes all the difference writing anything one likes, and not for an Editor" (*L2* 169).[3] Julia Briggs has recently argued that Woolf's investment in the "manufactured conventions of print" (cited in Hussey 253) directly influenced her experimental formalism in "Kew Gardens," the story's complex binary oppositions—between human and natural worlds; men and women; children and adults—reflecting her practice turning "folio sheets [. . .] into alternating sequences of recto and verso pages" (Briggs, "Writing by Numbers"). At the same time, however, Woolf was certainly no stranger to short fiction writing. Rather, it was a genre she had tried but abruptly abandoned several years earlier when, in 1910, Reginald Smith rejected one of the stories she had written, "Memoirs of a Novelist," for publication in the *Cornhill Magazine*. The rejection stung, not least because the *Cornhill* had held such strong paternal and literary patriarchal associations for Woolf: her father, Sir Leslie Stephen, had been its long-time editor, following in the footsteps of *his* father-in-law, William Makepeace Thackeray.

As a story that deals with the difficulties of both reading and writing women's lives, "Memoirs of a Novelist" usefully repositions the historical relevance of "Kew Gardens" to feminist narratology on two counts: first, because it was one among a series of overtly woman-centered short fictional experiments Woolf was composing before 1910 that coincided with the beginning of her long novelist's apprenticeship on *The Voyage Out* (1915); and second, because it was the very first *fictional* work she offered for publication that was also her most rhetorically ambitious exploration of narrative to date (Briggs, "Virginia Woolf and the 'Proper Writing of Lives' " 245). Its narrative complexity, and doubtless the reason Smith rejected it on the grounds of overt "cleverness" (Quentin Bell 154), stems from the imaginatively esoteric way Woolf strives to express the frustration of a woman reader. Woolf frames the story as a review of a biography of a fictional mid-Victorian sentimental novelist, Miss Willatt, by Willatt's equally fictionalized friend, Miss Linsett, the story/review becoming increasingly fraught as its reader/reviewer (whose gender is never remarked upon, but becomes progressively more marked as the "review" progresses) yearns for something other than the formulaic narrative of Willatt's life that Linsett offers.[4] Notably, the tableau featured in the story's final line invokes Kew Gardens in a gesture of mute yearning, transforming that familiar destination of the Edwardian day-tripper into the site where narrative closure gives way to emotional impasse, to an unfulfilled desire for a more sinuous, less laboriously self-conscious shape for narrative critique. At that moment, the reviewer's interactive and interrogative rereading finally gives way to discursive flirtation with a fictional, rather than a critically objective narrative voice, completely reinventing the circumstances of Linsett's emotional response to Willatt's death: "But afterwards, when she went home and had her breakfast, she felt lonely, for they had been in the habit of going to Kew Gardens together on Sundays" (*CSF* 79).

That the nature of the women's friendship and the speculative content of the conversations they exchange at Kew Gardens should fall literally outside the bounds of the story Woolf had intended to mark her public entré as a creative writer (a writer who, until then, had published only reviews) offers a suggestive allegory for any feminist narratological rereading of "Kew Gardens." With this story, Woolf marked her return to both the gardens and the short fictional genre, but this time as an accomplished, if fledgling, modernist. In rereading the story's reception history, we must be attuned to the kinds of audiences, critical and otherwise, that not only have overlooked the narratological feminism that grounds her modernism, but also have influenced the ways in which she shaped her fiction, a fact that Smith's rejection drove home for her as early as 1910, the year when, she later famously declared, "human character changed" (*E3* 421). With the history of feminist narratology now allegedly secure, it seems high time that we take another look at the writing and reception of "Kew Gardens," questioning not only how they comment on one another, but also how they deepen our understanding of Woolf's journey toward becoming a "high" modernist.

*　*　*

"Kew Gardens" is arguably Woolf's most widely read short story. A nicely compact piece of prose, it suits itself well to anthologies and to the syllabi of countless undergraduate English courses, a useful pedagogical introduction to Woolf's more "complex" works. Critics have tended to devote more singular attention to "Kew Gardens" than to any other piece of short fiction in Woolf's canon.[5] Taking their lead from Leonard Woolf's remark that "Kew Gardens" was "a microcosm of all [Woolf's] then unwritten novels, from *Jacob's Room* to *Between the Acts*," they have duly focused on the "rhythms, movements, imagery, [and] method" by which Leonard catalogued its distinction, irrefutable proof that "it could have been written by no one but Virginia" (*Downhill* 60). The most fascinating, if overlooked, aspect of the story's critical reception, however, is that it reads in large part like a primer for traditional narratology, its emphasis on form in lieu of content, on universal generalizations about style and method obscuring specific interrogations for how history, gender, and class drive the story's manifold innovations of narrative form.

Reading the gaps and often freely acknowledged hesitations in a representative sample of recent interpretations of the story, against the backdrop of the precedent-setting formulaic established by the 1919 *Times Literary Supplement* review, we can better orient an alternative reading of "Kew Gardens," one that reveals the precise grounds on which a feminist narratology applies to it. While this approach does not aim to disparage or displace earlier readings, even less to suggest their *a priori* theoretical importance, it does expose how the story's own elaborate patterning—its carefully demarcated oscillations between landscape and people, images and voices—might be said to ambivalently encourage structuralist interpretations. What becomes interesting, then, is to ask *why* conventional readings of such an *un*conventional story have held sway for so long: to determine which parts of its narrative have attracted the attention of certain kinds of reading, and which aspects have gone unheard, if not unread, despite their more overtly dialogic presence within the story. I argue that Woolf seems to be interrogating the idea that what gets read and what gets heard can be two very different things, adumbrated by gender's intervention in the hierarchical valuation placed on the written over the spoken word.

A feminist narratological rereading of "Kew Gardens" needs to address precisely those parts of its structure that conventional narratology, deaf to the sounds of gendered critique, tends to dismiss: its conversations. Bracketed within quotation marks, the conversations in Woolf's gardens speak the story's feminist modernist critique. Yet, unlike Woolf's novelistic use of the parenthetical to invert known power relations, the verbalized passages in "Kew Gardens" risk being diminished, not enlarged, by their typographical separateness. Melba Cuddy-Keane aptly reminds us that conversation can often appear liberating and inclusive simply because it democratically "encodes opposing views"; yet this very rhetorical porousness leaves open the possibility that "the culturally dominant view [will] easily be privileged by the naïve or resisting reader/listener. The radical writer who rejects authorial dominance takes the risk that a conventional reading will dominate instead" ("The Rhetoric of Feminist Conversation" 137–38).

Woolf's narratological risk-taking in "Kew Gardens" engages this double bind with a heightened awareness for what is at stake. It is not that she
naively believes all conversational modalities exist within direct quotations,
nor that she is hiding her polemical light under the gardens' luxuriant
foliage. Rather, by turning her readers into eavesdroppers straining to over-
hear tenuous and fragmentary conversations, she intensifies the culturally
symbolic preeminence of the garden itself to overwhelm or to subsume the
critical content of the overlapping, non-intersecting, speech acts. It takes a
lot of effort, in other words, to decipher what her conversationalists are saying. Without that effort, the hypnotic, somnambulistic effect of the gardens holds sway, precluding attentive consideration to the more ominous
implications of the free-floating "wordless voices" (*CSF* 95) that provide
such an alluringly ambient backdrop. Woolf, who described this story cryp-
tically as "a case of atmosphere" (*L2* 257), knew better than to expect, or
even to desire, instantaneous recognition of her emergent critique, the kind
of unwelcome attention that may well have ensured its rejection on
grounds of both form *and* content. Instead, she deftly replicates within the
story the kind of atmospheric static that mediates and distorts the articu-
lated voices as they compete for fair hearing in the silence, the alleged qui-
escence, of the gardens. Yet, perhaps not even Woolf could have foreseen
how long it would take for that hearing to be granted its broadest audience.

Ever since the first review of "Kew Gardens" appeared in May 1919, its
mixture of formal unity and impressionistic beauty has beguiled critics.
Harold Child, writing in the *Times Literary Supplement*, helped set a model
for the formalist critic when he admitted to being somewhat baffled by a
story which appeared to be based inauspiciously on a suburban public gardens; the story was "neither something nor nothing; neither formal nor
wild; neither old nor new; neither urban nor rural; neither popular nor
choice" (Majumdar and McLaurin 66–67). On second glance, however, he
concluded that its beauty must lie in its very ability to artistically transcend
its own mundanity; although "Mrs Woolf writes about Kew Gardens and a
snail and some stupid people," the story itself is "a work of art, made, 'created' [. . .] finished, four-square [. . .]" (Majumdar and McLaurin 66).
Child does rather uncannily hit on the story's hidden power: it does,
indeed, lie somewhere on a borderland between competing discourses, at
once removed from and near to alternative places and subjectivities, all held
in delicate counterpoint. Yet, his neither/nor paradigm still recalls the abso-
lutism of an either/or epistemology successive feminist critics have found
disabling. Giving up the ghost of critical comment, Child quotes at length
from the story as signature and salve of an exhausted reader, content to let
the excerpt speak the merits of the larger story. He concludes his review
by printing in full the last two paragraphs of "Kew Gardens," notably

privileging the phenomenological setting of the "wordless voices" while avoiding any reference to the conversational oddities of the "stupid people."
Unlike a literary critic, of course, Child's prerogative as a literary reviewer is to make such lengthy, unsupported quotation from his source in an effort to heighten its appeal. Yet, the technique can also come across as a kind of shorthand summary, a facile way of chasing off a professional obligation, even while reasserting the power of the *status quo*. Maintaining the inviolable beauty of the piece without tackling any of its elements that might rattle conventional assumptions about artistic autonomy, Child celebrates the non-radical aspects of the story, for himself and his readers. This said, however, Woolf certainly benefited from Child's admiration and was undoubtedly glad he *didn't* challenge her story for being too strangely avant-garde; it was this review, after all, that led to the outpouring of public interest in "Kew Gardens," which, in turn, launched the Hogarth Press toward commercial viability and Woolf, with time, onto the sometimes contradictory path of prosperous avant-gardism.[6] Taking experimental cover at Kew in 1919 was a smart artistic move.
Reinventing Child's position from a number of different angles, more contemporary critics of the story have continued to privilege formalist interpretations intent on precluding the disruptive presence of the gardens' human interlocutors. Avrom Fleishman, seeking rather notoriously (for 1980) to inject "a cool draft of formalism [. . .] in[to] the currently moist atmosphere of Woolf criticism" (46), divides Woolf's short fiction writing into "circular" or "linear" models of development; he praises "Kew Gardens" for its linear progression toward a concluding paragraph in which all the disparate voices find full expression and unity in a "common life" (57). For Fleishman, the people—"eight beings or kinds of beings" (56)—appear more mystical than real, a view that disarms in advance any thematic dissonance that might reside in what they actually say. Still, Fleishman himself gestures somewhat wryly to the limitations of his own formalist model. As if stunned by the story's formal beauty, he admits retreat from further interrogation of its content, punning on the risks to his own intellectual contentment:

> It is difficult to distinguish form and content in this beautiful piece; even the simplest description of the form verges on an interpretation of the content; and I must content myself on this occasion with singling out the linear progression by which "Kew Gardens" reaches its heights at the close. (57)

John Oakland similarly finds a "harmonious, organic optimism" (264) whereby a "cumulative theme-voice [. . .] generalize(s) character in a dramatically creative way that eventually leads to the universality of the voices in the final paragraph" (267). While offering good summaries of the four human episodes in full, Oakland links the dialogues by virtue of their similar preoccupations with time past and time present within the man/nature continuum. Despite admitting that these themes become "more confused" (269) as the dialogues progress, he leads inexorably back to the predetermined conclusion that "behind the diversity of people and things there lies an essential oneness" (267). Reacting against this kind of animistic reading, Dominic Head promises a more complex engagement with the story's fourfold dialogues, interpreting them in the context of Bakhtinian theory. A novel and academically updated approach, Head's methodology does, however, succumb to a common problem of using Bakhtin to address the tensions within dialogue, what Carla Kaplan describes as "[t]he tendency to universalize and abstract the social efficacy of the dialogic" where "the mere identification of 'heteroglossia' is itself a cause for celebration and proof of liberatory or subversive counterforces" (11). Head's dilemma is not so much that he assumes too readily the subversive potential of heteroglossia (without defining what precisely *is* the object of subversion), but rather that his observations end up privileging a celebratory, cohesive formalism long attendant on readings of "Kew Gardens."

While most of these contemporary critics therefore surpass Harold Child's initial assessment of the gardens' inhabitants as "stupid people," few interpret their speech patterns as more than just harmonic interludes reconciling life and death, past and present, age and youth. Edward L. Bishop, however, sees Woolf's experimentalism reaching beyond the phenomenology of the story itself. Although he too adopts a formalist approach, reading the story as something of an enclosed unit that reflects its own thematic unities, Bishop draws unique attention to two important aspects of its narratology relevant to a feminist narratological rereading. In the first instance, he notes that the four couples present at Kew Gardens are *not* random choices, but represent a carefully considered cross-section of age, class, and social relation; in the second, he argues that the story is as much about discourse and reading practices as it is about setting and situation. Bishop perceptively observes that Woolf's innovation in "Kew Gardens" is not so much an atmospheric utopianism, but rather a highly flexible narrative style that moves easily between the external world and the inner workings of consciousness, one whose inventiveness rests precisely on its ability to (re)enact a similarly fluid relationship between text and reader. By recognizing that "the reality Woolf conveys is apprehended through the *experience of reading*," Bishop illustrates how Woolf "gently forc[es] the reader out of *his* established perceptual habits, raising questions about the nature of discourse and the conventions used to render it" (112; my italics).

If Woolf is challenging conventional ways of reading with her writing of "Kew Gardens," the story bears witness not only to a new relationship between text and reader, but also to a new alliance between Woolf's reading practice and her narrative innovation. If, in "Memoirs of a Novelist," Woolf literalizes her reading of narrative's alienation of female experience through the trope of the review, it might be argued that in "Kew Gardens" she takes that almost editorial self-consciousness to the heart of the cultural mystique, retracing her steps to the roots of the original and originary garden myth in Genesis. Metaphorizing the setting of that most prescriptive of cultural mythologies, she invokes the gardens at Kew in defiance of former (literary, cultural, political) exclusions, no longer intimidated by or deluded about their ramifications. Her act of authorial assertion (or insertion) is, in part, an act of transgression, returning the woman writer/critic to her Edenic origins to better view how the myth has long given precedent to conventions, narrative or otherwise, that deny cultural authority to women. Her action can also be read more hopefully as a mature "embrace of reality" (Froula, "Rewriting Genesis" 211), an awareness that such myths are narrative constructs which have long privileged the sexual politics of a masculine reading, but are not impervious to change. On the threshold of modernist discovery, Woolf "at [almost] 40" is ready to embrace the narratological changes those challenges entail.

Not, of course, that such bravura is unqualified. The difficulty of reading the dialogues, I suggest, has as much to do with Woolf's awareness of the strenuousness of taking a stand against dominant narratologies as it does with her desire to keep something of the tenuousness and flexibility—the non-hegemonic potential—of the conversational mode alive. She may want to liberate the reciprocity of the spoken word from the fixity of the written, but only so long as it doesn't fall outside the frame of the materially documentable. Her timely access to the Hogarth Press and her active investment in hand-setting typeface for this story undoubtedly helped her to pit her speculative conversational critique against the solid authority of print; yet, as she reassembles her ingots into the voice of feminist interrogation, she also gains privileged access to the material power of print. Like the snail in her story who takes such a long time to reach its goal, with the interruptions of the angular green insect and the human passers-by continually altering its epistemological progress toward the "dead leaf" blocking its way, we might say that Woolf considers "every possible method" of addressing the dead weight of tradition that confronts her "without going around" or "climbing over" it (*CSF* 93) in her conception and eventual production of this story. Like the snail who eventually takes the leaf head-on, poking its head underneath to take stock of the leaf's height and diffuse light, she too comes to position her critique at the very center of the garden, exposing its dominant paradigms from within by adapting a rhetorical mode that had seemed so fugitive for the reader/reviewer of "Memoirs of a Novelist."

Mixing the necessity for invention felt by that frustrated reader with the speculative potential for what was left outside the text, Woolf devises a new narrative form based on conversation as creative critique that explains her sensitivity to the experience of reading, and to the role of the modernist reader in "Kew Gardens" as Edward L. Bishop depicts it. From one stand-point, the ability to draw readers into her text is vital to the dissemination of her critique and, as Elizabeth A. Flynn proves empirically, "Kew Gardens" does seem to possess a peculiar elixir that weakens the resistant reader.[7] Yet, it does not always mean, as the predominant reception history shows, that her radicalness has been heard as resoundingly as it might have been. But, there had to be a beginning. Since the first edition of this story also constituted Woolf's first independent publication from the Hogarth Press, it seems that the safe haven she had unearthed between the textual leaves of "Kew Gardens" found commensurate material sanction— appropriate "cover"—in the hand-painted paper wrappers and hand-sewn folio pages of that inaugural, if fragile booklet.[8] Finally, her feminist narrative critique had found its own narratological, no less material form, awaiting readers who might also be keen listeners.

*   *   *

Having argued that the dialogic complexity of "Kew Gardens" has been stifled for too long by conventionally formalist readings, it is helpful to keep in mind Carla Kaplan's cautionary words for the study of heteroglossia when pursuing a revisionary reading of its dialogues:

> Mapping the presence of and conflict between multiple textual voices is only one task; it cannot answer in advance the question of what conclusions we might draw about the particular forms taken by their presence and interac-tion, cannot answer the difficult questions about how—in concrete instances of dialogic exchange—conflicting agendas are negotiated and "footings" are rearranged. (11)

I argue that Woolf maps and interrogates orthodox intersections of romance, gender, class, and war through the concrete voices of this story, showing precisely how her characters negotiate and rearrange their discur-sive relationships—their "footings"—with respect to hierarchies of power and subordination. Lately, there have been encouraging signs that Woolf's garden voices are drawing the inventive attention they deserve. Melba

Cuddy-Keane has focused renewed interest on what she calls the underexplored "aurality" of "Kew Gardens," how the sounds of the gardens play as important a role in the story's gestalt as does the hypnotically impressionistic imagery. This is, after all, "a story about voices—voices of people we see before we can hear what they are saying, voices which pass out of earshot before the conversations are over" ("Virginia Woolf, Sound Technologies, and the New Aurality" 82). Cuddy-Keane gives a fresh interpretation of these fragmentary voices as experiential metaphors derived from new technologies of sound, specifically from radio.

Even critics who have written about the visual appeal of "Kew Gardens" have taken inspiration from the discursive qualities of the speaking voices. Edward L. Bishop, for instance, opens his article by citing the last of the four garden conversations, the exchange between the two young lovers:

> 'Lucky it isn't Friday,' he observed.
> 'Why? D'you believe in luck?'
> 'They make you pay sixpence on Friday.'
> 'What's sixpence anyway? Isn't it worth sixpence?'
> 'What's "it"—what do you mean by "it"?'
> 'O, anything—I mean—you know what I mean.' (*CSF* 94)

Pursuing this elusive "it," Bishop states that the reader knows "what the young woman means" (109) because this dialogue comes at the end of a story in which Woolf has "already captured 'it': the essence of the human and natural world of the garden" (109). While this interpretation values the integrative pleasures of the garden, in the precise context of the lovers' dialogue, "it" nonetheless carries a weight of social signification that goes beyond questions of essence; "it" encodes a critique of the economies of sexual exchange that underpin prevailing assumptions about patterns of courtship, romance, and marriage. These two lovers are in the process of negotiating, in Kaplan's sense of the phrase, their "conflicting agendas" about what it might mean to journey to Kew Gardens that day. If we tune in to a slightly different tonal frequency (adapting the spirit of Cuddy-Keane's work) we hear them talking at cross-purposes to the occasion at hand; we begin to apprehend a structural pattern intimating that the couple's increasingly interrogative exchange forms a discrete narratological unit that comes to refract each of the three preceding dialogues rather than just summarily concluding the story's depiction of a day spent at Kew.

When the woman asks her suitor if "it" is worth it, she is not referring to a detached contemplation of the flowers. Instead, she includes herself in the afternoon's enterprise, implicitly questioning whether she herself—as partner, as mate—is worth the sixpence cost of admission. She takes instinctive offence at the man's suggestion that he is especially pleased to be able to perambulate with her at Kew on a day when, as luck would have it, admission is reduced, perhaps even free. She reads his relief defensively as a sign of prevarication, a devaluation of a courtship that should, after all, be the subject of intention and hard work, not the vagaries of luck. If he were serious about her, shouldn't cost be an irrelevant consideration? Her doublespeak, those "words with short wings for their heavy body of meaning" (*CSF* 94), answers rhetorically that, of course, cost should be of no consequence; it is, therefore, of the utmost importance.

Woolf was well aware of the price differential for entry to Kew Gardens on Fridays. She writes in her diary on Friday, November 23, 1917 that she conceived a game for herself to test her decisiveness. If she discovers while out on her daily walk that "it was the 6d day at Kew [she] wouldn't hesitate but decide not to go in" (*D1* 81). Since admission to the Royal Botanic Gardens was sixpence on Fridays as well as Tuesdays, and only one penny the rest of the week, she decides on this occasion not to enter. Yet, such adherence to her own self-conviction is not something the young Trissie in "Kew Gardens" has learned to abide, caught up as she is in the machinations of the romance plot (and, it might be argued, manipulating its economic terms of engagement). The symbolic ramifications of the "sacred sixpence" to free a woman from unreal loyalties, both familial and marital, will return with a vengeance in Woolf's 1938 feminist-pacifist polemic, *Three Guineas*, where it comes to stand for the independent income of a working woman, distinct liberation from having to "charm or procure money from her father or brother" (131–32). Here, however, it is the image of a woman's economic servitude within the romance plot that triggers a chain reaction of anxieties for both the man and the woman, who harbor equally intense but ambivalent expectations of romantic fulfilment. Moreover, Trissie's name—as distinct from the Simons and Eleanors, Lilys, Huberts, and Carolines who otherwise take center stage at "Kew Gardens"—betrays her lower-middle-class, perhaps even working-class status (Trissie Selwood was Vanessa Bell's maid during the period Woolf wrote the story). Coupled with the man's anxiety that the price of admission would have materially affected their ability to visit the public gardens, Woolf highlights the manifold conflicting agendas over which both speakers are struggling to gain some (misplaced) control.

The activity that follows this exchange gives somatic weight to Trissie's half-articulated anxieties, even as it leaves her dangerously open to "purchase." As the lovers stand at the edge of the flowerbed, his hand covering hers as it rests on her parasol, the action of pressing that parasol "deep into the soft earth" (*CSF* 46) codes the sexual implications of their courtship, which require social legitimation through marriage. Their mutual discourse of courtship, underpinned by the language of economic transaction, merges with contemporary expectations that she become an object for sexual exchange within the marriage rite/right. This displacement is nowhere more clearly executed than when the man finally picks up the thread of her rhetoric—He: "[. . .] what do you mean by 'it'?"; She: "O anything— I mean—you know what I mean"—by initiating an uncomfortable reversal of desire, problematic for them both. He immediately translates the confusion and excitement of the sexual *frisson* between them into something materially quantifiable, consolidating his role as arbiter of an economic pact by finding "reality"—not to mention a reprieve from potentially unruly passion—in the sense of proleptic urgency that he will be required to pay the bill for tea:

> [. . .] there was a bill that he would pay with a real two shilling piece, and it was real, all real, he assured himself, fingering the coin in his pocket, real to everyone except to him and to her; even to him it began to seem real; and then—but it was too exciting to stand and think any longer, and he pulled the parasol out of the earth with a jerk and was impatient to find the place where one had tea with other people, like other people. (*CSF* 94)

The young man's impatience to assert his likeness to other people, now that an intimation of a sexual bond has been established, draws him back into a world where conventionality rules. The expected fusion of sexual and economic identity is no more markedly apparent than in that fingering of the two-shilling coin inside his trouser pocket. This mixture of eagerness with secrecy—the sense that he is being initiated into some private club where the other adult tea drinkers are members awaiting his entrance— anticipates Woolf's portrayal of Paul Rayley in *To the Lighthouse*, whose proffering to Mrs. Ramsay of a gold watch newly removed from its wash-leather case signals both his intention toward Minta and his capitulation to the rules of order governing Mrs. Ramsay's exclusive matchmaking club (127). In both cases, the men bear economic totems of their suitability to marry, and the women enter unions that anticipate a precarious loss of self and potential failure of the merger. In no time, Trissie's defensive interrogative posturing has turned on itself, and she becomes a passive observer of her own life, a somnambulist poised forever on the edge of awakened memory and orientalized desire:

> 'Wherever *does* one have one's tea?' she asked with the oddest thrill of excitement in her voice, looking vaguely round and letting herself be drawn on down the grass path, trailing her parasol, turning her head this way and that way, forgetting her tea, wishing to go down there and then down there,

remembering orchids and cranes among wild flowers, a Chinese pagoda and
a crimson-crested bird; but he bore her on. (*CSF* 95)

These apparent reversals—the woman's compulsion toward exploration
only after expressing her anxiety about the man's romantic intentions; the
man's identification with the economic trappings of ownership only after
admitting to sexual feeling—are not Woolf's expressions of gender essen-
tialism. Rather, the verbal and gestural pantomime through which the man
and woman communicate shows just how closely both enact and soon
become entrapped by intersecting orthodoxies: romantic, sexual, and economic. Moreover, the thinly veiled insistence, the repressed force, with
which the man leads the newly ambivalent woman on to tea is sufficiently
inconclusive that it directs the reader's attention *back* to the garden's other
romantic pair in search of a unifying circularity that actually leads to a
reassessment of marriage and desire. This romantic pair, the first of the four
couples to stroll through the gardens, is a married couple who, with their
children in tow, figure as harbingers of the bourgeois security the younger
couple perhaps hopes to attain by (paid) admission into the gardens.

Here, the orderly dispersal of the various couples throughout the
gardens, representing a cross-section of social class, generation, and familial relation (Bishop 110), takes on added narratological significance when
we notice that the two romantic couples, and the discourses that identify
their relationships, bookend the two single-sexed dialogues that are
exchanged between the two men (one aged and one youthful) followed by
the two women (one "stout and ponderous," the other "rosy-cheeked and
nimble") (*CSF* 93). That these interior dialogues—not coincidentally, the
most frequently overlooked or misread by Woolf's critics, beginning with
some of her earliest reviewers[9]—should code references to the Great War—
that great political conflict raging outside the garden—further complicates
conventional readings of the romantic liaisons between the male and female
pairs. By placing the war at the conversational core of the story, but
encrypting its presence there (as cleverly as any government war propagan-
dist although to decidedly different narratological ends), Woolf insinuates just
how closely personal and political, domestic and national ideologies inter-
twine; by unravelling one, she must necessarily critique the other. In her
previous writings, Woolf had certainly broached these connections before.
Dalloway's unwanted kiss to Rachel in *The Voyage Out* is, for instance, the
somatic coda to his warmongering. Yet, with "Kew Gardens," she finds a
detached, deceptively "lightweight" narrative formula that resides generi-
cally and bibliographically outside the frames of the conventional novel. In
this fusion of narratological and material freedom, the story's critical
conversations define the voice of Woolf's emergent modernism.

By making a structural and semantic link between the young lovers and Eleanor and Simon, the older married couple, as if they are avatars of what Trissie and her suitor hope to become, Woolf encourages a reappraisal of the melancholy that haunts the seamless alternation between the married couple's thought and speech. On the one hand, the sense of loss both express—Simon, for another woman; Eleanor, for her former youth—can be read as part of that benign regret which always accompanies maturation and compromise, the choice of one path inevitably closing off another. On the other hand, their longings point to very specific repressions which seem forever bound up in their marriage; the decisions made to honor conventional expectations of marriage and family are potentially second choices, at odds with prior, more individual and independent needs.

For the man, marriage to Eleanor is a secondary victory of sorts, having failed in his quest to convince Lily to marry him fifteen years earlier, despite having "begged her . . . all through the hot afternoon" (*CSF* 90). His remembrance of Lily's impatiently twitching shoe metonymically gestures Lily's intention not just to resist Simon's advances—to refuse to do what "Simon says"—but also to walk out of the marriage plot he, with the help of another fictional format, might have had her walk into. It is the first intimation in Woolf's writing of a shoe embodying the clash between individual freedom and societal constraint: an early incarnation of Jacob's empty shoes, emblem of a life wasted, literally blown off its feet, on the battlefield of war. As William Handley writes about *Jacob's Room*: "[w]hile Jacob's shoes point to his death in the Great War, they also suggest what the narrator has had to combat throughout the novel: the ways in which a militarized society robs human beings of bodies and voices for its own violent ends" (110). With a twitch of her toe, Lily escapes the romance plot that is here literal and metaphoric prologue to the war plot in which conscripted soldiers require women's conscription to the ideals of marriage and family to make meaningful their fight.

Although Lily may find her way out of the scripted love plot, Woolf ensures she remains an eponymic presence in Eleanor's thoughts of lost youth and unrealized desires. The water-lilies Eleanor paints as a child merge with the kiss of the old grey-haired woman—the "mother of all my kisses all my life" (*CSF* 91)—to show how suppression of a woman's creative independence is contingent on prior repressions, whether homoerotic or homosocial in their homage to the strength of maternal inheritance. According to Woolf's artistic creed in *A Room of One's Own*, "we think back through our mothers if we are women" (69). For Christine Froula, such repressions are precisely the legacy of the Genesis myth, generated in that mythological garden of Eden, where male appropriation of culture and history originates at that moment of symbolic acquisition of the "Word" at

costly expense of the "name of the mother" ("Rewriting Genesis" 198).
Woolf may even have chosen Lily's name as a feminist challenge to biblical
typology, the white lily being the floral emblem of Mary, mother of Jesus.
In her garden narrative, Woolf forsakes the connotations of chastity associated with the religious flower, favoring instead the free-floating red water-
lilies of Eleanor's remembrance: "Imagine six little girls sitting before their
easels twenty years ago, down by the side of the lake, painting water-lilies,
the first red water-lilies I'd ever seen" (*CSF* 91). A subtle syncretism of name
and vision, the two lilies of Woolf's gardens—the Lily who got away, and
the mnemonic lily of the woman who did not—critique the narratives of
development available to women in a patriarchal culture; they provide the
seed for fuller expression of the conflict between independence and marriage, art and mothering that Woolf later depicts in *To the Lighthouse*—her
painter protagonist, Lily Briscoe, only the most famous in a long line
of Lilies.

The iconography of the female painter and the white lily was, in fact,
close at hand the summer Woolf was writing "Kew Gardens." Her sister,
Vanessa Bell, had completed a painting entitled *The Madonna Lily* in July
1917 that Woolf displayed proudly in her dining room at Hogarth House.[10]
It was this painting that caused Woolf, in a now (in)famous letter to Bell in
July 1918, to reassess her aesthetic priorities when the painting, "so cool, so
exquisite, so harmonious" (*L2* 258), provoked a color clash with a chair cov-
ered in yellow check that Woolf had recently bought at the Omega
Workshop. What is usually overlooked in this letter is that the introduction
to Woolf's disquisition on the nature of aesthetic emotions begins with a reference to "Kew Gardens." Woolf is eager to analyze her response to *The
Madonna Lily*, but epistolary convention demands that she must first thank
Bell for the woodcut Bell has recently completed to illustrate Woolf's story.
Woolf attests that the woodcut brings consolation to her story: it is "a
most successful piece; and just in the mood I wanted" (*L2* 258). During a
summer in which Woolf is soliciting artwork for the projected publication
of a story that offers a trenchant critique of established narrative conventions
and of the woman artist in all her writerly or painterly guises, it is perhaps
no surprise that Woolf finds questions in *The Madonna Lily* that further dis-
turb aesthetic continuities. Little wonder that the most searching line in her
letter to Bell, where she speaks of "some sort of live instinct trying to come
into existence" (*L2* 259), suggests the birth of something far more textually
anarchic than a mere clash of color. It is as if the clash between chair and
painting displaces Woolf's deeper fears for the aesthetic coherence of her
own text, still a year from publication, awaiting its own moment of
confrontation with established artistic traditions.

If the two exterior dialogues in "Kew Gardens" mirror each other in their discourses on romance and marriage, their concerns and inhibitions are refracted through the interior dialogues that speak obliquely of war. This highly deliberate structural patterning suggests that in the discourses of dominance and submission and of economy and exchange, both of which govern the romantic relationships, there resides, however deeply buried, the narrative of war. The war's shadow falls most ominously across the conversation between the two men, its presence so subtly inscribed in the women's conversation it is perhaps not surprising that most critics, concerned primarily with reading the romance of Kew, have overlooked it altogether.[11] Between the men, there is a slight suggestion that the older man's delusions mime responses to war trauma, his desire to rationalize the enormous loss of life by invoking the spirit of the Greeks—"Heaven was known to the ancients as Thessaly" (*CSF* 92)—giving way to feverish attempts to adapt modern technology, responsible for such unprecedented destruction, to compensatory ends. He imagines the invention of a type of radio on whose airwaves wives might summon back the voices of their dead husbands. His allusion to the Greeks, tumbling headlong into a visual and syntactic hallucination whereby women and widows become interchangeable— "Women! Widows! Women in black—"(*CSF* 92)—draws an exclamatory trajectory from the education of men schooled heavily in the Greats to the institutional hazards of marriage, the terms of cont(r)act becoming clear only in the distorted haze of hallucination. It is as if the exclusivity of male education as a bastion of privilege separated from female influence achieves its highest and most perverse form of accreditation on the battlefield where death inevitably returns home, finding domestic expression in those black-shrouded women (still) left behind. Later in her career, Woolf will elaborate the old man's delusions as identifiable expressions of war-trauma in her portrayal of Septimus Smith, driven insane by a war that continues to haunt him through the recurring visions of his dead friend, Evans, whose hallucinatory visitations sing the song of the dead in Thessaly, a poignant intertextual allusion to her own "Kew Gardens."[12]

Compared to the imaginative confusion of the old man's thoughts, the fractured dialogue of the succeeding women's conversation appears deceptively innocent. Interlacing discussions of familial goings-on with grocery lists and recipe ingredients, the two women attempt to outdo each other in a discourse of domesticity.[13] Yet, in other ways, the rhetorical fragmentation of their exchange acts as a deliberate foil to the imaginative incoherence of the old man's thoughts, linking the contexts of both dialogues. In the singsong rhyming pattern of their speech, emphasized by the typographical formation of the words, Woolf invokes the war through her insistent repetition of the word "sugar":

> 'My Bert, Sis, Bill, Grandad, the old man, sugar,
> Sugar, flour, kippers, greens
> Sugar, sugar, sugar.' (CSF 93)

Sugar was a rationed commodity during the war, a fact Woolf knew all too keenly. In the same diary entry where she writes about refusing to visit Kew Gardens because it was the day they charged admission, she returns home and checks her sugar supplies, as if in defiant compensation: "I counted my lumps of sugar, 31: but Saxon came in, & took one [. . .]" (D1 81).[14] Earlier, on August 15, 1917, a terse diary entry reads hopefully, "The Co-ops will allow more sugar, so we can now make jam" (D1 42). These wartime restrictions sometimes tempted Woolf to break the embargo, writing conspiratorially to her sister in early July 1917 under cover of a "dull, domestic letter" about the limited supply of icing sugar, but offering to "get it & hoard it, unless you think its too expensive" (L2 169). Her story, written later that summer, connects the women's fragmentary rhetoric with the old man's racing thoughts by juxtaposing the "sugar" incantation with the list of interchangeable familial names, engendering a deceptive euphony. The narrative effect of that euphony blurs the possible allusion to the old man as one of a benign string of relatives—perhaps a husband or a father to one of the women ("My Bert, Sis, Bill, Grandad, the old man [. . .]") or even, in less benign class terms, to their domestic employer—with an exterior reference to the estranged old man himself, awkwardly sharing the same garden walk as the two women. They fold him deftly into their household discourse, just as easily as they will later fold ingredients into their evening recipes.

By means of these rhetorical devices—the play between internal and external points of reference mirroring the story's synesthetic oscillation between thought and speech (Bishop 112)—the women become implicated in the discourse of war, even as they speak of food and family. It is here that the class status of the two women, chattering about recipes and relatives, becomes relevant; Woolf explicitly depicts them as "two elderly women of the lower middle class" (CSF 93), a class tag she does not apply to any other couple. The women then come to represent more than a generalized personification of the domestic sphere, focalized by the old man as war widows. The implication is that these women are employed as servants in some larger upper-middle-class household, their black attire not widow's weeds, but their daily uniform. This description is not, however, a straightforward example of Woolf's class prejudice. The narrative context of the women's discourse suggests that, not just employed in domestic service, they also act in service to conventional expectations of middle- and upper-class marriage; they are what Eleanor acquires and perhaps Trissie can only fantasize as part of the marriage trousseaux. Linked rhetorically to the old man, the women become accessories after-the-fact of marriage in the same way his war-induced hallucinations assume an automatic elision, both visual and semantic, between women and widows: widowhood through war is simply another matrimonial accessory. Woolf seems to be gesturing here toward a critical aesthetic that will not emerge as full polemic until much later in her career (most notably in *Three Guineas*, written when Europe was once again faced with total war). As critique, it circles around the idea that, although all women may not be employed as servants, they are all, in complex ways, bound in service to the consequences of patriarchal ideology.

The summer before she composed "Kew Gardens," Woolf had broached tentatively an essayistic connection between men and women, war and domesticity in "Heard on the Downs: The Genesis of Myth," when she described the ominous booming of guns, heard on the English Downs from across the channel in France, as "the beating of gigantic carpets by gigantic women" (*E2* 40–42). These mythological goddess figures execute the world's house-cleaning chores in a way that confuses the distinction between women's detachment from and complicity with warfare, exposing how, as Susan Stanford Friedman describes it in her reading of *To the Lighthouse*, "the domestic realm enables war, while seeming to be its opposite" (*Mappings* 125). In Woolf's essay, however, her attempts to extract domestic metaphor and domesticated meaning from the horrors of war come across as waywardly romantic as much as she might have intended her goddess imagery to act as an antidote to the overblown masculinist rhetoric that opens the essay, to "the hammer stroke of Fate" and "the pulse of Destiny" (*E2* 40). Probably for this reason, Andrew McNeillie brackets this essay as a "distinctly odd piece of writing" (*E2* xiii). Yet, what the published context of the essay seems to preclude—given voice in that great conservative organ, the *Times*[15]—and what the generic form of the short story facilitates, is a more pliable (and private) space where Woolf can manipulate her narrative voices to expose the subtle links between patriarchy and paternalism, to defamiliarize the complex ties binding marriage, class, and war. When Woolf records in her diary a frightening night air raid in December 1917, she, Leonard, and their servants huddled in the basement of Hogarth House, and she records the moment she knew it would be impossible to go back to sleep—"guns apparently at Kew" (*D1* 85)—her words carry a weight of meaning the essay can address only by default: the seeds of war lie closer to home than we might otherwise presume.

That Woolf should circle in "Kew Gardens" around such radical ideas with the help of elaborate structural parallelisms and elliptical rhetorical overlaps may also betray, however, her discomfort with appropriating the women's discourse as lynchpin for the political aesthetics of her new narrative form. Biographers and critics frequently point to the anxiety Woolf expressed when members of the Richmond branch of the Women's Cooperative Guild pressed her for copies of the newly published story (Lee, *Virginia Woolf* 360–61). She wrote privately of her reservations: "But I don't want them to read the scene of the two women. Is that to the discredit of Kew Gardens? Perhaps a little" (*D1* 284). But her response is itself ambiguous. Is the scene itself to the discredit of the story, or is it Woolf's embarrassment at the guild members' request that does the story disservice? Perhaps, as Woolf herself might have sensed, a little of both. Notwithstanding that as an aesthetic device, the scene usefully consolidates a narratological perspective specific to feminist critique, on a social level it raises Woolf's self-consciousness about how truthfully she can identify with the experiences of working women. Her feminist narratological critique gains its voice from women Woolf would not have chosen to befriend. Additionally, there is a painful irony that a story partly generated from Woolf's literalized depiction of the frustrated woman reader, excluded from conventional narrative paradigms, should itself have become the source of projected anxiety about its own women readers.[16]

As always with Woolf, however, these reservations must be historicized to become credible depictions of her contemporary mindset. Woolf's concerns for the "scene of the two women" needs to be placed in the context of a further and earlier conversation. The previous month, she and Ernest Altounyan had met and, according to her account, he had offered her a "surfeit of praise for Kew Gardens—the best prose of the 20th century, surpassing Mark on the Wall, possessing transcendent virtues, save for one passage, between the women, & highly praised by Clive & Roger" (*D1* 276). This one reservation, relayed beside Altounyan's reported praise from Woolf's other more familiar—and familial—male admirers, would have been enough to linger in Woolf's thoughts about the piece, a salient reminder of the need as much as the instinct to divide her loyalties between the readership of the women's guild and the admiration of the male literary and artistic establishment closer to home. Woolf also knew that Altounyan's praise did not come without some self-interest. He was currently in the process of courting the Hogarth Press in the hopes that it would publish his novel. Considering his possible ulterior motives in flattering Woolf's writing, however, it is particularly striking that he criticized the *one* part of her story he felt confident would *not* breach any coterie understanding he might have shared with her (might, indeed, have enhanced it); the conversation between the two women of the "lower middle class" could be dispensed with, without jeopardizing Altounyan's "in" with the Woolfs. Altounyan's comments show how closely assessment of a narrative's "transcendent virtues" comes at the expense, even the sacrifice, of social critique (as much as they also illuminate Woolf's equally conflicted response to any perceived devaluation of her literary standing *as* social critic). As I have shown, this type of oversight has had historical implications for the literary-critical reception of "Kew Gardens," which has supported traditionally formalist readings of the story without reference to Woolf's own intellectual history, her development of a feminist narratology through her experiments in writing short fiction, or her role as printer and publisher of these formative modernist works. There was one reader of "Kew Gardens," however, who showed uncanny perception of the story's merits. In a single phrase, Katherine Mansfield captured the story's critical potential when she wrote in the *Athenaeum* that it was an exquisite example of "love at second sight" (*Novels and Novelists* 36).[17] In typically Mansfieldian way, the phrase evokes the poetic dimension of Woolf's critique without sacrificing elliptical reference to the darker corners of the sunny garden, and serious reflection on Woolf's personal and political motivations for writing. Describing the "disturbing beauty" of the gardens, where the world balances "on tiptoe" and "the secret life is half revealed" (*Novels and Novelists* 38), Mansfield rightly intuits that the story itself stands on tiptoe at an important threshold of Woolf's writing life.

NOTES

1. For a sample, see the articles by Lawrence, Little, Flint ("Revising *Jacob's Room*"), and Froula ("War, Civilization and the Conscience of Modernity").

2. For an excellent introduction to the history of feminist narratology and the diversity of work currently being produced by this "hybrid of an *ology* (the science of narratives) and an *ism* (the action of being a feminist)," see Mezei 1–17. See Warhol 340–41 for an illuminating synopsis of the field's contentious history and its current status as an accepted branch of narratology.

3. This remark appears in a letter Woolf wrote to Vanessa Bell in late July 1917, closely contemporaneous with her writing of "Kew Gardens." See Benzel for further typescript evidence dating the story's composition as early as August 1917, and for the narrative changes Woolf made between the typescript and its eventual publication in May 1919 ("Woolf's Early Experimentation").

4. Lyndall Gordon speculates that Miss Willatt may have derived from a Miss Willett of Brighton who Woolf mentions in *Moments of Being* as having written an ode comparing George Duckworth, Woolf's half-brother, to the Hermes of Praxiteles. His and Virginia's mother, Julia Stephen, apparently used

to keep the ode in the drawer of her writing table. Gordon makes the connection between Brighton and the imaginary seaside library mentioned at the end of "Memoirs of a Novelist"—the final resting place of the now unread biography (Gordon 95).

5. A fact made apparent by Thomas Jackson Rice whose index records that, by the mid-1980s, "Kew Gardens" shared with "The Mark on the Wall" the highest number of critical citations (253). Of course, since then, criticism on Woolf has risen exponentially with "Kew Gardens" continuing to draw a disproportionate amount of interest.

6. For Woolf's own account of the flurry of orders for "Kew Gardens" that succeeded Child's review, overflowing the hallway of Hogarth House upon her return with Leonard from Asheham, see *D1* 280–81. See also Leonard's comments on how the story's "immediate success" spurred the Hogarth Press on its journey toward becoming "a commercial publishing house" (*Downhill all the Way* 59–60).

7. Studying the responses of male and female first-year university students to three short stories, James Joyce's "Araby," Ernest Hemingway's "Hills Like White Elephants," and Virginia Woolf's "Kew Gardens," Flynn discovered that, in the first two stories, readings of the texts often revealed a "pattern of dominance [. . .] in some of the men's responses" where no such pattern appeared in the female responses, women tending to be better able "to resolve the tensions in the stories and form a consistent pattern of meaning" (276). But, in the case of "Kew Gardens," there was little evidence that *any* student tried to dominate the text along gender lines; both male and female students placed themselves within the text and "[d]omination became acceptance" (282). Flynn defines domination as a reader's resistance to the "alien thought or subject" confronted in a text, forcing judgments to be made on the basis of "previously established norms rather than empathetic engagement with and critical evaluation of the new material encountered" (268). A reader who dominates a text remains, in Flynn's assessment, "essentially unchanged by the reading experience" (268), something that "Kew Gardens"—as an expression of Woolf's own openness to the epistemological changes wrought by being an active reader—sought to counteract.

8. Although Woolf's story "The Mark on the Wall" had appeared two years earlier in the inaugural publication of the Hogarth Press, it was paired with Leonard's story "Three Jews" in a combined publication entitled *Two Stories*. "Kew Gardens" was, therefore, her first authorially independent production from the Press.

9. E. M. Forster's description of Woolf's method is here pertinent for its masculine rhetoric, partly enabling complete oversight of the single-sex dialogues in the story: "Flowers and men are the two items at which Mrs. Woolf is looking, and, at first, they seem strongly contrasted. The flowers are down in the bed with a snail, the men erect and sentient, are strolling past with their womenkind, and the possibility of tea. And the men sometimes look at the flowers whereas the flowers never look at the men" (Majumdar and McLaurin 69). Review dated July 31, 1919, *Daily News*.

10. Diane Gillespie reproduces this painting in her book on the relationship between Vanessa's painting and Virginia's writing (114) and she draws attention to Woolf's reference to it in the letter I cite above. While this letter from Woolf to Bell dates from the summer of 1918, a year *after* Woolf had written at least a draft of "Kew Gardens," Regina Marler's recent selection of Bell's letters confirms that Bell painted *The Madonna Lily* in July 1917 (Bell, Vanessa 205–06), allowing us to conclude that the composition of both Woolf's story and Bell's painting were closely contemporaneous, whether or not Bell discussed her conception for the painting with Woolf that summer.

    For further analysis of the iconography of the lily, especially its relationship to a woman's virtues and her proscribed reading practices, see Kate Flint's discussion of Dante Gabriel Rossetti's painting, *The Girlhood of Mary Virgin* (1848–49) in *The Woman Reader 1837–1914* (17–19).

11. The disparate critical attention afforded these two interior dialogues is neatly encapsulated in John Oakland's discrete response. While he acknowledges that the old man's ranting is not mere senility, but perhaps a sign of shell-shock, he sees only "domestic minutiae" in the words exchanged between the two women (270–71). Karen Levenbach, in an effort to prove the war's nondisruptive presence in "Kew Gardens," argues that "[t]he only evidence of war" in the story appears in the two men's dialogue, overlooking the possibility that it is also inscribed in what the women say (21). Linden Peach has recently explored how "the influence of the war on the public mood" affects passages of narrative description in the story (65), although he does not read its presence in the conversations.

12. While Septimus's delusions are usually read as symptoms of shell-shock, Elaine Showalter has suggested that their range and severity indicate a more systemic mental illness (*xl*). And if the actions of the old man in "Kew Gardens" anticipate Septimus Smith's suffering, his hallucinations may also have recalled Woolf's own experience of ill health during the early stages of the war. Hermione Lee draws the connection between the advent of the Great War and Woolf's second major breakdown in 1915, reading its imprint on "Kew Gardens": "In one paragraph, the story dares to touch [. . .] on what being deranged had felt like" (*Virginia Woolf* 375).

13. Woolf may even have decided to tone down the verbal sparring between the two women when she set the story into type. One of the major distinctions between the surviving typescript and the published text is an excised section of the typescript that expands on the women's dialogue, rendering it more of a competition than an exchange: "the small woman either from majority of relatives or superior fluency of speech conquered, and the ponderous one fell silent perforce" (*CSF* 298). Susan Dick suggests that Woolf may have omitted this passage "by mistake" (*CSF* 298). But since Woolf presumably had the option of reinserting it in later editions of the text (the second edition was rushed out less than a month after the first, owing to the initial outpouring of interest), its possible omission at the point of typesetting raises provocative questions. It might indicate the Press's power to intensify Woolf's feelings for

the complex dialectic between art and politics since in the typescript the passage has an existence that Woolf appears to have denied it in print, fraught as it was both with the problematic specter of female competitiveness and the use of class stereotypes for fictional critique. We must keep in mind, after all, the unprecedented degree of control Woolf exercised with this text, literally overseeing its entire production from manuscript to publication.

14. In fact, the "real" Kew Gardens was itself transformed by the demands of wartime restrictions on food. Sections of the gardens were set aside to cultivate potatoes (although not, as far as I can tell, the more poetically appropriate sugar-beet). See Raymond Desmond 376.

15. For a more complete study of editorial influence on Woolf's prose style, see Leila Brosnan 38–69.

16. As is now commonly acknowledged in Woolf criticism, Woolf would continue to have reservations about speaking not just about but *for* the working classes, eventually coming to terms with her own class status as a way of envisioning the collective power of all women who embrace their individual class experience. See Woolf, "Memories of a Working Women's Guild," her preface to Margaret Llewellyn Davies's edition of the memoirs of working class women, *Life As We Have Known It*. For her comments on the anachronism of an educated twentieth-century woman intervening in the lives of the working class as a substitute for challenging the limitations imposed by her own class status, see Woolf, *Three Guineas* (310).

17. Mansfield's review, apparently the only one by a woman at the time of the story's publication, was not collected by Robin Majumdar and Allen McLaurin in their 1975 study of Woolf's contemporary reception, nor does it appear in their updated 1997 edition. Eleanor McNees, however, does include it in her recent four-volume collection of critical reviews on Woolf that spans the contemporary responses to current academic appraisals (*Critical Assessments 2*, 3). The knowing approval Mansfield displays in her review of the story creates an even more complex historical interface, given Antony Alpers's suggestion that an exchange of letters between Mansfield and Woolf in the summer of 1917 may, in fact, have been the catalyst for the story (250–51). Mansfield was certainly one of the story's earliest readers, incorporating her private response to it in a letter written to Woolf in late August 1917 (*Selected Letters 1* 327).

Chapter 4

The Lesbian Intertext of Woolf's Short Fiction

Krystyna Colburn

"I've just written, or re-written, a nice little story about Sapphism," Virginia Woolf wrote in 1927 to Vita Sackville-West of her story "Moments of Being: Slater's Pins Have No Points" (*L3* 397). In fact, though, this was not a unique event: a Sapphic thread winds persistently in and out of Woolf's short stories from her narrative apprenticeship in 1906 to the later stories of her maturity in 1940.

Feminist scholars first wrote in general terms about the rich lesbian cross-currents in Woolf's novels and stories in the 1970s.[1] More recently, essays in *Virginia Woolf: Lesbian Readings* have analyzed the lesbian component of Woolf's fiction in more detail. Few Woolf critics, however, have focused specifically on the lesbian segments of the short stories, perhaps because only fourteen of the stories were published during Woolf's lifetime.[2] Most were published for the first time in 1985 from holograph manuscripts and typescripts left in Woolf's literary estate and edited by Susan Dick.[3]

Although missing the explicit and often sparkling erotic playfulness of Woolf's letters and diaries, the story, shorter and more allusive than the novels, gave Woolf the leeway to reveal the hidden and to imagine the as yet unsafe-in-public lesbian position. The short story is, as Clare Hanson posits it, a "vehicle for different *kinds* of knowledge, knowledge which may be in some way at odds with the 'story' of the dominant culture" (*Re-reading* 6); Corinne E. Blackmer links the genre more specifically to the lesbian reader: "To the extent that lesbians have been associated with the obscure, the neglected, and the marginal," she writes, "there is something quintessentially 'lesbian'" about focusing critical attention on Woolf's short fiction (78).

Certainly the intense and contradictory demands the short story makes on its readers invite a unique kind of readerly involvement. Calling attention to the writer–reader interaction demanded by short fiction, Ian Reid writes, "extratextual framing is unavoidable. No text can be understood apart from what readers bring to it" (310). Woolf herself repeatedly insists on the importance of readerly involvement in short fiction. Arguing that what gives Chekhov's short stories their power is precisely the interpretive involvement they demand from their readers, Woolf writes that they "provide a resting point for the mind—a solid object casting its shade of reflection and speculation" (*BP* 123). Elsewhere she writes that from such inconclusive stories, "the soul gains an astonishing sense of freedom" (*CR1* 182; see also Benzel and Hoberman's introduction as well as Skrbic's essay in this volume).

I want to suggest that in that "shade of reflection and speculation" there is a special space for the lesbian reader. Because the modern short story is so short, so allusive, so tantalizingly suggestive of a coherence and clarity it fails to provide, it invites the reader into a space at once intimate and unconfined, where reader and writer cooperate in the making of meaning. That process allows the lesbian reader to construct herself and her own desires in the act of reading Woolf. For lesbians, as Sally Munt suggests, "are particularly adept at extracting our own meanings, at highlighting a text's latent content, at reading 'dialectically,' at filling the gaps, at interpreting the narrative according to our introjected fictional fantasies, and at foregrounding the intertextuality of our identities" (xxi).

Virginia Woolf uses multiple strategies to signal Sapphist material in her short stories. These strategies are most easily accessible to those who read her, as Pamela Olano suggests, from a lesbian perspective, enriching the text with alternative meanings (see also Blackmer 80). Olano's essay about "reading Virginia Woolf as a lesbian" conflates writer and reader as lesbians, as I do here. The text is simultaneously the author's own, an independent entity, and the reader's own. And though Virginia Woolf clearly recognized the lesbian features of her work as evidenced by her comments about her "Sapphist story," the reader can legitimately find lesbian significance independent of the author's original impetus. "By reading against the grain of compulsory heterosexuality," Olano writes, "readers can, within the margins of lesbian narrative space created by the writer, become intertextual lesbians by affirming the homoeroticism of Woolf's narratives" (167). Reading on these terms becomes a subtle intertwining of lesbian sensibility and lesbian recognition.

Broadly speaking, the stories most amenable to such lesbian readings fall into two categories: dystopic marriage plots haunted by lesbian yearning, and utopian celebrations of lesbian love. Throughout, key motifs encode or evoke lesbian readings, among them what Terry Castle calls the "Apparitional Lesbian"; the spinster, her single state underlined by the title "miss"; an intense sensuality in the use of sound; traditionally lesbian floral and jewel imagery; and a climactic emphasis on the loving kiss between women. Many of these motifs appear in the novels as well: In *Mrs. Dalloway*, for example, Miss Kilman is the spinster, while the climactic kiss of Clarissa and Sally Seton, accompanied by lyrical flower imagery, celebrates lesbian eroticism. The difference is that in the novels, these motifs are mingled with other concerns and therefore resonate less suggestively than in the short fiction. Far from being "apparitional," Miss Kilman is so embodied she appears grotesque, while Sally grows away from her youthful lesbianism into middle-aged marriage. In the stories, on the other hand, readers share the narrator's mingled loss and yearning for Miss V. or Fanny's kiss with Julia Craye with no further plot developments to mitigate their resonance.

The stories' suggestiveness is enhanced by the revision process Woolf went through as she composed them. In many of them her repeated reworking of brief moments draws attention to her own uncertainties about what kind of relationship she wanted to depict. Often the stories' lesbian content turns more ghostly and elusive as drafts near publication. Paradoxically, this stripping away of lesbian presence forces the reader to delve more deeply into the story's texture, to experience that "astonishing sense of freedom" Woolf found in Chekhov's stories, as the soul—both the reader's and the story's—is evoked without being coerced or pigeonholed.

I want to look first at stories of dystopian marriage and lesbian yearning, several of which are among Woolf's earliest, unpublished work. In these stories, a ghostly lesbian presence is at once evoked and elided through the use of the honorific "miss," a term underlining not only the unmarriedness of a major character but also her lesbian desire. As Mieke Bal points out in the Miss Marple stories, the reader can "consider the 'Miss' a proper name" (123), a substitute for the risky "lesbian." Patricia Cramer more specifically identifies Woolf's "beloved spinster characters" as lesbians ("Notes" 178); these "misses" generally coexist with other hints of a lesbian presence; fully realized lesbian intimacy is precisely that which is "miss-ing."

The first of Woolf's previously unpublished stories, dated 1906 in the holograph version, is untitled in manuscript but called "Phyllis and Rosamond" by Dick (*CSF* 295). Exploring the idea of marriage resistance prevalent throughout Woolf's work, it tells the story of two upper-class sisters, Phyllis and Rosamond Hibbert, twenty-eight and twenty-four years old, whose fate is to be "in the market" for husbands, no matter what their own wishes may be. The story at first appears to be an extended husband search, but that overt line of narrative is undermined by a running commentary between the sisters, and one offered by the story's narrator. Caught in a time when marriage is the only "profession" available for women, they play their parts well, but the narrator insists that their private lives are their own by recording their private conversations about their potential suitors:

'Do you care for him?'
'Not in the least.'
'Could you marry him?'
'If her ladyship made me.' (*CSF* 22)

Their fate is to succumb to loveless marriages. Yet the sisters and the reader are at the same time conscious of what they term their "slavery," which contrasts with the freedom of Bloomsbury, and especially of Miss Tristram.

It is in Bloomsbury that the sisters meet Miss Tristram, who wears a "shooting jacket, with her arched little head held high" (24)—an androgynous or even masculine counterpoint to the Hibberts' strict femininity. Phyllis is attracted to the open conversation, the heady sense of selfhood, and once again verbalizes her lot: "You must remember that most young ladies are slaves; and you mustn't insult me because you happen to be free" (27). The lesbian reader can identify the cross-dressing of the host as a subversive hint. There is also an implied but clear condemnation of marriage: a sense that, even if not for these two women, there is an escape possible somewhere for others. There is the independence of Sylvia Tristram in her profession as a writer, an implication that her life may be successfully lived apart from men and marriage, a hope of a future that will be explored in subsequent Woolf stories. Woolf seems to be suggesting that there must be freedom from a life with men if any lesbian existence is to thrive.

This same implication is pursued in "The Mysterious Case of Miss V." (probably also 1906), where the elusive if unremarkable Miss V. suggests Castle's "apparitional lesbian." Castle posits that the "literary history of lesbianism [. . .]is first of all a history of derealization [. . .] One woman or the other must be a ghost, or on the way to becoming one" (34). Blackmer, following up on Castle's suggestion, labels Miss V. an "apparitional spinster," part of Woolf's exploration of the "psychological experience of attraction among women" (78). Always present, Miss V. is never part of the narrator's actual life; the narrator calls it a "tie of blood" that brings them into the same space so frequently. "No party or concert or gallery seemed quite complete unless the familiar grey shadow was part of it" (*CSF* 31). That assumed and comfortable situation changes when Miss V. no longer appears at events. The narrator looks for something missing, but she cannot identify a person or a name. The story, to this point, has a careful, slow, unfolding pace. But the rhythm of the piece changes with an epiphanic realization. "Then one morning early, wakening at dawn indeed, I cried aloud, Mary V. Mary V!!" (31). That exclamatory anapestic cry halts the flow of the text. The reader is forced to stop by the exclamation and the punctuation, and the suddenness of this change is disconcerting. The narrator then begins a search, desultory at first, that culminates in a decision to go to Miss V.'s home "to track down the shadow" (31). She likens her task to visiting the "shadow of a blue bell" or "catching the down from a dandelion at midnight in a meadow." The pace of the story quickens with this "fantastic expedition" ending at Miss V.'s home. The narrator/character hastens with a sense of anticipation to her destination, only to learn that Miss V. had died the previous morning "at the very hour when I called her name" (32). "So I shall never meet her shadow any more" (32), the narrator concludes. That final sentence, with its slowing pace, soft sounds and rare rhythm (a classical Greek fourth paeon) evokes Castle's notion of the apparitional lesbian as she-who-is-missed.

So, too, does the recurring word "shadow": suggesting an elusive, suggested-yet-absent presence, the word is related to that used by Woolf to characterize the distinctive function of the short story as a "solid object casting its shade of reflection and speculation" (*BP* 123). The story itself, like Miss V., is ungraspable. The reader, like the story's narrator, is left alone with her desire.

This desire—the excitement and nervousness of the potential lesbian connection—is eroticized in the story by pacing, imagery, and sounds. Once the narrator realizes her bond to Miss V., the connection is felt most intensely while she is in her bed. The narrator cries out Mary's name (the only use of her first name) from her bed on waking. The decision to go find Miss V. comes to her as she lies awake the next night. One is tempted to call the abrupt recognition an in-bedded text. On another level, the images of flowers and dandelion down that immediately follow that recognition epitomize Miss V.'s combination of elusiveness and desirability: "Consider how it would seem to set out in an omnibus to visit the shadow of a blue bell in Kew Gardens, when the sun stands halfway down the sky! Or to catch the down from a dandelion! At midnight in a Surrey meadow" (31). The imagery is soft, beautiful, romantic. The joy and excitement, the preparation for meeting, are those more of a lover than an acquaintance: "as I put on my clothes to start I laughed and laughed to think that such substantial preparation was needed for my task" (31). A telepathic communication underlines the closeness of these two women who had lived their lives apart. The orgasmic sequencing is evident in the pacing and rhythms of the story with its leisurely beginnings, the climactic exclamation of Mary V.'s name, and the denouement in which even the shadow of this most passionate connection is lost.

In an early version, interestingly, the two women actually confronted each other. The holograph version of this story has an earlier canceled ending when the narrator "walked straight in and saw Miss V. sitting at a table." But quite clearly any real meeting is doomed. How could Woolf write beyond the meeting after that intensity of the calling out, the excitement of the search? The lesbian content is close to the surface, but ultimately must be hidden. As Castle posits, the apparition stands in the stead of the woman-lover. The story is Woolf's touch of lesbian reality but without its caress.

In the 1909 story "Memoirs of a Novelist," Woolf becomes bolder in her treatment of women's love for each other (perhaps one reason Reginald Smith turned it down for *Cornhill* [*CSF* 296]), though still evoking an apparitional quality to encode their passion. The narrator tells of Miss Linsett, who is telling the story of another woman, Miss Willatt, who died in 1884 "after fourteen years of unbroken friendship" (69). The narrator reveals that Miss Linsett is "uneasy" and willing to tell her friend's story only because there was none closer in her friend's life. Their connection is socially recognized within the text—Miss Linsett is the person asked to write an "appreciation" for the newspaper. In a strange near-disclosure, she reports that she does not want this task and would prefer that someone else write it "as long as they did not 'break down the barriers' " (70). The quotation marks draw the reader's attention to these barriers, but there is no revelation as to what those boundaries conceal. Miss Linsett keeps them up intentionally, clearly unwilling to reveal what they hide. In another similar passage, Miss Linsett again holds back revealing elements. She begins to tell of an extraordinary experience of loss, then interjects, "so much we may say, more we may not" (73).

The external narrator immediately comments, "The most interesting event in Miss Willatt's life, owing to a nervous prudery and the dreary literary conventions of her friend, is thus a blank" (73). Woolf teases the reader with hints and subterfuges, then draws the curtain on these two women. She tantalizingly advances and then withdraws. She seduces the reader to revise the surface meanings, and one would say "to what end?" One feasible explanation is the concealed lesbian relationship. The frame story itself is confusing, as the reader must spend significant energy at some points to decipher who indeed is the immediate narrator and whose story is currently being told. The first narrator switches to the first person, wanting more detail from the memoir, and invites the reader to guess at what is hidden, even while identifying its source as the relationship between the two women. Everything else in the story is simply colorless. The letters of Miss Willatt that are quoted (but not verbatim) are labeled dull "because the word love and whole passages polluted by it, have shrunk into asterisks" (73). The dead Miss Willatt is no longer dangerous, but her words may still be so. She, too, is in the realm of the apparitional lesbian. Her friend can write her life and still preserve their reputations simply by leaving blanks where any scandal may lie. "The problem with Miss Linsett's work," one critic comments, "is that she views her duty to her beloved (and there are lesbian overtones to the story) to be to obfuscate the dreariness of the life" (Fox 165). The only excitement is the titillation of the concealed. The memoirs evoke a hidden relationship that is more important to the biographer than the elements of her subject's life.

The story's unstated lesbian core is also suggested by the very naming of the characters themselves. The two "misses" suggest a romantic relationship between them: Woolf supplies her leading characters in this story with no first names, no other relationships; they are Miss Willatt and Miss Linsett. The convention of two "misses" in conjunction with one another is one of the clues that Woolf leaves in her early stories to call attention both to the marriage resistance and to the woman-only romance of the characters.

Obviously the brevity of the short story form is uniquely suited to such allusiveness. But why is there such hiding or why such teasing of the lesbian reader with these near-revelations? This indirection typifies Woolf's depictions of relationships between women. As Janet Winston notes, this short story "shows women's intimate bonding as genuine, enduring, and to a large extent, reciprocal" (59), but ultimately a private concern. The world may wonder, but only from the other side of the barrier. The misses elect to keep their secrets hidden. This suggestion of lesbianism as that which must be hidden anticipates the "privacy of the soul" so valued by Mrs. Dalloway fifteen years later. This is the space—figured in the text by her own small room, as well as that of the old woman opposite—that allows Clarissa to become a lesbian reader of her own past, able to decode the "match burning in a crocus" that evokes her own sexual responsiveness to women. Perhaps, in fact, what becomes clearest as one reads Woolf's stories from a lesbian standpoint is the extent to which the acts of reading and interpretation are coextensive with the enactment of lesbian desire.

This intermingling of reading and desire is clearest in two stories Woolf wrote about mis-reading: "Sympathy" (probably 1919 [CSF 299]) and "The Legacy" (1940). Collectively they are a kind of lesson in reading-as-a-lesbian. In both, standard readings of their plots assume the centrality of marriage to their meaning. But suppose these readings only mirror the "compulsory heterosexuality" of the dominant culture (see Rich)? Reading as a lesbian produces quite a different plot line: one focused yet again on a dystopic marriage and lesbian desire.

"Sympathy" was never published in Woolf's lifetime. The narrator of the story reads an obituary of Humphry Hammond and proceeds to daydream about him and then about Celia, the (presumed) widow. The only Celia the reader comes to know is the one of the narrator's imagination. "Celia. Yes . . . I see her, and then not. There is a moment I can't fancy: the moment in other people's lives that one always leaves out; the moment from which all that we know them by proceeds" (108).

But the "fancy," as Woolf names it, includes the narrator in a very particular positioning, not with "Mrs. Hammond," the widow, but with "Celia," the woman. They are together in an idyllic fantasy revel:

> Now I see her more distinctly [. . .] There I follow her; no longer with envy. [. . .] Can one offer her—a day's walk in the hills? Striking our boots sturdily upon the high road we start out, jump the fence and so across the field and up into the wood. There she flings herself upon the anemones and picks them 'for Humphry'; and refrains, saying that they will be fresher in the evening. We sit down and look at the triangular space of yellow-green field beneath us through the arch of bramble twigs which divides them so queerly. (*CSF* 109)

The narrator returns to reality, concluding that it is all fancy, all a dream world. The delightful and captivating fantasy of the escapade collapses on contact with the real world as the narrator receives a reply to her letter of condolence. The widow is not widowed. The Humphry who died was her father-in-law.

Instead of feeling relief, the narrator reacts with dismay. The following revision reflects Woolf's indecision, for she wrote multiple versions, and in fact, crossed the following: "Do you mean to tell me that Humphry is alive after alland [sic] you never open the bedroom door or pick the anemones, [. . .]; death never was behind the tree; and I'm to dine with you, with years and years in which to ask questions about the furniture. Humphry, Humphry you ought to have died." Most tellingly, the typescript's last crossed-out phrase, "Humphry, Humphry you ought to have died," is replaced in the published version with "O why did you deceive me?" (Woolf, CD-ROM, "Sympathy" typescript MH/A24.d). The narrator wants Celia to be the widow of her fantasy.

The complication of the ending, the multiple rewrites of the simple last sentence, the exclamatory tone, the clear wish for Celia to be available, all point to a story with an unpublishable longing, that of the narrator for Celia. Celia herself serves as yet another apparitional lesbian, who, though not dead like Miss V. and Miss Willatt, is part of a fantasy escapade rather than the real world. The lesbian reader discerns the echoes of longing, the dissolving image, as traditional tropes of lesbian desire.

The narrator's mistaking one man's name for his son's anticipates the reader's own possible mistaking lesbian desire for conventional "sympathy." Along similar lines, in "The Legacy" a widower initially misreads his wife's death as an accident; the reader senses what finally becomes clear to the widower, that it was a suicide in response to the death of her (male) lover. But I want to propose yet another reading: a story of lesbian love. Inviting the reader toward this third reading is the fact that the story was heavily revised. Susan Dick reveals, "one holograph draft, two complete typescripts, and fragments from at least six other typescript drafts have survived" (*CSF* 311). While the final version depicts a husband who, reading through his newly dead wife's diaries, discovers that she had a male lover and may well have killed herself for love of him, a careful look at the story's various drafts leads to a more complex understanding of the passionate relationships depicted.

The story's opening words, read by Gilbert Claydon, the husband, are these: "For Sissy Miller." These words refer to a pearl brooch left by the dead woman, Angela, to her friend. Reaching us through the consciousness of Angela's husband Gilbert, these words suggest a legacy diverted from husband not to a male but to a female lover, a point reinforced by the paragraph's closing words: "For Sissy Miller, with my love" (*CSF* 281).

Sissy Miller turns out to have been Angela Claydon's personal secretary of many years. When she arrives at Gilbert's behest, he pities her, yet his thoughts may mean more than he intends. "She was terribly distressed, and no wonder. Angela had been much more to her than an employer. She had been a friend" (282). But study of the story's multiple versions suggests that at least at moments in the compositional process, Sissy had been more than a friend as well. In the latest revision, Woolf writes, " 'I've been so happy here,' [Sissy] said, looking around. Her eyes rested on a writing table behind him. It was there they had worked—she and Angela" (282). But in an earlier draft, the passage reads: "She was gazing, he noticed, still at the table, where she had sat at her typewriter, where the diary lay. And lost in some recollection of Angela, she did not answer his suggestion that he should help her. She seemed for a moment not to understand" (Woolf, CD-ROM, "The Legacy" typescript M81). And a third version ruminates: "She was thinking, no doubt, of Angela; that explained the [. . .], the rather awkward pause that followed his [. . .] question" (Woolf, CD-ROM, "The Legacy" typescript M80). It is clear that this is a passage Woolf worked on carefully, refining it more than most of the text. The subject that she struggles to present is the nature of the relationship between the two women.

Gilbert, of course, has no idea of what has passed between the two women, and Sissy reveals neither her thoughts nor her memories. There is another more awkward reworking of this same passage. It is clear that the connection is an important one and that the brooch means more than a simple remembrance:

> [Gilbert] said how his wife had [. . .] always spoken of Miss Miller as a friend: she had felt her more than a always spoken in her highest terms of Miss Miller. She had felt that she was a friend. She had [. . .] left her a token of her regard. [. . .] "This brooch"—he took it from the hearth [?] [. . .] & Miss Miller It looked incongruous, he cd not help feeling [. . .] It lay in the palm of her hand. Oh, she said, she wd always value it. (Woolf, CD-ROM, *A Haunted House*: "The Legacy" holograph M79)

It is the brooch that is the key to this story. It is Angela's specified gift to Sissy and explicitly pearl. Paula Bennett has suggested that many lesbian writers use what she calls a "clitoral coding" involving small precious objects such as diamonds and pearls. After Clarissa kisses Sally Seton in *Mrs. Dalloway*, for example, she feels she has been given "a diamond, something infinitely precious" (35). Here, Sissy holds the pearl brooch in her hand. "For Sissy Miller, with my love": set off by quotation marks three times in the latest version, these words are strikingly soft (with their sibilants and liquids and perfect iambic tetrameter). They also contain the only direct statement of love in the entire story. While Gilbert learns from his wife's elusive diary fragments of an apparent affair between her and a mysterious "B.M.," who turns out to be Sissy's brother, the story's subtext underlines Sissy's own love for Angela. At story's end, when Sissy asks Gilbert, "Is there [. . .] anything that I can explain?" Gilbert responds, "Nothing!" (287), sure that he has finally seen the whole truth of his legacy: his cuckolding by a male rival. But the reader, especially the reader privy to the multiple reworkings, can conclude otherwise.

Related to these dystopic marriages is the cluster of stories involving Mrs. Dalloway's party. The stories resemble a collage of persons at the party with the reader as an eavesdropper on their conversations and consciousnesses. Not meant as chapters in a larger piece but as independent entities focusing on individuals in the same time and place, the stories defy classification in terms of genre; Woolf herself commented, "I am less & less sure that they *are* stories, or what they are. Only I do feel fairly sure that I am grazing as near as I can to my own ideas" (*D2* 325). The party is society writ small and Mrs. Dalloway herself is the linchpin. Underlying all the stories is a sharp contrast between societally mandated heterosexuality and the desires of individual women. As the specifics of the following stories make clear, here at her party, women invitees share Clarissa's own sense of a hidden life, of important moments just beneath the surface of what can be seen and heard.

"Mrs Dalloway in Bond Street" began in 1922 as the opening chapter of a book to be called *At Home: or The Party* (*CSF* 302). In it, Clarissa walks, enters a shop, and buys a pair of gloves; underlying these seemingly inconsequential actions is a sensual subplot of two women recognizing each other's erotic potential.

> 'Good morning,' said Clarissa in her charming voice. 'Gloves,' she said with her exquisite friendliness and putting her bag on the counter began, very slowly, to undo the buttons. 'White gloves,' she said. 'Above the elbow,' and she looked straight into the shop-woman's face—but this was not the girl she remembered? She looked quite old. (*CSF* 156)

This is the Clarissa who remembers a younger woman with whom she had a connection, and the slow taking off of the gloves reveals skin in an unhurried exposé. The grammar of the sentences exposes more than her hands. The "very slowly" separated by commas from the rest of the sentence and using no plosive or dentive consonants makes this nearly a seduction, of the reader if not of the shop-woman. The reader is in the position of watching Clarissa slowly unbutton, watching her gaze at the shop-woman. In addition, the syntax leaves just what is being unbuttoned ambiguous. This play of words resembles the privately coded messages of lovers in the company of strangers. (Woolf, CD-ROM, "The Man Who Loved His Kind" holograph and typescript M106)

The hinting continues. They speak of gloves with pearl buttons and Clarissa's mind concludes "perfectly simple—how French" (25). The pearl buttons—those clitoral surrogates—radiate lesbian associations reinforced by their Frenchness, which evokes the famously free French lesbians of Natalie Barney's salon. The shop-girl then intensifies the erotic component as her next words call attention to the slenderness of Clarissa's hands, and thus, by implication, to their role as instruments of female pleasure.

Clarissa thinks about their both being older, noticing the "little brown spots" now on her own arm, noting their very different lives, juxtaposing her memories of twenty years before with the woman she now sees. "Yes, thought Clarissa, if it's the girl I remember, she's twenty years older . . ." (*CSF* 156). And though earlier drafts of the story compress the time between the earlier erotic impulse and the present, Clarissa's mind keeps moving closer and then backing away in imagining the girl's life and then returning to her own. The movement has a wave-like rhythm that keeps bringing the reader to the point of lesbian desire and then moving away. The reader is left with a hint but not a climax of sensuality. An earlier draft of this story includes the words "It's imagination we women want." It is the imagination of the lesbian reader that Woolf counts on to span the ellipses between past and present. The plot of the piece is very much in the present. But Clarissa's mind travels to another pre-marriage time, which was less socially and sexually circumscribed.

The party as depicted in the stories is itself a sequence of disconnections. Despite the apparent ease of the people in the room, the reader sees beneath the visible flourishes to the agitated minds of the guests, who vie for our attention and our sympathy. Prominent among these are the individual women guests who are part of the scene but very much anchored in their own worlds instead of this aggregate. The women carve their own moments into our minds and emerge from the crowded room to claim their own space and singularity. The lesbian is separate from the "party" that is society.

In "The Man Who Loved His Kind," for example, a "Miss" O'Keefe challenges the arrogant Prickett Ellis (and what a name *that* is). Instead of a demure woman who admires him, he is faced with a woman who challenges not just his words but his life choices and his soul. His internal response threatens this uppity woman: "feeling something rise within him which would decapitate this young woman, make a victim of her, massacre her" (*CSF* 198). Woolf clearly intends the raw violence of this sentence. In an earlier draft she had written "make her an example" (M106), crossed the words out, and replaced them with the horrifying "make a victim of her." Their parting, after a conversation with no communication, offers no resolution, only a continuation of the conflict between the sexes. " 'I am afraid I am one of those very ordinary people,' he said, getting up, 'who love their kind.' Upon which Miss O'Keefe almost shouted: 'So do I' " (200). The ritualized gendered points of view end on this note, as the "lovers of their kind" cannot cross the chasm between them.

These stories of dystopic marriages and hinted at but unexpressed lesbian desire persist from the earliest moments of Woolf's career through its final days. Woolf's quasi-utopian stories of love between women, on the other hand, grow out of particular relationships at particular moments. Throughout Woolf's stories the ideal grouping is a female one, with women understanding one another in an intimacy inaccessible to men, in terms reminiscent of Woolf's own comment, "Much preferring my own sex, as I do. [. . .] [I] intend to cultivate women's society entirely in the future" (*L3* 164). But the stories I am about to discuss go further than most of her work in evoking such a female utopia, first, by depicting it within the story—either as fantasy or as contained within a single, momentary kiss—and second by enmeshing the story at the extratextual level in female–female relationships.

Take, for example, the earliest of these stories, the unpublished "Friendship's Gallery." This was a private biography given by Woolf to her beloved friend, Violet Dickinson. Woolf herself identified her relationship with Violet as a "romantic friendship" (*L1* 75). She wrote to Violet of her "tender memories of a long embrace, in a bedroom" (*L1* 71). Blanche Cook acknowledges the lesbian content in "Friendship's Gallery," describing it as "[a] fantasy of an erotic and nurturing female utopia" (719), while Jane Marcus calls it "only one of many lesbian utopias" (89) written by Woolf. Virginia sent the story typed in violet and bound in violet leather, with the firm demand that it was to be only for the eyes of Violet and one other friend. The story is full of fun and foolishness and fantasy, much as *Orlando* would be some twenty years later. It is a farcical biography, beginning with the ostensible lusty cries of the newborn Violet. This fictional Violet grows outlandishly tall and plain, and strides a plot line reminiscent of *Orlando* (or is it perhaps the other way round?) in tone and even in wording. Nothing is chronologically linear in this story—time is where one wants it to be. The sense of play is outrageous and meant to be so.

This is to be a women's world. Violet herself in the story has boundless energy. Violet strides; she springs over a gate. "Violet's eye was charged with fire and her lips moved with decision" ("Friendship's" 289). The final section of the story, though, has nothing to do with earlier parts; it fancies two goddesses alighting in the east as saviors. A sea monster appears and the two become jesting as well as jousting heroines. "Now they had just made up their minds to be devoured when the two Princesses came down to the seashore and bewitched the monster by making passes with certain magic wands called 'Umbrellas'" (300). The two women are apart from anyone else and together in their exploits. Each is the only possible peer for the other. Their reckless fun and laughter echo in the lives of their listeners. In "Friendship's Gallery," Virginia presents this gift, encapsulates this lesbian moment, and flings it to her love, its intensity enhanced by its brevity.

While "Friendship's Gallery" was written for a friend, several of Woolf's stories written for publication also hint at the pleasures of a fully realized lesbian relationship. The proper word, however, is hint: the stories' climactic kisses as well as their sensual imagery evoke momentary ecstasies that are not sustained. These kisses, which Stimpson claims bear "metonymic responsibilities"(99), represent lesbian sexuality in terms of ecstatic, even orgasmic moments. Unlike *Mrs. Dalloway*, however, where most of the novel writes over its subtext of lesbian love, these stories, because of their brevity and lyricism, can evoke this love without submerging it in more conventional plot lines.

"Kew Gardens" (1919), as critics have noted, diverges from the typical narrative of the short story. Instead of a comprehensively linear account, the story is a visual display with tightly focused close-ups of the gardens in bloom, and a mid-length camera view of people who pass by: first a man and a woman, then two men, then two women, and finally another man and woman. There is no plot; the unifying principle is the locus rather than character. The story begins literally with a snail's eye view of the grass and flowers, which are depicted with corresponding size and perspective. While critics have long noted the story's stylistic innovativeness, a closer look reveals that its lavish play with words and sounds is joined to a visually loaded lesbian imagery.

To read its opening sentence aloud is a distinctive experience:

> From the oval-shaped flower-bed there rose perhaps a hundred stalks spreading into heart-shaped or tongue-shaped leaves half way up and unfurling at the tip red or blue or yellow petals marked with spots of colour raised upon the surface. (*CSF* 90)

The preponderance of sibilant and liquid sounds, the way the tongue must move in the mouth to form them (rolling around the sounds), the way the vowels elongate the time needed to speak the words—all these combine to stress the passage's—and story's—sensuality. A bit further on:

> [. . .] the light now settled upon the flesh of a leaf, revealing the branching thread of fibre beneath the surface, and again it moved on and spread its illumination in the vast green spaces beneath the dome of the heart-shaped and tongue-shaped leaves. (90)

A lesbian reading of these words cannot ignore the erotic component of the sibilant sounds, the slow movement of the words, the very explicit images of tongue and flesh and light moving over the plants as a lover over the beloved's body. The words not only invoke lovemaking, they make love to the reader.

Woolf published "Kew Gardens" four times in her lifetime, giving it a singular place among her works. Unlike most of her other stories, this was published with visual accompaniment, illustrated by Virginia's sister, Vanessa Bell.[4] The 1919 printing contained two woodcuts, and the 1927 printing lavishes its attention on the visual: each page of twenty-two is illustrated by Bell. Of these, the page depicting two women is the most elaborate. A flower extends within the typography, emerging from the page to become part of the text itself. It extends from the earth, which is itself the lower border of the page. The words surround this blossom with its "heart-shaped, tongue-shaped leaves," becoming part of the image.

Catherine Stimpson has argued that flowers are a standard trope for lesbian passion (103). In Woolf's fiction, flowers recur during lesbian moments: carnations ("Moments of Being: Slater's Pins Have No Points"), wisteria ("The Evening Party"), anemones ("Sympathy"). Olano goes so far as to claim that the "flower imagery in Woolf's fiction, just as in her letters, often signals the start of the lesbian narrative" (31). Cramer tracks the lesbian floral connection in general, and in romantic meetings between Virginia and Vita Sackville-West in particular, through *The Years'* luxurious detail ("Pearls" 225–26). In "Kew Gardens" the association is even clearer as Woolf connects flowers and tongue-shaped leaves with an intricate delicacy.

"Kew Gardens" is also the site of a crucial kiss: as the first couple strolls, they report memories to each other. While the man remembers proposing to a woman who turned him down, the woman recalls a kiss on the back of her neck, a kiss so emotionally powerful it made her hands shake for the rest of the afternoon: "I took out my watch and marked the hour when I would allow myself to think of the kiss for five minutes only—it was so precious—the kiss of an old grey-haired woman with a wart on her nose, the mother of all my kisses all my life" (*CSF* 91). It is as if the narrator of "The Mysterious Case of Miss V.," who dreamed of visiting "the shadow of a blue bell in Kew Gardens," had finally completed her journey and found her "miss."

Both kiss and flowers reappear in "A Woman's College from Outside" (1920). Sent as a gift to the Women's Union of Edinburgh University, the story illuminates, like the moonlight within the story, young women's faces and lives. It begins with the "feathery-white moon" that keeps a light in the sky so that "all night the chestnut blossoms were white in the green":

> There, in the garden, if she needed space to wander, she might find it among the trees; and as none but women's faces could meet her face, she might unveil it blank, featureless, and gaze into rooms where at that hour, blank, featureless, eyelids white over eyes, ringless hands extended upon sheets, slept innumerable women. (*CSF* 145).

The first paragraph sets up a separate women's space. Angela, the central character, is alone in her room in a moment of quiet contentment. There is no plot or even chronological sequence to ground the reader's understanding as would be necessary in a novel; the scene merely shifts to a nearby room full of women students whose "soft laughter [comes] from behind a door" (146). The laughter, "seeming to bubble up from the depths and gently waft away the hour" (146), moves outward to the garden and influences it with its own sense of peace, floating over everything, imbuing every fragment with its "fertilizing, yet formless" haze (147).

What little there is in the story of talk and action affirms both the women's delight in each other, and their erotic self-awareness. There is talk of a woman seen slipping out the back gate, defended by the women because "we're not eunuchs" (146); this is followed by a crucial kiss that we learn of only in retrospect, as Angela, now back in her room again, remembers the moment when Alice

> [. . .] stooping, kissed her, at least touched her head with her hand, and Angela, positively unable to sit still [. . .] roamed up and down the room . . . throwing her arms out to relieve this excitement, this astonishment at the incredible stooping of the miraculous tree with the golden fruit at its summit— hadn't it dropped in her arms? She held it glowing to her breast, a thing not to be touched, thought of, or spoken about, but left to glow there. (147)

In the sentences immediately following, Angela realizes that the world lies beneath her, "all good; all lovable" (147). The excitement of the moment after the kiss and the holding on to it, the identification of the kiss with something small and precious and not to be forgotten, echoes the kiss in "Kew Gardens" and anticipates the one in *Mrs. Dalloway* between Clarissa and Sally. Like those kisses, its pleasure is intense but unsustainable; when she sees the morning coming, Angela cries out in pain. The moment is passing and the women's world is giving way to the everyday; life is returning to "normal," and that is to be mourned.

"Moments of Being: 'Slater's Pins Have No Points'," Woolf's most explicitly "Sapphist story" (*L3* 431), was written during the height of her love affair with Vita Sackville-West. Apparently based on an actual comment about Slater's pins made by her tutor when Woolf herself was young, it is the story most often perceived by critics as lesbian. The five-page story's actual durational time is a matter of minutes, and most of the story consists of the speculations of the pupil, Fanny Wilmot, as she looks for a dropped pin that had just previously held a flower on a dress. Her thoughts, and we are privy to them, are about her teacher, Miss Craye. Fanny surmises that there is "something odd" about Julia Craye. The thought pattern is interrupted when she notices that Julia has picked up the carnation. Her thoughts here have "something odd" about them as well:

> She crushed it, Fanny felt, voluptuously in her smooth, veined hands stuck about with water-coloured rings set in pearls. The pressure of her fingers seemed to increase all that was most brilliant in the flower; to set it off; to make it more frilled, fresh, immaculate. (217)

Fanny notes that Julia had never married, then finds the missing pin and returns from contemplating Julia's past to her presence at that moment, recognizing that Julia is "steadily, blissfully, if only for a moment, a happy woman. Fanny had surprised her in a moment of ecstasy" (220). And the corresponding moment of ecstasy for Fanny follows: "She saw Julia open her arms; saw her blaze; saw her kindle. Out of the night she burnt like a dead white star. Julia kissed her. Julia possessed her," after which Fanny pins the flower "to her breast with trembling fingers" (220).

As early as 1974, Avrom Fleishman recognized this as a representation of lesbian passion: "It seems crass to labor the point," writes Fleishman, "but this intuition of homosexuality is part of the total vision of Julia which Fanny achieves" (61). The flowers, the pearls, the sensuous immediacy of Julia's hands, the insistence on her identity as "miss" and marriage-resistant, the mood of passionate reverie climaxing in a kiss are all coded referents to lesbian lovemaking familiar from other Woolf stories.

In *Mrs. Dalloway*, Clarissa experiences Sally's kiss as "a present, wrapped up." She'd been told "just to keep it, not to look at it—a diamond, something infinitely precious, wrapped up, which, as they walked [. . .] she uncovered, the radiance burnt through, the revelation, the religious feeling" (35). Judith Roof points out that like the match burning in the crocus, Woolf's other image for this kiss, the wrapped diamond suggests both layers that can be stripped away and, ultimately, concealment: what's underneath the covering is a feeling rather than anything that can be seen: a radiance or fire, which glows within the crocus as within the wrapped diamond. This covered radiance, Roof suggests, is a metaphor for lesbian sexuality: "hiding within radiating petals is something indescribable, something other than the phallus" (111). The kiss in "A Woman's College from Outside" is similar; Angela feels a "golden fruit" has dropped into her arms and holds it "glowing to her breast, a thing not to be touched, thought of, or spoken about, but left to glow there" (*CSF* 147). Like Clarissa's sense, when aroused by women, of an "inner meaning almost expressed" (*MD* 32), these images imply a fire deeply felt because deep within, a fire inevitably private and inexpressible. To make such a feeling explicit is to betray its very nature. The short story, at once offering and withholding its meaning, resembles just such a golden fruit, glowing yet elusive.

Woolf's use of imagery, sound, and erotic symbolism places her in the long line of lesbian authors who celebrate their love in their writings. Woolf wanted to "be friendly with women, what a pleasure—the relationship so secret and private compared with relations with men. Why not write about it truthfully?" (*D2* 320). In fact, Woolf did write about it truthfully in diverse and sensitive ways. The short stories, with more suggestiveness than her novels, invest the words with a blushing delight in women-relatedness, the lesbian eroticism carefully teased in and out of the text. The short story offers Woolf a unique opportunity to create lingering textual echoes and recurring lesbian images. The short story provides Woolf with a way to affirm women's love for each other and to communicate such love with a multi-layered and multi-textured voice. She limns her lines with the tenderness of a lesbian quill.

Notes

1. Among those pioneer women were Blanche Wiesen Cook and Jane Marcus. Their work has provided a sound bedrock for later critical exploration of feminist and lesbian themes in Virginia Woolf's work. See Eileen Barrett for a more complete history of the lesbian work. *Virginia Woolf: Lesbian Readings* has both original essays of the 1990s and an extensive bibliography invaluable for any scholar doing research on this topic.
2. Important lesbian readings of Woolf's short fiction include those by Blackmer, Cox, Winston, and Levy.
3. Susan Dick's study is invaluable for tracing multiple drafts of the short stories and I owe her a debt of gratitude for pointing me in this direction.
4. Diane Gillespie investigates the collaboration between Virginia Woolf and Vanessa Bell in *The Sisters' Arts*. In particular, see her chapter "Criticism and Collaboration" for a fuller analysis of the "Kew Gardens" illustrations.

Chapter 5

Collecting, Shopping, and Reading: Virginia Woolf's Stories About Objects

Ruth Hoberman

In "The Work of Art in an Age of Mechanical Reproduction," Walter Benjamin defines "aura" as the quality possessed by objects to the extent that they are unique and authentic, still steeped in their original relation to tradition and ritual. In his own age, he writes, this aura has decayed: when the vast majority of objects and aesthetic experiences are mechanically reproduced (movies and photographs, e.g., as well as consumer goods), they gain meaning not from their uniqueness, but from their relation to an audience or consumer. In such an atmosphere, according to Susan Stewart, those eager to separate themselves from the shopping masses form collections. They collect the old-fashioned kind of unreproducible object, whose value rests solely on its authenticity, its relation to its origins. Unlike the marketplace, where everything is available to everyone at prices set by demand rather than intrinsic worth, Stewart points out, collections offer a "nostalgic myth of contact and presence" (133), their components radiating precisely that "aura" lacking in mass-produced objects.[1] This contrast between the collector of auratic objects and the consumer of mass-produced goods underlies many of Woolf's short stories. In her short fiction, I want to argue, Woolf enacts an anti-collecting aesthetic that not only privileges the shopper over the collector, but also redefines the act of reading as a kind of shopping.

In her relatively positive treatment of shoppers, Woolf sets herself apart from many male modernists, who, as consumption was increasingly seen as women's work (Richards 206), began to define themselves against a mass culture they perceived as female and consumption-crazed (Huyssen 44–64; Felski 61–90).[2] While Woolf often mentioned her personal dislike of shopping in letters and diary entries, she depicts London shoppers affectionately in a number of stories and essays, as well as, most famously, in *Mrs. Dalloway*. In all of them shopping is depicted in terms of what Jennifer Wicke calls "market modernism": a market perceived in Keynesian terms as chaotic, charged with "a fluid magic, feminized, anarchic, yet interconnected, playful at its best" and fueled by consumption ("Mrs. Dalloway" 20–21), which is construed in positive, rather than threatening terms. More recently, Michael Tratner has argued that *Mrs. Dalloway* and *Three Guineas* between them posit the institution of the cooperative—where consumers are also owners, whose every purchase contributes to the store's dividends, in which they have a share—as an alternative to imperialism. If the rich hoard and the poor lack the means to spend, Britain must rely on expanding markets for economic growth; if the rich spend, on the other hand, and the poor share in the profits produced by their own consumption, money and goods will circulate freely (91–98). These positive understandings of shopping underlie my own argument, that Woolf in her short fiction contrasts the socially interactive and constructive act of shopping with the egotism and sterility of the collector.

Tratner contrasts twentieth-century delight in pleasure, spending, and self-indulgence with nineteenth-century respect for labor, saving, and self-restraint (both economic and sexual), positing the 1890s aesthete as a transitional figure (9). I would argue for a crucial qualification, however: the aesthete's consumption is best described not as shopping but as collecting. Fictional late-nineteenth-century collectors like Gilbert Osmond, of Henry James's *The Portrait of a Lady*, Mrs. Gareth, of *The Spoils of Poynton*, and Wilde's Dorian Gray spend in the name of aesthetic pleasure, but invest in museum-quality objects—which are "above" the marketplace—rather than in consumer goods like clothing or refrigerators, that lose value when sold. These collectors' purchases are defined very much against the "cheap gimcracks" characteristic of what Mrs. Gareth calls "this awful age" (31).

When Woolf writes of shopping, she does so in contrast not with the ethos of productivity and saving associated with Victorian seriousness, but with the ethos of collecting: an ethos that involves adventurous forays into exotic locales and auction houses; the extrication—often amid competition and conflict—of valuable objects from the hands of the "unworthy"; and the construction of the exquisitely decorated home, whose aura-laden objects tell and retell the story of their own origins, while serving collectively to mirror their owner's ego.

In contrast to collecting, the acts of window-shopping, buying, spending, and selling create a social environment in which the mind wanders freely over the spectacles supplied by shops, goods, and shoppers; meditates on loss and desire; and enters into sympathetic, if temporary, relationships with others, for consumption, as Arjun Appadurai points out, is "eminently social, relational, and active" (31). Woolf herself depicts such a quasi-utopian vision of the streets in "Street Haunting," a 1927 essay describing her late-afternoon quest for a pencil. Leaving her room—that "shell-like covering which our souls have excreted to house themselves"—she becomes a "central oyster of perceptiveness, an enormous eye," as she delightedly meanders through Oxford Street on the way to the Strand for a pencil (*DM* 21–22): "Passing, glimpsing, everything seems accidentally but miraculously sprinkled with beauty, as if the tide of trade which deposits its burden so punctually and prosaically upon the shores of Oxford Street had this night cast up nothing but treasure" (27).

The street-haunting shopper finds excitement and anonymity outside, in contrast to the solipsistically self-contained world of home, where "we sit surrounded by objects which perpetually express the oddity of our own temperaments and enforce the memories of our own experience." These objects are aura-laden, freighted with meaning, serving to preserve a past moment—with which they are "stamped like a coin indelibly among a million that slipped by imperceptibly"—and to shore up the "self our friends know us by" (21). Typical of these collectibles is the "bowl on the mantelpiece," bought at Mantua and still redolent with the conflict that surrounded its purchase:

> We were leaving the shop when the sinister old woman plucked at our skirts and said she would find herself starving one of these days, but, "Take it!" she cried, and thrust the blue and white china bowl into our hands as if she never wanted to be reminded of her quixotic generosity. So, guiltily, but suspecting nevertheless how badly we had been fleeced, we carried it back to the little hotel where, in the middle of the night, the innkeeper quarreled so violently with his wife that we all leant out into the courtyard to look. (21)

Acquired amid conflict and distrust, the collected object's uniqueness ensures that it retains its power to "express" its past and "enforce" its owner's identity. The innkeeper's quarrel with his wife echoes the agon of the collector, who must wrest his objects from a resistant environment.

The pencil, on the other hand, which the narrator painlessly acquires from the stationer's shop, bears no such burden. And in fact the story of its purchase reverses the bowl-narrative. The stationer and his wife, quarreling when the narrator enters the shop, become reconciled as she makes her purchase; the shopper even prolongs her decision—"one had to be particular in one's choice of pencils; this was too soft, that too hard"—in order to keep them "standing side by side in forced neutrality" (34) until finally, "without a word said on either side, the quarrel was made up" (35). The essay concludes with the narrator home again with her only "spoil," a pencil.

This is not to say that Woolf's vision of shopping is wholly or simply positive. Pointing out that Woolf's persona returns home with relief, exhausted by her expedition, Leslie Hankins places "Street Haunting" on an "ideological faultline," between "the ivory tower and the market economy" (21). In fact, Woolf's ambivalence in the essay is evident not only in her retreat homeward, but also in her treatment of consumption itself. For as she gazes into windows, the narrator experiments with, then rejects ownership: "one may build up all the chambers of an imaginary house and furnish them at one's will with sofa, table, carpet," she thinks, looking into windows. "But, having built and furnished the house, one is happily under no obligation to possess it; one can dismantle it in the twinkling of an eye, and build and furnish another house with other chairs and other glasses" (27). Shopping, ironically, is valued for the opportunity it provides not to acquire objects, but to imaginatively strip oneself of the old ones and try on the new without committing oneself. Reginald Abbott, pointing out how little actually gets bought in *Mrs. Dalloway*, argues it is characterized by an "acommodity aesthetic" that reveals Woolf's "ambivalent response, her aristocratic demur to commodity culture" (208). I would argue, however, that Woolf's ambivalence derives less from aristocratic snobbery than a pervasive distrust of ownership. Her identity suspended between what she owns but might discard and what she might—but might not—buy, Woolf's narrator is optimally receptive to the spectacle around her: a spectacle of exchange and interaction yet not possession. For modernity means, for Woolf, a process of buying and losing, of building and tearing down, a flux devoid of the stability implied by mere ownership: "The charm of modern London," she writes in "Oxford Street Tide," "is that it is not built to last; [. . .] We knock down and rebuild as we expect to be knocked down and rebuilt. It is an impulse that makes for creation and fertility" (*London* 19–20).[3]

Collectors, horrified—like the hypothetical "moralist" of "Oxford Street Tide"—by this spectacle of flux, surround themselves protectively with possessions that mirror back to them their own (fallacious) solidity and depth. Shoppers, on the other hand, especially to the extent that they look without buying, embrace the uncertainties and superficialities of commodity spectacle.[4] This is the contrast Woolf explores in four of her short stories: "Solid Objects," "Mrs Dalloway in Bond Street," "The Lady in the Looking-Glass," and "The Duchess and the Jeweller." Two of the stories depict people who collect and hoard objects; two depict people who buy or sell them. This contrast matters, for Woolf, because it involves not only two differing responses to modernity, but also two differing accounts of the artist's relation to her/his work and public. In fact, through her depictions of collectors and consumers, Woolf explores two versions of modernist art: one that turns its back on the marketplace and conceptualizes art as the sum of heroically collected and preserved fragments of life; another that defines itself in and through the marketplace, its meanings multiple, negotiated, and coproduced by its consumers.

In "Solid Objects," John and his friend Charles, both politicians, sit on a beach. Aimlessly digging into the sand, John comes up with a lump of glass. He keeps it and becomes so haunted by its form that he seeks out other lumps—a piece of china, a lump of iron. As he spends all his time hunting for more things, John abandons his constituents and loses his election for Parliament. At the end of the story he is totally isolated, his mantel full of collected objects. His friend Charles stops by and asks, referring to his parliamentary career,

> 'What made you give it up like that all in a second?'
> 'I've not given it up,' John replied.
> 'But you've not a ghost of a chance now,' said Charles roughly.
> 'I don't agree with you there,' said John with conviction.

Charles leaves with "a queer sense that they were talking about different things," as indeed they were: John still has high hopes for his collection of objects, not his parliamentary career. "Pretty stones," Charles says, as he heads out the door, clearly convinced his friend is crazy (*CSF* 106–07).

The story has been read variously as a comment on artist Mark Gertler's "obsession with form" (Baldwin 20; Lee 370), Woolf's own taste for glass (Lee 370), Roger Fry's description of the "creative vision" in a 1919 *Athenaeum* article (Reid Broughton 55–56), Fry's insistence on the separation of art from life (Reid 240–41), and the desire of modernist artists to see themselves as producers of "solid objects" rather than useless aesthetes (Mao 38–39). Without contesting any of these readings, I want to argue additionally that the story explores—in part—the problem of the artist in an "age of mechanical reproduction."

John is the collector described by Susan Stewart who seeks in objects a "nostalgic myth of contact and presence"(133). Because his objects are wrested with difficulty from a world which fails to recognize their value and uniqueness, John can find in them all those qualities lacking in the mass-produced objects on sale in stores, particularly the intense and reciprocal relationship offered only by the auratic object. The aura, Benjamin explains, "rests on the transposition of a response common in human relationships to the relationship between the inanimate or natural object and man. [. . .] To perceive the aura of an object we look at means to invest it with the ability to look at us in return" (188). John's lumps of glass, china, and metal—worn, broken, and thus unique—are deep and meaning-laden in a way that mass-produced objects, with their unstable, arbitrary value and multiplicity could never be.

Once hooked on collecting by his first lump of glass, John provides himself with "a bag and a long stick fitted with an adaptable hook" and "ransack[s] all deposits of earth" for his finds (106), which he places on his mantel: "Anything, so long as it was an object of some kind, more or less round, perhaps with a dying flame deep sunk in its mass, anything—china, glass, amber, rock, marble—even the smooth oval egg of a prehistoric bird would do" (104). Personifying his objects, John imagines they delight in being rescued (104) and spends all his time either collecting or contemplating them, fascinated, for example by the "contrast between the china so vivid and alert, and the glass so mute and contemplative" (105).

John's objects could hardly be further from the consumer goods for sale in the marketplace. They are either found in nature, or, if manufactured, have been broken and discarded. They are devoid of exchange value, for his eccentricity consists in the fact that he wants them at all; certainly no one else does. And he wants more and more of them; he has "serious ambitions" to find better and better objects (106). In fact, John's mantelpiece display resembles the "insane" collection defined by Stewart. The "proper" collection, Stewart writes, is always potentially redeemable, while the insane collection, resembling the worthless accumulations of the packrat, "refuses the very *system* of objects and thus metonymically refuses the entire political economy that serves as the foundation for the system and the only domain within which the system acquires meaning" (154). Theorists of material culture divide objects into three categories: rubbish, transients (consumer goods like clothing or refrigerators that lose value when sold), and durables (collectables, "above" the marketplace, bought by museums and collectors) (Pearce 34–35). To treat rubbish as durables—as John does—is to threaten the entire marketplace hierarchy.

Mao points out that John's eccentric collecting can be read in the context of Pater's conclusion to *Studies of the Renaissance*, which urges readers to respond intently to every possible gleam of beauty in the world around them.[5] He goes on to argue, though, that the story borrows from, in order to transcend Paterian aestheticism, exemplifying Woolf's—and other modernists'—efforts to construe artists as hardworking producers by linking art to "solid objects." His argument that modernist artists claim a "moral [. . .] high ground by turning from aesthetic experience as end, with its threat to the production imperative, to the work of art as fruit of

inspired labor" makes sense (38). But while I find Mao's point about modernism in general convincing, I find his reading of Woolf's story less so. For Woolf, by emphasizing John's isolation, undercuts any sense we might get of his productivity and underlines the danger modernist artists run when they overvalue the work of art itself—however hard they emphasize the labor involved—in isolation from its consumption by readers or buyers.

John's wholesale rejection of the rules and values of marketplace, in fact, resembles that not of Woolf herself, but of the traditional modernist, who, as Huyssen points out, tended to define himself against an "increasingly consuming and engulfing mass culture" (vii). Finding that modernity meant flux (as money and commodities changed hands and value fluctuated, creating a world where, as Marshall Berman suggests quoting Marx, "all that is solid melts into air"), many modernists saw their artistic task as the collecting of fragments to form a compensatory and autonomous wholeness.[6] Take Conrad, for example, who in 1897 describes the artist's task as the heroic rescue of "a passing phase of life" from "the remorseless rush of time" (xiv); or Lytton Strachey, who writes in his 1918 *Eminent Victorians* that the task of the modern biographer is to:

> [. . .] row out over that great ocean of material, and lower down into it, here and there, a little bucket, which will bring up to the light of day some characteristic specimen, from those far depths, to be examined with a careful curiosity. (v)

T. S. Eliot, in "The Waste Land" (1922), gathers allusive fragments to shore against his ruin, much as James Joyce collected epiphanies in his notebook, which he then turns into *A Portrait of the Artist as a Young Man*.[7] Like them, John has created a collection of fragments innocent of any contact with the marketplace, with their auras magically intact.

John's home is thus the ultimate ivory tower, untouched by commodification and mass culture. It is also a kind of trap. Fascinated by the intricate interplay of forms, of resemblances and differences created by his juxtaposed lumps, John neglects to reinsert his objects into the world of human discourse; their only audience is himself—"People gave up visiting him." Nor can he talk to others about his "serious ambitions" (106). The story ends in a miscommunication, as Charles assumes the "it" he has not given up refers to his political ambitions, when in fact John means his collecting. And the auratic objects with which John has a rich personal relationship are to Charles only "pretty stones." The occupational hazard of the collector, as for the modernist writer, is solipsism. As Jean Baudrillard writes, the collection enacts a fantasy where the "projected detail comes to stand for the ego, and the rest of the world is then organized around it" (79). To place an object in a collection is to turn it into a mirror of the self. "What you really collect," Baudrillard writes, "is always yourself" (91).

Woolf began "Solid Objects" in 1918, publishing it in the *Athenaeum* in 1920 (*CSF* 299). "The Lady in the Looking-Glass" was written in 1929 and published in *Harper's Magazine* at the end of that year (*CSF* 306), shortly after "Street Haunting" was written in 1927 (Squier 46). It, too, reflects the way people turn their homes into encrustations, their possessions both revealing and trapping them.[8] It is written from the point of view of a narrator who observes her friend Isabella Tyson's drawing room both directly and through a looking glass that hangs in the hall. The direct view is full of movement, suggestion, association; the looking glass, on the other hand, freezes and frames. Interpretation has focused on whether one view or the other of Isabella is correct: the narrator speculates about her friend's fascinating life based on the insides of the furniture, of letters, of surfaces; the final view we get of her, however, is through the looking glass, in which she looks stark, flat, and empty, the final confirmation of her emptiness coming through her failure to open her letters, which, the narrator concludes, "were all bills" (225). Baldwin and Chapman argue that the looking glass is right; it provides the insight allowed by aesthetic detachment and framing; it "composes and holds," according to Baldwin (56). Barzilai and Dick, on the other hand, argue that the dialectic is not resolved by the story's conclusion, that the looking-glass view is merely another aspect of the onlooker's viewpoint and no more authoritative than her imaginative version (Barzilai 28; Dick, "I Am Not" 37).

All these readings overlook the fact that Isabella Tyson is a collector, and that her collecting is part of what the story is about. Dick links Isabella to the artist Ethel Sands, whom Woolf visited in Dieppe in 1927. Woolf's *Diary* notes, "How many little stories come into my head! For instance: Ethel Sands not looking at her letters" (*CSF* 306; *D3* 157). I would juxtapose another entry from a month before, just after the visit, in which Woolf emphasizes two things: Ethel's "brittle & acid" personality and the care with which her house has been assembled. Ethel's house, Woolf writes, is "laid with pale bright Samarcand rugs, & painted greens & blues, with love 'pieces,' & great pots of carefully designed flowers" (*D3* 151). The ending of "The Lady in the Looking-Glass" evokes both points of this entry: standing bare and exposed in her beautiful house, in a light Woolf compares to "acid," Isabella fails to open her letters, leaving the onlooker to conclude she is "perfectly empty" (225). In fact, Isabella's emptiness is inseparable from her identity as a collector of beautiful objects.

This becomes evident if "The Lady in the Looking-Glass" is read in the light of an earlier story about a collecting woman, Henry James's *The Spoils of Poynton*. In this novel, based—according to Lady Ottoline Morrell—on her mother-in-law (Baron 53), Mrs. Gareth has, with her late husband, spent a lifetime filling her house, Poynton, with objets d'art. Denied the house by her husband's will, Mrs. Gareth resists turning it over to an inartistic daughter-in-law. For Poynton is not just a beautiful house, but its owner's life, "written in great syllables of colour and form, the tongues of other countries and the hands of rare artists" (22). The objects Mrs. Gareth and her husband have collected with patience and cunning are placed in explicit contrast to the mechanically reproduced consumer goods. Endowed with that auratic ability to "look back" at their owner, Mrs Gareth's objects are "living things"; they "know me," she says, "they return the touch of my hand" (31). This intense relationship with objects comes at the expense of other, more conventional ones: Mrs. Gareth's "ruling passion," the narrator comments, "had in a manner despoiled her of her humanity" (37). As a good friend of both Henry James and Lady Ottoline Morrell, Ethel Sands was aware of the story's connection to her friend's family (Baron 43). Woolf, involved in the same circles, might well have associated Sands's decorating talents with James's account of collecting at the expense of human relationships.

Derived as she is from Ethel Sands, Isabella Tyson suggests a conflation of artist and collector. Like both John and Conrad, she has gathered about her carefully chosen pieces and performed heroic tasks in rescuing them from their original contexts. Her possessions have been "collected with her own hands—often in the most obscure corners of the world and at great risk from poisonous stings and Oriental diseases" (222). If the looking-glass image is correct, however, she has, in the process, cut herself off from human relationships. "Sometimes it seemed," the narrator comments of her possessions, "as if they knew more about her than we, who sat on them, wrote at them, and trod on them so carefully, were allowed to know" (222). In relying on her possessions for a mirror image of factitious wholeness, she has cut herself off from others.

The narrator recognizes this identity between Isabella and her collected objects, thinking that Isabella is "full of locked drawers, stuffed with letters, like her cabinets" (225). She recognizes the objects' auratic power to "look back." The furniture comes to seem "hieroglyphic" and the day's letters, "tablets graven with eternal truth" (223). The entire room seems animate and potentially revelatory, full of objects as charged with meaning as John's.

But, as for John, the promise of coherence and mastery offered by the collection is illusory, for it is incommunicable. The collector, Baudrillard writes, "strives to reconstitute a discourse that is transparent to him, a discourse whose signifiers he controls and whose referent par excellence is himself" (105). The narrator thinks about gaining access to that discourse: "If she concealed so much and knew so much one must prize her open with the first tool that came to hand—the imagination"(223), but concludes, "To talk of 'prizing her open' as if she were an oyster, to use any but the finest and subtlest and most pliable tools upon her was impious and absurd" (225). The objects are valued for the stability of their meaning, but that stability depends on their forming a hermetically sealed system. If they were to circulate (i.e., as objects to go on the market; as words to be used in common discourse), their meanings—or value—would no longer be fixed. The oyster comparison, of course, echoes "Street Haunting"; there the oyster emerges from the shell only when she descends from her room into the street to shop. Collectors, however, acquire without the ordinary kind of shopping; they buy at auctions or in exotic locales and thus keep their shells intact.

While I agree with Baldwin and Chapman that the looking-glass view of Isabella Tyson is revealing (why else would its revelatory quality be compared at the story's start to open checkbooks and letters of confession?), the interesting question neither addresses is why Isabella would be "empty" in the first place. I would argue that as a collector, she has projected herself into her possessions, turned them into a kind of mirror (i.e., "what you collect is always yourself" [91]) and private language and thus preempted the human relationships that would give her substance.

In both "Solid Objects" and "The Lady in the Looking-Glass," the collector figure is contrasted with a narrative voice that is all "enormous eye," drawing attention to the challenges posed by the act of perception. In "The Lady in the Looking-Glass," the narrator is particularly prominent; as in "The Mark on the Wall," "An Unwritten Novel," and "Sympathy," the story consists precisely of the narrator's efforts to make sense of what she sees. Tantalized by Isabella's "mask-like indifference," the narrator suggests, "one must put oneself in her shoes" (224), but of course ultimately fails as she realizes her reflections mirror her own mind more than Isabella's.

The story's subtitle, "A Reflection," draws attention not only to this failure to penetrate Isabella's inner life but also to the inevitable multivalence of thought, vision, and language. For the word "reflection" could denote the narrator's thoughts, or Isabella's reflection in the mirror, or the narrator's own self-mirroring, or the story's role as mirror to the reader, or the story as mis-en-abime: a hall of mirrors in which the reader sees an endless series of multiplied, tantalizing yet unrevealing images that at once encourage and rebuke reverie. For Woolf's narrative "eye" involves the reader as coauthor, as synthesizer of the inconclusive images it reflects. As such, the narrative eye, like the reader it evokes, is the opposite of the collector; in love with surfaces, it wants only to play with meanings, not possess them or control them. "Let us [. . .] be content still with surfaces only," Woolf's narrator urges in "Street Haunting": "the glossy brilliance of the motor omnibuses; the carnal splendour of the butchers' shops with their yellow flanks and purple steaks; the blue and red bunches of flowers burning so bravely through the plate glass of the florists' windows" (*DM* 23). The reader resembles the street-haunting shopper, looking at once at and through plate glass shop windows, seeing displayed objects, street scenes, and her own image all mingled, shifting, and resistant to closure.[9]

In these two stories of collectors, the narrator's and reader's shopping sensibility contrasts with the quest for stability enacted by their protagonists. On the other hand, in "Mrs Dalloway in Bond Street" (published in the *Dial* in 1923) and "The Duchess and the Jeweller," the protagonists do the buying and selling, while the narrator is relatively invisible. Told for the most part through Mrs. Dalloway's perceptions of her shopping trip in quest of gloves, "Mrs Dalloway in Bond Street" is a fictional if somewhat more elegiac counterpart to "Street Haunting." Mrs. Dalloway's oyster-like consciousness responds imaginatively to all she sees, but is also itself haunted by thoughts of death, aging, and World War I. As the precursor to *Mrs. Dalloway*, of course, the story includes much of what Wicke analyzes in the novel as "market modernism"—consciousness itself depicted as oscillating, volatile (like Keynes's notion of the market itself), and exquisitely responsive to goods displayed for sale; a positive treatment of consumption as a kind of sacralizing gift ("Mrs. Dalloway" 19), moments of shared consciousness and interconnections between strangers "around sometimes invisible processes of exchange" (17). By focusing solely on the shopping trip (this time for gloves rather than flowers as in the novel), the story makes these points more explicitly than the novel, but also, I think, more problematically.

In many ways "Mrs Dalloway in Bond Street" delights in the new ways of looking and thinking offered by urban modernity. "The stream was endless—endless—endless," Mrs. Dalloway thinks, referring interchangeably to the street scene, the many shops she passes, and her own memories and associations (154). Mrs. Dalloway resembles the flaneur Baudelaire and Benjamin describe: the connoisseur of street life with his mobile, distracted gaze. While the flaneur, like the collector, is traditionally male, a number of recent theorists have argued that with the development of department stores, a female version, the flaneuse emerges (Friedberg 34; Felski 70).[10] In fact, Mrs. Dalloway scrutinizes the women she sees, not, as Baudelaire does, with sexual desire, but as a consumer weighing her fashion choices:

> No! No! No! Clarissa smiled good-naturedly. The fat lady had taken every sort of trouble, but diamonds! Orchids! At this hour of the morning! [. . .] Another motor car passed. How utterly unattractive! Why should a girl of that age paint black round her eyes? (*CSF* 155)

As in "Street Haunting," the strolling consumer experiments with her own identity as she measures her judgments against other strollers', remembers past purchases, and plans future ones. As Clarissa sees Lady Bexborough in a carriage, the narrator comments, she "would have given anything to be like that, the mistress of Clarefield, talking politics, like a man" (156). If collecting is a way of building up and fixing one's identity, shopping dismantles and metamorphoses it. Woolf's "oyster of perceptiveness" is the distracted eye of the modernist consumer, working out the consequences of possible purchases, sent into flights of reverie by the objects displayed in shop windows.

Once in the shop, Mrs. Dalloway's reveries over her gloves are appealingly responsive to those around her. She recognizes the sales girl's interiority ("She had her own sorrows quite separate" [*CSF* 157]), worries about her comfort (thinking this might be "the one day in the month . . . when it's agony to stand" [157]), thinks about offering to finance a vacation for her, and, linking the age spots on her own arm to the human condition of aging, suffering, and death, doubts the existence of God (158). But, she concludes, "she would go on. But why, if one doesn't believe? For the sake of others, she thought, taking the glove in her hand. The girl would be much more unhappy if she didn't believe" (158).

Mrs. Dalloway's purchase is thus depicted as a kind of noble sacrifice; her spending keeps the market going, much as her keeping up appearances keeps England stable. "Gloves have never been so reliable since the war," the shop-girl says to a customer who has torn a glove by tugging it. But Mrs. Dalloway shows her faith in them nonetheless; "Thousands of young men had died that things might go on," Mrs. Dalloway thinks, as if her purchase will make their sacrifice worthwhile (*CSF* 158–59).

Mrs. Dalloway's act of consumption is, as Appadurai says, "social, relational, and active." Unlike the more isolating and agonistic act of collecting, shopping involves conversation, interaction, and cooperation; and the objects acquired in the process—generally machine reproduced—are devoid of aura. Human relationships rather than the objects' values dominate the interaction. Clarissa and the shop girl discuss the gloves' quality and price, and while the girl's power is certainly limited by her class position, she is able to affect the interaction through both her tact and her slowness. Much of the plot's tension involves Mrs. Dalloway's initial recognition of but failure to remember the name of a fellow shopper, reinforcing the extent to which human contact is the story's subject. When a car backfires outside, the explosion suggests the violence that pushes people apart, but it also supplies the jolt that helps Clarissa remember the name. Postwar shopping, like the act of remembering another's name, becomes a way of reconnecting in the face of loss.

Of course Mrs. Dalloway's purchase also, as Reginald Abbott points out, reinscribes social barriers.[11] Throughout, Mrs. Dalloway is very much a product of her class: smug about empire and monarch, about her taste ("If you had lived with pictures, [. . .] you can't be taken in by a joke," she says dismissively of an "odd French" painting that sounds Post-Impressionist [*CSF* 156]); deferential toward Lady Bexborough, inwardly impatient—despite her initial sympathy—with the shop girl. And her shopping is inseparable from her classism: "A lady is known by her gloves and her shoes," she thinks of her uncle as having said and asks for the French gloves that had been available before the war. But Clarissa's limitations only highlight the momentary connection forged by her interaction with the shop girl; "The city of women," Wicke writes, "—Clarissa's London, for instance—is the site not only of all the hierarchies and divisions of the gendered social world, but also their liquefaction in gifts of consumption" ("Mrs. Dalloway" 19). At a 1913 Fabian conference Woolf jotted down, "Nothing ignoble in being a consumer. . . . Man wage-earner can make his power felt, woman consumer very little power" (quoted in Lee, *Virginia Woolf* 324). Far from being ignoble, Mrs. Dalloway's shopping trip allows her to identify—if only momentarily—with the various women and potential selves she encounters.

My final shopping story, "The Duchess and the Jeweller," also involves a redemptive purchase. Rarely written about, perhaps because of its uncharacteristically simple technique and anti-Semitic subtext, the story, according to Dick, was probably begun in 1932, as part of a series of "caricatures" and published in *Harpers Bazaar* in 1938 (*CSF* 308–09). In initial versions, the protagonist was Jewish (identifiable by his name, accent, and memories of childhood), but Woolf removed these links at the request of her New York agent (Dick, *CSF* 309). As Oliver Bacon, born poor in Whitechapel, endowed with an elephant-like nose and a talent for accumulating wealth in the jewelry business, the hero remains linked to Jewish stereotypes, but then the fat, gambling, overdressed Duchess is a bit overdrawn as well. These are certainly caricatures, as the story's all too pervasive animal similes suggest. (In keeping with his not so kosher name, the dissatisfied jeweler is compared to a hog seeking truffles.)

When juxtaposed with the two collector stories and "Mrs. Dalloway in Bond Street," however, this somewhat heavy-handed story takes on new interest. In it, the most successful jeweler in the world is visited by the Duchess, who wants to sell him her pearls. Despite his intuition that they are fake and despite the imagined warnings of his dead mother (as represented in a painting on a wall), Mr. Bacon agrees to buy them, tempted by the Duchess's offer of a long weekend at her estate in the company of her daughter, whom he loves. On the one hand, Oliver is a repellent social climber, delighting in his power to exploit the Mayfair aristocracy and, in the process, be assimilated into it. On the other, he sacrifices his cash to buy the pearls he knows are fake, out of a desire for connectedness and love.

Wicke describes Mrs. Dalloway as an anti-Midas because she is willing to consume rather than horde. Oliver Bacon, in contrast, seems much like Midas, as he gazes rapturously on the jewels he keeps in his safe:

> All safe, shining, cool, yet burning, eternally, with their own compressed light.
> 'Tears!' said Oliver, looking at the pearls.
> 'Heart's blood!' he said, looking at the rubies.
> 'Gunpowder!' he continued, rattling the diamonds so that they flashed and blazed. (*CSF* 250)

Like John's objects, the jewels have taken on personalities of their own. Removed from the marketplace, authentic, priceless, they are charged with the aura that only "durables" can have. Bacon's greed is also Midas-like: he always wants one more truffle. His acquisitiveness is conveyed by the narrator's emphasis on his mouth; his lips in childhood were like "wet cherries" (250), his eyes like "licked stones" (251). When he speaks to the duchess, he "lick[s] the words" (252). This greed is what motivates him to deal with the duchess.

Yet they also share a communion of sorts. "You have all my secrets," she tells him, and as she cries "tears like diamonds" fall down her "cherry-blossom cheeks" (252), the diamonds and cherries linking her to Bacon. They call each other "old friend," and as he seems about to yield and buy her pearls, she calls him by his first name. She gambles, and he sees his success in terms of his having "won my bet." She manipulates him, but he recognizes the possibility: they are deeply akin and interdependent in their temperament and needs.

Ultimately, Oliver Bacon is a Midas who reforms in an act of consumption. Like Mrs. Dalloway he sees through the conventions of the exchange, yet keeps up appearances rather than let the charade collapse. In the process he must reject the caution he associates with his mother, who periodically surfaces in his mind wailing, "Oh, Oliver! When will you have sense, my son?" (248)

Is he sorry he has bought the pearls when he finally ascertains that they are, in fact, fake? The truffle, we're told through his consciousness at the end, is "rotten at the core!" And he asks his mother's picture to forgive him, "For [. . .] it is to be a long week-end" (253). This is not a story that can be read too deeply; neither character is treated sympathetically enough to suggest he or she could undergo any deep transformation or insight. But in an understated way, it seems to me, Woolf is depicting the stereotypically Jewish role of financial middleman in a positive way. If consumption is a positive, even creative act, the jeweler's investment in fake pearls to facilitate the Duchess's spending is as generous a sacrifice as Mrs. Dalloway's.

Finally, despite her occasionally expressed distaste for mass consumption—her criticism of oversimplified movies, for example in "Cinema," and of popular writers in "Life and the Novelist"—and her personal dislike of shopping, Woolf depicts consumption in an age of mechanical reproduction as an act of generosity and openness, starkly opposed to the narcissistic nostalgia of her collectors. Both Oliver Bacon and Clarissa Dalloway are, of course, limited and class-bound. But their openness to exchange signals a deeper receptiveness, a recognition that identity and language are as permeable, unstable, and interactive as commodities.

Indeed, Woolf's own choices of profession, genre, and style are linked to her preference for marketplace over ivory tower. As printer and publisher, she had an unusually intimate relation with her audience, sometimes literally packing and mailing her own books to buyers (Lee, *Virginia Woolf* 359). As a reviewer, she served to link potential readers with the books they might buy; as a friend and sister of artists, she went to galleries, discussed picture prices and sales. She shopped at her friend Roger Fry's Omega Workshop, which aimed at bringing craftspeople, beautiful objects, and the general public closer together; Fry, Woolf wrote in her biography of him, called it his experiment with "free trade" in art (*RF* 187). In May 1921, Woolf fantasized to Vanessa about a combination teashop/bookshop gallery that she and Leonard had talked about (*L2* fn. 470). All these activities suggest her interest in not only the production but the marketing of art.

Woolf's writing of short fiction was, from the first, linked to her interest in reproducing and distributing her work. Her first published story, "The Mark on the Wall," was inspired by the purchase of a printing press (Lee, *Virginia Woolf* 360). Woolf often sold single stories to magazines—in fact all those discussed here were published soon after their composition in mass-market publications. Simply because they took less time to write and publish, Woolf's short stories brought the acts of writing, selling, and reading closer together than did her novels. Short fiction thus offered Woolf a particularly intense awareness of her reader—as both buyer and co-conspirator.

For the reader is very much the cocreator of Woolf's short fiction. In her 1937 "Craftsmanship," Woolf talks about the way words' meanings and associations "shuffle and change" (*DM* 199). Unlike Conrad, who worried that ordinary words were worn out—"old, old words, worn thin, defaced by ages of careless usage" (xv), Woolf writes that even the oldest words are "full of echoes, of memories, of associations" (203). It is in the nature of words, she writes, "not to express one simple statement but a thousand possibilities" (200). Words hate to have their meanings pinned down:

> It is because the truth they try to catch is many-sided, and they convey it by being themselves many-sided, flashing this way, then that. Thus they mean one thing to one person, another thing to another person. (207)

Such a view of language suggests that the reader will inevitability construct a text's meaning in an individual way. Woolf's ideal reader is thus much like her ideal shopper, willing to browse, to speculate, to try on, perhaps even to make a purchase. Unlike the collector, who is concerned with authenticity and long-term value, the shopper accepts value as negotiated and unfixed. She may buy one interpretation or another, but she doesn't get too invested in it. And she is happy with reproductions rather than "originals." By this I mean she accepts the unmoored nature of words, the fact that their meanings change over time and in various contexts, much as she accepts the notion of exchange value, the fact that a commodity's value lies in demand for it rather than in its intrinsic worth.

The short story itself is a "solid object," Woolf writes in "The Russian Background," written in 1919, the same year she wrote her story "Solid Objects." But the story as solid object casts a "shade of reflection and speculation" (DM 123). Its meaning, in other words, is not self-contained, but defined through its impact on a reader, through its reverberations. The terms "reflection" and "speculation" suggest mirroring, multiplicity, and even, with "speculation," a hint of financial risk.

As mass production, department stores, and advertising made mass culture an increasingly defining presence, Woolf could look nostalgically backward to a time before the "age of mechanical reproduction" and align herself with the artist-as-collector; or she could align herself with the marketplace and the artist-as-purveyor, providing a range of possible experiences which only take shape once they are purchased by a consumer. To make the latter choice is to abandon the appeal to authenticity and transcendence in favor of the "common reader," who creates meaning and value as she interacts with the text. For Woolf, finally, both writer and reader do best when they make meaning much as they buy pencils: casually, tentatively, cooperatively.

Notes

1. Museums function much the same way, as an effort to compensate for the large-scale, society-wide "decline of the aura" that Benjamin sees as pervading

late-nineteenth-century Europe. Major museums served, according to Philip Fisher, as "storage areas for authenticity and uniqueness per se," flourishing most in those cities where mass production was strongest, where they were most needed as "counter-institutions to the factory" (29).

2. Recent critics have challenged this high/low art dichotomy, pointing out ways in which "high art" practitioners like Conrad, Eliot, and Joyce borrowed from mass and popular culture (see North, Chinitz, and Wicke *Advertising*, among others). But as Chinitz points out, their borrowings were often fraught with anxiety precisely because early-twentieth-century discourse "treats mass culture as a feminine object" (321).

3. On the impermanence of Oxford Street and its rhetorical implications, see Pamela Caughie's analysis of the *London Scene* essays in *Virginia Woolf and Postmodernism* (119–37). There Caughie argues that Woolf's depictions of "The London Docks" and "Oxford Street Tide" represent differing socioeconomic and rhetorical orientations. The docks, solid, productive, and useful, supply the goods that are then sold on flimsy, superficial Oxford Street. "Instead of accumulating useful products," she writes, "Oxford Street values using things up, selling things quickly, changing things frequently" (126). Caughie links these differing orientations to differing attitudes toward language: the docks invite purposive, referential language, while "emphasis on rhetorical flourish over referential use is what Oxford Street displays" (129).

4. The shopping eye, Woolf points out in "Street Haunting," is neither miner nor diver (*DM* 22), suggesting it pursues neither spoils nor depths.

5. Mao even sees echoes of Pater's "hard, gem-like flame" in John's glass with "a dying flame deep sunk in its mass" (36).

6. Mao recognizes modernists' insistence on the autonomy of art but argues it originates, ironically, in efforts "to justify the artist's activity as a part of a society's total work, at a time when removal from production no longer seemed to be anyone's prerogative" (39–40).

7. Joyce's *Ulysses*, of course, as Wicke and others have pointed out, is immersed in the language of advertisement and consumer culture (see Wicke, *Advertising*). But his Stephen Dedalus, determined to escape the nets of language, nationality, and religion, shares John's purist isolationism.

8. Dick links the story to Woolf's discussion of "scene making" in her diary, starting in 1927, when she decided her talent lay there, rather than in plots (*CSF* 34).

9. For "it is vain to try to come to a conclusion in Oxford Street," Woolf writes in the ironic final sentence of "Oxford Street Tide" (*London* 22).

10. See also Bowlby, Wolff (34–46) and Rappaport (7). Leslie Hankins makes a similar link between "Street Haunting" and the flaneuse, though she argues that the image is problematic, since women's gender made them uniquely vulnerable in urban streets, in ways unknown to the flaneur; "the flaneuse, unlike the flaneur," she writes, "was a moving target" (19); see also Minow-Pinkney (165).

11. Abbott points out that in *Mrs. Dalloway*, characters do not have the opportunity to change their identity through shopping, but in fact shop in ways determined by their social group (198). Clarissa, Abbott argues of the novel, "transforms the commodity before her [flowers] into part of her past, her own identity, rather than relying on the commodity as a signifier of her lifestyle or as something to transform her lifestyle" (200)

Part II

Crossing Generic Boundaries

Chapter 6

"A corridor leading from Mrs. Dalloway to a new book": Transforming Stories, Bending Genres

Beth Rigel Daugherty

Until recently, short story criticism has often suffered from what might be called genre anxiety; to justify the genre (or perhaps the critic's interest in it), the criticism generally included statements about neglect, efforts at genre definition, and/or calls for more rigorous theory.[1] Valerie Shaw uses a comment from Katherine Mansfield about what she wrote—"only short stories"—in her introduction to *The Short Story: A Critical Introduction*, for example, to indicate how severely this anxiety infected even an author who set out to revolutionize the genre. Many writers, critics, and publishers, she continues, persist in the "widespread notion that unless it can be seen as useful apprentice work for budding novelists, short-story writing must be a compromise of some sort" (2). Understandably, then, short story critics eager to elevate the short story's status often de-emphasized the relationship between story and novel and concentrated on stories in and of themselves. But Susan Lohafer, in her 1998 introduction to *The Tales We Tell: Perspectives on the Short Story*, suggests that short story critics are moving beyond such genre anxiety and its accompanying strategies:

> Students of the form are looking askance now at the very boundaries that brought the field into existence (tale versus sketch, novel versus story, oral versus written . . .). We're losing our defensiveness about genre; we're bored by taxonomies. Indeed, discussions of the short story tend now to be genre-bending and interdisciplinary. (xi)

The reception of Woolf's short stories has occurred, of course, within this larger context of short story reception history. Both Dean Baldwin and Joanne Trautmann Banks comment on the lack of attention paid to Woolf's short stories (xi, 57), and even a cursory glance at Woolf studies sources shows that their perception is accurate. Though not ignored entirely, the stories averaged about three entries a year in the *MLA Bibliography* between 1990 and 2003 (ranging from a low of one to a high of eight); one to two articles (out of approximately forty-five) in the annual Woolf conference *Selected Papers*; and one essay, one manuscript transcription, and one essay on the short fictions editorially labeled "Portraits" in the nine volumes of *Woolf Studies Annual* to date.[2] When Woolf critics have turned to the short stories, it has often been to support a claim about the novels or to follow up on Susan Dick's suggestion that Woolf's "short fiction was often a testing ground where she experimented with narrative techniques that she would use and develop further in her longer fictions" (*CSF* 3). Yet other Woolf critics have insisted that Woolf's short stories should be studied on their own, apart from the novels. Avrom Fleishman, for example, perhaps the first to criticize the practice of using Woolf's short stories as "quarry for the longer works" (44), asserted that the stories should be seen "within the modern history of the genre"; he then categorized and defined the various forms of the Woolfian short story.[3] Now, however, as short story critics within Woolf studies have begun to see the complexity and instability of Woolf's stories as challenges to genre boundaries, they, too, are moving from genre anxiety to genre-bending.

Woolf critics may have ignored her short stories in the past at least partly because Woolf's own attitudes and practices can so easily be interpreted as dismissive. As Susan Dick points out, Woolf published only eighteen of the forty-six short stories she wrote during her lifetime (*CSF* 1), and Dean Baldwin, author of the only long study of Woolf's short stories, notes Woolf's lack of interest in publishing her short work and lack of theoretical commentary about the genre (3, xii; see also Skrbic's essay in this volume). Many of Woolf's comments in her diaries and letters also suggest she did not take her stories seriously. She often emphasizes her stories' provisional, dashed-off feel by referring to them as sketches, little stories, scenes. She writes that the stories between *Mrs. Dalloway* and *To the Lighthouse* were "scrambled [. . .] down untidily" (*D3* 29); extreme ease and speed marked their progress. She frankly admits to writing some stories for money, commenting in a letter to Vanessa, for example, that she is following Vanessa's advice and will write "The Duchess and the Jeweller" "only if money is paid beforehand" (*L6* 157). She also recognizes their experimental value— "I daresay one ought to invent a completely new form. Anyhow its very amusing to try with these short things" (*L2* 167)—but often describes that value in terms of fun. Her stories are amusing, escapades, diversions, treats, even guilty pleasures: "I'm *ashamed* to think how many stories I've written this month" (*L3* 185; my emphasis). But perhaps these attitudes and practices do not so much reveal a dismissal as conceal a radical freedom—playing, inventing without pressure, and not publishing all protect Woolf's freedom to challenge genre norms.

Susan Dick's title for her edition of Virginia Woolf's short stories itself questions genre norms: not *Collected*, but *Complete*; not *Short*, but *Shorter*; not *Short Stories*, but *Shorter Fiction*. The edition challenges publishing customs as well, bringing together in a lively chronological mix *all* of Woolf's stories, whether complete or incomplete holograph drafts, corrected typescripts, or previously published stories. Dick makes clear, through her editorial apparatus and notes, that she has often made choices for publication from among several versions of a story—drafts, typescripts, published and/or reprinted—and that she has sometimes combined a holograph draft and a typescript to arrive at a copy text.[4] That she was able to bring to fruition such an unusual publishing project in 1985 with the first edition of *The Complete Shorter Fiction* and then again in 1989 with a new, corrected edition results from not only her extensive editorial efforts and acumen but also the interest in Woolf's manuscript drafts she helped create with the publication of her *To the Lighthouse* holograph draft transcription in 1982.[5] The publication of Woolf's manuscripts led to intense interest in her writing and revising process, close attention to her decisions about "what to leave in, what to leave out" (Seger), and stimulating suggestions about what Donald Reiman calls "versioning" (quoted in Silver 196). As Brenda Silver has pointed out, our awareness of these manuscripts and our study of Woolf's revising practices result in a blurring of the distinction between "final" version and draft, making us question the nature of the "text" and making us see Woolf's works as palimpsests in which no layer is silenced (217; see also Wussow ix, xi). When Susan Dick published Woolf's short stories in this context and chose to mix unrevised with finished stories in chronological order (5), she again called attention to Woolf's revising practices, and her decision has had the same effect Silver notes: no matter how many times Susan Dick cautions us otherwise, the distinctions among manuscript drafts, typescripts, and published stories, while there, also blur.

Woolf's writing and revising practice, as shown in her comments about the short stories she wrote between *Mrs. Dalloway* and *To the Lighthouse* and in the stories themselves, reveals yet another blurring, that between story and novel. Seeing her own stories in a multiplicity of ways, Woolf calls into question the distinction between her stories as *either* practice for the novel *or* an end in themselves. Her practice reveals a writer who bends

genre, who views her stories as both independent and interdependent; they
retain generic identity at the same time they have permeable boundaries.

As Woolf finished *Mrs. Dalloway*, she jotted down some "Notes for
stories—&c."[6] dated March 6 and 14, 1925 in a small notebook labeled
"Notes for Writing": "This book will consist of the stories of people at
Mrs. D's party" (*TTL Holograph*, App. A 44). She then listed four possible
topics and continued,

> My idea is that these sketches will be a corridor leading from Mrs. Dalloway
> to a new book. What I expect to happen is that some two figures will detach
> themselves from the party & go off independently into another volume; but
> I have no notion of this at present. The book of stories ought to be complete
> in itself. It must have some unity, though I want to publish each character
> separately. (44–45)

After again listing titles or notes for several stories, she writes, "It strikes me
that it might all end with a picture. These stories about people would fill
half the book; & then the other thing would loom up; & we should step
into quite a different place & people? But what?" (47). One page later, as
she seems to answer her question "But what?" with plans for *To the
Lighthouse* (Woolf, *TTL Holograph*, App. A 47n.), a startling transformation of this corridor image occurs: "Two blocks joined by a corridor" (*TTL
Holograph*, App. A 48). Thus, in the space of a few pages, Woolf transforms
an image of her *product*—the short stories themselves—and of her revising
process—starting in one place and moving through a corridor to another
place—into an image for her next novel's *structure*.[7] The two original
blocks, *Mrs. Dalloway* and the new book, joined by a corridor of short
stories, have become the structure of the new book, and the place originally
occupied by the short stories has become the place occupied by "Time
Passes." Woolf has literally turned one thing into another.

But nothing stays the same for very long in Woolf's planning process as
detailed here; all is fluid, with categories—stories, books, parts, characters,
volumes—metamorphosing into each other in a sometimes disconcerting
way. The meaning of the phrase *new work*, for example, seems to shift back
and forth between the collection of short stories and another book, and the
nature of that other book keeps changing; at one point, Woolf gives up on
the language of genre entirely, using the word "thing." *Mrs. Dalloway* is
overflowing its boundaries, the short stories either lead into *To the
Lighthouse* or are some part of it, and then the image of the new work
reassembles it all differently. In these few notebook pages, Woolf refers to
the planned short stories in at least five different ways: separate entities; a
unified collection; a corridor leading from one novel to another; the new

book's first half; and the new book's corridor. Genre identity is indeed in flux. Such unstable genre identity extends well beyond her plan, however, since Woolf's stories, when written, actually function in the multiple ways she names here: (1) as individual stories, each from the point of view of a character or two; (2) as a short story sequence, tied together by theme, language, and characters; (3) as a corridor that becomes a place of transformation, extends *Mrs. Dalloway*, and reaches into *To the Lighthouse*; (4) as a rough draft for "The Window"; and (5) in a metaphorical transformation, as "Time Passes" or pure process, the corridor that paradoxically works to undermine form as it holds form together.

Woolf wrote eight stories between finishing *Mrs. Dalloway* and beginning *To the Lighthouse*: "The New Dress," "Happiness," "Ancestors," "The Introduction," "Together and Apart," "The Man Who Loved His Kind," "A Simple Melody," and "A Summing Up" (*CSF* 170–211). She planned them as character studies, the "stories of people at Mrs. D's party" and their "[s]tates of mind" (*TTL Holograph*, App. A 44). As she continued to think on paper, she further noted, "Each separate from the other" (*TTL Holograph*, App. A 44), aptly describing not only the characters, who have difficulty establishing any connection to each other, but also the stories, each of which is self-contained.[8] Each story focuses on one character's state of mind, though we may also gain access to another character's mind and still other characters may be present and talking. Each has an intriguing *in medias res* opening that keeps the reader reading. Each illuminates a conflict, usually internal, but sometimes external as well. Each feels concluded, though as Baldwin points out, not because conflicts are resolved (50). And each has a Woolfian moment of being and/or recognition. Later in her notes, Woolf says her book of stories "must have some unity," but that she "want[s] to publish each character separately" (*TTL Holograph*, App. A 45), a comment suggesting she contemplated publishing these stories in two ways, grouped together in a book and placed individually in journals. Certainly the quality of the individual stories as they stand in Susan Dick's edition, even the seven still in manuscript or typescript draft, indicate she could have done so, and Leonard Woolf's decision to publish three of the typescripts in *The Haunted House and Other Short Stories* in 1944, albeit "with some hesitation" (vi), supports such a contention.

In each of the eight stories, Woolf introduces the reader to different guests at Mrs. Dalloway's party, ones we do not meet in *Mrs. Dalloway*, and moves those guests from the background to the foreground by presenting their "[s]tates of mind" (*Woolf, TTL Holograph*, App. A 44). "The New Dress" features Mabel Waring and her self-consciousness about a dress that seemed so right at the dressmaker's and so wrong at the party. In "Happiness," Stuart Elton, as he converses with Mrs. Sutton, both imagines himself pursued by famished wolves and contemplates the nature of happiness (*CSF* 178). Mrs. Vallance idealizes the past, her parents, and her relationship with them in "Ancestors" as she both suffers in and scorns the present. In "The Introduction," Lily Everit is introduced not only to Bob Brinsley but also to her role as a woman and the oppression of the patriarchy, which "fell like a yoke about her neck" (*CSF* 186). Mrs. Dalloway introduces Miss Anning to Mr. Serle in "Together and Apart," and their brief dialogue about Canterbury calls up a multitude of feelings and memories in each of them, though they end up in "that paralysing blankness of feeling, when nothing bursts from the mind" (*CSF* 193). In "The Man Who Loved His Kind," Prickett Ellis inwardly criticizes the guests at the party (*CSF* 196) and the society that supports such an "appalling entertainment" (195), but ironically misses the opportunity to connect with Miss O'Keefe, who actually agrees with him in a fundamental way, because he "let[s] her have it" over her questions about art and beauty (199). Mr. Carslake looks at a picture of a heath in "A Simple Melody" and imagines walking there with several people at the party, convinced that walking to Norwich and talking on the way would allow them to set aside their dissatisfactions and bring them understanding, "an increase of life" (*CSF* 204). "A Summing Up" features Sasha Latham, whose inner, complex vision of civilization ("which view is the true one?" [*CSF* 210]) is juxtaposed with Bertram Pritchard's simple "conclusion that he liked Mr Wallace, but disliked his wife" (211).[9] Each story, then, as it presents the reader with the vivid interior life of a character or two, can stand on its own *as* a story.[10]

Although each story functions "separately," the group of eight stories also has "some unity" (*TTL Holograph*, App. A 45). Susan Dick based her arrangement of the stories on the order of the holograph drafts in Woolf's manuscript books, the list of story titles and topics Woolf created in her "Notes for stories—&c.," and chronology, as best as she could determine. Put in the order discussed above, the stories can, in fact, be seen as a book "complete in itself" (*TTL Holograph*, App. A 45); one can easily read the eight stories as a short story sequence.[11] Although she did not publish this story sequence as a book,[12] Woolf experiments here with a form literally on the boundary between story and novel.

Several themes unify the eight stories, probably the most important being the contrast between external social appearances and internal private realities. Characters think one thing, say another. Almost all "hug" something to themselves, some core identity that exists outside the party where the characters feel they live more fully and authentically, an identity threatened by the social world: Mabel Waring's "soul of herself" in "The New Dress" (*CSF* 172), for example, or Lily Everit's essay marked with "three red stars; First rate" in "The Introduction" (*CSF* 184). When, in "A Simple

Melody," Mr. Carslake describes his "sense of being in two places at once," physically at a London party and yet on the heath (*CSF* 205), he describes all the other characters' divided selves as well. Also, when he understands that "all thinking was an effort to make thought escape from the thinker's mind past all obstacles as completely as possible: all society is an attempt to seize and influence and coerce each thought as it appears and force it to yield to another" (*CSF* 206), he summarizes a theme running throughout the sequence. In addition, all the stories are haunted by the desire to communicate and the inability to do so. Although sudden and inexplicable communion sometimes illuminates people's lives, the moment never lasts and the sense of isolation afterward is often more intense. The sequence also reveals the human inability to "read" others accurately, as Woolf repeatedly portrays characters misinterpreting each other. For example, in "The Introduction" Mrs. Dalloway thinks Bob Brinsley has "the carefulness of women latent in all men" (*CSF* 187), but he's actually condescending to Lily, self-absorbed, and mocking toward women (187–88).

Characters' inward complaints about the inadequacy of language to describe deep emotion (such as Mr. Carslake's in "A Simple Melody" [*CSF* 197]) also tie the stories together thematically, and Woolf, too, searches for the language to capture the transitory nature of happiness against a backdrop of human suffering. In "The New Dress" Mabel realizes her "delicious moments" come unexpectedly, not when everything's arranged (*CSF* 175–76). In "Happiness" Stuart Elton thinks that "In happiness there is always this terrific exaltation [. . .], a mystic state, a trance" that sets him free, but he also understands that "if it came so inexplicably, so it might go" (*CSF* 180). Mrs. Vallance in "Ancestors" believes she would have been "perfectly happy" if the life created by her parents "could have gone on forever" (*CSF* 182–83). In "The Introduction" Lily remembers her mind filling with "rapture and wonder" at the sight of "little ceremonies which had no audience" on her long walks in the woods and on the moors (*CSF* 186). In "Together and Apart" Mr. Serle and Miss Anning feel "the old ecstasy of life" when they suddenly communicate without words (*CSF* 192–93). In "The Man Who Loved His Kind" Miss O'Keefe hopes that beauty and happiness are "dirt cheap" (*CSF* 199), and Prickett Ellis enjoys lying "on his back in a field" once a year (197). In "A Simple Melody" Mr. Carslake muses that one wants happiness "here and now," not in Heaven (*CSF* 204), and for him that means walking where "thoughts were half sky" (206). In "A Summing Up" though Sasha Latham must return to the "prosaic daylight" where a party is "nothing but people, in evening dress," she can also temporarily endow nature, civilization, and people with "dripping gold" out of an admiration for humanity's achievements (*CSF* 209–10).

Recurring words and images also connect the stories. For example, in both "The New Dress" and "Happiness," being happy is referred to as "delicious" or "divine," and Mabel Waring exclaims "This is it!" to herself when happy (*CSF* 176), whereas Stuart Elton is relieved to realize "He had it still" (180). Miss Anning in "Together and Apart" has "that," a "cluster of miracles" consisting of Sarah, Arthur, the cottage, and the chow (*CSF* 190). In "The New Dress" Mabel refers to her "wretched self" (*CSF* 176) and Lily in "The Introduction" feels like a "naked wretch" (*CSF* 188). Miss Anning uses a phrase in "Together and Apart"—"On, Stanley, on" (*CSF* 190)—to encourage herself to converse with Mr. Serle, a phrase echoed in Sasha Latham's admiration in "A Summing Up" for the courageous adventurers "who, set about with dangers, sail on" (*CSF* 209). Mabel imagines herself and the others at the party as flies unsuccessfully struggling to climb out of a saucer of milk in "The New Dress" (*CSF* 171), so that when Lily Everit either sees or imagines Bob Brinsley tearing the wings off a fly in "The Introduction" (*CSF* 187–88), the image seems even more brutal. Lily feels turned out of a garden in "The Introduction" (*CSF* 188), Miss O'Keefe observes a woman and her children locked out of a garden square in "The Man Who Loved His Kind" (*CSF* 197), and Sasha Latham perceives Mrs. Dalloway's garden in "A Summing Up," at least at first, as a refuge from the party (*CSF* 208–09). Mrs. Vallance in "Ancestors" reads "all Shelley between the ages of twelve and fifteen" (*CSF* 182), and Bob Brinsley can "talk about Shelley" in "The Introduction" (*CSF* 185). Images of nature—the sky, flowers, trees, the sea, insects, rabbits, birds—or metaphors of human beings *as* nature—struggling flies, clamoring cormorants, pursuing wolves, unmated widow birds, swimming fish, unbound butterflies, lovely cherry trees—occur surprisingly often throughout the sequence and are intense against the dull backdrop of pillows, mirrors, sofas, and arm chairs in Mr. and Mrs. Dalloway's home. In "Ancestors" Mrs. Vallance sees "human beings packed on top of each other in little boxes" in London (*CSF* 182) and in "A Simple Melody" Mr. Carslake thinks that "[p]eople pressed upon each other" in London drawing rooms (*CSF* 206).

Characters featured in one story never actually join characters featured in another, yet characters and readers make connections across stories.[13] Mabel Waring, suddenly self-conscious and anxious about her new dress's color and old-fashioned design as she walks into the party (*CSF* 170), is noticed later in "A Simple Melody" by Mr. Carslake, who observes her "pretty yellow dress" and wonders why she is unhappy (*CSF* 201–02). The reader also wonders whether Jack Renshaw likes Mabel Waring's dress when he exclaims "What a lovely frock!" to Mrs. Vallance as someone passes by in "Ancestors" (*CSF* 182). But because Mrs. Vallance refers first to "women's clothes" (*CSF* 182) and then to "the girl whose clothes he admired" (183), the identity of the person wearing the dress remains uncertain. In "A Simple Melody" Mr. Carslake also knows Mabel's "way of doing something suddenly quite out of her character, rather startling and dashing" and realizes that such impulses often do not succeed, but plunge her "deeper into gloom" (*CSF* 204), which is exactly what has happened with the new dress. In "A New Dress" Mabel unhappily "slouche[s]" across the room and looks "at a picture [. . .]. As if one went to a party to look at a picture!" (*CSF* 173). Prickett Ellis, however, knowing only two people at the party, also "examine[s] the pictures" in "The Man Who Loved His Kind" (*CSF* 196), and Mr. Carslake happily spends most of his time at the party gazing at *one* picture, not feeling any of Mabel's humiliation or Prickett's isolation. Prickett Ellis rebukes "well fed, well dressed women" for talking about beauty, and as Miss O'Keefe's lips twitch, "for she was thin, and her dress not up to standard" (199), the reader thinks of Mabel Waring in "The New Dress," who cannot afford a dress in the height of fashion (*CSF* 170), and then is reminded of both Mabel and Miss O'Keefe when introduced to Sasha Latham, who feels "perfectly inadequate and gauche when she had to say something at a party" in "A Summing Up" (*CSF* 208). In "Together and Apart" Mr. Serle has a great facility for talk, which he realizes is his undoing (*CSF* 191) and Bertram Pritchard can "be trusted, even out of doors, to talk without stopping" in "A Summing Up" (*CSF* 208). Mr. Carslake observes and thinks about Stuart Elton and Prickett Ellis in "A Simple Melody," intuiting Stuart's worry about his soul's "extreme unlikeness to anyone else's" and seeing Prickett's "glaring" anger (*CSF* 205).

Despite these interconnections, however, Woolf never published these stories in a separate book as she had planned; rather, she wrote them at top speed, revised them (sometimes extensively), and then set them aside, her frequent pattern with short fiction. Woolf began these stories as individual character studies and planned and organized them as a story sequence, but in the process of writing, they become a "corridor leading from Mrs. Dalloway to a new book" (*TTL Holograph*, App. A 44–45). Narrow and restricted, a corridor opens out into more space, and so seems similar to the "tunnelling process" Woolf used to connect her "beautiful caves" in *Mrs. Dalloway* (*D2* 263, 272). The corridor suggests a place "between," not a destination itself, but a passage through which one must go to arrive; a place that establishes relationship; a place that allows one to leave *and* return; a place of transition where one journeys from one place to another and where changes may occur, so that the "one" arriving differs from the "one" embarking—in other words, a place of process. Woolf's corridor image also reflects her use of the genre of the short story to move *toward* a novel of the open sea in which the idea of a journey, going *to*, becomes paramount. In this image, the stories shift from product to process and function as a place of transformation between the two novels, just as the corridor between two blocks in the planned novel becomes "Time Passes," another place of transformation. In her corridor of short stories, in her writing process, Woolf transforms one novel into another, continues *Mrs. Dalloway*, and begins working on *To the Lighthouse*.

We can see Woolf's transformations in several specific examples. Mrs. Dalloway's parents are almost nonexistent in *Mrs. Dalloway* (and Clarissa's motherhood seems almost incidental). In several of the stories, Woolf begins to transform the vague icon of a mother in "Ancestors" into the more fully realized mother who appears in *To the Lighthouse*. Mabel Waring, in "The New Dress" for example, has Mrs. Ramsay's sense of an untouched core self, desire to hold on to moments when everything comes together, and belief that her self-love deserves punishment (*CSF* 172, 175–76, 171). Mrs. Dalloway's matchmaking in "The Introduction" foreshadows Mrs. Ramsay's compulsion to make people marry. Miss O'Keefe's fury and impotence at seeing a woman and her children shut out of a square in "The Man Who Loved His Kind" (197–98) become Mrs. Ramsay's frustration at the differences between people. Mabel Waring ("The New Dress") and Miss Anning ("Together and Apart") use repetitive phrases (*CSF* 171, 177, 190, 192). In "A Simple Melody" Mr. Carslake feels trapped into repeating a phrase with "God" in it (*CSF* 203), and Mr. Serle and Miss Anning are both relieved to be alone at the end of "Together and Apart" (194), all traits belonging to Mrs. Ramsay. Thus, a barely mentioned Mrs. Parry in *Mrs. Dalloway* becomes transformed into a maternal presence that permeates *To the Lighthouse*.

Woolf also transforms art as she moves from novel to novel. The importance of art, present in *Mrs. Dalloway* as Septimus gains some peace from making a hat, increases in "A Simple Melody," where a painting "[has] the power to compose and tranquillize [Mr. Carslake's] mind" (*CSF* 201) and stimulates a vision of people walking on a heath and resolving their differences; the stories almost "end with a picture" (*TTL Holograph*, App. A 47). In *To the Lighthouse*, the *painting* of a picture at the end becomes a way to heal. Thus, the brief respite with a hat has been transformed into the making of art as a central theme. The hat being made in *Mrs. Dalloway* (process) becomes the picture being viewed in "A Simple Melody" (product), which becomes the picture being painted in *To the Lighthouse* (process). Perhaps this transformation of art reflects the instability of genre itself as the short stories also change from a process (planning and writing) to a product (stories and possible book) and back to a process (a corridor in which something else is made).

Woolf's transformations affect her techniques, too. In *Mrs. Dalloway*, Woolf attempts to make "luminous" both Clarissa's and Septimus's minds, show the nature of sane and insane truth (*Hours*, App. 2, 412), and give "[a] general view of the world" (Wussow xii). In her first notes under the heading of *To the Lighthouse*, she writes, "All character—*not* a view of the world" (*TTL Holograph*, App. A 48). In the short stories, her emphasis shifts from Mrs. Dalloway to her guests, and Woolf rapidly introduces character after character, practicing her "tunnelling process" (*D2* 272) on more people, giving them all points of view and pasts. Then in *To the Lighthouse*, she, like Lily, goes on "tunnelling her way into her picture, into the past" (173), examining the pasts that affect various selves. As Susan Dick puts it, "In [*To the Lighthouse*] she made brilliant use of the narrative method these stories had helped her to perfect" (*CSF* 3). *Mrs. Dalloway*, though it examines several characters from within, focuses mainly on two individuals as it moves back and forth between Clarissa and Septimus. In the stories, Woolf often pairs characters whose contrasting thoughts are available to the reader as they talk to each other. Then in *To the Lighthouse*, she assembles a large cast and gives an inner world to major and minor characters alike, increasing the crosscurrents and contradictions, and thus the complexity of perception.

The point of view framing the two novels shifts drastically: in *Mrs. Dalloway*, an adult woman in the present looks back at her young womanhood; in the first part of *To the Lighthouse*, the reader is *in* the world of the child's past. As Hermione Lee puts it, *To the Lighthouse* "uncover[s] and appease[s]" childhood memory (*Virginia Woolf* 475), rather than just recalls it. Woolf begins that shift to childhood memory in a scene from "Ancestors." There, Woolf uses a similar point of view to Mrs. Dalloway's as she creates a middle-aged woman, Mrs. Vallance, who looks nostalgically back at her past. But in Woolf's creation of a vivid scene in which Mrs. Vallance in "Ancestors" remembers being a little girl in a cotton frock, looking at her father shaving as she recited Shelley, she momentarily anticipates a shift to the gaze of the daughter, the gaze providing the impetus for *To the Lighthouse*. Not only does Woolf use the point of view of children in her next novel (James as a young boy and both James and Cam as adolescents) and the point of view of the grown-up surrogate daughter (Lily Briscoe), but she herself stands outside the novel as the daughter, gazing at her parents, recreating her parents' world, and trying to make readers, as Mrs. Vallance puts it, "understand what her father, what her mother and she herself too [. . .], felt" (*CSF* 181). Thus, the short story gives her a glimpse of the framing point of view she will use in *To the Lighthouse*; rather than using an older female to narrate her memories of the parents and herself, Woolf brings the parents to life. Having written a story in which the gaze of the daughter emerges, Woolf transforms *Mrs. Dalloway*—a novel in which adolescent memories live on in the present—into *To the*

Lighthouse—a novel in which childhood memories *are* the present and then *become* the past.

A final extended example of Woolf's transformation strategy can be seen as Woolf transforms Elizabeth Dalloway into Lily Briscoe. Elizabeth Dalloway has nothing to do, barely appears in *Mrs. Dalloway*, and has Chinese eyes and an air of "Oriental mystery" (123); she enjoys the country more than she does parties (134–35), "but they would compare her to lilies," and such comparisons "made her life a burden to her" (134). In "The Introduction" Lily Everit has written a first rate essay (*CSF* 184), has a story to herself, is lovely, and enjoys nature more than she does parties. She is painfully initiated into a society with "no sanctuaries, or butterflies" (*CSF* 188), a society that demands, through the "chivalries and respects of the drawing room" (*CSF* 185), that she put on the role of a woman—it has something to do with what happens when a woman drops a handkerchief (*CSF* 186). By the end of the story, she feels "crushed" by "the weight of the world" (*CSF* 188). Lily Briscoe paints and is a major character in *To the Lighthouse*; she is plain but has Chinese eyes.[14] Older and more rebellious, she wonders what would happen if women did not help men assert themselves and if men did not let women out of the burning tube first (91). Occasionally burdened by patriarchal expectations, she asserts her independence ("I'm happy like this" [175]), sees clearly how such expectations wore Mrs. Ramsay down (149), and finds a way to interact with Mr. Ramsay that does not involve "self-surrender" (153–54, 150). At the end of the novel, she triumphs: "I have had my vision" (209). In the corridor of a short story Elizabeth Dalloway, the shy girl who cannot imagine even discussing a profession with her mother (*MD* 137), has been transformed into a woman who uses her painting to withstand patriarchal pressures.

The corridor of short stories, then, has functioned as a place of transformation. In addition, as critics have often noted, Woolf's novels grow out of her stories.[15] Woolf herself provided evidence for that process when she wrote to Ethel Smyth: "The Unwritten Novel was the great discovery, however. That—again in one second—showed me how I could embody all my deposit of experience in a shape that fitted it [. . .]. I saw, branching out of the tunnel I made, when I discovered that method of approach, Jacobs Room, Mrs Dalloway etc—How I trembled with excitement" (*L4* 231). Less often noted, however, is the evidence for the reverse also being true, that the novels serve as drafts or impetus for the stories. Woolf points out that writing *Night and Day* generated the stories in *Monday or Tuesday*: "These little pieces [. . .] were written by way of diversion; they were the treats I allowed myself when I had done my exercise in the conventional style. I shall never forget the day I wrote The Mark on the Wall—all in a flash, as if flying, after being kept stone breaking for months" (*L4* 231). In

April 1925, after finishing *Mrs. Dalloway*, she wrote that stories are "welling up in me" (*D3* 12); by May, she confessed to Vita Sackville-West that she "cant stop writing. I'm ashamed to think how many stories I've written this month" (*L3* 185). As she finished *To the Lighthouse*, she wrote, "*As usual*, side stories are sprouting in great variety as I wind this up" (*D3* 106; my emphasis). Even as she contemplated her own end, Woolf ended *Between the Acts* with an invitation to more fiction making, and she was working on several short stories, two of which, "The Symbol" and "The Watering Place," seem complete and are in Susan Dick's edition, and three of which, "Winter's Night," "Another Sixpence," and "English Youth" were in process and left unfinished (see *CSF* 337–38). Woolf's novel manuscripts and stories (in their various stages) make clear something crucial about Woolf's writing practice: novels grow out of short stories and short stories grow out of novels in an ongoing process of making and revising fiction. Thus, the stories in her corridor not only function as a place of transformation, but they also touch both novels, functioning simultaneously as a continuation of *Mrs. Dalloway* and a source for *To the Lighthouse*.

Thus, the corridor of short stories means that Woolf does not really have to "finish" *Mrs. Dalloway*; the corridor perpetuates the process of fiction making, expanding the boundaries of both the stories and the novels around them. In the stories, we are still at Mrs. Dalloway's party, though a party at which Septimus's suicide does not seem to have occurred. The stories describe characters who, in their isolation, remind us of Septimus, sharing his belief that "communication is health; communication is happiness" (*MD* 93) but also his inability to reveal himself. The stories continue *Mrs. Dalloway* in other ways, too. When Mr. Dalloway runs into Prickett Ellis in "The Man Who Loved His Kind," invites him to the party, and says as he walks away, "Good—till this evening then" (*CSF* 195), the reader remembers Mrs. Dalloway's last-minute invitation to Peter and her cry, "Remember my party to-night!" (*MD* 48). Prickett, like Peter, scorns the idea of such a party; surely, too, their first names are related! Mabel Waring in "The Introduction" seems a continuation of Ellie Henderson, and Bob Brinsley, who has "read everything and could talk about Shelley" (*CSF* 185), is a young version of Professor Brierly, "who knows everything in the world about Milton" (*MD* 177). Finally, Miss Milan in "The New Dress" and Prickett Ellis and Miss O'Keefe in "The Man Who Loved His Kind" bring a more complex class analysis to the party than Miss Kilman and Septimus can sustain in *Mrs. Dalloway*. The short stories thus allowed Woolf to work further with the people and issues in *Mrs. Dalloway*, yet move away from the *character* of Mrs. Dalloway.

The stories also allowed Woolf to move toward the people and issues of *To the Lighthouse*, becoming a resource for Woolf and her novel by providing the time and material necessary to her writing process. Woolf used them to keep herself from rushing to the new work before she was ready. After her first description of *To the Lighthouse* in her diary on May 14, 1925, she wrote, "However, I must refrain. I must write a few little stories first, & let the Lighthouse simmer [. . .]" (*D3* 19). Two weeks later, she wrote to Vita Sackville-West that she "can hardly bear to keep my fingers off a new novel, but swear I won't start till August" (*L3* 185). And in fact, she did not begin the novel until August 6. Woolf may also have learned her novel's real focus from the short stories. When she sketched out *To the Lighthouse* on May 14, 1925, she said her father's character would be at the center (*D3* 18–19), but by August 6, when she made her first notes for the novel in her manuscript notebook, she had decided, "The dominating impression is to be of Mrs. R's character" (*TTL Holograph* MS2). In making that switch, Woolf followed the proportions she established in the eight stories: someone like Mr. Ramsay appears only once, as John Ellis Rattray in "Ancestors," whereas someone with a trait of Mrs. Ramsay's appears in nearly all the stories.

Many of the characters, phrases, and themes of *To the Lighthouse* also grow out of the stories.[16] At least six characters in the novel have precursors in the stories: Mr. and Mrs. Ramsay, Mr. Bankes, Mr. Carmichael, Charles Tansley, and Lily Briscoe. John Ellis Rattray in "Ancestors," the already mentioned rough draft of Mr. Ramsay, wears a white linen coat, smokes, listens to his young daughter recite Shelley while he shaves, and is "full of reverence for women" (*CSF* 182). Catherine Macdonald, a version of Mrs. Ramsay, is a beautiful woman who loves flowers, seems always to be herself, and sits in the garden dreaming of the past (182). These characters, almost caricatures of Mr. and Mrs. Ramsay, create a childhood from which their daughter, the middle-aged Mrs. Vallance, cannot escape. As discussed earlier, a more realistic Mrs. Ramsay begins to emerge out of the character traits Woolf created for several women (Mabel Waring, Mrs. Dalloway, Miss O'Keefe, and Miss Anning) and two men (Mr. Serle and Mr. Carslake) in six of the other stories. Most noticeable is the way Mrs. Ramsay's compulsion to make people marry is prefigured by Mrs. Dalloway's matchmaking in "The Introduction," where she "bears" down on the shy Lily Everit (*CSF* 184), consciously pairing the "clever" young woman with Bob Brinsley, a "young man just down from Oxford" (185), saying "Both of you love Shelley" (187). She thinks she sees in Brinsley "the tenderness, the goodness, the carefulness of women latent in all men" (187), and seeing the shy, startled look on Lily's face at the moment of introduction, thinks about the

> loveliest and most ancient of all fires [. . .] and man feeling this for woman, and woman that for man, and there flowing from that contact all those homes, trials, sorrows, profound joy and ultimate staunchness in the face of

catastrophe, humanity was sweet at its heart [. . .] and her own life (to introduce a couple made her think of meeting Richard for the first time!) infinitely blessed. (187)

She thus cheerfully sacrifices Lily to the heavy yoke of the patriarchy, doing her part to perpetuate it. She, like Mrs. Ramsay after her, does not really understand Lily's interests (Swift, not Shelley) and seems unaware of the damage done not only to younger women but also to herself by the social system she so ardently supports.

Woolf also hints at Mr. Bankes and Mr. Carmichael in "A Simple Melody," "Happiness," and "Ancestors." Surely Mr. Bankes grows out of Woolf's portrayal of Mr. Carslake. He is kind, thoughtful, and calm—and perhaps the most genuinely happy character in the stories; he realizes that landscapes outlast people, but refuses to feel sad about it (*CSF* 202); is thought a "queer fish" by others (207), but does not "bother his head" about it (205); and spends most of the story gazing at a picture (see *TTL* 20, 93). In Stuart Elton's self-possession and flight from women who want to know more about it in "Happiness" (*CSF* 179) and in an old Mr. Rogers who is the "ideal of a Greek sage" in "Ancestors" (*CSF* 181), Woolf begins to sketch Mr. Carmichael.

But only "two figures [. . .] detach themselves from the party & go off independently" into the new novel (*TTL Holograph*, App. A 45): Bob Brinsley/Prickett Ellis and Lily Everit walk straight out of the stories and into *To the Lighthouse* as Charles Tansley and Lily Briscoe. When Bob Brinsley sneers at Lily Everit's writing in "The Introduction" (*CSF* 187), Charles Tansley's "women can't write, women can't paint" comes immediately to mind (*TTL* 86). In addition, Tansley's spartan habits, including shag tobacco (12), his anger at the hypocrisy of the Ramsay dinner party (85), his social ineptitude and resulting defensiveness (12), his inability to respond to beauty (8, 13), and his "denouncing [. . .] condemning" speeches about brotherly love during the war (197) all originate in Prickett Ellis's character in "The Man Who Loved His Kind."

Many traits Woolf creates for the young Lily Everit in "The Introduction" become part of the older Lily Briscoe.[17] For example, both want to avoid revealing their work to others (*TTL* 17–18; *CSF* 185); both are aware of patriarchal power (*TTL* 91; *CSF* 187–88); and both feel helpless in the face of a powerful maternal figure (*TTL* 176; *CSF* 184, 185). The most startling similarity, however, is that both women "hug" their work and its importance to themselves in the midst of uncomfortable social situations: Lily Everit's achievement of three red stars for her essay on Dean Swift's character at Mrs. Dalloway's party (*CSF* 184) and Lily Briscoe's solution to the problem in her painting at the Ramsay dinner party (*TTL* 86, 93, 102).

Woolf's novel also echoes phrases she uses in her eight stories. For example, Mrs. Ramsay's "It is enough!" (*TTL* 65) echoes Mabel Waring's "This is it!" in "The New Dress" (*CSF* 176). The sense Lily Briscoe has of Mrs. Ramsay's being relieved of the patriarchal burden, "relieved for a moment of the weight that the world had put on her" (*TTL* 181), is first the sense of Lily Everit's taking up that burden: "Lily looked 'as if she had the weight of the world upon her shoulders' " in "The Introduction" (*CSF* 188). James Ramsay's question about the lighthouse ("So that was the Lighthouse was it?" [*TTL* 186]) can be heard in Mr. Carslake's question about similarity and difference in "A Simple Melody" ("and which is the more profound?" [*CSF* 206]) and in Sasha Latham's humble question about civilization near the end of "A Summing Up" ("which view is the true one?" [210]). In "Together and Apart" Miss Anning's use of "on, Stanley, on" in social situations (*CSF* 190, 192) prefigures Mrs. Ramsay's "giving herself the little shake that one gives a watch that has stopped" and saying to herself "And so on and so on" at the beginning of her dinner party (*TTL* 83). Certainly James Ramsay's description of his father's destructive influence— "It was in this world that the wheel went over the person's foot" (*TTL* 185)— echoes Mrs. Vallance's description of her suffering in a world without her parents in "Ancestors": "life had passed over her like a wheel" (*CSF* 182).

Finally, Woolf's stories allow her to try out several of her novel's themes. Art's healing power is important in "A Simple Melody"; the importance of the past and the function of memory are major themes in "The New Dress," "Ancestors," and "Together and Apart"; the patriarchy's effect on relationships between men and women colors "Happiness," "Ancestors," "The Introduction," "Together and Apart," and "The Man Who Loved His Kind"; and class differences underlie "The New Dress," "The Man Who Loved His Kind," and "A Summing Up." All the stories focus on different views of the same "reality" to question whether any one view is right. "A Summing Up" ends, as Baldwin notes, with "two visions" coexisting, "the one of society and civilization as a high attainment, the other of these as dull and indifferent," and these visions "continue but do not resolve the problems posed in earlier stories" (49–50). Thus, the stories move toward the "answer" of *To the Lighthouse*, which also does not resolve: "So that was the Lighthouse, was it? No, the other was also the Lighthouse. For nothing was simply one thing" (186).

At the same time genre remains fluid within the corridor, the stories function in yet another way, as part of *To the Lighthouse*. As mentioned earlier, the nature of Woolf's terms keeps changing during her planning process, so that when she writes, "These stories about people would fill half the book; & then the other thing would loom up; & we should step into quite a different place & people? But what?" (*TTL Holograph*, App. A 47), at least two possible meanings emerge. First, as the just-completed discussion indicates and as most commentators surmise, Woolf could mean that the stories about people fill half the planned book of short stories, and then the new book looms up, and we step into the world of *To the Lighthouse*. But she could also mean that the stories about people fill half the new book, "The Window," and then the other thing, "Time Passes," looms up, and we step into quite a different place and people, the postwar world of "The Lighthouse." In the second reading, which anticipates Woolf's description of her novel's structure as "[t]wo blocks joined by a corridor," the stories in the corridor are moved to another location and become a "block," and in being transformed from corridor to block, are also transformed from process to product; that is, the stories providing a transition *between* novels have become part *of* the new novel. Woolf, by placing the stories in the spot later identified as "The Window" in her structure, suggests they in some way function as a rough draft for that part of her novel, and thus bends genre once more.

These stories do not, however, function as a rough draft in the sense that Woolf spreads them out in front of her and begins marking them up until they take on some resemblance to the holograph draft of "The Window" in *To the Lighthouse*. Rather, the stories as a whole provide Woolf with an idea of what she might do in "The Window." The dinner party at the end of "The Window" is another version, more focused and unified, of Mrs. Dalloway's party in the stories. The stories, after all, when viewed as a whole, bring together a group of people in one place, and those people, as Baldwin notes, include "a number of social types and ranks" (50). The same holds true for "The Window," in which numerous people are brought together in one place and then participate in one special occasion, the dinner party. In the stories, Woolf goes from person to person, pair to pair, exploring their perceptions as they talk with each other. In the first part of *To the Lighthouse*, she still moves from person to person, making sure she provides the reader with multiple points of view, but it is as though she has removed the boundaries between characters that exist in the story sequence: erasing separate story titles, doing away with the necessity of ending one story and starting another, removing self-contained episodes. The characters in the first part of *To the Lighthouse* thus seem closer, more related to each other, than do the characters at Mrs. Dalloway's party (even though the characters in the novel are spread out over more space and divided on many issues). Instead of overtly using the device of a hostess to introduce all the guests to each other and to readers, Woolf uses her narrative in "The Window" to perform the same function; we are unaware of the hostess because she has been moved to the background, incorporated into the narrative. In the stories, Woolf introduces us to several points of view and allows some connections among characters to develop during the party. In "The Window," it is as though Woolf has taken those stories and fledgling connections and placed them into a far wider context; in her novel, the dinner party exists in a web of relationships that goes backward and forward in time. Woolf has taken people's isolated struggles to establish and maintain communion within a party's time constraints and used them again in the dinner party in "The Window," but they are reworked in the context of ongoing relationships that both readers and the characters know about. Examined as a whole, the stories provide in embryo much of what will emerge in "The Window": an overall view of a world filled with multiple and contradictory points of view; the sense of a full, bustling world; the inner questioning; the desire to assert and the desire to unify; the observer trying to balance opposing views; the creator suspecting her creation may not be worth much; the minor characters; the children; the gender struggle; the class struggle; and so on. Thus, although these eight stories in the corridor between *Mrs. Dalloway* and *To the Lighthouse* do not become the literal block that begins *To the Lighthouse*, they function as a preliminary version of it.

When Woolf ends her "Notes for stories—&c." with the idea that "These stories about people would fill half the book; & then the other thing would loom up; & we should step into quite a different place & people? But what?" (*TTL Holograph*, App. A 44, 47), she has not only proposed her stories as the opening of her new book but also unconsciously drafted the plan for *To the Lighthouse* that appears on the next page. There, her metaphor for the new novel's structure, the "[t]wo blocks joined by a corridor," shifts everything yet again. Woolf bends genre one more time as she transforms the corridor of stories between two novels into "Time Passes," the corridor between the two blocks of *To the Lighthouse* where time and process "loom up." Using the corridor of short stories as a transformative space provides her with the distinguishing trait of her *novel's* corridor: in it, process, transformation, and change link the past to potential; formlessness challenges form; distinctions blur, boundaries dissolve, and genres bend.

In fact, the transformation of her corridor of short stories into the corridor between the two blocks of *To the Lighthouse* suggests an affinity between the two corridors *as* corridors. Both corridors function in multiple ways, for example. The stories can be read as a separately conceived sequence, yet they also function as a corridor, linking two novels. Similarly, "Time Passes" can be read as a separate narrative, and an earlier version of it was published as such in France (Haule "Le Temps passe"), yet it functions as a corridor, linking the two worlds and times of the novel. Both corridors, the stories and "Time Passes," reveal relationships between the two "blocks" at either end. As corridor the stories function as process for Woolf; for all her plans, she never turns the stories into a product. Rather, the drafting, writing, and revising of them, the time passing as she wrote, seem to have been useful to her, and the stories lead her from one novel to the next. Similarly, "Time Passes" functions as process in her novel, where all human activity and achievement is threatened, including the novel itself, and yet it literally holds the two parts of the novel together. The stories in the corridor remain themselves, with identifiable stages and drafts and locations in Woolf's papers, just as "Time Passes" remains comprehensible prose, with identifiable sections, narratives, and sentences. Yet the stories also become something other than themselves, and their shifting nature confuses, just as "Time Passes" confuses and disconcerts as it shifts between human and nonhuman narration. The stories in the corridor challenge genre—are they stories, a story sequence, a passage between two novels, a draft for part of her new novel, pure process, or what?—at the same time they have shape. "Time Passes" challenges form—Woolf writes that she "cannot make it out—here is the most difficult abstract piece of writing— I have to give an empty house, no people's characters, the passage of time, all eyeless & featureless with nothing to cling to" (*D3* 76)—at the same time it is rigidly structured and provides structure. Thus, both corridors threaten to pull asunder and work to join together.

For Woolf, the corridor represents a major structural shift from the basically binary structure of *Mrs. Dalloway* (with its back and forth movement between two main characters) to the tripartite structure of *To the Lighthouse*. Adding the corridor changes Woolf's underlying logic from "either/or" to "both/and." By adding that third piece, the passage, Woolf metaphorically adds the writing process, revision, transformation itself to the thing written. She metaphorically adds process, the threat to all form, to the thing formed. When she literally and metaphorically adds "and," she illustrates how opposites actually participate in each other and are joined. That move threatens; that move breaks down categories, distinctions, hierarchies, divisions, definitions; that move bends genre: the short stories in the corridor are both short stories *and* the corridor in a novel. Adding the corridor, the "and," also makes all endings provisional, including the one she writes for *To the Lighthouse*; vision, form, genre, and fiction making itself will be challenged once again in yet another corridor.

Woolf commented, at the end of 1924 when she was finishing *Mrs. Dalloway* and *The Common Reader*, that she would soon be "[f]ree at least to write out one or two more stories which have accumulated. I am less & less sure that they *are* stories, or what they are. Only I do feel fairly sure that I am grazing as near as I can to my own ideas, & getting a tolerable shape for them" (*D2* 325). As it turned out, she wrote eight stories, not one or two, and they gave shape to her ideas, several shapes: individual stories, story sequence, corridor between two novels, draft of the new novel's first part, and corridor of the new novel. Woolf challenges genre in her corridor of stories by using her stories in at least five different ways, shifting them from genre to genre, and thus calling attention to the nature of transformation and the process of fiction making. Ultimately, her corridor of stories leads her to include an "abstract" corridor of "eyeless & featureless" process, "the thing itself before it has been made anything" (*TTL* 193), within her novel; within her fiction, she includes "the thing" against which fiction is made and makes genre's constructed nature evident.

Woolf's writing and revising practice, then, just as it makes us question the nature of "text" and see her texts as palimpsests, should also make us question the nature of "genre" and see her genres on a continuum of fiction making; her practice both uses genre and questions its usefulness. The sometimes close relationship between short stories and novels in Woolf's canon does not belittle the short stories, but instead reflects Woolf's lifelong questioning of genre[18] and indeed, her lifelong questioning of boundaries and hierarchies of all sorts. "Have no screens," she once wrote, though she admitted we probably need the "screen making habit" for our sanity. "But," she added, "the screens are in the excess; not the sympathy" (*D3* 104). Certainly critics often associate the short story genre itself with challenges to social boundaries. Lohafer points out the short story's "alignment [. . .] with the marginalized speaker" ("Introduction" xii) and its close relationship to the classroom through the "utilitarian" textbook ("Introduction to Part I" 5), Ferguson explores the language of class as it intersects with genre ("Rise of the Short Story"), and Mary Eagleton comments on how many of the genre's traits— "not the primary literary form," holding a "marginal and ambiguous position in literary culture," filled with characters "at odds with the dominant culture"—seem linked to gender, to "the position of women in a patriarchal society" (62). Katherine Mansfield's comment that she wrote "only short stories" testifies to the genre's "marginal" state, which Hanson reinforces in her suggestion that the short story is "a form of the margins," "the chosen form of the exile," and the "preferred form" for women writers with "squint vision" (*Re-reading* 2–5). If we agree with Hanson that the short story's formal properties, "disjunction, inconclusiveness, obliquity," relate to its "ideological marginality" and that "the form may be used to express something suppressed/repressed in mainstream literature" (6), then Woolf's challenges to genre imply even more radical questions about class and gender.

In our discussions of Woolf's short stories, then, we might take our cue from her—"I am less & less sure that they *are* stories, or what they are" (*D2* 325). We need not stop our examinations of Woolf's shorter fiction *as* short stories—after all, she also called them that, and they continue to function as such, in her papers and in publications since. But they function in other ways as well, reminding us that genre definitions are not stable in her work—they shift and change and become transformed in the corridor of Woolf's writing practice, the corridor of process where the writer never finishes making fiction but is always going *to* . . . what?

NOTES

1. Daniel Burke's comment that making a statement about the short story's neglect has become conventional (3) suggests how frequently such statements have occurred in the criticism. The focus on definition may have stemmed from the relatively late acknowledgment that the novel and the short story might be "separate entities" (Shaw 3). Shaw suggests that "a firm definition of the short story is impossible" (21), and Suzanne Ferguson suggests that defining the short story has "proven surprisingly resistant to critical effort" ("Defining" 287). Clare Hanson notes that much short story definition limits itself to defining the story "against" the novel, "the major form and the norm in fiction" (" 'Things Out of Words' " 23), and Lohafer says the question dividing short story critics is whether the short story differs from the novel "in kind or only in degree" ("Introduction to Part IV" 173). May's two collections of short story theory reflect the demand for more, and more rigorous, theory. By 1989, Lohafer could identify "a scattered but committed group of [. . .] short story theorists" ("Introduction to Part I" 10), yet Norman Friedman could still suggest that short story critics should be more systematic and coherent in their approaches ("Recent Short Story Theories" 13–31). Although Head still claims in 1992 that existing theory is "patchy and repetitive" (8) and that the modern short story "has *not* been subjected to the systematic attentions of literary theory" (x), both Sarah Hardy and Gerald Prince argue in 1993 that such complaints and calls to arms are no longer necessary (326, 327).
2. A recent example of this neglect is *The Cambridge Companion to Virginia Woolf.* The book's blurb says *The Companion* provides "original, new readings of all nine novels and fresh insight into Woolf's letters, diaries and essays [. . .]." Several chapters are devoted to the novels, and the essays receive a chapter, as do the letters and diaries, but no chapter exists for the short stories; focused attention on them is limited to a short discussion of eight stories (169–77) *within* Roe's chapter on Post-Impressionism's impact on Woolf.
3. Other critics who insist or assume that Woolf's stories are "valuable to consider in their own right" (Baldwin 4) are Dean Baldwin, Joanne Trautmann Banks, Susan Dick, Shuli Barzilai, Selma Meyerowitz, Alice Staveley, Kathryn N. Benzel, and Sandra Kemp. Some recent critics also continue to use a short story to support a reading encompassing more and/or longer works, such as Tracy Seeley's essay on "The Lady in the Looking-Glass."
4. Dick often goes back to the typescripts or to the texts published in magazines to establish her copy texts rather than use the versions published by Stella McNichol in *Mrs. Dalloway's Party* or by Leonard Woolf in *A Haunted House* ("Editorial Procedures" 7–13).

In Dick's edition, the text of "A Simple Melody" is a transcription of a holograph; the texts of "Happiness," "The Introduction," "Together and Apart," and "The Man Who Loved His Kind" are transcriptions of typescripts with holograph revisions; the texts of "Ancestors" and "A Summing Up" are transcriptions of typescripts combined with holograph portions; and the text of "The New Dress" is the version published in *Forum*.

To establish these copy texts, Dick used three manuscript books from the Berg Collection, a notebook labeled November 22, 1924 (*VW Manuscripts—Berg*, Mrs. Dalloway M20, reel 6), a notebook labeled Articles, Essays, Fiction, and Reviews and dated April 21, 1925 (*VW Manuscripts—Berg*, M1.1, reel 4), and another notebook with the same label but dated May 22, 1925 (*VW Manuscripts—Berg*, M1.2, reel 4); a folder of typescripts in the *Mrs. Dalloway* materials (*VW Manuscripts—Berg*, M106, reel 11); and typescripts at the University of Sussex (*VW Manuscripts—Monks House*, B.4, reel 3 and B.9, reel 4).

5. Wallace Hildick and Charles G. Hoffmann paved the way in the 1960s for this explosion of interest in Woolf's manuscripts. John W. Graham brought out his edition of two holograph drafts of the *Waves* in 1976, and special issues of *Twentieth Century Literature* (25 [1979]) and the *Bulletin of the New York Public Library* (82 [1979]) gave readers access to various shorter manuscripts. Louise DeSalvo's work on *The Voyage Out*, Grace Radin's work on *The Years* and Mitchell A. Leaska's work on *The Pargiters*, the essay portion of *The Years*, and *Between the Acts* continued the trend.

6. Dick reads this heading as "Notes for stories—e." However, the mark after the dash is probably Woolf's abbreviation for et cetera, the ampersand followed by a "c": &c.

7. I argued thus in an earlier version of this essay presented at a Midwest Modern Language Association double session on "Literary Women Working: Writing, Revising, and Publishing" in 1991. Wussow agrees, noting that the stories written after *Mrs. Dalloway* "provide a channel from *Mrs. Dalloway* to *To the Lighthouse*, a corridor similar to that formed by the 'Time Passes' section in the latter novel" (x).

8. Baldwin suggests that "A Simple Melody" is not as self-sufficient, depending "perhaps too much on others in the series" (46). But although knowledge of three other stories enriches "A Simple Melody," such knowledge is not required to read it on its own and grasp its meaning.

9. See Baldwin's fuller discussion of these stories (36–50).

10. Jean Guiguet calls "The New Dress" a "perfectly self-contained narrative, with its own progress and peripeteia" (337), and Meyerowitz shows how to use "The Introduction" (249–51) in a Women's Studies class, but any of these stories could be studied for narrative techniques, modernism, character development, social implications, and/or generic traits.

11. Baldwin writes that "Individually, the stories may not strike the reader as great short fiction, but collectively they represent a considerable achievement in a rarely practiced and seldom analyzed form—the story sequence" (50). Robert M. Luscher and Nicole Ward Jouve both explore the nature of a short story sequence, and Staveley notes the neglect of *Monday or Tuesday* "as a collected work" ("Voicing" 263).

A thematic consideration, "the party consciousness," led Stella McNichol to publish her edition of *Mrs. Dalloway's Party: A Short Story Sequence* in 1973. Focusing on the *Mrs. Dalloway* materials, without the benefit of either the published letters and diaries or the subsequent sorting of the voluminous mass of manuscripts in the Berg and at Sussex and without realizing that notes about these stories existed in the *To the Lighthouse* notebooks, McNichol put six of them (four of which had been published by Leonard Woolf in *A Haunted House*) with "Mrs Dalloway in Bond Street," a story Woolf wrote *before* she began *Mrs. Dalloway*, for an edition of seven stories. In her introduction, McNichol mistakenly suggests that "The New Dress" is "connected with the genesis of the novel *Mrs. Dalloway*" (14) and justifies her arrangement of the stories ("Mrs. Dalloway in Bond Street," "The Man Who Loved His Kind," "The Introduction," "Ancestors," "Together and Apart," "The New Dress," and "A Summing Up") based on "a simple narrative and chronological unity" (14): the first two stories "anticipate the party," and the next five are "at the party" (15). John F. Hulcoop criticizes McNichol for not providing more information about the manuscripts and editorial procedures she used, and McNichol provides only partial documentation in her reply. Because Dick locates all known versions of each story, uses internal and external evidence to date the versions, and then puts the latest versions of the stories in chronological order, her edition establishes a more reliable text of Woolf's short story sequence, although not, of course, in the form of a separate book.

Regrettably, Harcourt uses Stella McNichol's *Mrs. Dalloway's Party* rather than Susan Dick's arrangement in its recent publication, *The Mrs. Dalloway Reader,* and compounds the error by claiming on its book jacket that *Mrs. Dalloway's Party* "is a kind of writer's notebook, containing many outtakes from Woolf's initial attempt to write *Mrs. Dalloway*." Francine Prose's introduction also implies that all the stories were written before the novel. Worse yet, neither the editing work of Stella McNichol nor the subsequent careful dating of the story manuscripts by Susan Dick is acknowledged.

12. Of the stories written between *Mrs. Dalloway* and *To the Lighthouse,* Woolf herself published only "The New Dress," and only in the United States, in *Forum* in May 1927.

13. Baldwin also points out connections, seeing "Happiness" as a contrast to "The New Dress," with Stuart Elton's self-satisfaction opposed to Mabel Waring's insecurity (37–48), and "Ancestors" as a "companion piece" to "Happiness" because Mrs. Vallance and Stuart Elton both have an "aloof detachment" (38). He also notes that characters in both "The Introduction" and "Together and Apart" are brought together by Mrs. Dalloway and argues that all the stories up through "The Man Who Loved His Kind" are about the forces that separate people, whereas "A Simple Melody" portrays an attempt to find people's "common humanity" (47).

14. Patricia Laurence explores Woolf's allusions to Chinese eyes in *Lily Briscoe's Chinese Eyes: Bloomsbury, Modernism, and China.*

15. Joanne Trautmann Banks suggests, for example, that all the "great experimental novels" continue "many of the same methods and themes as [. . .] her shorter

pieces" (82) and points out Woolf's plan for *Jacob's Room*: "conceive mark on the wall, K[ew]. G[ardens]. & unwritten novel taking hands & dancing in unity" (*D2* 14). Charles Hoffmann notes that Woolf wrote "Mrs Dalloway in Bond Street" and "The Prime Minister" as short stories before using them as the first "chapters" of the novel that follows ("From Short Story to Novel" 171–72), and Susan Dick suggests that Woolf explores the tension between immersion in and resistance to narrative in the three short stories she wrote immediately before *The Waves* ("Three Short Fictions" 162–63).

16. Lee writes that the "eight stories which formed the bridge between *Mrs. Dalloway* and *To the Lighthouse* are all set at Mrs. Dalloway's party, but the tunes of *To the Lighthouse* are beginning to be played in them" and discusses specific pre-figurings ("*Lighthouse* Introduction" 163–64). See also Hulcoop, who says the stories "anticipate, in thematic material, recurrent images, names and other innumerable details, *To the Lighthouse*" (4).

17. Some of Mr. Carslake's ideas about art, particularly its value, also belong to Lily.

18. See Head's chapter on Woolf (79–108), and Kemp, who notes "Woolf's attempt to blur the generic spectrum" (xvii).

Chapter 7

"A view of one's own": Writing Women's Lives and the Early Short Stories

Anna Snaith

Due to changes in the literary marketplace the 1890s witnessed a burgeon-ing of the short story genre. The collapse of the triple-decker novel in 1894, the waning of the circulating libraries and their powers of censorship, and a proliferation of periodicals helped to create this climate (Ledger 187). The advertising space available in the new periodicals meant that writers were relatively well paid for their short stories. For women writers, in particular, the genre was attractive: demands on time as well as relative ease of publi-cation meant the *fin-de-siècle* periodicals were full of short stories by women (Bennett xiv). In addition, many women writers (George Egerton, Olive Schreiner, Kate Chopin, Vernon Lee, Ada Leverson to name only a few) saw the genre as releasing them from the conventional constraints of the novel. "The fragmentary and inconclusive nature of the short story made it the ideal vehicle for some of the most successful fictional explo-rations of modern women and feminism" (Miller, Jane Eldridge 24). Seen in opposition to the baggy, epic Victorian novel, the economy of the short story appealed to women writers concerned with the glimpse rather than the survey. Many New Women writers favored a "marginalized" genre to express their marginalized status as women.[1] The potential inconclusiveness of the genre added to its subversive possibilities. The use of allegory, dream, and fantasy in the stories of Egerton and Schreiner, for example, constitute an early modernism: their experimentation needs to be linked to Woolf's own short story writing in the first decade of the twentieth century.[2]

There are, of course, many reasons Woolf's fictional debut took the short story form. Having published reviews and essays up until this point, she may well have had ease of publication in mind: an ease disproved when "Memoirs of a Novelist" was rejected by *Cornhill Magazine* in 1909. She would certainly have been familiar with the short stories by women in the periodical press during the late nineteenth century and early twentieth century. She would have been familiar with the ways in which these women writers, Schreiner in particular, used the short story to experiment with form, stylistics, and subject matter. I want to argue that, along with many of the New Women writers, Woolf was attracted to the flexibility of the short story genre, but that she used the form for a specific purpose: her rethinking of women's history and the writing of women's lives.

In October 1909, when Clive Bell called Virginia Woolf's short story "Memoirs of a Novelist" "a new medium," he identified the blurring of the genres of essay, review, biography, and short story which is that text (Woolf, Monks House Papers). This story is one of several of Woolf's early short stories, written between 1906 and 1909, in which she reconceives generic boundaries. Although she writes to Bell in 1908 about *The Voyage Out* that she will "re-form the novel," her explorations with the short story did not require such self-conscious alterations (*L1* 356). The form already allowed for diversity.

In another of Woolf's letters to Clive Bell about *The Voyage Out*, she wrote that it represented "a view of one's own" (*L1* 383). This phrase could equally well apply to the departures Woolf was making in the short stories she was writing at this time: indeed, I want to argue that the generic innovations involved in writing women's lives found in her later texts are expressed, *not* in embryonic or juvenile form, in her early short stories.[3] That this phrase, "a view of one's own," predates the famous "a room of one's own" by twenty years, parallels the ways in which many of the ideas in her 1929 essay had been rehearsed years earlier in the first decade of the century.

Woolf's early short stories (I look here specifically at "Phyllis and Rosamond," "The Journal of Mistress Joan Martyn," and "Memoirs of a Novelist") are so often overlooked in favor of her later, more obviously "modernist" stories that critics often ignore what the genre first meant to her, and its links to her ideas on women's history. Although Dominic Head is right to argue that "Woolf never did finally abandon the conventional short story [. . .] her experiments in the genre depend upon the adaptation, often the subversion of existing forms and conventions," a look at these early stories would have confirmed his thesis (Head 79). Many other conventional genres underpin the stories: nineteenth-century biography, the journal, the essay, and the review. The absence of stylistic experiment— something that has sent critics to "The Mark on the Wall" and "Kew

Gardens"—does not preclude other kinds of generic experimentation. Dean Baldwin, in his study of the short fiction, accepts Jean Guiguet's division of the stories into three periods, the first of which starts at 1917 (Baldwin 4). Although he does discuss the early fiction, he notes that these stories "differ" from the "mature short fiction" (10). These stories are not juvenilia, failed projects, or test runs for later works; we need to reevaluate them as central to her ideas on life writing and women's history, and how these are both determined and reconceived through genre. Their incomplete or unpublished status does not undermine or eradicate this importance.

The tradition of auto/biographical writing in Woolf's own family, including her father's editorship of the *Dictionary of National Biography*, foregrounded for her the revisions she needed to make in order to write women's lives. Rather than being able to think back through their mothers, Woolf's ancestors on the Stephen side handed down a tradition of male life-writing. Her great grandfather, James Stephen, wrote his *Memoirs* for his children during the 1820s, just as his grandson, Leslie Stephen, Woolf's father, wrote his autobiographical *Mausoleum Book* for his children in 1895 after his wife's (Julia Stephen) death. Two of great grandfather James Stephen's sons wrote their own autobiographies: George Stephen wrote his *Anti-Slavery Recollections* in 1854, and the second son, another James Stephen (Leslie's father), wrote his *Diary* in 1846, as well as *Essays in Ecclesiastical Biography*. Leslie Stephen, in addition to his autobiographical *Mausoleum Book* wrote *Some Early Impressions* (1903) and a biography of his brother, James Fitzjames Stephen.[4] The proliferations of Jameses and Stephens parallel the proliferations of autobiographical texts: a significant family tradition of autobiographical writing with which Woolf would have been familiar. She would have also been well aware how these familial texts fit into a tradition of male nineteenth-century auto/biographers including Ruskin, Carlyle, and Mill.

Her essays and reviews of the period 1905–09 show Woolf reading a substantial number of memoirs, diaries, and letters by women, including *Letters and Memorials of Jane Welsh Carlyle, The Memoirs of Lady Ann Fanshawe, Memoirs of Sarah Bernhardt*, and *The Family Letters of Christina Rossetti*. She was, however, reevaluating the conventions of life-writing by men *and* women. Her ideas of newness resulted from an awareness of male traditions, particularly familial, of auto/biography. She also knew that despite the many memoirs written by women, she lacked a sense of a female tradition. "Until the late 1970s, critics focused on the familiar male canon: Mill, Newman, Ruskin, Trollope and Carlyle [. . .] Harriet Martineau and Margaret Oliphant were the women most often admitted into this literary version of the male clubland" (Sanders 153). Woolf would also have felt directly the pressures of convention when writing a biographical sketch of her father in 1904 for Frederic Maitland's *The Life and Letters of Leslie Stephen*. The sketch, by focusing on Stephen's literary taste, achieves the right amount of "delicacy and reserve" and thereby contrasts sharply with Woolf's later portraits of her father (*L1* 151).[5]

Woolf played a central role in the early-twentieth-century reevaluation of the biographer or autobiographer as artist rather than chronicler (*CE4* 231). Woolf coined the term "new biography" in her 1927 essay/review of Harold Nicolson's *Some People*. She writes that it is time to get beyond the "draperies and decencies" (*CE4* 230) of Victorian biography with its emphasis on eulogy, monumental moments, and public events. In line with Lytton Strachey's *Eminent Victorians* (1918), Woolf calls for more freedom, a loosening of the form. The new biography will have room for satire, for fiction, for the psychological, and for a more democratic relationship between biographer and subject. The biographer, rather than "toiling even slavishly in the footsteps of his hero" will be "an equal" (*CE4* 231).

In her later essay, "The Art of Biography" (1938), Woolf appears to be much less optimistic about the marriage of fact and fiction that she had gestured toward in "The New Biography." In "The Art of Biography," in the context of Strachey's *Elizabeth and Essex*, she writes, "the combination proved unworkable; fact and fiction refused to mix" (*CE4* 224). The implication of the essay, however, is that biography needs to move away from such a distinction. She is interested in "the creative fact; the fertile fact; the fact that suggests and engenders" (*CE4* 228). Biography as it stands is at an impasse, but both essays speak of the potential of a new form of biography, one that will be much more wide-ranging in its scope and its attention, thereby erasing distinctions between publicly known facts and fictional account. To this end, biography needs to uncover the lives of the obscure: "is not anyone who has lived a life and left a record of that life, worthy of biography" (*CE4* 226). Biography will "enlarge its scope by hanging up looking glasses at odd corners," thus blurring the line between private and public lives, making the private public (*CE4* 226).

Throughout her life, Woolf deliberated on biography and its potential. She particularly liked a biography of Stopford Brooke because it included "the record of the things that change rather than of the things that happen" (*E2* 184). In an essay review of the biography, Woolf writes: "he [the reader] will be wise, we think, not to attempt to sum up Stopford Brooke as this, that, or the other until he has read to the end, when the desire for such definitions may have left him" (*E2* 183). Biography needs to avoid fixity, both interpretative fixity and fixity of content. Rather than "the majority of Victorian biographies" which are "like the wax figures now preserved in Westminster Abbey [. . .] effigies that have only a smooth superficial likeness to the body in the coffin" (*CE4* 222), new biographies need to show the living, contradictory self. As Laura Marcus points out, Woolf portrays Victorian biography as much more homogenous than it was, but that construction allowed her to have a view of her own (93).

Such rethinking of biography is crucial to Woolf's feminism. In 1940 Woolf wrote to the composer Ethel Smyth: "I was thinking the other night that there's never been a womans autobiography. Nothing to compare with Rousseau. [. . .] Now why shouldnt you be not only the first woman to write an opera, but equally the first to tell truths about herself? [. . .] I should like an analysis of your sex life. [. . .] More introspection. More intimacy" (L6 453). Woolf, for many reasons, was unable to write this autobiography herself. She shied away from such explicit exposure, but also her stylistic and imaginative vision took her to places other than the unequivocally stable "I" of a conventional autobiography. Her redressing of patriarchal dominance was intimately linked to generic, stylistic, and conceptual revision. She felt that, as we see in *Orlando*, a written account of a life may have a somewhat looser and more complex relationship to the life it is representing. Fiction may play a part in that representation. A request to write a "conventional" biography of Roger Fry caused her much turmoil because she was obliged to stick to facts and to present a coherent and focused portrait. She felt the work was "too minute & tied down & documented," and she proposed something "more fictitious" when she entered the biography herself in 1909 (D5 155). With *Roger Fry* we see Woolf straining against the restrictions of the genre, longing to mix accuracy with imagination. It is possible, then, to trace Woolf's revisions to the conventions of biography, but I want to suggest that years before this biography, and her essays on biography, she was using the short story genre to reconfigure life-writing. We need to go back to her early short stories to contextualize these later comments.

The narrator of Virginia Woolf's earliest short story "Phyllis and Rosamond," written in June 1906, meditates on the early-twentieth-century interest in biography, in "pictures of people" (CSF 17). The emphasis is on the veracity of these portraits, she comments, the accurate and faithful reporting of, for example, "how the door keeper at the Globe [. . .] passed Saturday March 18th in the year of our Lord 1568" (17). The narrator notes, however, the absence of such historical and biographical portraits for "those many women who cluster in the shade" (17). Novelists and historians have only just begun to shine a "partial light" on the "obscure figures" occupying the "dark and crowded place behind the scenes," the narrator remarks, thereby setting the premise for the story to follow and affording writers of fiction as much authority to fill the gap as historians (17).

The narrator presents the story of the Miss Hibbert's liberating journey from Kensington to Bloomsbury as both informative and representative: an essential addition to the many images of male experience. The story, then, is sociological: "we intend to look as steadily as we can at a little group" and historical: "which lives at this moment (the 20th June, 1906)" (17). The narrator refers to the "facts" of the case, the "excellent material" for "enquiry" found in their situation, and also to the topical phrase "daughters of the home" which encapsulates their position (18). The women's lives are typical, a "common case" and "epitomise the qualities of many" (17). Woolf has set up a factual and historical framework for the piece; it will have the same function as the portrait of the doorkeeper at the Globe. Despite this clear historical agenda, Woolf, or Virginia Stephen as she was then, also makes explicit the fictional element of the piece. The narrator picks the characters' names randomly: "Phyllis and Rosamond, we will call them" (18).

Another layer to the story is the autobiographical element available to those readers aware that Woolf herself grew up in a Victorian home in Kensington and moved to Bloomsbury after the death of her parents. The story is about that transition: Woolf is both Phyllis and Rosamond, denied a formal education, existing as ornaments in the home, *as well as* the Miss Tristrams, whose party is reminiscent of Thursday evening gatherings at 46 Gordon Square, Bloomsbury. The reason that Woolf can so confidently present the piece as a sociological and historical case study is that it is based on her own experience, but experience that she has reworked, transmuted, and spread among the various characters. The story, although most obviously fiction, sits also at the intersection of autobiography, biography, and history and begins Woolf's complex revisioning of these categories. Woolf fictionalizes fragments of her own life *and* a representative English, upper-middle-class woman's life in 1906 through a conceptualized and an actual crossover between fact and fiction. As the text shifts in tone from an empirical study to a fictional narrative, and free indirect discourse moves the reader from the position of detached observer into Phyllis's mind, Woolf enacts the blurring of history and fiction that she is to theorize in "The Journal of Mistress Joan Martyn." The first person narrator, who acts as both chronicler and artist, becomes less and less obtrusive. Comments to the reader such as: "you must be in a position to follow these young ladies home" (18) are replaced by: "the stucco fronts, the irreproachable rows of Belgravia and South Kensington seemed to Phyllis the type of her lot; of a life trained to grow in an ugly pattern" (24).

In August 1906, just after she wrote "Phyllis and Rosamond," Woolf was twenty-four and holidaying with her sister Vanessa in Blo' Norton Hall in Norfolk. Here, she wrote an unfinished piece, posthumously entitled "The Journal of Mistress Joan Martyn," in which she continues the discussion begun in her first story about the representation of women's lives, reactions to those representations, and the concomitant negotiations between fact and fiction that were to preoccupy her throughout her life. The text deals with feminist historian Rosamond Merridew, who researches land tenure systems of the thirteenth, fourteenth, and fifteenth centuries and who comes across the journal of a Miss Joan Martyn dated 1480. The piece is a double fictional autobiography in that Merridew writes about herself and then the second half of the text is a transcription of Joan Martyn's journal. Merridew introduces herself in terms of the "lives of the obscure"; although her readers may find her obscure, she has "won considerable fame" for her work: "Berlin has heard my name; Frankfurt would give a soiree in my honour; and I am not absolutely unknown in one or two secluded rooms in Oxford and in Cambridge" (33). Woolf undoes the scenario she set up in "Phyllis and Rosamond": here is a woman who is not in the shade. In order to do this, Merridew has "exchanged a husband and a family and a house" (33). Her maternal passion is transferred to her "fragments of yellow parchment" (33). Merridew's assertion of choices other than marriage and motherhood for women and her challenge to the then male world of academia is present not only in her career but in her methodology and independence. As an independent historian she is in competition with historians working within universities. The state system "robs my poor private voice of all its persuasion" (33). Her private, female voice is up against the masculine conglomerate of the state. The private documents, some of them by women, which Merridew relies on are being inspected by government officials who will, like its owner, dismiss Joan's journal.

The main challenges and obstacles Merridew both presents and faces, however, have to do with her methodology and her subject matter. First, she is interested in women's history and second in the private, individual lives of her subjects. She wants to study the "intricacies of land tenure [. . .] in relation to the life of the time" (34). Descriptions of "Dame Elinor, at work with her needle" are integral to her representation of medieval history (34). Her mixture of public records with private life, however, means mixing fact and fictional recreation, based on historical evidence. Merridew wants to present the time as "vividly as in a picture" and acknowledges that the absence of private documentation and records necessitates the use of imagination "like any other storyteller" (34, 35). Merridew in her historical research, just like Woolf with her Fry biography, wants to move beyond the strictures of facts. Bringing to life the past necessarily means embellishment and creative imagining. Woolf, through Merridew, is questioning the boundaries of genre, the limits of historical research, the interplay of fact and fiction. This, of course, is what Merridew's critics object to, claiming she has no documentation to "stiffen these words into any semblance of the truth" (35). The phallic image belies a philosophy alien to Merridew's feminist revision. She does not want the words stiffened; she wants them freefloating, suggesting, intimating rather than pointing. Woolf takes the fact/fiction combination from "Phyllis and Rosamond" and places it in the mouth of a feminist historian.

Merridew recognizes the value of Joan Martyn's journal, regardless of its owner's, John Martyn's, dismissive comments. John, an expert regarding his ancestors, has time only for the male line. He values public achievement, and is scathingly dismissive of Mistress Joan's diary. The Stud book of Willoughby and the Household Books of Jasper make more interesting reading for John Martyn than Joan's private journal. When Merridew asks to borrow the journal, Martyn replies, "I don't think you'll find anything out of the way in her [. . .] as far as I can see, not remarkable" (45). His interest in his family history does not encompass women's experience. Critics have noted the discrepancies in the dates in the text. The manuscript, dated 1480, is said by John Martyn to have been written by Joan Martyn, born in 1495, when she was twenty-five. Susan Dick notes that if Woolf had revised the text she would "undoubtedly have noticed the inconsistencies" (*CSF* 296). Bernd Engler uses this and other "mistakes" to argue that Woolf is satirizing Merridew for her shoddy and unprofessional methods and means us to suspect that the journal is a forgery. Engler's unconvincing and rather tortuous argument seems to miss Woolf's point entirely, particularly when he argues that Merridew's search for privately owned documents "clearly shows that Rosamond has no genuinely academic interests at all" (12): journals like Joan's are not publicly available. Engler also accuses Merridew of overlooking the Stud Book and Jasper Martyn's household book, choosing instead Joan's journal with its "complete lack of usable data" (14). It is Engler's historical methodology, with its strict division of accuracy and falsity, its notions of academic rigor, and its dismissal of private texts that Woolf is arguing against.

A more convincing reason for the discrepancies is that put forward by Jan VanStavern. The mistakes come from John Martyn and point to his ignorance about his female ancestors, when he has blithely stated that "any fool knows his own ancestors" (39). Ancestors, for John and for Joan's father, mean the male line. Woolf throws "into question men's ability to record or remember women's position in history" (VanStavern 255). Joan Martyn's is one of the "lives of the obscure" that Woolf was so intent on recovering, be it in fact or fiction. Merridew bypasses the books of records written by men, for the autobiographical recording of a woman's life.

The second half of the text is a transcription of Joan's journal, reinforcing the importance not just of noticing, but of publishing women's accounts of their lives. The structure of text within text (Rosamond Merridew's voice takes on the voice of Joan Martyn) suggests performed identity. Joan herself takes on the voices of other women. She is soon to be married off and so retreats into narrative: into the stories of women such as

Helen of Troy. She finds inspiration in stories of "Knights and Ladies [. . .] of whispers, and sighs, and lovers' laments" (*CSF* 56). Instead of following her imagination, Joan is forced to learn the management of the home and farm, the accounts and records, in readiness for her husband's absence. These will take precedence over her private journal, just as the household accounts did for John Martyn. Joan finds it difficult to secure a place in her life for either her own narrative or the narrative of other women. In portraying this difficulty, Woolf's text itself "inscribes both the history of narrative and the role of narrative in history" (Cuddy-Keane, "Virgina Woolf and the Varieties" 67).

Joan needs privacy for her writing: "confusion came over me when he asked me what I wrote, and stammering that it was a 'Diary' I covered the pages with my hands" (60). Joan's father values her writing, but wishes that his male ancestors had written their lives, and pulls her away from her journal to visit her grandfather's tomb. Her writing is secondary to the immortalization of her male ancestors, as both her father and John Martyn make clear.

Woolf's unfinished story is even more revealing, however, when viewed alongside her journal entries from August 1906. Finding herself in a new location, Woolf set out to represent the life of the land: its geography, its history, the social configurations of its inhabitants. The boundary between animate and inanimate blurs: Woolf meditates on her characterization of Norfolk in biographical terms. The land is "strange, grey green, undulating, dreaming, philosophising & remembering" (*PA* 312). The adjectives move the reader into Woolf's anthropomorphization of the countryside, hence the relevance of her comments to her simultaneous meditations on women's biography and autobiography in "The Journal of Mistress Joan Martyn." Indeed, Woolf makes explicit that the process of written description works the same "for a place as for a person" (312). She goes further, however, figuring the land as "some noble untamed woman conscious that she has no beauty to vaunt, that nobody very much wants her" (313). The largely uninhabited areas of Norfolk in which Woolf spent her holiday parallel the lives of the obscure, the undocumented lives of women. The concern with the lives of women continues when she examines the gravestones at Kenninghall church. She copies down the inscription on a Mrs. Susan Batt's tomb and meditates on the epitaph as an encapsulation of a life: a "solid lump of truth" (314). Again Woolf turns to the lives of obscure women and the process and means by which one might record those lives.

Woolf writes to Violet at this time: "I tramp the country for miles with a map, leap ditches, scale walls and desecrate churches, making out beautiful brilliant stories every step of the way" (*L1* 234). Woolf is trespasser here, reveling in her freedom to walk the countryside, to *cross* those boundary markers. This freedom, this deviation from conventional roads and pathways both parallels and makes possible her stories. Imaginative freedom necessitates physical freedom. All her work at this time is to do with land—controlled and bounded land—women's bodies, and writing.

Similarly, Joan Martyn's fifteenth-century journal depicts a world under siege. Just as Joan reads Helen and the Siege of Troy to her mother and their servants—a story of both military siege and a besieged female body—so her own environment is troubled by civil war and her own body is to be sold in marriage.[6] It is no coincidence then that Woolf portrays Merridew as a historian of land tenure systems: documenting land controlled by feudal laws—very different from Woolf's experience of walking freely across the countryside. For Joan, although her family own the surrounding land, the world outside her gates is dangerous and she is forbidden to walk freely. She has recourse only to her imagination to recreate the journey to London that her father makes, but that she cannot make herself.

As the journal progresses we see Joan accepting her forthcoming marriage and taking on her mother's role as overseer of the house in her husband's absence. In the first paragraph of the journal, Joan sees the gates around their house as restraining rather than protecting. She is "bold and impatient," feeling the need for the "free and beautiful place" outside the gates as a hunger: "We are starving!" she tells her mother (45). Rather than a place of exploration and opportunity she must learn the responsibility of land. She knows "already what lands and monies" she owns and consequently that "the burden of [. . .] great lands" will be on her (51). This means adopting the attitudes of her mother. We see her taking on the required views on the "peasants" as subhuman "pests" to "rule; and tread under foot" in order to prevent uprisings (53). It is only when she makes a midsummer pilgrimage alone that she sees the land as "soft and luxurious," to be crossed freely (58). As for Woolf, her walk across country means imaginative freedom, "nothing [. . .] keep[ing] her to the road" (57). At this point she is glad of the communion with other classes, thinking "it was terrible that flash and [fens?] should divide us" (59). Physical freedom equals freedom from intolerance.

Her mother's "theory of ownership" envisages peace and prosperity and the gates of the great houses open to all, but this will come about through cultivation, taming, and controlling (59). Throughout the journal the manor is seen as an island; the wild, turbulent waters are the land outside the gates.[7] Joan knows there is something amiss with her mother's view of "equality," which depends on her role as the "Ruler of a small island" (59): an equality and peace gained through control and constraint.

In the journal, then, we see a woman imprisoned, both literally and metaphorically, struggling between acceptance and resistance. Woolf's freedom during her stay in Norfolk—freedom to roam and to write—contrasts with Joan's looming responsibilities and with Merridew's struggle to find space for her own historical methodology. That methodology is all about imaginative freedom: not being confined to the road, not being bounded by tradition. It means listening to journals like Joan's just as Joan listens to Old Anne, her nurse, who knows "the history of each chair and table or piece of tapestry" (46).

In this early text, Woolf, through Merridew, questions the possibility of including fiction, and the private journal, within the public, factual realm of history. Woolf demonstrates that "the imagination can have historical authority" (Lee, *Virgina Woolf* 15). Making the text half Merridew's autobiographical account of her work and the finding of the journal, and half a transcription of that journal, doubles the emphasis on the importance of women's experience. Both Rosamond and Joan's accounts are historical documents within the fictional framework of the text, and both emphasize the importance of private narrative, within women's history in particular. Woolf chose the short story as the genre most conducive to experimentation. When she places the journal within the short story, the short story itself then comprises two autobiographical texts. Merridew's section is also a preface and an essay on historical methodology. We see Woolf playing with the genre of "The Journal of Mistress Joan Martyn" in her letter to Violet Dickinson when she writes that the story is being transferred to paper at that moment: which "might mean that this letter was it" (*L1* 234).

In "Phyllis and Rosamond" and "The Journal of Mistress Joan Martyn," Woolf writes women's biographies while simultaneously questioning the conventions or traditions by which they operate. She questions the genres of biography and autobiography themselves by focusing on how they might be inappropriate for the writing of women's lives based on what they traditionally cannot include. In "Memoirs of a Novelist," another early short story written in 1909, Woolf is more direct in her attack (*CSF* 297). Here, in this essay/review of a biography of Miss Willatt, a novelist, written by her friend Miss Linsett (both fictional women), Woolf simultaneously inscribes and undercuts discourses of Victorian biography.

The story is about a writer of romances, Miss Willatt, who dies in 1884 and her friend, Miss Linsett, who publishes a two-volume biography of Willatt's *Life and Letters*. In this story, which itself blurs the boundaries between autobiography, biography, short story, essay, and review, Woolf, in critiquing Linsett's biography of Willatt, also offers a biography of both these women, novelist and biographer. Again, as in these two other short stories, Woolf makes very clear that she is dealing with lives of the obscure: Linsett's biography of Willatt lies hidden on the dusty shelves of a bookshop, and Willatt's own novels lie "upon the topmost shelves of little seaside libraries, so that one has to take a ladder to reach them, and a cloth to wipe off the dust"

(*CSF* 70). This story prefigures Woolf's two essays entitled "The Lives of the Obscure" about the "Taylors and Edgeworths" and "Laetitia Pilkington." In these pieces, which also abound with images of dusty books that are "faded, out-of-date, obsolete," Woolf uses fictional devices of imagined conversations and interior thought to "rescue some stranded ghost" (*CR1* 147). In "Memoirs of a Novelist," by reassessing the biography of this obscure female novelist, the narrator affirms the importance of such biographies in the first place. Again genre is crucial to the short story. The text is essentially a review of Linsett's memoir, but in critiquing the memoir the reviewer actually writes an alternative one, not only of Miss Willatt but of Linsett as well. As we gradually get a biography of the biographer, Woolf makes us increasingly conscious of the "reviewer's" own agenda—the Miss Willatt she wants to emerge—highlighting the subjectivity of history and life-writing.

Again, as in "The Journal of Mistress Joan Martyn," there is a male relation, Willatt's brother William, who agrees to Linsett's suggestion that she write his sister's life as long as she doesn't " 'break down the barriers' " (70). Despite this order that she not "expose" or "undermine" his sister, William's contribution to the biography actually goes a long way to tear down these barriers. He tells a story of her mistaking the pigsty for the washhouse because she had her nose in a book, realizing her mistake only when an old black sow ate the book out of her hands. In "The New Biography," written years later, Woolf describes how anecdote, presented "in one passage of brilliant description," makes redundant whole chapters of Victorian biography (*CE4* 232).

In contrast, Linsett is the one who feels the most allegiance to Victorian codes of behavior and biographical writing. In particular, the narrator questions Linsett's portrayal of Willatt's early years. Willatt becomes an absence in the biography, since Linsett talks around her subject. The subject has, according to Linsett, done nothing of importance in her early years, so Linsett provides information on the achievements of male relatives instead. We read, for example, of Willatt's two uncles, their careers and their inventions. Linsett's biography tells the reader nothing of Willatt's mother, who died when Willatt was sixteen—the biography is concerned with the male line and Willatt's mother is another absence, another silence in the text, a gap that is filled in, to some extent, by the reviewer.

In "Memoirs of a Novelist," the Victorian biography is a carapace that prevents access to the subject.[8] The narrator becomes increasingly frustrated with Linsett's biography and so turns to Willatt's own letters—thereby letting Willatt speak for herself—and to imagination. Repeatedly the narrator uses phrases like "we can imagine," "we may theorize," and because all Linsett says of Willatt's first ball is that it occurred, the narrator offers a lengthy imaginative recreation of the ball for us. Woolf is interested in a biography that provides subjective experience rather than factual evidence.

Linsett in a sense conceals more about Willatt than she reveals due to the conventions of both Victorian biography and Victorian morality. Victorian biography is "dominated by the idea of goodness," as Woolf writes in 1927, again looking back to these short stories (*CE4* 231). In "Memoirs of a Novelist" Woolf's narrator quotes from Linsett's biography: "No one who has read the book (*Life's Crucifix*) can doubt that the heart which conceived the sorrows of Ethel Eden in her unhappy attachment had felt some of the pangs so feelingly described *itself*; so much we may say, more we may not." And then comments: "The most interesting event in Miss Willatt's life, owing to the nervous prudery and the dreary literary conventions of her friend, is thus a blank" (*CSF* 73). Eventually, "it is clear that one must abandon Miss Linsett altogether or take the greatest liberties with her text" (74). Victorian biography appears to erase rather than express life. As Woolf makes clear—the biography tells more about Linsett than Willatt—the narrator must read between the lines to find "the signs that Miss Willatt was not what she seemed" (74). On the blank pages at the back of Willatt's diary, the private space of a private genre, Woolf's narrator finds Willatt questioning her religion and her philanthropic work: "To imagine her then, as the sleek sober woman that her friend paints her, doing good wearily but with steadfast faith, is quite untrue; on the contrary she was a restless and discontented woman" (75). In Linsett's hands, Willatt becomes "a wax work [. . .] preserved under glass" (74). The idea that Linsett actually denies life to her biographical subject is furthered by her obsession with Willatt's death. True to Victorian convention, Linsett is fascinated with death, and the deathbed scene is prominent in the biography.[9] The "narrative slackens to a funeral pace" (78) and is full of "random flourishes" and "inappropriate detail" (79).

In this story Woolf explores the ways in which writing can obscure life (women's lives in particular) ways that fiction and imagination can bring such women back to life, and the need to find alternative ways of life-writing to Victorian biographies of great men, which focus on public events. This public forum is inappropriate for Miss Willatt, as it is in her private life where she has experience and records it. Having said this, the narrator is aware of the value of Linsett's biography over no biography at all. Only through this less than perfect document can the narrator offer an alternative history. As Woolf writes in one of her essays on biography: "There are some stories which have to be retold by each generation" (*DM* 78). As methods, traditions, and conventions change, histories need to be rewritten: "the new biography can be made by dismantling the old" (Briggs, "Virgina Woolf" 254). Woolf is conscious also of the narrativity of history: the narrator in "Memoirs of a Novelist" offers equally as subjective and partial an account of Willatt as does Linsett. The narrator's version of events is just as governed by conventions—here of modernity and modern biography—as Linsett's account.

Through familiarity with traditions of nineteenth-century biography, Woolf was able, at an early stage in her career, to rethink the ways in which women's lives might be represented—through interdisciplinarity, hybridity of genre, and interplay between the private and the public and between fact and fiction. At the end of "The New Biography" Woolf writes that a "little fiction mixed with fact can be made to transmit personality very effectively" (*CE4* 233). She points toward a possible "mixture of biography and auto-biography, of fact and fiction" (235) when, of course, she herself has been enacting in her writing just such a complex negotiation throughout her life.

NOTES

1. See Hanson, *Rereading* 3.
2. Much work on the modernist short story (Flora, Head, and Reid) overlooks its association with New Women writers. For exploration of such links see Ledger (177–98) and Ardis (2–9).
3. In, for example, *Orlando, The Waves, The Pargiters, A Room of One's Own* and *Three Guineas*.
4. See Dahl.
5. See *Moments of Being* 109.
6. Engler is right to point out that in 1480, the date of the journal, England was enjoying relative peace during the second half of Edward IV's reign (1471–83).
7. In a letter from this period Woolf describes exploring the countryside as a "dive beneath the sea" (*LI* 235).
8. Woolf's biographical portrait of her friend Violet Dickinson, written in 1907 in violet ink and bound in violet leather (Hawkes 272), works in partnership with "Memoirs of a Novelist" in its deconstruction of Victorian biographical conventions employed by Linsett. Dickinson's own nonconformity—her "decided opinions"—parallel the nonconformity of the text (277). Woolf's mock biography, full of the fantastical, anticipates *Orlando* and the narrator's insistence that the project is "no novel but a sober chronicle" (279); that she herself is "the most capricious of chroniclers" only adds to the irony and the playfulness of the text (284).

    Generically playful, the text is divided into three chapters, each resembling a short story, but none more so than the third chapter, "A Story to Make You Sleep," a Japanese story told by mother to child. Like the *Mausoleum Book*, in which Leslie Stephen addresses his children, and "Reminiscences," also written in 1907 and addressed to Julian Bell, Woolf embeds both the short story genre and the oral tradition of storytelling into the text. Again, the generic makeup is indeterminate.
9. See Laura Marcus 94.

Chapter 8

Virginia Woolf's Shorter Fictional Explorations of the External World: "closely united . . . immensely divided"

Michelle Levy

While received notions of Virginia Woolf as a writer primarily if not exclusively concerned with mapping the contours of the internal world have been steadily eroded in recent years, the reception of Woolf as a writer of interiority has been so entrenched that James Mepham, in his 1992 survey of Woolf criticism, writes, "until recently [. . .] the consensus view was that Woolf was not interested in the external world" (25). While Alex Zwerdling's *Virginia Woolf and the Real World* (1986) initiated a major reconsideration of Woolf's fiction, offering her "account of [the] complex relationship between the interior life and the life of society," much remained to be said about her exploration of the nonhuman world (3). And though Douglas Mao, in a book that derives its title from one of Woolf's short stories, *Solid Objects: Modernism and the Test of Production*, focuses our attention on centrality of the object to Woolf and other modernists, this is by no means exhaustive of Woolf's fictional encounters with the external world, which range far beyond the inanimate object to include all of nature.[1] This essay aims to redirect our attention to how Woolf used short fictional forms to achieve her most sustained exploration of the human relation to the external world, as she found the genre at once sufficiently capacious and circumscribed to accommodate the nonhuman presence in narrative.

For Woolf, the human and nonhuman worlds were, as she imagined
Elizabeth Barrett Browning and her dog Flush, at once "closely united" and
"immensely divided": the great difficulty was to find the appropriate form
in which she could explore the relation between them. Woolf was acutely
aware of the "assumption that fiction is more intimately and humbly
attached to the service of human beings than the other arts," and sought
actively to refute this assumption through her experiments in short fiction
(*CE2* 54).[2] In *A Room of One's Own* (1929), Woolf expresses her dissatis-
faction with the present state of fiction, encouraging women to invigorate
literature by "see[ing] human beings not always in relation to each other
but in relation to reality; and the sky too, and the trees or whatever it may
be in themselves" (107). Yet, by and large, we continue to read Woolf's
fiction by seeing human beings "always in relation to each other," ignoring
her repeated attempts to write fiction that saw human beings "in relation
to reality." This lack of critical attention in part reflects our failure to examine
her short fiction. From her first published story, "The Mark on the Wall"
(1917), to "Gipsy, the Mongrel" (1940), an unpublished story written in
the year before her death, Woolf's short fiction attests to her abiding interest
in the worth and integrity of the external world.[3]

"The Mark on the Wall" offers a masterful exploration of the relation of
the human mind to the external world, as the narrator's observation of a
mark on the wall and uncertainty about its origin and nature prompts a
rich series of reflections and speculations on topics ranging from life and
death to trees and furniture, from Shakespeare to Whitaker's Table of
Precedency. Throughout, the narrator's attempt to move beyond her subjective impressions is fraught with hesitation and uncertainty:

> I might get up, but if I got up and looked at it, ten to one I shouldn't be able
> to say for certain; because once a thing's done, no one ever knows how it
> happened. Oh! dear me, the mystery of life; the inaccuracy of thought! The
> ignorance of humanity! (*CSF* 83–84)

> No, no, nothing is proved, nothing is known. And if I were to get up at this
> very moment and ascertain that the mark on the wall is really—what shall I
> say?—the head of a gigantic old nail [. . .] what should I gain? Knowledge?
> Matter for further speculation? [. . .] And what is knowledge? (87)

Despite her skepticism, Woolf resists, as S. P. Rosenbaum has persuasively
argued, philosophical idealism. The intrusion of the real world at the story's
close—when a man, closely resembling Leonard Woolf, interrupts the narrator's musings to complain bitterly about the war and the snail on the
wall—asserts the independent existence of the external world. What interests Woolf in this story, and what will preoccupy her throughout her career,
is the frustrating but fruitful interaction between the imaginative powers of

the human mind and facticity of the external world, "the interrelations of thought *and* external reality, of consciousness *and* the objects of consciousness" (Rosenbaum 324–25). Knowledge of the external world is important because it offers the impetus for thought and imagination *and* because it imposes crucial constraints on the life of the mind.

Though the narrator's return to the mark on the wall circumscribes her mental wanderings, this restraint is embraced rather than lamented. The narrator continues:

> Indeed, now that I have fixed my eyes upon it, I feel that I have grasped a plank in the sea; I feel a satisfying sense of reality [. . .]. Here is something definite, something real. Thus, waking from a midnight dream of horror, one hastily turns on the light and lies quiescent, worshipping solidity, worshipping reality, worshipping the impersonal world which is proof of some existence other than ours. That is what one wants to be sure of. . . . (*CSF* 88)

Like the young Wordsworth, who recalled as a schoolboy having "grasped at a wall or tree to recall myself from this abyss of idealism to the reality," it is the "real solid world / Of images," to use Wordsworth's words again, that offers Woolf particular comfort (Wordsworth, *Fenwick Notes* 161; *The Prelude* VIII 604–05). The proof of a world that endures beyond human existence is especially consoling in the face of the catastrophic suffering of World War I, alluded to in "The Mark on the Wall," and the horrific violence that was soon to be unleashed in World War II. In her notebook to *Between the Acts*, titled "London in War," Woolf finds solace in the thought that even if town life were to end, indeed if all human life were to cease, "Nature prevails. I suppose badgers & foxes wd. come back if this went on, & owls & nightingales" (quoted in Lee, *Virginia Woolf* 718).[4] In *Between the Acts*, Mrs. Swithin speaks for Woolf in her observation that "what makes a view so sad [. . .]. And so beautiful" is that "it'll be there [. . .] when we're not" (49).

The nonhuman world promises to survive in part because it is not susceptible to the human propensity for classification and hierarchy. The narrator in "The Mark on the Wall" recalls how, even as a child, she thought the "the thing itself, the standard thing" was "leading articles, cabinet ministers—a whole class of things indeed [. . .] from which one could not depart save at the risk of nameless damnation" (*CSF* 86). And now, as an adult, "those real standard things" have been replaced by other, though equally corrupt, conceptions of "the thing itself," by "the masculine point of view which governs our lives, which sets the standard, which establishes Whitaker's Table of Precedency" (86). Bernard Blackstone, one of Woolf's earliest and most perceptive critics, believed that she "was more interested by the life of things, such as snails and trees, than with the life of societies, such as churches and banks and schools" (248). Woolf values the lives of snails and trees because they are unencumbered by the rules (in the narrator's childhood "there was a rule for everything" [*CSF* 86]) and the hierarchies (in Whitaker's Table of Precedency "everybody follows somebody [. . .] and the great thing is to know who follows whom" [88]) that permeate the human world. And it is these very structures that, as Woolf argued in *Three Guineas* (1937), led to the very global conflict that intervenes to put an end to the reveries of the narrator in "The Mark on the Wall," and, finally, to Woolf herself. Unlike the human world, which for Woolf seemed determined to destroy itself, the nonhuman world was worthy of worship because of its potential to survive post-history, just as it flourished for millions of years of prehistory.

"Sympathy" (probably written in the spring of 1919) and "An Unwritten Novel" (written in January 1920 and published in July 1920) follow the same trajectory as "The Mark on the Wall." The narrator of "Sympathy" conjectures about a newspaper obituary, whereas the narrator of "An Unwritten Novel" surmises about a fellow train passenger. Both narrators' musings are proven to be incorrect. In "Sympathy," the narrator believes the "Humphry Hammond" referred to in an obituary is her friend's husband, prompting a meditation on "how death has changed everything" (*CSF* 109). As the narrator of "Sympathy" thinks about the dead man's armchair, the endurance of the world of objects offers consolation:

> There is the yellow arm chair in which he sat, shabby but still solid enough, sur-
> viving us all; and the mantelpiece strewn with glass and silver, but he is
> ephemeral as the dusty light which stripes the wall and carpet. So will the sun
> shine on glass and silver the day I die. The sun stripes a million years into the
> future; a broad yellow path; passing an infinite distance beyond this house and
> town; passing so far that nothing but sea remains, stretching flat with its infin-
> ity of creases beneath the sunlight. Humphry Hammond—who was Humphry
> Hammond?—a curious sound, now crinkled now smooth as a sea shell. (111)

An armchair outlasts Humphry Hammond, glass and silver will survive the narrator, and the sun and sea will persist for millions of years into the future. When the narrator receives a letter from her friend and discovers that the deceased is her friend's father-in-law, not her friend's husband, she feels as though she has been deceived. Nevertheless, her reflections on death are not vitiated; they simply need to be redirected to their proper object. The external world (as manifested in the obituary and letter) performs a necessary role in both provoking and circumscribing the imagination.

In "An Unwritten Novel," the narrator scrutinizes a woman whom she encounters on the train, attributing to her the name of "Minnie Marsh" and a life of bitter spinsterhood and poverty. When the woman disembarks and is greeted by her son, the narrator is confounded, exclaiming, "Well, my world's done for! What do I stand on? What do I know? That's not Minnie. [. . .] Who am I? Life's bare as bone" (*CSF* 121). Here the narrator's mental reveries are comically deflated, as are similar speculations by the narrators in "The Mark on the Wall" and "Sympathy." Woolf insists upon the existence of a knowable external world that exists independently of the mind: the mark on the wall is a snail; Humphry Hammond the elder is the deceased; and the woman on the train is a wife and mother. But "An Unwritten Novel" makes a critical claim about the interdependence of imagination and its objects: without imagination, life appears "bare as bone," whereas without the external world, life lacks solidity and a "satisfying sense of reality."

In "Solid Objects" (began at the end of 1918 and published in 1920), Woolf pursues her exploration of how the mind interacts with the world of objects, and in particular how the artist reconfigures the relation between subject and object. The story begins as follows:

> The only thing that moved upon the vast semicircle of the beach was one small black spot. As it came nearer to the ribs and spine of the stranded pilchard boat, it became apparent from a certain tenuity in its blackness that this spot possessed four legs; and moment by moment it become more unmistakable that it was composed of the persons of two young men. (*CSF* 102)

Like "the small round mark, black upon a white wall" that initiates the narrator's musings in "A Mark on the Wall," the "one small black spot" that the narrator of "Solid Objects" observes becomes "the persons of two young men" (102). Robert Watson correctly remarks on the way that the story "diagrams not only fictional technique, but the author's odd relations with the things of the world, the interpretive relations that produce stories" (120). The beginning of the story introduces what becomes John's lifelong ambition, and a central trope of many of Woolf's shorter narratives, the investment of objects with subjectivity. In "Solid Objects," the narrator transforms objects into subjects, as the black spot sprouts "four legs" and the abandoned boat grows "ribs and spine." John, likewise, transforms a stone he finds on the beach into a subject, thereby permanently altering the course of his future life, imagining "that the heart of the stone leaps with joy when it sees itself chosen from a million like it, to enjoy this bliss instead of a life of cold and wet upon the high road" (*CSF* 104). He completes this transformation by endowing the stone with language: "It might so easily have been any other of the millions of stones," he imagines the stone saying, "but it was I, I, I!" (104).

But John takes his identification with solid objects to extremes, neglecting his burgeoning political career and ultimately isolating himself from the human community as he searches for increasingly unusual bits of glass and broken pieces of china in dumps and condemned buildings. The implements of John's new career, a stick with a hook on the end and a carpetbag, are, as Robert Watson notes, those of the artist.[5] Indeed, John is modeled on Woolf's acquaintance the painter Mark Gertler, who, like John, was obsessed with solid objects.[6] The story not only features Gertler as a character, but also responds to a complaint he made about fiction. In "A Sketch of the Past" (1939), Woolf recollects that Gertler denounced the inferiority of literature as compared to painting because the former "always deals with Mr. and Mrs. Brown," that is with the human subject, "the personal, the trivial," a criticism which for Woolf had "its sting and its chill" (*MOB* 95). In her characterization of Gertler as John, Woolf dramatizes the consequences of complete immersion in the world of objects: she had herself counseled Gertler in 1918 to "put sheets of glass between him and his matter," and she dramatizes the dangers of failing to heed this advice in "Solid Objects."[7] Thus while the artist must imagine objects as subjects, he must finally appreciate that objects are *not* subjects. Likewise, it is hazardous to commit oneself utterly to a world exclusively comprised of either subjects or objects. Thus John's political career, an endeavor consumed only with subjects, would have been just as perilous as John's chosen pursuit of objects to the exclusion of all human interaction.

In her fiction, Woolf sought to demonstrate the need to maintain a balance between subjects and objects. But since, as Gertler had correctly if cuttingly pointed out, fiction was generally too concerned with the human subject, what Woolf needed was to pay greater attention to objects in her narratives. To do so, Woolf employs narratological shifts similar to John's, with the narrator of "The Mark on the Wall," for example, imagining life from the point of view of a tree:

> Wood is a pleasant thing to think about. It comes from a tree; and trees grow, and we don't know how they grow. For years and years they grow, without paying any attention to us, in meadows, in forests, and by the side of rivers [. . .]. I like to think of the tree itself: first the close dry sensation of being wood; then the grinding of the storm; then the slow, delicious ooze of sap. I like to think of it, too, on winter's nights standing in the empty field with all leaves close-furled, nothing tender exposed to the iron bullets of the moon, a naked mast upon an earth that goes tumbling, tumbling all night long. The song of birds must sound very loud and strange in June; and how cold the feet of insects must feel upon it, as they make laborious progresses up the creases of the bark [. . .]. (*CSF* 88–89)

The narrator imagines the tree as tactile and auditory, that is, as being sensate. Woolf, in drawing our attention to death and decomposition as natural processes that reduce all forms of life, human, plant, and animal, to organic matter, further elides differences between human beings and trees:

> But after life. The slow pulling down of thick green stalks so that the cup of the flower, as it turns over, deluges one with purple and red light. Why, after all, should one not be born there as one is born here, helpless, speechless, unable to focus one's eyesight, groping at the roots of the grass, at the toes of the Giants? As for saying which are trees, and which are men and women, or whether there are such things, that one won't be in a condition to do for fifty years or so. (84)

This inability to distinguish between different forms of matter—between trees and human beings, men and women, the living and the dead—discloses important continuities between subject and object.

But, unlike John in "Solid Objects," Woolf appreciates that stones and trees are, ultimately, different than human beings, though to her mind the natural world in many respects has the advantage. "The very stone one kicks with one's boot," Mr. Ramsay muses in *To the Lighthouse*, "will outlast Shakespeare" (50). Similarly, the narrator in "The Mark on the Wall" observes that trees grow for "years and years" and do so "without paying any attention to us" (*CSF* 88). The endurance of the natural world, and its independence from and indifference to human affairs, both attracts and alienates us. Unlike human beings, trees have a recognizable afterlife: "Even so, life isn't done with; there are a million patient, watchful lives still for a tree, all over the world, in bedrooms, in ships, on the pavement, lining rooms, where men and women sit after tea, smoking cigarettes" (89). But even though the tree survives, and Woolf continues to imagine the tree as being watchful, it has nevertheless been restored to its status as an object, to wood. Thus though Woolf can imagine the perceptions of a tree, this shift cannot be indefinitely sustained, both because it is difficult to maintain the fiction of being a tree or a stone and because such shifts tend to obscure inevitable differences between human beings and objects. Shorter fictional forms enable Woolf to express what were necessarily temporary shifts in point of view and to present a philosophical narrative voice that could contemplate the vexed but fascinating relations between subject and object.

In "Kew Gardens" (1919) and "In the Orchard" (1923), Woolf continues her project of decentering the human presence in fiction by devoting equal attention to human beings and to their surroundings, a garden, a house and an orchard, as well as to the nonhuman forms of life that inhabit these places: snails, flowers, trees, and birds. In her essay "Women and Fiction" (1929), Woolf had argued that women writers were "perpetually wishing to alter the established values—to make serious what appears insignificant," and the same may be said of the attention she bestows on diminutive forms of life (*CE2* 146). Obeying her own admonition in "Modern Fiction" that we ought "not [to] take for granted that life exists more fully in what is commonly thought big than in what is commonly thought small" (*CE2* 107), Woolf effects in her short stories what Bernard Blackstone describes as a "reversal of values":

> More than any other novelist I know Virginia Woolf has the gift of making us see the thing in itself, and the interpenetration of the thing with human life. The older novelists, she seems to say, busy with plots, busy with propaganda, have missed something. But let man and nature exist on equal terms, and then let us see what happens [. . .]. What happens is a reversal of values. (152)

Sandra Kemp has likewise observed that a "new status [. . .] given to the objects of the outside world is another feature of Virginia Woolf's experimentation; of dismantling the old narrative hierarchies of character and plot" (xxiii). In these stories, human characters are no longer the exclusive focus; by allowing nonhuman forms of life and objects to share the same stage with human characters, Woolf expresses a vision of life in which the human presence no longer dominates but is simply part of a larger whole.

Just as in "Solid Objects" and "The Mark on the Wall" Woolf decenters the human subject in her fiction by shifting narratological perspectives, in "Kew Gardens" and "In the Orchard" she achieves the same result by varying visual perspectives. Woolf's awareness, as Lily Briscoe in *To the Lighthouse* remarks when observing the sailboat recede into the bay, that "so much depends [. . .] on distance" is exploited in her short fiction. We saw how Woolf uses this technique in "Solid Objects," where as the narrator draws closer to the black dot, it is transformed into two men. As Bernard Blackstone has noted, this was a favorite device of Woolf's:

> The shifting of values and change of proportion is a device that Virginia Woolf praises in the writers she likes—Sterne, Defoe, the Russians—and employs constantly in her own work. She will take her characters up a mountain, and show them the vastness of the earth, or set them on the sea, and show them the insignificance of the land, or set them under the sea, and show them another world altogether; in their moments of greatest anguish or ecstasy, she will direct her readers' attention away from them and show how, surrounding all human passion, the quiet seasons continue and the wind blows a little dust about the floor. (220–21)

In "Kew Gardens," one of Woolf's earliest and most popular stories, Woolf attempts to shift values by shifting perspectives, blurring the line between subject and object, as human beings are transformed into natural objects, taking on the properties of flowers and butterflies, and objects are personified, with flowers given "heart-shaped or tongue-shaped leaves," "throats," and "flesh" (*CSF* 90).[8] Woolf further adds shifts in spatial perspective, thereby demonstrating her point that our judgment of the relative worth of things depends on our view of them. In "Kew Gardens," we are given a snail's eye view of the world, as the snail commences his journey at the base of flower bed and proceeds across a treacherous path, strewn with puddles ("brown cliffs with deep green lakes in the hollows"), grass ("flat blade-like trees"), and pebbles ("boulders of grey stone") (91–92). What appears small to us is, of course, enormous to a snail. But the same may be said of human beings when viewed from a sufficient distance. Hence as the visitors leave the gardens for tea, from the vantage point of the gardens they disappear, "dissolving like drops of water" over the horizon (95). And Kew Gardens itself, when viewed from a distance, is simply one of "a vast nest of Chinese boxes" surrounded by a larger metropolis (95).

"In the Orchard" traces another narrative trajectory, as the narrative perspective ascends into the sky and descends into the center of the earth. The aerial view, because of its tendency to diminish the centrality of the human subject, was a favorite of Woolf's.[9] As Miranda sleeps in the orchard, the narrator (who may be Miranda dreaming) observes her(self) first from the ground, then from "four feet in the air over her head [where] the apples hung," from "the very topmost leaves of the apple-tree.[. . .] thirty feet above the earth," from "two hundred feet" and then finally from "miles above" (*CSF* 149–50). At this distance, Miranda shrinks to occupy "a space as big as the eye of a needle" (150). The sounds that are perceptible alter at each altitude: at four feet she hears children saying multiplication tables and a drunk man crying; at thirty feet she hears a church organ; at two hundred feet she hears the parish bells; and above that she hears only the wind itself, similarly reflecting the attenuation of the human presence at higher altitudes (150). Distance from the earth adds sights and sounds to one's experience, bringing about a fuller appreciation of life on the earth. Once again, Woolf is following her own advice, this time from "The Narrow Bridge of Art" (1927), where she enjoins writers to "[stand] back from life, because in that way a larger view is to be obtained of some important features of it" (*CE2* 228). From hearing the intermingling of all of these sounds, Miranda experiences "an extraordinary ecstasy," believing that "she heard life itself" (*CSF* 150). Miranda then lets "her body sink all its weight on to the enormous earth" which carries her, she thinks, "as if I were a leaf, or a queen" (150). The narrator travels deep into the earth, which "for miles beneath [. . .] was clamped together" (151). Woolf intimates that it is only by imagining ourselves traveling above the earth and beneath its surface, by paying attention to both the nonhuman world of fruit trees and horses, birds and cows, and the human community of farmers, children and churchgoers, that one may comprehend "life itself."

In "Nurse Lugton's Curtain," "The Widow and the Parrot: A True Story," "Lappin and Lapinova," *Flush: A Biography*, and "Gipsy, the Mongrel," Woolf gives prominence to animals, inverting conventional morality as animals model virtuous behavior for human readers. "Nurse Lugton's Curtain" (written for Woolf's niece Ann Stephen, probably in 1924) exemplifies this reversal of values. As Nurse Lugton sleeps, the pattern on the fabric she is stitching comes to life: "the blue stuff turned to blue air; the trees waved; you could hear the water of the lake breaking," and the animals, of various species, revive (*CSF* 160). The story makes explicit that it is a dream world in which humans and animals interact peaceably, that is worthy of our attention and emulation. The life of the animals, in a splendid place Woolf calls "Millamarchmantopolis," is vastly more rich and lively than the dull and insipid world inhabited by Nurse Lugton. In Millamarchmantopolis, "nobody harmed the lovely beasts," who are free to roam and to interact peaceably with the human population (161). By contrast, the waking world, inhabited by people like Nurse Lugton who has animals "in her toils," is also the contemporary world of zoos, in which animals are caged and harassed by spectators (161). Nurse Lugton's experience of life is impoverished because she "s[ees] nothing at all" of the vast panorama that marches over her lap. Her alienation from the animal world means that "even a little black beetle made her jump" (161). She is described as a "great ogress" because she condemns the animals to lifelessness: "every animal which strayed into her territories she froze alive, so that all day they stood stock still on her knee, but when she fell asleep, then they were released" (161). In this story, Woolf dramatizes the dangers to human beings of anthropocentricity, and suggests what we may gain by allowing animals greater freedom and respect.

"The Widow and the Parrot: A True Story" (the story first appeared in *The Charleston Bulletin*, a newspaper produced by the Bell children in the 1920s) may properly be thought of as another of Woolf's children's stories. Like "Nurse Lugton's Curtain," the story condemns cruelty and recommends kindness to animals.[10] The story features a widow who "in spite of her poverty [. . .] was devoted to animals" (*CSF* 162). She is selfless, and "often went short herself rather than stint her dog of his bone" (162). When she travels to collect the legacy her brother has bequeathed to her— a house and three thousand pounds—she learns from the solicitor that the house is decrepit and worthless and that the money cannot be located. Her only inheritance is her brother's parrot. Angered by her brother's deception, she recalls his cruelty to insects as a child, when he had, among other things, "trim[med] a hairy caterpillar with a pair of scissors" (164). Walking back to her lodgings after meeting with the solicitor she becomes lost. She is saved by the illumination provided by a fire in town, which turns out to be her newly inherited cottage going up in flames (165). Her only concern is for the parrot, whom she attempts to save, having to be restrained by the townspeople from entering the burning cottage. The parrot later turns up, quite alive, and gestures for her to follow him to the house where, by wildly gesticulating, he directs her to the three thousand sovereigns buried under the kitchen floor. On her deathbed, the widow explains that she is certain that the parrot, aware of her dangers on the riverbank, deliberately set the house on fire to save her. "Such," she reflects, "is the reward of kindness to animals" (169). In the story, human beings like the widow's brother are capable of disloyalty and even cruelty, whereas animals like the parrot are faithful and beneficent. Moreover, it is animals that are, quite literally, responsible for the lives and livelihood of humans.

Flush: A Biography (1933), Woolf's biography of Elizabeth Barrett Browning's spaniel, is her best known animal story and her most sustained examination of life from the point of view of an animal. Though considerably longer than her other short stories, Woolf refers to it in her diary entry for January 26, 1933 as one of her "little stories" (145). Moreover, one month prior, on December 23, 1932, Woolf suggests that *Flush* was too long—"it's not the right subject for that length"—suggesting that she saw the work formally as a short story (134). *Flush* has also received the critical fate of many of Woolf's short stories, having been, as Kate Flint observes, "largely written off by critics" ("Introduction" xliii). The few scholars who have engaged in more serious examinations of the text, Flint and Susan Squier, have tended to read the story allegorically, arguing that Woolf co-opts the animal world to explore the imbalance of power pervasive in gender, class, and even race relations. While many of their arguments are compelling, particularly in regard to Woolf's sense of the interdependence of all oppressions, these readings ignore what is most striking about the story—that Woolf wrote a biography of a dog.

Illustrating Flush's life with photographs, sketches, and an etching of a farmhouse entitled "Flush's birthplace," Woolf endows Flush's life with a narrative treatment generally reserved for human beings. Yet Woolf never fully anthropomorphizes Flush, constantly reminding us of the differences between dogs and humans, the vastly different "moral code of dogs" (13) that which governs their sexual conduct, the way the earth feels under the bare, "soft pads" of their feet (11), and the sense of smell in which they "mostly lived" (124). The first meeting between Flush and Elizabeth Barrett Browning revisits the epistemological problems that inevitably arise when humans attempt to know the nonhuman world:

Broken asunder, yet made in the same mold, could it be that each completed what was dormant in the other? She might have been—all that; and he—But no. Between them lay the widest gulf that can separate one being from

another. She spoke. He was dumb. She was a woman; he was a dog. Thus
closely united, thus immensely divided, they gazed at one another. Then
with one bound Flush sprang on to the sofa and laid himself where he was
to lie for ever after—on the rug at Miss Barrett's feet. (24)

One of the critical divisions between humans and animals results from
the inability of animals to speak a language we can comprehend. To Woolf,
however, this fact does not assist us in our ability to know and express a dog's
sense of smell, for we possess "no more than two words and one-half for
what we smell" such that "[t]o describe [Flush's] simplest experience with
the daily chop or biscuit is beyond our power" (124–25). Flush's dumbness,
moreover, does not lower him beneath us, nor even beneath poets who possess an exceptional facility with words; in fact, the reverse may true, in that
for Flush "[n]ot a single one of his myriad sensations ever submitted itself to
the deformity of words" (127). Nor is Flush's inability to communicate
through language an insurmountable impediment to communication,
with the narrator speculating that this barrier may even create a closer bond.
Moreover, Woolf suggests that Flush possesses an innate knowledge of what
is necessary for human happiness: for not only is Flush's happiness dependent on Barrett Browning, but her happiness is dependent on him, as he
forces her to overcome her life of oppressed invalidism, first by encouraging
her to leave her stuffy sitting room, and then by enabling her to open herself to love and the delights of true freedom in Italy.

In two of Woolf's later stories, "Lappin and Lapinova" (1939) and
"Gipsy, the Mongrel" (written in early 1940 and unpublished), human
beings are likewise figured as dependent on animals for their well-being.
"Lappin and Lapinova" examines the effect of marriage on women, but it
does so by condemning all forms of hunting and entrapment, whether per-
petrated by men on women or by human beings on animals. In "Lappin
and Lapinova," Rosalind, recently married, attempts to "get used to the fact
that she was Mrs Ernest Thorburn" by imagining the resemblance between
her husband and her pet rabbit (*CSF* 261). Not fond of the name Ernest,
she renames him King Lappin, and enjoys telling great tales of the Lappin
tribe. Ernest soon compares her to a female hare, and names her Lapinova.
After their honeymoon, they come to possess "a private world, inhabited,
save for the one white hare, entirely by rabbits," amusing themselves and
making "them feel, more even than most young married couples, in league
together against the rest of the world" (263). Rosalind, for her part, wonders how "[w]ithout that world [. . .] that winter could she have lived at all?"
for "she was not happy" (263–64). At a dinner party with Ernest's immense
family—they "breed so," as one guest puts it—Rosalind is saved from
despair when she sees her husband's nose twitch: she transforms the table

into a gigantic moor, her father-in-law into a poacher, her mother-in-law into a squire, and her sister-in-law into a ferret. She tells Ernest "if your nose hadn't twitched just at that moment, I should have been trapped" (266). But as the years go by, Ernest's nose twitches less and less often, until finally, Rosalind tells Ernest that Lapinova is lost, to which he replies, "'Yes [. . .] Poor Lapinova . . . ' [. . .] 'Caught in a trap [. . .] killed'" (268). "So that," the story concludes, "was the end of the marriage" (268). Only by imagining herself and Ernest as rabbits does Rosalind survive the trap of marriage. As in "Nurse Lugton's Curtain" and *Flush*, the world of humans, their institutions and practices, is frequently one of "damnable servility" in which both humans and animals are entrapped; human happiness is largely dependent on the ability to imagine human beings, like their animal counterparts, in a natural state of independence and freedom.[11]

In "Gipsy, the Mongrel," many of the ethical themes of the previous stories converge as Tom and Lucy Bagot tell their guests about their dog, named after the gypsies who had left her behind. Borrowing heavily from *Flush*, the story of Gipsy's existence is, as Tom describes it, a "character study" (*CSF* 273). The story is a difficult one for Tom to tell, so much so that his guest, Mary Bridger, comes to realize that "it was a love story he was telling": "It is difficult for a man to say why he fell in love with a woman, but it is still more difficult to say why he fell in love with a mongrel terrier" (274). Mary also reflects that "there is nothing like a dog story for bringing out people's characters" (275). Gipsy is charming, a good judge of character and wily, having saved himself from several attempts on his life. The Bagots learn from Gipsy that "A dog has a character just as we have, and it shows itself just as ours do, by what we say, by all sorts of little things" (277). They often found themselves examining Gipsy's psychology "just as if she were a human being": "I've often wondered," Tom says, "what was she thinking of us—down there among all the boots and old matches on the hearthrug? What was her world? Do dogs see what we see or is it something different?" (277). The four human characters look down and try to imagine life from the point of view of a dog, but ultimately they "couldn't answer that question" (278). The Bagots attempt to explain Gipsy's "tragedy"—her running away from them after hearing the whistle of the gypsies—as shame for behaving badly to a new dog they receive as a gift. The problem, they think, is again one of language: unlike human beings, who "can say 'I'm sorry' and there's an end of it. But with a dog it's different. Dogs can't talk. But dogs [. . .] remember," Bagot says, and Lucy continues, "If only she could have spoken! Then we could have reasoned with her, tried to persuade her" (279). The Bagots, in their love for Gipsy and inability to make sense of her leaving, long to cross the divide that inevitably separates them.

In *A Room of One's Own*, Woolf suggests that in the future, a "shorter, more concentrated fiction" will be needed to win a female readership, who have few extended periods of time for reading.[12] In "The Narrow Bridge of Art," Woolf suggests that the fiction of the future needs to be short in order to more closely "resemble poetry," which it must in order to "give not only or mainly people's relations to each other and their activities together, as the novel has hitherto done," but "the relations of man to nature, to fate; his imagination; his dreams" (CE2 225). Although Terence Hewitt in The Voyage Out muses about writing a novel about silence, Woolf was never able to write a novel in which human characters were substantially displaced by the nonhuman world. In part, this tendency may be attributed to the fact that Woolf's strategies for decentering the human presence in fiction were not sustainable throughout the length of a novel. Instead, Woolf came to realize the "more impersonal relationship" she had predicted as the new course for literature in her own shorter narratives. Indeed, Woolf recognized that short fiction possessed a special capacity to represent the mind's relation to the external world, so much so that she uses short narratives even within her novels.

The capacity of shorter fiction for greater density and lyricism, that is, to approach poetry more closely, was attractive to Woolf in her desire to establish the independence and grace of the nonhuman world. Sandra Kemp says "[t]he poeticism of the short stories [. . .] leads Woolf directly to the high modernism of the later novels (the 'Time Passes' section of To The Lighthouse, and the interlude sequences of The Waves)" (xxi). These sections—"Time Passes" and the interludes—are themselves shorter fictional narratives that could stand independently of the novels. Indeed, "Time Passes" was originally published on its own, in a French translation in the Paris periodical Commerce in 1926 (one year before the publication of the novel).[13] Woolf was well aware of the poetic quality of "Time Passes," writing in her diary that she had collected all of "the lyric portions" together such that they did not "interfere with the text so much as usual" (D3 106–07). That Woolf employs short narratives in her novels to convey aspects of the nonhuman world substantiates the extent to which she relied on the genre to express the complicated relation between the human and nonhuman.

"Time Passes" is in many ways the culmination of the vision and technique Woolf had developed in her short fiction. Woolf places at the literal center of the novel a house that knows no sustained human presence. She brings together the narratological, perspectival, and linguistic innovations that she utilized in her short stories to celebrate the external world that survives beyond human existence: human characters are pushed to the periphery; natural forces, like darkness, wind and waves, are given personality; and nonhuman forms of life—the butterflies and poppies, the artichokes and weeds, "the fertility, the insensibility of nature"— are given new prominence (187). The writing of "Time Passes" proved challenging for Woolf,

who wrote in her diary on April 18, 1926: "I cannot make it out—here is the most difficult abstract piece of writing—I have to give an empty house, no people's characters, the passage of time, all eyeless & featureless with nothing to cling to" (76). The impossibility of extricating the human subject from her fiction meant that she had to use, as Ellen Tremper observes, qualifying expressions, "as if" and "seemed," to "self-consciously draw attention to the approximateness or partial reliability of the figurative language the narrative voice is deploying" (171). This device in fact originates in Woolf's first short story, "The Mark on the Wall," where the repeated comments by the narrator—"I like to think"—when imagining life from a tree's perspective, shatter the illusion that the tree's thoughts and sensations are being recorded, reminding us once again that knowledge of the external world is inevitably tethered to a human perspective.

Ultimately Woolf aligns herself with Bernard in *The Waves*, who asks, "how describe the world as seen without a self?" and responds, "There are no words" (239). In thinking about what elements characterized a Romantic poem in her essay "Romance," Woolf suggested, "perhaps we most constantly feel that the writer is thinking more of the effect of the thing upon his mind than of the thing itself. And up to a point there is nothing more real than the effect of the thing upon one's mind" (*E2* 75). The interludes in *The Waves* represent the beauty of the thing itself, the nonhuman world of the sun, waves, and birds, while at the same time drawing attention to the way that this is necessarily a human apprehension of the external world: the artifice of the sections is inscribed in the italicized typescript, the qualifying expressions, and the excessively elaborate personifications. Woolf's examination of the relation between the thing itself and the effect of the thing on the human mind is therefore crucial to the "high modernism" of both a later work like *The Waves* and early experimental short pieces like "Solid Objects" and "The Mark on the Wall." "The Mark on the Wall" and the interludes in *The Waves*, like bookends framing Woolf's career, reveal that the peremptory need Woolf felt to explore the unity and division between the human and nonhuman worlds found its most perfect expression in shorter fictional forms.

NOTES

1. Mao also considers only one of the dozens of short narratives Woolf wrote during her life. Some writers who have considered Woolf's short fiction at greater length are Bernard Blackstone, S. P. Rosenbaum, Avrom Fleishman, Clare Hanson, and Dominic Head. Though many of these writers consider the importance of the natural world to Woolf, they have not offered a comprehensive reading of her short fictional explorations of this issue.

2. This quotation is from Woolf's review of E. M. Forster's *Aspects of the Novel*, and therefore the "assumption" to which Woolf refers is that specifically of Forster.

3. I follow Dick's dating of the stories and rely on the publication information she provides. "The Mark on the Wall" was first published in July 1917 with Leonard Woolf's short story "Three Jews" in *Two Stories*. It was also the first publication of the Hogarth Press (*CSF* 297).

4. Lee's source is Woolf's Monk's House Papers, A 20.

5. Woolf frequently uses similar analogies to describe the creative process. In "Professions for Women," a young woman writer is compared to a fisherman:

> I want you to figure yourself a girl sitting with a pen in your hand, which for minutes, and indeed hours, she never dips into the inkpot. The image that comes to my mind when I think of this girl is the image of a fisherman lying sunk in dreams on the verge of a deep lake with a rod held out over the water. She was letting her imagination sweep unchecked round every rock and cranny of the world that lies submerged in the depth of our unconscious being. (*CE2* 287)

6. A partial diary entry for July 29, 1918 is as follows: "Form obsesses him [. . .] Ever since he was a child the solidity & the shapes of objects have tortured him. I advised him, for arts sake, to keep sane; to grasp, & not exaggerate, & put sheets of glass between him and his matter" (*D1* 176).

7. Although Gertler made this remark in 1939 (Woolf, in her entry in "A Sketch of the Past" for May 15, 1939 says he had dined with them the night before), it seems likely that this was a long-standing position of his, and one that Woolf would have been aware of when she wrote "Solid Objects."

8. John Oakland (268, 271) and Dominic Head (99–102) make several similar observations.

9. Although Woolf herself never flew in an airplane, the recurrence of airplanes in her fiction suggests a deep fascination with flight and its opportunities for new perspectives. See Gillian Beer, "The Island and the Aeroplane" (152).

10. Such cultural critiques, especially in relation to animals, were so conventional in children's literature that Quentin Bell recalls being quite disappointed in the story. In his afterword to the 1988 publication of the story, he explains that when he "commissioned" the story from his aunt at age twelve or thirteen, both he and his brother Julian were shocked by her submission: "We had hoped vaguely for something as funny, as subversive, and as frivolous as Virginia's conversation. Knowing this, she sent us an 'improving story' with a moral, based on the very worst Victorian examples." Woolf no doubt would have been amused by the Bell boys' reaction; after solemn reflection they decided it would be "unkind to reject the story" (Woolf, *Widow*).

11. Susan Dick links the genesis of this story to the following comment in a letter to Vanessa Bell, dated October 24, 1938: "marriage, as I suddenly for the first time realised walking in the Square, reduces one to damnable servility. Cant be helped. Im going to write a comedy about it" (*CSF* 309–10).

12. This phrase comes from *A Room of One's Own*, in which Woolf speculates that the "future of fiction" for women has to be "concerned by physical conditions" (101). For Woolf, this meant that "the book has somehow to be adapted to the body, and at a venture one would say that women's books should be shorter, more concentrated, than those of men, and framed so that they do not need long hours of steady and uninterrupted work. For interruptions there will always be" (101). Thus, in addition to the many reasons why short fiction appealed to Woolf, she also believed that short fiction served the interests of her female readers.

13. James Haule offers a superb analysis of the various revisions made to this earlier publication of "Time Passes." According to Haule, "Woolf altered the antimale aggressor and antiwar focus of this pivotal section" by drastically reducing the direct references to the war and eliminating the direct identification of the war with male destructiveness and sexual brutality. Thus the only remaining reference to the Great War is "the silent apparition of an ashen-coloured ship [. . .] come, gone" and "a purplish stain upon the bland surface of the sea" (182). These revisions shift the focus from a specific historic and geographic perspective to a timeless one, in which the earth, long accustomed to war and destruction, fails to mark its significance. Human events are thereby restored to a cosmic sense of proportion.

perception, some heightened sensibility or cognition (*E3* 340). Generally the "narration" in her short fiction draws the reader away from short story conventions of character or plot and fixes on a figural consciousness, a pattern of thought that develops as the text unfolds; this evolution provides organization not in any chronological sense but in the sense of an idea progressively developing, becoming multifaceted and richer. When readers contemplate this recorded consciousness, they become inextricably linked to the narrator's perceptions and apprehensions and combine their efforts with the narrator's story telling, piecing the story together by whatever means, through bits and fragments. As Woolf describes in "Impassioned Prose," "[. . .] it is not the actual sight or sound itself that matters, but the reverberations that it makes as it travels through our minds. These are often to be found far away, strangely transformed; but it is only by gathering up and putting together these echoes and fragments that we arrive at the true nature of our experience" (*E4* 367).

In her 1921 short story collection, *Monday or Tuesday*, Woolf uses such experience-telling in a lyrical way to represent the human consciousness at work, and in doing so, she confronts and explores the difficulty of such representation in literature. Woolf describes the effects of this lyrical representation in her essay "On Not Knowing Greek":

> For words, when opposed to such a blast of meaning, must give out, must be blown astray, and only by collecting in companies convey the meaning which each one separately is too weak to express. Connecting them in a rapid flight of the mind we know instantly and instinctively what they mean, but could not decant that meaning afresh into any other words. There is an ambiguity which is the mark of the highest poetry; we cannot know exactly what it means. (*E4* 44–5)[2]

As the narrators in the *Monday or Tuesday* stories reflect on their immediate experience, they engage the reader in such an intense realization of consciousness, a consciousness that does not so much explain the working of the mind as demonstrate its changeability and variation. The objects of attention in the stories are minimized in favor of a consciousness perceiving and contemplating the subject; there are rapid perceptions, associative contemplation, and imaginative speculation. Woolf's essay "Phases of Fiction" compares such story-telling to the process of reading; as the "flight of mind" transforms itself into a "moment of being," the reader momentarily realizes that "[i]t is as though there were two faces to every situation; one full in the light so that it can be described as accurately and examined as minutely as possible; the other half in shadow so that it can be described only in a moment of faith and vision by the use of metaphor" (*GR* 139).

Chapter 9

Verbal Painting in "Blue & Green" and "Monday or Tuesday"

Kathryn N. Benzel

There has been much attention given to the lyricism in Virginia Woolf's novels as a technique to explore the representation of consciousness: the "Time Passes" section in *To the Lighthouse*; the interlude passages in *The Waves*; and Isa the poet in *Between the Acts*. Even in her first novel, *The Voyage Out*, there are stream of consciousness passages depicting Rachel Vinrace's reveries about the Amazon River as meditations on silence and self. There has been much less attention given to lyricism in her short fiction, perhaps because the issue of the short story as form becomes so problematic with Woolf; often her better known stories, "The Mark on the Wall" and "Kew Gardens," are questioned in terms of being short stories at all. Does a woman's contemplation of a spot on a wall create enough "plot" to constitute a short story? Does the narrative "voice" of a snail suggest that a story is being told? Even some of her lesser-known short stories are labeled as sketches or caricatures rather than short stories. "A Haunted House," "Blue & Green," "Monday or Tuesday," and "The String Quartet" are stories that seem to defy definition as sketches or caricatures or short stories.[1] To read these pieces is not to accumulate details in the conventional narrative sense of plot and characterization, but to experience a visionary moment that "startles us into a flash of understanding," as Woolf says in "On Re-reading Novels," one that replicates an immediate emotion, a sense

Thus in the *Monday or Tuesday* stories, Woolf disrupts conventional elements of the short story by using lyrical strategies, especially metaphors of visual art (color, line, spatial relations), to represent the mind's complexity and obstinacy. Woolf's use of these painterly qualities, creates this lyrical atmosphere that combines perception of ordinary objects and the imaginative conceptualization of the objects. She describes this technique in her *Diary*:

> The idea has come to me that what I want now to do is to saturate every atom. I mean to eliminate all waste, deadness, superfluity: to give the moment whole; whatever it includes. Say that the moment is a combination of thought; sensation; the voice of the sea. Waste, deadness, come from the inclusion of things that dont belong to the moment; this appalling narrative business of the realist: getting on from lunch to dinner: it is false, unreal, merely conventional. Why admit any thing to literature that is not poetry—by which I mean saturated? Is that not my grudge against novel[ist]s—that they select nothing? The poets succeeding by simplifying: practically everything is left out. I want to put practically everything in: yet to saturate. (*D3* 209–10)

In order to saturate the moment, Woolf focuses the angle of vision through narrators whose thoughts shift at random, sporadically, and without consequence. Woolf uses the narrators' ambiguous perceptions to reconceive this human consciousness in a verbal text and to suggest not only the human consciousness but also its uncertainty. Several features of these stories encourage this ambiguity: refusal to name places and things; resistance to obvious or fixed meanings; lack or uncertainty of closure or completion; the narrative voice's lack of focus; and sensory, impressionistic details in exposition. Finally it is through such ambiguity that readers are able to experience multiple states of consciousness—perception, cognition, reflection, and imagination—Woolf's "flight of mind."

By adhering to this phenomenological approach, Woolf refuses some modernists' call for a "unified sensibility," a midway between reason and emotion that returns to the discipline of classicism as opposed to emotionalism. Woolf rejects T. S. Eliot's emphasis on a literary tradition that uses classic features of narrative to model human behavior in prescriptive ways; for example, when Eliot privileges rationality of language over emotion, he adheres to classicism's attempts to escape emotion and to externalize a writer's inner feelings (Eliot's "objective correlative").[3] Because Woolf is skeptical about language/literature's capacity to represent accurately human consciousness, she seeks other means to characterize the totality of the human world. Thus, contrary to T. S. Eliot's notion of "dissociation of sensibility," Woolf represents consciousness by combining emotion and reason, feeling and thought, through impressionistic descriptions that incorporate artistic metaphors of color, space, and line to present human consciousness.[4] Using visual art as a metaphor, she says that she will emerge from the dark "underground" of conventional narrative structure to "discover what new colours and shadows are showing in them now that they are exposed to the outer world" (*GR* 82).[5]

Woolf's reference to color and her interest in visual art here are not accidental. Her personal and professional connections with painters fuel her interest in the relationship between visual arts and narrative form. Her sister Vanessa Bell and other Bloomsbury artists, Duncan Grant, Clive Bell, and Roger Fry, encouraged discussions about painting and its techniques. Even in her youth she tried her hand at the visual arts as she worked alongside her sister maintaining the family tradition of drawing after dinner. Pleased with her drawing skills when she was twenty-two, she writes to her friend Violet Dickinson: "I shall give up literature and take to art, I am already a draughtsman of great promise. I draw for 2 hours every evening after dinner, and make copies of all kinds of pictures, which Nessa says show a remarkable feeling for line. Pictures are easier to understand than subtle literature, so I think I shall become an artist to the public, and keep my writing to myself" (*L1* 172).[6] Though Woolf gives up her attempts at painting and drawing by 1918, she maintains her interest in visual arts throughout her life. She writes about artists and their struggles to bring the artistic vision into an aesthetic form—for example, Lily in *To the Lighthouse*. She experiments with her own verbal painting—the interludes in *The Waves*. She also writes art criticism: commentary in exhibition catalogues, essays about such artists as Walter Sickert, reviews of contemporary art criticism.[7] Often Woolf talks about her own writing as if it were a creative process similar to painting. From her early journals, she describes her practice at writing:

> I have sketched faint outlines with a pencil. But the only use of this book is that it shall serve for a sketch book; as an artist fills his pages with scraps & fragments, studies of drapery—legs, arms & noses—useful to him no doubt, but of no meaning to anyone else—so I [ ] take up my pen & trace here whatever shapes I happen to have in my head. [ ] It is an exercise—training for eye & hand. (*PA* 186–87, square brackets added by editor)

Woolf's interest in the relationship between painting and writing was chiefly reinforced by her friendship and collaborations with Roger Fry and his study of art and aesthetics.[8] For a time Fry was attracted to the idea of creating an aesthetic that would encompass both literature and painting: "I think that in proportion as poetry becomes more intense the content is entirely remade by the form and has no separate value at all. You see, the sense of poetry is analogous to the things represented in painting" (*Letters of Roger Fry* 362). He continues that both arts are inspired and initiated by emotions in "An Essay in Aesthetics": "the imaginative life is distinguished by the greater clearness of its perception, and the greater purity and freedom of its emotion" (*Vision and Design* 17). Using emotion as its source, Fry maps out an aesthetics by comparing "the emotional colours of life, to something which underlies all the particular and specialized emotions of actual life" (*Artist and Psycho-analysis* 364–65). Fry outlines ways that the artist "arouses our emotions": a "drawn line is the record of a gesture, and that gesture is modified by the artist's feeling which is thus communicated to us directly," and color "has a direct emotional effect [that] is evident from such words as gay, dull, melancholy, in relation to colour" ("An Essay in Aesthetics" 23–34). The viewer, Fry's "true spectator," apprehends these connections between emotion and painting through "creative vision," similar to the artist's vision; contemplating "the particular field of vision, the [. . .] chaotic and accidental conjunction of forms and colours begin to crystallise into a harmony" ("The Artist's Vision" 35–36). Thus Roger Fry concentrates his aesthetic experience not on a product per se but on the process whereby the viewer contemplates the formal features of painting in order to discover and experience the harmony of the work's total aesthetic effect. The viewer's pleasure in discovering the formal synthesis in painting is increased by a simultaneous discovery of its emotional values that Fry states are the focus of Post-Impressionists.

Significantly, the 1910 exhibition in London, *Manet and the Post-Impressionists*, reiterates this discussion about the synthesis of thought and emotion in art. Desmond MacCarthy's introduction to the exhibition catalog defines Post-Impressionism as an exploration and expression of "that emotional significance that lies in things, and is the most important subject matter of art" (9). Discussing Matisse as representative of Post-Impressionist painting, he emphasizes the synthetic quality of this painting: "*synthesis* in design; [. . .] to subordinate consciously [Matisse's] power of representing the parts of his picture as plausibly as possible, to the expressiveness of the whole design" (12 MacCarthy's emphasis). Fry elaborates this idea in a lecture closing the famous 1910 exhibition: the "visual language of the imagination" is the means to "discover [. . .] what arrangements of form and colour are calculated to stir the imagination most deeply through the stimulus given to the sense of sight" ("Post Impressionism" 100). Again, he says that "[p]articular rhythms of line and particular harmonies of colour have their spiritual correspondences, and tend to rouse now one set of feelings, now another. The artist plays upon us by the rhythm of line, by colour, by abstract form, and by the quality of the matter he employs" (105). These rhythms and harmonies of color and line, however, are not fixed or static but continually shifting and changing perspective and purpose from both the painter's and viewer's perspectives. As these painters attempt to represent their worlds, they "speak directly to the imagination through images created, not because of the likeness to external nature, but because of their fitness to appeal to the imaginative and contemplative life" (105). Through their various perspectives, Post-Impressionist painters create their understanding of ambiguity and variety in the real world; Monet's many "Water Lilies" paintings or Van Gogh's sunflower paintings or Cezanne's stylized still lifes epitomize such attempts.

Impressionism's and Post-Impressionism's concerns with the value of color, light, and line, provide an outline for Woolf's short fiction as well as for painters. Both Seurat's pointillist techniques—tiny dots of color—and Renoir's use of visible brushstrokes separate an individual color into tones and hues. Light also creates highlights and shadows that enhance this separation of colors. By breaking up colors into particles, Impressionist painters keep form indeterminate; spatial relations are not clearly defined and the focus is on the space separating the colors rather than a large mass of color. This indeterminate perspective challenges the illusion of density and outline and distance in Seurat's and Renoir's paintings where foreground and background seem to lie on the same plane. Such painting techniques create complex surface designs that engage the viewer in creating a coherent image from the bits of color and line and implication of mass and space; these techniques invite the viewer to actively participate in creating the aesthetic experience by replicating the artist's immediate and urgent perceptions in the act of creation, imagining possible harmony.

Post-Impressionism continues use of these techniques and adds another dimension that emphasizes the formulation of ideas, the conceptualization of the "life or spirit, truth or reality [. . .] the essential thing" (*E4* 160), as Woolf describes in "Modern Fiction." Post-Impressionism also manipulates design in order to create a tension between reality and appearance and to encourage reflection on some "significant form" or harmony (as Roger Fry suggests). Instead of experimentation with technique on the canvas surface, Post-Impressionism seeks an order or harmony beneath the surface appearance, some conceptual design that holds the picture together. For instance, Picasso and Matisse deconstruct and reconceptualize their subjects through interplay of color and light, geometric shapes, and perspective. The viewer, unable to use familiar or conventional terms (such as the curve of a nose or the corner of a room) to identify the subject in the picture, sees the subject transformed as the artist decomposes the conventional relations among color, line, shape, and perspective. Without conventional cues, such as perspective from the corner of a room or natural relations among facial parts, the viewer reconciles inconsistencies by reconceptualizing the object and its essence. The gaps and absences are not seen as negative space but used as "playgrounds" where the painting's parts can be reassembled by the viewer. In this way, the observer shares, coexists, with the artist in the conception of the painting's subject.

Through Woolf's "flights of mind" in *The Monday or Tuesday* stories, readers discover similar "emotional elements of design" (Fry, "An Essay in Aesthetics" 23) in a verbal context. As readers recognize the text's formalist features and apprehend the emotions found in the narrator's presentation, they enact an intimate dialectic with the thoughts and feelings in the text. In a 1925 essay, "Pictures," Woolf says writers as well as readers need to recognize this dialectic:

> The whole scene, however solidly and pictorially built up, is always dominated by an emotion which has nothing to do with the eye. But it is the eye that has fertilised their thought; it is the eye [. . .] that has come to the help of the other senses, combined with them, and produced effects of extreme beauty, and of a subtlety hitherto unknown. (*E4* 244)

In this manner Woolf's collection of short pieces in *Monday or Tuesday* and her emerging theory about reading focus on Post-Impressionist aesthetics.[9] Even in her 1926 essay, "The Cinema," she acknowledges the connection between emotion and thought in art: "But if so much of our thinking and feeling is connected with seeing there must be some residue of visual emotion not seized by artist or painter-poet which may await the cinema" (*E4* 351). When Woolf challenges writers to represent the connection between thought and feeling, to "[e]xamine [. . .] this unknown and uncircumscribed spirit" (*E4* 160), she calls for new techniques with the capability of bringing forth writers' perceptions of the real world—"to contrive a means of being free to set down what [we choose]" (*E3* 35). If writers are "constrained [. . .] by some powerful and unscrupulous tyrant who has him in thrall to provide a plot" (*E4* 160) (such as stagnant plot formulae and worn-out characterizations), then their representations of the human consciousness will not represent the mind's continuous work of shifting perspectives and modifying conclusions.

In calling for a lyrical means of representation, Woolf brings together the literary dialectic (form and content) with a concept of reading that combines emotion and thought. In "Byron and Mr Briggs," a 1919 unpublished essay, a proposed introduction to a book on reading, she addresses the process of reading, the purpose of reading, the pleasure of reading, and kinship between readers and writers (similarities arise with Roger Fry's "significant form" and true "spectatorship").[10] She prepares readers for their own imaginative creation of a work: "[. . .] to make a whole—that's what readers have in common. [. . .] to add to a single impression, the others that go to complete it. [. . .] to complete, to supply background, relationship, motivation" (*E3* 482–83). She continues, "all this is nothing but a random game" that creates a whole at the center of which is "some quite unimaginable end" (*E3* 485). In this new context, readers are faced with discovering new subtleties of form and then reconceiving the act of reading.[11] The act of reading then is not an accumulation of details but a visionary moment as stated in "On Re-Reading Novels": "A sudden intensity of phrase, something which for good reasons or for bad we feel to be emphatic, startles us into a flash of understanding. We see now why the story was written. [. . .] There the 'book itself' is not form which you see, but emotion which you feel" (*E3* 340). The reader's visual reconstruction of the writer's imaginings prompts recognition of the placement and arrangement of both literary features and aesthetic emotions within a text, and thus the reader is at once aware of the construction of the text and is responding to its aesthetic qualities.[12] Similar to the way that Post-Impressionist paintings are viewed, literary readers identify various literary features—metaphors, imagery, characterization, setting, even plot—through an apprehension of attached emotions and then combine them into a unique harmony of the particular text. By inviting connections between life and art, vision and expression, these emotions connect the reader and writer in a shared moment of creativity, a combined sympathetic interaction with/in the text. Such reading demands that the reader carefully discriminate, so that meaning comes only "after hard [. . .] exercise of the brain" (*E3* 488).

Woolf's short pieces in *Monday or Tuesday* demonstrate her borrowings from Impressionistic and Post-Impressionistic painting techniques, using lyrical strategies that engage readers in combining verbal elements of the text. Much short story criticism suggests that because of its brevity, the short story inherently contains lyrical qualities: foregrounding point of view; emphasizing interiority (moods and feelings); using metaphor to represent conventional narrative elements; rejecting chronological ordering; economizing form and style.[13] As these lyrical qualities appear in the *Monday or Tuesday* stories, they enable Woolf to represent the uncertainty of the mind at work, both as subject of the stories and through the reading experience. These strategies are especially important in reading "Blue & Green" and "Monday or Tuesday," where Woolf experiments with a kind of verbal painting that creates a poetics of reading.

In "Blue & Green" and "Monday or Tuesday," Woolf lyricizes narrative conventions of plot and point of view. Often called prose poems and prose sketches, these narratives do not fit neatly into conventional definitions of the short story, which rely on plot or characterization. There is no action in the conventional narrative sense where a character acts toward some goal, finds impediments, and overcomes them. Instead these short pieces are characterized by a high sensitivity to sensory impressions in the lyrical fashion, "the emotional elements of design," with the narrative perspective focused in the narrator's mind. Woolf's use of Post-Impressionist painterly concepts, like metaphors for spatial relations, color and light, and line, emphasizes a narrative organization that moves on two levels: on the horizontal level as readers scan across the surface of the page, noting organization though visual repetitions and frames; and on a vertical level as readers discover the depth of meaning in symbols and metaphors. Susan Stanford Friedman's "Spatialization, Narrative Theory, and Virginia Woolf's *The Voyage Out*" discusses these levels of reading with regard to Woolf's novels. Friedman's theoretical construction is useful in explaining these short pieces as corollaries to Impressionistic surface perception and Post-Impressionistic depth of conception. "Blue & Green" is an example of surface play where Woolf represents perception through the animation of color; the green and blue are transformed through their movement ("slips," "drops," "drips," "sweeps") and relation to other objects. In a more complex way "Monday or Tuesday" represents the process of conceptualization as the narrator contemplates the nature of truth relative to her immediate perceptions and metaphoric renderings, which both are vague and indeterminate as well as suggest gaps and absences. Together "Blue & Green" and "Monday or Tuesday" encapsulate Woolf's poetics of reading by authorizing the reader as someone who reads with insight, imagination, and judgment.

Both stories are brief; "Blue & Green" is 264 words with two separately titled sections facing each other in the original publication ("Green" is on the left page, and "Blue" on the right) , and "Monday or Tuesday" is 315 words in length, with six short paragraphs.[14] Both stories seem self-generated with no typical narrative cues: no direct reference to people speaking or thinking or acting as characters; no reference to plot as character action or time passing or passed; no tags like "she thought," "she said," "she wondered"; no narrative or speaking voice is clearly identified. They begin *in medias res*, in the middle of the narrator's thoughts. There doesn't appear to be any motivating emotional context such as hope or fear in either story. A typical reader's expectations for narrative conventions are removed and the reader identifies consciousness through the use of lyrical patterns that deconstruct and then transform familiar objects like the Impressionist and Post-Impressionist painters mentioned above.

"Blue & Green" experiments primarily with Impressionistic techniques. Woolf uses the colors green and blue to organize the random thoughts of the narrator's perception of a Tiffany-type lamp with hanging glass pendants. The hanging pendants reflect green as the sun reflects through the lamp during the day and then they change to blue in the evening when the lamp is turned on. Because each section is titled separately and appears on opposite pages in the original printing of *Monday or Tuesday*, the reflected light of the "Green" section is juxtaposed with the refracted light of the "Blue" section. Water imagery and representations of animals also animate the colors and make them whimsical and even erratic rather than constant; the colors drip and sweep, are turned into camels, frogs, a sea-monster, and iron scraps. The reader follows the narrator's developing perception as she free-associates the immediate color and shapes with her past experiences and perceptions. Though the present tense reinforces the immediacy and urgency of perception, the narrative itself takes place throughout the period of an entire day. Nowhere in "Blue & Green" does the narrator identify the subject as a lamp, so that readers discover this object in the text by recognizing shapes in the changes and patterns in the color found in the diurnal cycle. First, green's shadow changes shape on the marble tabletop, and the color becomes animated, like the feathers of a parakeet, then palm branches and pine needles, and then camels and frogs. In addition, water imagery reinforces the plasticity of the color: the "ruffled surface of the ocean," "the aimless waves." Then the green fades, and in the "Blue" narrative the lighted lamp becomes a "snub-nosed monster" spouting water "fiery-white in the centre," with a "fringe of blue beads" (CSF 142). The monster is beached among other "blues": the gray scales, scraps of rusty iron, a wrecked boat, and blue bells. When the blue progresses up the beach, it suggests a more substantive, permanent object—a cathedral—and finally the imagined "veils of madonnas." In perceiving the play between light and color, we conceptualize these colors and their sources and then imaginatively extend the concepts to other possible objects, even imagined ones.

Beginning in "Green," the glass pendants reflect green as the color changes from hard glass to a liquid pool to animated fingers to parakeet feathers to palm fronds to pine needles. Then the color green suggests an oasis in the middle of a desert, perhaps suggesting the placement of the lamp in the middle of the marble table. Green is even associated with not-green objects—camels, a white blossom—as well as green of weeds and rushes and frogs. When evening comes, the green needles, the lamp's glass pendants, transform into blue. As readers process these transformations of thought, they actually feel as if they are experiencing these thoughts rather than thoughts mediated by a speaker. It's only when the narrator uses metaphors and similes, that we have an inkling of characterized narrative voice. These metaphors suggest something about the narrator's consciousness and character—prone toward exoticism, very imaginative, and concerned about representing the color accurately. As we progress through the narrator's various kinds of consciousness—perception, imagination, and cognition—we recognize a sense of profound delight as the narrator creates versions of each color. As we contemplate and discover shapes of these colors, we reason that because colored mass suggests an object to know, we can know this object, by knowing its color. We reflect on its knowability and ask the question, can we decipher this color into something meaningful? An object? A concept?

These underlying questions persist in the "Blue" paragraph, where the narrator enacts another imaginative representation—of blue. The color blue seems to seep up from the underground rather than to flash to our attention; the "ruffled surface of the ocean" and "aimless waves" which are green in paragraph one, change into black in the snub-nosed monster's hide and white in a spray of waves; both are traced with blue rather than dominated by the color. The entire beach scene is tinged with blue color but is not itself blue; blue waves cross over the sea monster that sheds his blue scales on the beach cluttered with blue stains in rusty scraps. In the last two sentences, the scene moves up the beach to the blue bells (perhaps flowers or the cathedral bells) and then to a faint blue atmosphere in a cathedral. The blue bells become a metaphoric link between the two settings, transferring the blue from the beach to the cathedral. The "cathedral's different, cold, incense laden, faint blue" suggests that the lamp has been extinguished and the residual effect of seeing the lamp's color remains in the reader's eye as veiled and impressionistic. This final image of blue "veils of madonnas" moves from the concrete objects (iron scraps, boat) to a metaphor for emotion (blue veils). This movement of thought from perception to conceptualization combines the emotion and thought that Woolf sees as the essence of the reading experience. As readers move through both "Green" and "Blue," they experience the mind exercising its faculties. Without even being in the room where the lamp is located, readers perceive the colors green and blue, they experience an oasis, a beach, and finally a cathedral; and they imagine such a trip as a grand flight of fantasy through implication and imagination.

The reader's understanding of these colors green and blue is deepened by the narrator's metaphoric descriptions that give the glass objects a feeling of life, through their association with animals, and emotion, through the pleasure of imagining the colors as such. When the glass pendants are defamiliarized through various associations they simultaneously suggest sameness and difference—the green is both hard glass and liquid pool; the blue is blue spray and dry scales. Yet in spite of these paradoxes, the entire story is held together by the references to water imagery—pool of green, ocean, waves, water frogs and monsters, water spray, polished pebbles on a beach. The "aimless waves" in "Green" become water spouts spraying "off into a fringe of blue beads" in "Blue." "The snub-nosed monster" in "Blue" inhabits the "ruffled surface of the ocean" in "Green." Finally in "Blue," the narrator's point of view shifts from the water with a monster floundering on the beach to a wrecked boat to a field of blue bells to the inside of a cathedral; the wrecked boat with ribs like gothic arches foreshadows the cathedral. The verbal signal "But" jolts us into the recognition that the color is yet again changing into something very different—the blue bells, perhaps flowers, change into church bells inside a cold cathedral, incense-laden. This sudden shift from the expanse of the beach to the inside of a cathedral draws attention to the difference between color as dynamic space and color as containment. In fact readers "see" the colors blue and green as constantly changing rather than absolutely defining and confining. Thus the reader's realization of these changes not only becomes a metaphor for the continually changing consciousness of the narrator but also suggests the essential power of the reader's imagination as plastic and adaptive.

"Monday or Tuesday" both literally and metaphorically echoes a similar aesthetic of reading that is also grounded in the narrator's consciousness and the reader's discovery of the story. The story begins with an anonymous narrator looking out a window and seeing a heron fly across the sky and merge with the clouds. As she looks out the window, the narrator's thoughts shift and change from the exterior sights of sky and sounds of the street to the interior tearoom scene. The subject of writing is brought to bear as the anonymous narrator develops a writer's consciousness, and seemingly random and disconnected images, in fact, reveal the difficult process of "distilling" an idea into words, presenting the process of conceptualization. In addition, a never-answered, repeated question about searching for truth complicates both the narrator's expression of uncertainty and the reader's expectation of wholeness or completeness: "Desiring truth, awaiting it, laboriously distilling a few words, for ever desiring—[. . .]—for ever desir-ing truth. [. . .]—and truth?" (*CSF* 137). Similar to "Blue & Green," "Monday or Tuesday" continually changes shape, line, and direction in its desire for representation, and the reader again is challenged to seek out the story's meaning through defamiliarized objects, ambiguous perspectives, and imaginative reflections.

Whereas color in "Blue & Green" provides the reader with a visual means for reconstructing the story's development and connecting the reader and the writer, in "Monday or Tuesday" the story's cloud imagery works to this end. As the narrator looks out the window, she imagines shapes in the clouds as they change and shift: the sky "covers and uncovers, moves and remains"; clouds form lake, mountain, ferns, feathers, "Down that falls" (137). Perhaps not coincidentally, the clouds' disintegration sym-bolizes the narrator's scattered thoughts and the reader's continually shifting position in the text. In the fourth paragraph, when the clouds reassemble, visual images of "sun gold," "ferns," and "feathers" combine with adjectival abstractions like "leaf-light" and redirect the organic image from the first paragraph. And then again the clouds are "gathered, scattered, squandered"

(137). Nowhere does the narrator identify these images as clouds; we understand them as clouds only because we have played the same imaginative game in viewing clouds.[15] Without naming the clouds as such, the narrator engages us as active participants in creating both the objects in the story and their meanings. Again, we locate the visual patterns of shape, color, and line in the clouds and then watch those patterns shift and change to no end. The traditional reliance on the narrator's authority is undercut when she cannot sustain or complete her speculations and imaginings. They all seem to come to nothing; yet, this is something. That is, the narrator's thoughts replicate the mind at work, differentiating, assimilating, speculating, and imagining in response to the view outside the window.

In the second paragraph, the narrator's speculations about a writer truthfully representing such a thought process, "desiring truth, awaiting it, laboriously distilling a few words," are interrupted by the physical world, suggested by sounds of human cries and traffic noises in the street outside (137). The tension between the exterior, physical world and the narrator's imagined world is emphasized by the loud disruptions: "a cry starts to the left, another to the right. Wheels strike divergently" (137). As these immediate sounds disrupt her concentration on the cloud picture framed by the window, her thoughts move inside to a smaller, more intimate tea scene around a fireplace. Even as she attempts to draw herself back to her speculations about the clouds and truth, the sensory world interrupts any conclusion to her questions; she shifts from imaginative contemplation to a more urgent perception of her physical surroundings.

In the third paragraph, those partaking in tea are described not as actual people but metaphorically as large splashes of black, red, and gold color and pointed and round lines, and this metaphoric description signals a shift from perception to conceptualization. Teatime conversation is abbreviated and placed in parentheses with no tags, suggesting such talk is typical of teatime (weather, tea). Without any actual speakers, the talk remains generalized and suggests a mood of politeness rather than providing characterization. The parenthetical observation represents another interruption of the narrator's thoughts by the perception of voices. Again sounds from the present moment ("outside a van discharges") disrupt the narrator's thoughts as she imagines a clerical worker taking tea at her desk in a business office, perhaps across the street from her window. At the end of paragraph three, the imagined physical scene is left incomplete, punctuated with a dash, and the scene disintegrates and dissolves like the clouds in paragraph one. This scene's indeterminate description (who is wearing the shoes and speaking?) suggests the writer's difficulty in rendering the scene's emotion in words; that is, the difficulty of combining emotion and thought in a single scripted event.

Next, the narrator refocuses on the clouds as they merge with the street scene, "drifting at corners, blown across wheels," and she questions again whether the entire scene evidences any truth: "and truth?" Now both her imagined scenes of the clouds and her perceptions of the room's colors and sounds merge in the metaphor of the clouds' dynamics, "swept up, down, torn, sunk." The clouds' further changes are matters of signification rather than pictorial images. In paragraph five the whiteness of the clouds is concretized as a white square of marble in the fireplace, which transforms into a book, which disappears up the chimney as smoke, which drifts cloud-like to an imagined scene in India. Finally in the last paragraph the clouds reappear in a night sky as they drift across the stars. As we follow the narrator's mental transformations throughout the day (similar to the diurnal pattern in "Blue & Green"), they are mirrored in the cloud changes, and we begin to apprehend the underlying structure that signifies Woolf's "moment of being": the combination of thought and emotion. Through this discovery, readers are able to "perform" the text and authorize their own readings. Thus by the end of the story, as readers interact with the narrator's cloud metaphors, they also enter into the process of creating and interpreting the questions about truth.

Yet the reader–writer collaboration is often hesitant, and the resultant tension, the inability to fix meaning to either the actual or imagined world, reinforces the writer and reader's sympathetic realization of the indecipherability of life. The white marble square symbolizes this uncertainty as it changes from the hard, permanent, decorative, and structural character of the fireplace to the soft, fragile pages of a book: "From ivory depths words rising shed their blackness, blossom and penetrate" (137). When the words become less concrete, more abstract, even abstruse, they provide space for the reader's imagination to play with potential meaning. This transformation of white, in the same manner as colors in "Blue & Green," is then visualized as the marble decomposing and changing its shape, line, and color into an altogether different substance. White changes from the marble square to a piece of paper or a book with ivory pages and black words and then dissolves into the fire as its words imaginatively go up in smoke and rise through the chimney: "Fallen the book, in the flame, in the smoke, in the momentary sparks" (137). Neither reality—the tangible, present world—nor the transient imaginings can represent the sought-after truth. Here realization in the text is momentary, like the "flashes" of understanding or significance. At the end of paragraph five, the reader is left to infer from the cloud transformations cum marble square that reading can only approximate meaning and the writer and reader must be "content with closeness" to meaning (137). Woolf suggests such in a

later *Diary* entry:

> Now is life very solid, or very shifting? I am haunted by the two contradictions. This has gone on for ever: will last for ever; goes down to the bottom of the world—this moment I stand on. Also it is transitory, flying, diaphanous. I shall pass like a cloud on the waves. Perhaps it may be that though we change; one flying after another, so quick, so quick, yet we are somehow successive and continuous—we human beings; & show the light through. But what is the light? I am impressed by the transitoriness of human life to such an extent that I am often saying a farewell— (*D3* 218)

Finally, the return of the heron brings us back home, like the final repeated melody in a symphony; yet the moment is incomplete. The seeming pleasantness of fulfillment is undercut when the question about truth remains unanswered. We are left with a sky full of stars, and the unlimited possibility of translating these into more imaginative visions.

Signification in "Monday or Tuesday" is more ambiguous than in "Blue & Green" because of the higher level of abstraction—immutability of life metaphorized in clouds in "Monday or Tuesday" versus the transformation of colored glass of "Blue & Green." As we view the verbal painting in "Blue & Green" and "Monday or Tuesday" as a means to represent human consciousness, both stories paradoxically deconstruct expectations for certainty. In literature as in painting, color and line are points of visual reference for the reader; we can tell the time of day or weather or climate by an intense white, dark gray, or brilliant green. Color can be used as metaphor for characterization: blue for sadness; gray for indifference or death; red for passion. Line can suggest distance, division, direction, and perspective in painting, and similarly in literature it is used to delineate space and determine connections. However, Woolf subverts the conventional uses of color and line in order to create a paradox of perception in which the reader experiences the simultaneity and spontaneity of consciousness and creates spaces of ambiguity to explore, narrative spaces for meditation and reflection instead of definition and demarcation.

Woolf's attempts to translate painterly elements into writing encourage a new way of reading/looking at the verbal text, and readers create meaning in these short pieces much as we do when we view paintings. The lyrical qualities become prompts for recognizing connections between thought and emotion within a text or a visual image, and in this way thought and emotion are linked in a distinct aesthetic experience. Woolf, through her use of color and her lyrical strategies, invents a new type of narrative that disregards the conventional dichotomy between reason and emotion. This innovative, lyrical story transfers authority to the reader for imagining and creating a text, thus creating a new readership that becomes embedded in the text itself. In "A Sketch of the Past," Woolf represents this moment as "a revelation of some order" in which "we [the writers and readers] are the words; we are the music; we are the thing itself" (*MOB* 72).

Finally the underlying irony in these stories underlines our unusual perspective as readers inside and outside the stories, performing the reading and observing the text. One consistent feature of "Blue & Green" is the sense of transparency throughout; light is reflected or refracted by the lamp. Much of the meaning of this story is dependent on our expectation that this light will "illuminate" the story's subject/object, make it more definite and easier to comprehend. However, as the light reflects through the lamp's glass shade, it does not make anything clearer, and the meaning of this story is not so very transparent. When we look to the narrator to guide us, we get multiple suggestions about color but no distinct outline. In fact, the colors presented in both sections "Green" and "Blue" defy any precise definition exactly because the use of color does not delineate any object; instead, the lyrical strategies confound our ability to rationally delineate the objects. This irony continues in "Monday or Tuesday" when the reader's expectations for conventional narrative are never fulfilled. Readers see the spontaneous shapes of the clouds and the lively colors of afternoon light and hear the sounds of the street and teatime conversation and expect a description of setting and character; however, readers are never given a sequence of events, a main character, or a setting. When the reader cannot draw conclusions about the narrator's perceptions and meditations or about the story elements, the narrative seems failed. Thus the question about truth remains at the story's end.

Implicit in the reading of each story are dialectics between narrative and lyric and between reader and writer; between sequence and simultaneity; between story and point of view. The reader's search for some structure of events is thwarted by the countless deceptive images and ambiguous metaphors of color. The resultant tension provides the motivation for readers to view the stories in new ways that combine reason and emotion into a single aesthetic experience. In "The Narrow Bridge of Art," Woolf sums up the essence of this experience shared by writer and reader: "Every moment is the centre and meeting-place of an extraordinary number of perceptions which have not yet been expressed. Life is always and inevitably much richer than we who try to express it" (*GR* 23). Woolf's goal has been to create a word image that represents the complexity of the aesthetic experience, one that combines emotion and reason—to "attain a different kind of beauty, achieve a symmetry by means of infinite discords, showing all the traces of the minds passage through the world; & achieve in the end, some kind of whole made of shivering fragments; to me this seems the natural process; the flight of the mind" (*PA* 393).

NOTES

1. *Carlyle's House and Other Sketches* is a recent publication of some of Woolf's unknown "shorts." Doris Lessing's Foreword and David Bradshaw's Introduction reiterate the experimental nature of Woolf's short fiction.
2. Woolf began reading for the essay "On Not Knowing Greek" in the winter of 1922, just as *Monday or Tuesday* was published. It was included in *Common Reader, First Series* (1925).
3. See T. S. Eliot's essays "Hamlet," "The Metaphysical Poets" and "Tradition and the Individual Talent."
4. In spite of Woolf's theoretical differences with Eliot's literary dicta, they were colleagues and friends; she addresses him as "My dear Tom" in letters. He helped publish some of her essays in the *Criterion*, and the Woolfs' Hogarth Press published Eliot's *The Waste Land* (1923) typeset by Woolf herself; it is "one of the Hogarth Press's greatest books" (Willis 68).
5. Susan Stanford Friedman's essay "Lyric Subversion in Narrative in Women's Writing: Virginia Woolf and the Tyranny of Plot" suggests that Woolf's use of lyric is characteristic not only of her modernism but also her rebellion against patriarchal literary structures.
6. It is interesting to note that the artists that she copied, Dante Rossetti and William Blake, exhibited dual creativity themselves, combining interests and talents in both visual and verbal arts.
7. See Benzel, "Modern In(ter)vention"
8. In her "Preface" to *Orlando: A Biography*, Woolf credits Roger Fry with her understanding of painting: "To my unrivalled sympathy and imagination of Roger Fry, I owe whatever understanding of the art of painting I may possess" (iii). Also Woolf's biography of Fry reiterates her appreciation of his interest in connections between painting and literature.
9. Panthea Reid's biography of Woolf, *Art and Affection*, identifies Post-Impressionism as a significant influence on Woolf's writing. In addition, Diane Gillespie's *The Sisters' Arts* and her edited collection *The Multiple Muses of Virginia Woolf* demonstrate Woolf's involvement with intersections of the visual and verbal in her collaborations with her sister Vanessa Bell. Both Reid and Gillespie reveal Woolf's writing process as organic, replicating life's uncertainties through its own ambiguous and ambivalent stylistics.
10. Beth Carole Rosenberg's *Virginia Woolf and Samuel Johnson: Common Readers* takes up this dialogic relationship between reader and writer; Woolf's common reader "becomes a metaphor for a rhetorical technique that, like dialogue, allows for flux, freedom, and the lack of stable meaning" (xxi). The reader becomes "interactive and interdependent [in] the process of creation and interpretation" (xxi).
11. See Benzel, "Reading Readers in Virginia Woolf's *Orlando: A Biography*," for discussion of the reader as collaborator.
12. See James Phelan's *Reading People, Reading Plots* and Peter Rabinowitz's *Before Reading* for discussions of the reader's dual role as both reader and author of the text.

13. See Eileen Baldeshwiler, Suzanne C. Ferguson "Defining the Short Story: Impressionism and Form," Wendell V. Harris, Charles May, "Chekhov and the Modern Short Story."

14. "Blue & Green" and "Monday or Tuesday" were first published in the 1921 collection *Monday or Tuesday* and did not appear again until Susan Dick's edition of Woolf's shorter fiction in 1985.

15. Simon Winchester in *Krakatoa* explains that in the mid-1800s advanced technology provided ordinary people with the means to predict and measure their weather conditions.

Chapter 10

"Cut deep and scored thick with meaning": Frame and Focus in Woolf's Later Short Stories

Julia Briggs

"I w[oul]d. like to write a dream story about the top of a mountain. Now why? About lying in the snow; about rings of colour; silence . . . & the solitude," wrote Woolf in June 1937, as she labored over the arguments of *Three Guineas*. "I cant though. But shant I, one of these days, indulge myself in some short releases into that world? Short now for ever. No more long grinds: only sudden intensities. [. . .] And its useless to repeat my old experiments: they must be new to be experiments" (*D5* 95–96). For Woolf, as for other nineteenth- and twentieth-century novelists, the short story was a playground, or else a sketchbook where she renewed her search for "the essential thing," developing through fiction her thoughts on the connections between experience, perception, and imagination, and their expression in words (or paintings). Because she used her stories to carry her thinking forward, their publication was comparatively unimportant: she published eight of them in *Monday or Tuesday* (1921), while others (e.g., "The Evening Party" and "Sympathy"—by no means the slightest) remained uncollected and unpublished during her lifetime. "Lappin and Lapinova," dating from the same period, was published in the United States in 1939, when she felt short of money. Often the stories clustered significantly around a novel. *Mrs. Dalloway* began and ended in short stories: growing out of "Mrs Dalloway in Bond Street" and "The Prime Minister," it was followed by a series of further episodes from Clarissa's party as viewed by different individuals. They are tinged with social satire such as Woolf had used in her first two novels, and in "A Society" and "The Evening Party."

This essay examines three groups of short stories, from the last twelve years of Woolf's life: the first three, a kind of tuning-up for *The Waves*, provide self-reflexive commentary on the nature and outcome of the creative process. Two of three stories written after *The Waves* are uncharacteristically melodramatic, creating a surprisingly violent satire on the English establishment; their distance from Woolf's usual inwardness suggesting a parody that never becomes explicit. The last two stories, from the end of Woolf's life, revert to questions of art and imagination, now seen in relation to the workings of memory, or the "shock-receiving capacity" behind the impulse to write that Woolf had explored in her "Sketch of the Past" (*MOB* 72).

Late in May 1929, Woolf interrogated herself "about this book, The Moths. How am I to begin it? And what is it to be? I feel no great impulse; no fever; only a great pressure of difficulty. Why write it then? Why write at all? Every morning I write a little sketch to amuse myself" (*D3* 229). One of these was "The Lady in the Looking-Glass," a fantasia woven around the painter Ethel Sands coming in from her garden and not reading her letters. One of its typescripts is dated May 28, 1929, the date of the diary entry, while that of "The Fascination of the Pool" is dated the following day, May 29, 1929 (*CSF* 306). "Three Pictures," written that June, according to Leonard Woolf (*DM* 14), followed them closely. Bracing herself to begin her "very serious, mystical, poetical work" (*D3* 131), revisiting the "abstract" mode of the "Time Passes" section of *To the Lighthouse*, Woolf used these three stories to explore a series of conceptual problems that she often returned to: the relation of experience to imagination, and the crystallization of meaning, both in the mind and in a work of art. The complex vision of "The Lady in the Looking-Glass" gives place to the simpler and more individual voices of "The Fascination of the Pool." "Three Pictures" is the most conventional, its setting and ironic twists recalling Thomas Hardy, yet it also explores the way apparently static "pictures" suggest "narratives."

"The Lady in the Looking-Glass," with its punning subtitle, "A Reflection," plays with the cliché of art as a mirror of life, bringing out both the mastery and the loss involved in the act of recording. The mirror's frame, with its sharp exclusions (it cuts and slices off), holds a static world, a world already fixed and finished. It also suggests the way in which paintings differ from writing. The story sets up a series of binary opposites: life and art; room and garden; inside and outside (the frame); words and pictures; imagination and reality; change and stillness; light and shadow; convolvulus and aster; convolvulus and wall (or fantasy and truth). The world of the mirror is opposed to the constant motion of living thoughts as they flush and darken, in rhythm with the fluctuating feelings within the room.

In a reversal of normal expectation, it is the inside of the house (the imagination) that is full of forms of life, fantastic creatures pirouetting or stepping delicately, while "in the looking-glass things had ceased to breathe and lay still in the trance of immortality" (*CSF* 222).

As the changeless work of art, the looking-glass exaggerates what is lost between conception and expression. Woolf had pictured "the greatest book in the world" as one "made entirely solely & with integrity of one's thoughts. Suppose one could catch them before they became 'works of art'? Catch them hot & sudden as they rise in the mind—" (*D3* 102). Lily Briscoe echoes her creator's insight, and frustration: "Beautiful pictures. Beautiful phrases. But what she wished to get hold of was that very jar on the nerves, the thing itself before it has been made anything" (*TTL* 209).

With a glance back at *Jacob's Room*, the Lady's room, like her shoes ("very narrow and long and fashionable" [*CSF* 224]), contains her imagined presence. As in several early short stories, Woolf celebrates the potential of imagination at the expense of achieved art: the figure of the Lady is mysterious, suggesting secrets within secrets, hidden, like her letters; tied with bows of ribbon; shut within the little drawers of her cabinets. The arrival of further letters, delivered by a "large black form," a harbinger of change or death from the temporal world outside, is at once interrupting and confusing. At first the messages seem part of the mirrored world, a "packet of marble tablets"; then they briefly share in the changing life of the room, and are "all dripping with light and colour." Restored once more to the mirror's world, they become "tablets graven with eternal truth," their pages "cut deep and scored with meaning" (*CSF* 223). When the Lady returns from the garden, the fantasies that have accumulated around her absence suddenly collapse, as such fantasies do in earlier stories such as "The Mark on the Wall" or "An Unwritten Novel." Interrupted, the rich world of the imagination falls in on itself. Finally, "Everything dropped from her." The looking-glass exposes the Lady entirely drained of meaning, "naked in that pitiless light. And there was nothing. Isabella was perfectly empty. [. . .] no thoughts. [. . .] no friends. [. . .] nobody. As for her letters, they were all bills" (*CSF* 225).

"The Fascination of the Pool" extends and transforms that contrast between the reflective surface and "the brooding, the ruminating of a mind" (*CSF* 226) at the heart of "The Lady in the Looking-Glass." While the looking-glass had evoked the stillness of the plastic arts as opposed to the flux of words, this story begins with a scene suggesting the various paintings by Vanessa Bell, Duncan Grant, and Roger Fry of the pool at Charleston, with their play of light across the water.[1] Again, there is a contrast between depth and surface appearance—in this case, the water's rippling reflection of a poster advertising a sale, a figure for the "here and now," the immediate material focus of consciousness ("farm horses, agricultural implements and young heifers"). But if the surface is visual, the depths are figured as voices, half-heard voices from the past, like those of "A Haunted House." The disembodied voices of 1851, 1662, 1805—voices of pleasure, love, sorrow—rise from a shared unconscious. Behind them seems to lie some ultimate voice that might lift the others "as a spoon lifts all the things in a bowl of water"—yet this too is an illusion, for "There was always another face, another voice" (*CSF* 227). As the mind floats upward, the pool becomes a painter's image once again, its surface a reflection of the poster pinned to a tree stump.

"Three Pictures" juxtaposes pictures and voices, the painter and the writer, in a third formulation. This time, the picture-forming habit is explicitly defined as an illusion, but an inevitable one: "We cannot possibly break out of the frame of the picture by speaking actual words." The narrator, apparently the village blacksmith (Rodmell's Mr. Dean? see *D5* 247), (mis)interprets the "you" in a car (Woolf herself?) as "a picture of old luxurious aristocratical England" (*CSF* 228). "The Lady in the Looking-Glass" had contrasted the Post-Impressionist flushes of color in the room with their unchanging reflection in the mirror (photography? traditional painting?). "The Fascination of the Pool" set the Post-Impressionist reflections on the surface with the words spoken from the depths. "Three Pictures," by contrast, invokes Victorian "genre" painting: the first represents "The Sailor's Homecoming," complete with neighbors, "a cottage garden ablaze with flowers," and a young wife expecting a baby—a picture heavy with ideological content, designed to makes life "sweeter," "more enviable." Paradoxically, the second picture is not seen but heard,—a cry in the night followed by "dead silence," creating fear and apprehension in the hearer (*CSF* 229). In the third picture (actually several), the peace and stability of the summer are disrupted, have become "a little unreal," torn by that cry. The narrator calls up further scenes of the sailor's homecoming, "so that one picture after another of happiness and satisfaction might be laid over that unrest, that hideous cry, until it was crushed and silenced." Descending into the village (Rodmell), and the churchyard (at the back of Monk's House), we see a grave being dug, while the gravedigger's family picnics beside it—" 'Here, Tommy, you're all covered with earth!' " (*CSF* 230). The grave is for the sailor; the cry was that of his bereaved wife.

Now the three pictures form a new and tragic sequence, constructing a narrative meaning different from its constituent elements. The story illustrates how we continually rewrite the tales we tell ourselves about what goes on around us, commenting self-reflexively on the making of private fictions, as "Sympathy" and "An Unwritten Novel" had done earlier. And as in those two stories, Woolf uses the short story's traditional "twist in the tail," in this case to bind the three pictures into a close-knit plot. The workings of the imagination, its delight in its own richness, and its ability to fill up the emptiness of the material world anticipate *The Waves*, as does the linking of art and loss, and the blend of individual voice with communal consciousness. The Lady's room, emptied of the creatures of the imagination, anticipates the deserted room, house, garden, and landscape of the interludes.

If the stories that precede *The Waves* participate in its abstraction, its exploration of inner consciousness, those that follow focus, as if to compensate, on the fabric of the material and social world: on dials and telescopes, dead pheasants "with soft warm bodies, with limp claws, and still lustrous eyes" (*CSF* 255), on fake pearls. At the end of 1931, exhausted from finishing *The Waves*, Woolf lapsed into a pensiveness, rich with possibilities: "Books come gently surging round me, like icebergs. I could write a book of caricatures" (*D4* 57). In January and February 1932, she wrote three "caricatures," but then abandoned the project. Six years later, two of them—"The Shooting Party" and "The Duchess and the Jeweller"—were published in *Harper's Bazaar*. A third, "Scenes from the Life of a British Naval Officer," remained unpublished. But she had not exhausted her impulse to satire, and in 1937, with *The Years* finally dispatched, she began writing a sequence of short "Portraits" for a book with Vanessa, to be called "Faces & Voices." Eight have survived, and the last four (along with "Uncle Vanya," dating from the same period) are written as self-justifying soliloquies, miniature versions of Alan Bennett's "Talking Heads" (*CSF* 244–47).[2] The popularity of fictional satire (by Huxley, Orwell, Waugh, Wyndham Lewis, and others) may have encouraged such experiments.

Woolf's "Caricatures" or "Scenes from English Life" portray stereotypes satirizing aspects of the British establishment—in particular, its militarism, capitalism, patriarchy, and decaying aristocracy. Woolf's response to "the inherited glory of the rich" was ambivalent: while Vita Sackville-West and her ancestral home at Knole (celebrated in *Orlando*), and various society hostesses—Ottoline Morrell, Sybil Colefax, Christabel Aberconway—appealed to Woolf's sense of tradition, she disliked their imperialist and conservative politics, and suspected them of being Philistines. Like Martin Pargiter in *The Years*, she could sneer at their lack of taste, while enjoying their hospitality (*TY* 191–93). On the issues of patriarchy and militarism, however, Woolf's views are clear: she would analyze their pernicious nature in *Three Guineas*.

The sketchiest of these, "Scenes from the Life of a British Naval Officer," is also the one most closely connected with the previous group through its focus on "seeing," and in particular, a mode of seeing that occludes imagination and perception, and so prevents sympathy for, and even relation with others. One point of origin for it was the comic yet sinister

"Dreadnought Hoax" of 1910, in which the young Virginia Stephen and her brother Adrian, bearded and blacked up, had posed as the retinue of Abyssinian royalty—part of an elaborate practical joke played on the British navy by Adrian's friend Horace Cole. In its day, the Dreadnought battleship represented the height of technology, the pride of the Admiralty. Absurdly disguised, Virginia, Adrian, Duncan Grant, Cole himself, and two others were given an official reception and a tour of the ship by members of the Royal Navy, including Virginia's first cousin Willy (later, Sir William) Fisher (who never forgave her—*D5* 100). Near the end of her life, Woolf turned the story into a comic history to amuse the Rodmell Women's Institute (*D5* 303), yet it left her with a profound horror of battleships, evident in the fifth chapter of *The Voyage Out*, where the British Mediterranean Fleet consists of "two sinister grey vessels, low in the water, and bald as bone, one closely following the other with the look of eyeless beasts seeking their prey" (*VO* 60). It returns in *To the Lighthouse*—the "silent apparition of an ashen-coloured ship" that comes and goes, leaving "a purplish stain upon the bland surface of the sea as if something had boiled and bled, invisibly, beneath" (*TTL* 146). Closer than these in its concern with military precision is the episode from *Jacob's Room* where "The battleships ray out over the North Sea, keeping their stations accurately apart. At a given signal all the guns are trained on a target which (the master gunner counts the seconds, watch in hand—at the sixth he looks up) flames into splinters" (*JR* 136).

In "Scenes from the Life of a British Naval officer" Captain Brace is discovered seated in his cabin, with a map in front of him and a wall of dials behind him, drawing figures with extreme exactness on squared paper. When the ship's gong is struck, he marches with measured tread onto the deck, salutes his crew, and marches to the dining room, his officers falling into step behind him. Here he leaves them, preferring to dine alone, rejecting the muddle of human relationships (*CSF* 232–33). The final paragraph explores the nature of his viewpoint, at once rigid and piercing. As he places a telescope to his eye, as if emphasizing his alien view of the world, it becomes "a horn casing that had formed itself to enclose the penetration of his sight. When he moved the telescope up and down it seemed as if his own long horn-covered eye were moving" (*CSF* 234). The Captain is thus transformed from a creature of flesh and blood into some kind of armored monster—a snail, whose eye on its long stalk, far from demonstrating a Keatsian "snailhorn sensibility,"[3] is rigid and hard, like the bony extrusion of a dinosaur. Though analogies between extinct dinosaurs and over-armored military regimes were not yet commonplace, Woolf exposes how military attitudes deny the wincing tenderness of the human body, figuring its servants as invincibly armored machines. *Three Guineas*, with its critique of militarism, its processions marching in mindless conformity toward destruction, is never far off.

Very little "happens" in this story, and its meaning partly depends on the significance of "seeing," of perception and viewpoint in Woolf's work. In the two remaining "Caricatures," almost too much happens, and events carry more of the meaning than usual. Both stories satirize wealthy Edwardian life, with its lavish weekend shooting parties, its extravagance, and "upstairs, downstairs" mentality. "The Great Jeweller," later "The Duchess and the Jeweller," is in some ways the more disturbing, its explicit anti-Semitism being considered the key critical issue. Like "The Shooting Party," it comprehends social extremes only to acknowledging their distance.

"[T]he richest jeweller in England" is a social climber, a Jew living in a fashionable flat looking out onto Green Park and Piccadilly—and thus very far from the "filthy little alley" in the East End where he grew up. In fact, it is less far than he supposes, since the Jew[eller] is haunted by memories of his own origins that are liable to disrupt his consciousness. He is constantly admonished by the voice of his mother, whose picture hangs on the wall in front of him (*CSF* 248–49). At his shop off Bond Street, the Duchess of Lambourne persuades him to hand over twenty thousand pounds for ten pearls and an invitation to her weekend house party, knowing that he is infatuated with her daughter Diana. Though his mother's voice warns him against it, he allows himself to be deceived. On closer inspection, the pearls turn out to be fake, but he has saved the Duchess's "honor." The Jew pays to maintain the aristocratic society he is in love with, while recognizing its dishonesty: like the fake pearls, it is "Rotten at the centre—rotten at the core!" (*CSF* 253)

Both the Duchess and the Jeweller are crudely drawn—the Duchess is "very large, very fat, tightly girt in pink taffeta, and past her prime" (*CSF* 251). The Jew combines two equally threatening, though usually antithetical racial stereotypes: that of poor refugees, overcrowded and breeding in the East End slums—he began his career by selling stolen dogs in Whitechapel (with an echo of the fourth chapter of *Flush*); but he also belongs to the (imagined) international conspiracy of bankers, masterminding world finance, and familiar from Eliot's "Bleistein," Pound's "Usura" and the caricatures of Nazi propaganda. His racial identity, and even his "character" are exposed by his physical appearance:

> [. . .] his nose, which was long and flexible, like an elephant's trunk, seemed to say by its curious quiver at the nostrils (but it seemed as if the whole nose quivered, not only the nostrils) that he was not satisfied yet; still smelt something under the ground a little further off. Imagine a giant hog in a pasture rich with truffles; after unearthing this truffle and that, still it smells a bigger, blacker truffle under the ground further off. (*CSF* 249)

The jeweler's nose is only the most obvious of a series of traits and gestures that betray his origins. It is a traditional source of racist jokes, the phallic connotations of the nose revealing scarcely suppressed anxieties about sexual contamination. Woolf's description develops that theme by comparing the jeweler to a truffle-hunting pig, not only implying his greed, but also referring to the pig's uncleanness and the Jewish taboo against eating pork (itself a further mark of racial difference). Originally Theorodoric or Isidore Oliver, Woolf would rename the jeweler Oliver Bacon. And while it is the nobly born English duchess who sells him the fake pearls, an early draft of the story refers to the "crowds of Jewesses" remembered from his youth, "beautiful women, with their false pearls, with their false hair" (*CSF* 309). It was customary among East-End Polish Jews for the women to shave their heads on marrying, thereafter wearing wigs—another marker of visible difference.

Woolf was unexpectedly unconscious of her anti-Semitism. In 1937, the year she revised this story, she published *The Years*: it includes a quite different but equally disturbing episode in which the crippled Sara complains to her nephew North of sharing her bath with a Jew—Mr. Abrahamson, her fellow lodger, who leaves a grease mark and hairs around the edge. This time, the Jew is more explicitly associated with contamination. Its defenders maintain that the scene offers a critique rather than an endorsement of anti-Semitic myth, but Sara's singsong repetition, " 'all because of a Jew in my bath, all because of a Jew'," and North's " 'Pah!' " evoke a mood of disgust that the narrative does not attempt to extenuate (*TY* 248–50).[4]

Revising this story in August 1937, Woolf felt "a moment of the old rapture—think of it!—over copying The Duchess & the Jeweller [. . .] there was the old excitement, even in that little extravagant flash" (*D5* 107). She had been working at *Three Guineas* since the beginning of that year, struggling to construct arguments and illustrations, so that a brief escape into "the space & irresponsibility of fiction" (*D5* 109) delighted her. But *Three Guineas*, by contrast, adopts a very different attitude to Jews, comparing their persecution as outsiders to the oppression of women. Readers are warned that under fascism they risk suffering as their mothers did, "because you are Jews, because you are democrats, because of race, because of religion. [. . .]The whole iniquity of dictatorship, whether in Oxford or Cambridge, in Whitehall or Downing Street, against Jews or against women, in England, or in Germany, in Italy or in Spain is now apparent to you" (*TG* 228).

If Woolf herself failed to notice the prejudice reflected in "The Duchess and the Jeweller," it was evident enough to the New York agent Jacques Chambrun who commissioned it, or else to his client. After accepting her synopsis, he backed down, explaining that a "psychological study of a Jew" would be unacceptable to his client (at this point Chambrun himself attracted a racist slur—"that maroon coloured sharper, as we suspect him"

[*D5* 107, 112–13; see also Lee, *Virginia Woolf* 679]). It was Leonard who intervened to effect a compromise, persuading Virginia to remove the more explicit references to the jeweler's Jewishness, and Chambrun to accept her changes.

Leonard was also indirectly responsible for Woolf's crude stereotype. At Cambridge he had absorbed the anti-Semitism of his upper middle-class English friends, and it is reflected in his early fiction. It was Leonard's description of the Jewish nose in his short story "Three Jews," Leonard's assertion of Jewish energy in his novel *The Wise Virgins* that Virginia had echoed, feeling (if she thought about it at all) that if Leonard wrote thus about his own race, there could be "no offence, no offence in the world" in following his example.[5] Despite, or even because of, her love for Leonard, Virginia found her mother-in-law and relatives by marriage at best tedious, and at worst distasteful, as successive diary entries reveal. It may or may not be an accident that the name of the Jew in the bath is Abrahamson: obviously a generic name for the sons of Abraham, it was also the name of Leonard's most successful cousin, Sir Martin Abrahamson (*D5* 117). The Jew in "The Duchess and the Jeweller," like Abrahamson in *The Years* episode, may articulate suppressed irritation with her in-laws, who no doubt figured all that she found most alien in Leonard (as in-laws usually do).[6] If that is so, there may be an analogy to be drawn with the figure of the Duchess of Lambourne who recalls another "mother-in-law" figure, in this case, Vita's mother, Lady Sackville-West. For Woolf's story reworks elements of a scene of four years earlier, when Lady Sackville-West accused her daughter of having changed twelve of her pearls for fakes.

Woolf consistently linked Vita with pearls, picturing her as "pink glowing, grape clustered, pearl hung" (*D3* 52). When she sat on the floor beside her at Tavistock Square, Virginia would knot "her pearls into heaps of great lustrous eggs" (*D3* 117). The ten pearls in the story, rolled from a wash-leather pouch that "looked like a lean yellow ferret," resemble "the eggs of some heavenly bird" as they roll out of "the slit in the ferret's belly" (*CSF* 252).[7] On April 18, 1928, while Vita was visiting the family solicitor, her mother turned up and started to scream abuse at her: "Give me your pearls, . . . twelve of them belong to me, and I wish to see how many you have changed, you thief" (as Suzanne Raitt has shown, she was obsessed with the idea that her jewellery was fake [113–18]). Lady Sackville-West marched back to her Rolls, sending her chauffeur to order Vita to go to the jeweler and have twelve pearls cut from her necklace. Vita went straight out to her mother's car, and there and then cut up the pearl necklace in front of her, handing over the twelve largest pearls to her in the middle of the street. Later that afternoon, Vita visited Virginia, who recounted the episode in her diary, commenting, "The woman is said to be mad" (*D3* 180; Glendinning 192–93).

If Lady Sackville-West was indeed a model for the Duchess, Woolf's position in loving her daughter (Diana/Vita) is analogous to that of the Jew. A further verbal echo suggests that she may have shared the Jeweller's subversive desire to blow up the existing social order. Gloating over his jewels, he sees them as

'Tears!' said Oliver, looking at the pearls.
'Heart's blood!' he said, looking at the rubies.
'Gunpowder!' he continued, rattling the diamonds so that they flashed and blazed.
'Gunpowder enough to blow up Mayfair—sky high, high, high!' (*CSF* 250)

Woolf's diary for February 1932, the month she drafted "The Great Jeweller," refers to her feminist sequel to *A Room of One's Own*, "for which I have collected enough powder to blow up St. Paul's" (*D4* 77). The jeweler also resembles Woolf in being haunted by the voice of his dead mother, as she was before she exorcised it by writing *To the Lighthouse* (*MOB* 80–81). And Phyllis Lassner has noticed that the jeweler's original name—Isidore Oliver—becomes that of "Isa Oliver," the very English heroine of *Between the Acts*, and the victim, not of racial, but of gender oppression (138–39).

Preparing "The Duchess and the Jeweller" and "The Shooting Party" for Jacques Chambrun, Woolf may have supposed that an American audience might find satire on the English class system more sympathetic. In the event, they appeared simultaneously in the London and the New York editions of *Harper's Bazaar* in the spring of 1938. If one source for "The Duchess and the Jeweller" lies in Vita's biography, that of "The Shooting Party" seems to be recorded in a diary entry for December 29, 1931: "Christabel's story of the Hall Caines suggested a caricature of Country house life, with the red-brown pheasants" (*D4* 57). Christabel (the Hon. Mrs Henry Maclaren, soon to be Lady Aberconway) was a society hostess who had visited Virginia earlier that month. Thomas Hall Caine wrote cheap popular novels and lived on the Isle of Man until his recent death in his late seventies. But what exactly was the story that Christabel told Woolf? The Hall Caines lived at Greeba Castle—not an ancestral home (as in Woolf's story), but merely a crenellated house that Hall Caine had acquired and restored to provide himself with the kind of home suited to his success. The single link between Hall Caine and Woolf's story was a scandal concerning an illegitimate son, said to have been born to one of his domestic staff, though this scarcely explains the centrality of "the red-brown pheasants" in both diary entry and story.

"The Shooting Party" (or "Scenes from Country Life") may be Woolf's least typical fiction, in terms of setting, characters, and violent denouement, yet it finds a curious echo in *Three Guineas* (written five years later). Observing that, before 1919, marriage "was the only profession open" to women, Woolf added, "The influence of the pheasant upon love alone deserves a chapter to itself." An endnote explains that a mother's concern to marry off her daughters was potentially in conflict with a father's requirement that a shooting party guest should be a "decent shot" (*TG* 160, 288). But though heaps of dead pheasants lie at the center of "The Shooting Party," it has little to say about courtship or love. Instead, it links the degeneracy of the upper classes with what Woolf saw as the wanton—and essentially masculine—destructiveness of hunting. As *Three Guineas* had pointed out, "Scarcely a human being in the course of history has fallen to a woman's rifle; the vast majority of birds and beasts have been killed by you [i.e. men], not by us [women]" (*TG* 120). Within Woolf's immediate circle it was another in-law—her brother-in-law Clive Bell—who went in for shooting. In 1908, Vanessa wrote to her sister from Scotland, "Clive killed three rabbits. Oh Billy! poor little furry beasts. It surpasses my imagination entirely, this wish to kill—does it yours?" (Bell, Vanessa 69). The cruelty of pheasant shooting also occurs in fiction, most memorably, perhaps, in Hardy's *Tess of the D'Urbervilles*, where it is used to make a similar point about the carelessness of the British upper classes.[8]

"The Shooting Party" represents the killing of large numbers of pheasants as an example of wanton brutality, an indulgence in mass destruction that ultimately recoils upon those who practice it—in this case, the (suggestively named) Rashleighs, an old English family, whose last members stay on in their decaying stately home on the family estate. Their way of life dramatizes the danger of separate spheres that Woolf would expose in *Three Guineas*: the men are preoccupied with war, womanizing, or hunting and shooting, while their womenfolk sit by the fire and sew, complacently, even complicitly, gloating over their brother's sexual exploits. Powerless to resist his violence, they are also a little proud of him. A younger generation has died violently on the battle or the hunting field, and now only the squire and his two aging sisters survive. The sisters, confined to the house, are clawed and feathered like the pheasants, and like them, helpless victims, as stupid as they are doomed. When the squire returns from the shoot, his three huge gun dogs set upon their spaniel (does he, significantly in 1937, let "slip the dogs of war?"). As the squire curses and lays about him with a whip, in his efforts to regain control of his dogs, he knocks his elder sister into the fireplace, where the family shield falls on top of her and kills her. The emblems on the shield—grapes, mermaids, spears—indicate the family weaknesses for drinking, womanizing, and war making. Upper-class English life is here characterized by a passion for imperial conquest and pillage, reflected in miniature in the enthusiasm for blood sports. The fall of more than the house of Rashleigh seems foretold by the final sentence: "The wind lashed the panes of glass; shots volleyed in the Park and a tree fell. And then King Edward in the silver frame slid, toppled and fell too" (*CSF* 270).

The original holograph and the earlier typescript of "The Shooting Party" are both dated January 19, 1932 (*CSF* 309), the day after the Woolfs drove to Ham Spray to see the dying Lytton Strachey. That version begins with Miss Antonia embroidering as she listens to the firing of the shooting party growing ever closer to home. It introduces Wing, the keeper, and Milly Masters, the handsome housekeeper, with a long scar along her jaw— the squire's mistress, and mother of his illegitimate son. It ends with the words quoted above. Rereading the story in July 1937, before sending it to Chambrun, Woolf must have found it inadequate, since she now added some framing paragraphs at the beginning and the end, resorting to a familiar figure from earlier work: the middle-aged woman sitting in the corner of a railway carriage, who appears in "An Unwritten Novel" (1920), in chapter III of *Jacob's Room* (1922), and, most famously, in her essay "Mr. Bennett and Mrs. Brown" (1924).

The published text thus begins with a woman "telling over the story now, lying back in her corner" (*CSF* 254). The initials on her suitcase, "M. M.," the long scar on her jaw and the brace of pheasants identify her as Milly Masters, the Rashleighs' housekeeper. "[L]ike somebody imitating the noise that someone else makes, she made a little click at the back of her throat: 'Chk. Chk.' "—precisely the noise Miss Antonia made while embroidering, and itself an echo of the whirring cries of the doomed pheasants. "[W]hy should not the eyes there, gleaming, moving, be the ghost of a family, of an age, of a civilization dancing over the grave?" (CSF 260). Milly Masters, in the railway carriage, seems to contemplate the fall of the family with a certain grim satisfaction.

Revising "The Shooting Party," Woolf suddenly

> [. . .] saw the form of a new novel. Its to be first the statement of the theme: then the restatement: & so on: repeating the same story: singling out this and then that: until the central idea is stated. [. . .] What happened was this: when I finished the S[hooting]. P[arty]. I thought, now that the woman [Milly Masters] has called a taxi; I will go on to meet, say, Christabel [Aberconway, who had originally told her the story], at T[avistock]. Square who tells the story again: or I will expatiate upon my own idea in telling the story; or I will find some other person at the S[hooting]. P[arty]. whose life I will tell: but all the scenes must be controlled, & radiate to a centre. [. . .] c[oul]d. be a concentrated small book: c[oul]d. contain many varieties of mood. [. . .] I must keep the idea at the back of my mind for a year or two, while I do Roger [Fry] &c. (*D5* 114–15)

The search for a frame that would enhance the significance of her story suggests that Woolf was uncertain whether she had communicated everything she had in mind, even after the addition of the scene on the train (her phrase, "the woman has called a taxi," picks up more or less where the published short story leaves off). The concern to provide a clarifying frame recalls Woolf's "novel-essay," *The Pargiters*, the initial draft of the 1880 section of *The Years*, in which fictional episodes alternate with a framing commentary on their social significance (an experiment abandoned a few months later). If "The Shooting Party" also required further exposition, Woolf had in mind for it a subtler method of framing and interrogating her narrative, and one that would allow for further reflections on her art, the theme at the heart of so many of her short stories. Such a scheme is further connected with *The Years* through the image of a circle with spokes that "radiate to a centre," a motif that recurs in the novel (indeed, C. Ruth Miller considers it the novel's organizing principle [33]). It is, perhaps, regrettable that Woolf never found an opportunity to try out this new form.

Several late short stories create frames or draw on images of focusing to explore how the casual accidents of life can be endowed with the force and pressure of a work of art. The most fully achieved of these is "The Searchlight," "the old Henry Taylor telescope story that's been humming in my mind these 10 years," Woolf called it at the end of January 1939, turning to it from her biography of Roger Fry (*D5* 204). The telescope, employed in "Scenes from the Life of a British Naval Officer" and elsewhere, focuses on a distant object, isolating, enlarging, and enclosing it in a circular frame, but as Woolf worked on successive drafts of this story,[9] she combined it with the image of the searchlight, a more up-to-date version of the lighthouse beam, which also focuses upon and illuminates its object, as does the process of fiction making. Holly Henry, in contextualizing this story, points out that both the telescope and the searchlight had been developed for military purposes, and that Woolf particularly associated the searchlight with war (65). As its "rods of light wheeled across the sky," we learn that "It was peace then; the air force was practising; searching for enemy aircraft in the sky" (*CSF* 269).

Setting the action of "The Searchlight" between the wars is one of several links with Woolf's last novel *Between the Acts*, which also takes place as war approaches. It, too, begins on a summer's night, and is steeped in theatrical imagery. "The Searchlight" adopts a deliberately theatrical style and setting: it is played out on the balcony of one of London's Pall Mall clubs, looking out on the backdrop of Green Park and the play of the searchlight/spotlight. And as in *Between the Acts*, the narrative itself is merely an overture or "curtain-raiser" to another play that will take place offstage. Mrs. Ivimey (almost the only character named) promises her listeners a story: "If they liked, she would try to tell it. There was still time before the play" (*CSF* 269). It trails off in mystery—"The light [. . .] only falls here and there (272)."

"The searchlight had passed on. [. . .] And it was time they went on to the play" (*CSF* 272). Within the time allowed, Mrs. Ivimey performs her story with a strong sense of drama, though at one point she is interrupted by a fragment from a different play:

> Then a voice behind them said:
> 'Right you are. Friday.'
> They all turned, shifted, felt dropped down on to the balcony again. (*CSF* 271)

"The Searchlight" plays upon time and space, their complex correspondences and drastic foreshortening, not merely through acts of memory but through more mechanical means of expansion or illumination. As the searchlight strikes the balcony, highlighting a single "bright disc," Mrs. Ivimey "sees" the bright disc of her great-grandfather's telescope, thus prompting her to relate the story (*CSF* 268).[10] Her listeners are transported to a ruined tower looking out onto the "green and blue" distance of the Yorkshire moors, and the Ivimeys' party is replaced by a lonely boy, a hundred years earlier, for the telescope's action of making far-off things close seems to operate through time as well as space, and what is framed and focused in its circular field acquires the intensity, stillness, and permanence of a work of art.

"So much depends then, thought Lily Briscoe, [. . .] upon distance: whether people are near us or far from us" (*TTL* 207). The story's romantic vision of a decaying tower and a lonely boy recreates a distant, timeless world, corresponding to "that great Cathedral space which was childhood" (*MOB* 81). Gazing up at the stars ("very permanent, very unchanging"), the boy wonders about their origins, and his own: " 'What are they? Why are they? And who am I?' " Then he turns the telescope onto the earth, and "focussed it," growing ever lower and closer to the unknown object of his search (*CSF* 270–71). What he ultimately sees, with all the intimacy that the telescope can confer, is a man and a woman kissing—metaphorically, a primal scene—his own point of origin, as it is more explicitly Mrs. Ivimey's: " 'if there hadn't been a telescope [. . .] I shouldn't be sitting here now!' " (CSF 270). And just as his excitement carries the boy across the moors to the girl, so Mrs. Ivimey then becomes the girl that awaits him, her own great-grandmother, encountering the boy in the theatrically lit circle of the searchlight: "A shaft of light fell upon Mrs Ivimey as if someone had focussed the lens of a telescope upon her. [. . .] She had risen. She had something blue on her head. She had raised her hand, as if she stood in a doorway, amazed" (*CSF* 272). Between them, searchlight and telescope have fulfilled the purposes of art, crossing and overcoming the cold distances of time and space, focusing upon and illuminating our origins.

Between the Acts ends with the approach of war and the possibilities of new life. When it was virtually finished, Woolf turned to a short story she had kept in mind for three years or more: "I shall brew some moments of high pressure. I think of taking my mountain top—that persistent vision—as a starting point" (*D5* 341). The outcome of that impulse, "The Symbol," is evidently provisional and unfinished compared to "The Searchlight," but like the earlier story, it brings distant events into close-up, this time through the use of field glasses. More explicitly than in "The Searchlight," "The Symbol" takes place on a balcony that overlooks "the main street of the Alpine summer resort, like a box at a theatre." As in the sitting room of "The Lady and the Looking-Glass," there is "something fantastic" about the street entertainments played out below, something "airy, inconclusive." Beyond the street stands the mountain, immutable and inescapable: " 'The mountain,' the lady wrote, sitting on the balcony of her hotel, 'is a symbol . . .' She paused. She could see the topmost height through her [field] glasses. She focussed the lens, as if to see what the symbol was" (*CSF* 288).

As in "The Searchlight," "so much depends . . . upon distance": the mountain changes its appearance, from white to blood red; sometimes appearing close, at other times distant as a cloud, yet it never disappears. Its looming presence is at once oppressive, yet longed for—in the letter she is writing, the lady links the summit of the mountain with her own yearning for freedom as her mother lay dying, imagining that "when I reach that point—I have never told anyone for it seemed so heartless; I shall be at the top" (*CSF* 289). Both her letter, and Woolf's several drafts of the story repeatedly try to pin down the meaning of the mountain: it was "a cliché [. . .]The symbol of effort," yet it was also "not at all a cliché: in fact it was something that far from running into ink spontaneously, remained almost unspeakable even to herself" (*CSF* 312). Whether that "something . . . almost unspeakable" refers to the lady's long-suppressed yearning for freedom, or to the mountain's phallic appearance or to its nature as a source of sudden death remains obscure. In alternative versions, the lady would "be happy to die. . . . in the crater," would "find the answer" there. And in the same version, she goes on to wonder why we want "to climb to the top of the mountain. Why [. . .] have we the desire? Who gave it us?" (*CSF* 313).

Woolf adds to the metafictional dimension of "The Symbol," a story about a woman writing, a specific connection with the process of writing itself: in "The Lady in the Looking-Glass," the letters had acted as messages from a temporal world beyond. In this story, the lady's struggle against cliché as she writes reflects the writer's sustained commitment "To purify the dialect of the tribe."[11] And her letter enacts the writer's imaginative intimacy with violence and sudden death, echoing Woolf's own sense that "the shock-receiving capacity is what makes me a writer" (*MOB* 72). The sudden disappearance of the climbers from the lady's field of vision finds its equivalence on the written page:

> [. . .]'They are now crossing a crevasse . . .' The pen fell from her hand, and the drop of ink straggled in a zig zag line down the page. The young men had disappeared. (*CSF* 290)

Here, the printed marks across the page, echoing the ink marks of the lady's letter, reproduce the disaster visually—the climbers are like the dots of the aposiopesis, momentarily strung out across the page. When they fall, they form a zig zag repeated by the movement of her pen.

"The Symbol" explores the obscure connections between desire—the longing for the unattainable—death, and language, as the pen- and print-marks directly record the climbers' fall. In this, almost her last short story, Woolf reaches through a series of different frames—theatrical, epistolary— to focus upon the permanent mystery of our surroundings, and the continual shock of death. Returning to her interrupted letter, the lady writes, "They died in an attempt to discover . . . ," but she does not know how to end either the sentence, or her letter: "There seemed no fitting conclusion" (290). The date on the typescript is March 1, 1941.

NOTES

1. See, e.g., Vanessa Bell: *Charleston Pond*, 1916 (Charleston Trust); Duncan Grant: *Landscape, Sussex*, 1920 (Tate Britain) and *The Barn by the Pond*, 1925 (Aberdeen Art Gallery); Roger Fry: *Farm Pond, Charleston*, 1918 (Wakefield Art Gallery), all reproduced Naylor 247, 246, 215, 214.
2. For a recent account of these, see Humm.
3. "To [. . .] select from [Roger Fry's writings on art history] so as to show his snail-horn sensibility trembling this way and that would require the skill of a trained hand," Woolf wrote of Fry (*RF* 96), echoing Keats's phrase, "that trembling delicate and snail-horn perception of Beauty" (from his letter to Benjamin Haydon, April 8, 1818).
4. See e.g. Bradshaw, "Hyams Place."
5. See the description of the cemetery-keeper's nose in "Three Jews" 11 (reprinted in *Virginia Woolf Bulletin* 7): "a nose, by Jove, Sir, one of the best, one of those noses, white and shiny . . . immensely broad, curving down, like a broad highroad from between the bushy eye-brows down over the lips. And side face, it was colossal; it stood out like an elephant's trunk with its florid curves and scrolls" and the end of ch. III of *The Wise Virgins* 51–52.
6. See Lee, *Virginia Woolf* 314–35.

7. In "Sketch of the Past," Woolf recalled Mr. Gibbs giving "Vanessa and myself two ermine skins, with slits down the middle out of which poured endless wealth—streams of silver" (*MOB* 74).

8. See the end of chapter xli as well as Hardy's "Triolet" and "The Puzzled Game-Birds" in *Collected Poems* 135.

9. For an account of these, see Graham 379–93.

10. Woolf discusses "seeing" ("by wh[ich]. I mean the sudden state when something moves one") in a diary entry for November 1, 1937 (*D5* 118).

11. T. S. Eliot, *Little Gidding*, § 2, line 127, translating Stéphane Mallarmé's "Donner un sens plus pur aux mots de la tribu," "Le Tombeau d'Edgar Poe," line 6 (and one aim of modernism).

Works Cited

Abbott, Reginald. "What Miss Kilman's Petticoat Means: Virginia Woolf, Shopping, and Spectacle." *Modern Fiction Studies* 38 (Spring 1993): 193–216.

Alexander, Jean. *The Venture of Form in the Novels of Virginia Woolf.* Port Washington NY: Kennikat, 1974.

Alpers, Antony. *The Life of Katherine Mansfield.* Oxford: Oxford University Press, 1982.

Appadurai, Arjun, ed. *The Social Life of Things: Commodities in Cultural Perspective.* Cambridge: Cambridge University Press, 1986.

Ardis, Ann. *New Women, New Novels: Feminism and Early Modernism.* New Brunswick: Rutgers University Press, 1990.

Bal, Mieke. *Narratology. Introduction to the Theory of Narrative.* Second edition. Toronto: University of Toronto Press, 1997.

Baldeshwiler, Eileen. "The Lyric Short Story: The Sketch of a History." May, *New* 231–44.

Baldwin, Dean R. *Virginia Woolf: A Study of the Short Fiction.* Boston: Twayne, 1989.

Banks, Joanne Trautmann. "Virginia Woolf and Katherine Mansfield." *The English Short Story: 1880–1945.* Ed. Joseph Flora. Boston: Twayne, 1985. 57–82.

Barnes, Julian. *Flaubert's Parrot.* London: Picador, 2003.

Barolsky, Paul. "Water Pater and Bernard Berenson." *New Criterion* 2 (April 1984): 47–57.

Baron, Wendy. *Ethel Sands and Her Circle.* London: Peter Owen, 1977.

Barrett, Eileen and Patricia Cramer, eds. *Virginia Woolf: Lesbian Readings.* New York: New York University Press, 1997.

———, eds. *Re:Reading, Re:Writing, Re:Teaching Virginia Woolf.* New York: Pace University Press, 1995.

Barzilai, Shuli. "Virginia Woolf's Pursuit of Truth: 'Monday or Tuesday,' 'Moments of Being' and 'The Lady in the Looking-Glass.'" *The Journal of Narrative Technique* 18 (1988): 199–210.

———. "Virginia Woolf's Pursuit of Truth: 'Monday or Tuesday,' 'Moments of Being' and 'the Lady in the Looking-Glass.'" McNees II. 19–30.

Baudrillard, Jean. *The System of Objects.* Trans. James Benedict. London: Verso, 1996.

Bazin, Nancy Topping. *Virginia Woolf and the Androgynous Vision.* New Brunswick: Rutgers University Press, 1973.

Beer, Gillian. "The Island and the Aeroplane: The Case of Virginia Woolf." *Virginia Woolf: The Common Ground: Essays by Gillian Beer.* Edinburgh: Edinburgh University Press, 1996. 149–78.

Bell, Clive. *Art.* 1913 New York: Capricorn Books, 1995.

Bell, Quentin. *Virginia Woolf: A Biography.* New York: Harcourt Brace Jovanovich, 1972.

Bell, Vanessa. *The Selected Letters of Vanessa Bell.* Ed. Regina Marler. New York: Pantheon Books, 1994.

Benjamin, Walter. *Illuminations.* Trans. Harry Zohn. New York: Schocken, 1969.

Bennett, Bridget, ed. *Ripples of Dissent: Women's Stories of Marriage in the 1890s.* London: J. M. Dent & Sons, 1996.

Bennett, Paula. "Critical Cliterodectomy: Female Sexual Imagery and Feminist Psychoanalytic Theory." *Signs. Journal of Women and Culture in Society* 18 (1993): 235–59.

Benzel, Kathryn N. "Modern In(ter)vention: Reading the Visual." *Visual Resources* 19:4 (Fall 2003): 321–38.

———. "Reading Readers in Virginia Woolf's *Orlando: A Biography.*" *Style* 28:2 (Summer 1994): 169–82.

———. "Verbal Painting in Virginia Woolf's Short Fiction: 'Monday or Tuesday' and 'Blue and Green.'" Discovering Virginia Woolf's Short Fiction. M/MLA Convention. Regal Riverfront Hotel, St. Louis. 5 Nov. 1998.

———. "Woolf's Early Experimentation with Consciousness: 'Kew Gardens,' Typescript to Publication, 1917–1919." *Virginia Woolf: Turning the Centuries: Selected Papers from the Ninth Annual Conference on Virginia Woolf.* Ed. Ann Ardis and Bonnie Kime Scott. New York: Pace University Press, 2000. 192–99.

Berman, Marshall. *All That Is Solid Melts into Air: The Experience of Modernity.* New York: Penguin, 1982.

Bishop, Edward. "Pursuing 'It' through 'Kew Gardens.'" Baldwin, 109–16.

———. "Pursuing 'It' Through 'Kew Gardens'." *Studies in Short Fiction* 19.3 (1982): 269–75.

Blackmer, Corinne E. "Lesbian Modernism in the Shorter Fiction of Virginia Woolf and Gertrude Stein." Barrett and Cramer, 78–94.

Blackstone, Bernard. *Virginia Woolf: A Commentary.* London: Hogarth Press, 1949.

Bowen, Elizabeth. "The Faber Book of Modern Short Stories." May, *New* 256–62.

Bowlby, Rachel. *Just Looking: Consumer Culture in Dreiser, Gissing and Zola.* New York: Methuen, 1985.

Bradshaw, David. "Hyam's Place: *The Years,* the Jews and the British Union of Fascists." *Women Writers of the 1930s: Gender, Politics and History.* Ed. Maroula Joannou. Edinburgh: Edinburgh University Press, 1999. 179–89.

———. "Introduction." *Carlyle's House and Other Sketches.* Ed. David Bradshaw. London: Hesperus Press Limited, 2003. xiii–xxv.

Briggs, Julia. "Virginia Woolf and 'The Proper Writing of Lives.'" *The Art of Literary Biography.* Ed. John Batchelor. Oxford: Clarendon, 1995. 245–66.

———. "Writing by Numbers: An Exploration of Woolf's Revisionary Practices" (unpublished paper 2003)

Brosnan, Leila. *Reading Virginia Woolf's Essays and Journalism.* Edinburgh: Edinburgh University Press, 1997.

Broughton, Panthea Reid. "The Blasphemy of Art: Fry's Aesthetics and Woolf's Non-'Literary' Stories." Gillespie, *Multiple Muses* 36–57.

Brussof, Valery. "In the Mirror." *The Republic of the Southern Cross and Other Stories.* London: Constable, 1918. 55–72.

Burke, Daniel, FSC. *Beyond Interpretation: Studies in the Modern Short Story.* Troy, NY: Whitston, 1991.

Castle, Terry. *The Apparitional Lesbian: Female Homosexuality and Modern Culture.* New York: Columbia University Press, 1993.

Caughie, Pamela L. *Virginia Woolf and Postmodernism: Literature in Quest and Question of Itself.* Urbana: University of Illinois Press, 1991.

———, ed. *Virginia Woolf in the Age of Mechanical Reproduction.* New York: Garland, 2000.

Chapman, R. T. "The Lady in the Looking-Glass: Modes of Perception in a Short Story by Virginia Woolf." *Modern Fiction Studies* 18 (1972): 331–37.

Chekhov, Anton. "Gusev." *The Witch and Other Stories.* Trans. Constance Black Garnett. Project Gutenberg Etext. 1999. 15 May 2004. (http://gutenberg.net/etext/1944).

———. "Happiness." Project Gutenberg Etext. 1999. 15 May 2004. (http://gutenberg.net/etext/1944).

———. *Letters on the Short Story, the Drama and Other Literary Topics.* Ed. Louis S. Friedland. London: Vision Press, 1965.

Chinitz, David. " 'Dance, Little Lady': Poets, Flappers, and the Gendering of Jazz." In *Modernism, Gender, and Culture: A Cultural Studies Approach.* Ed. Lisa Rado. New York: Garland, 1997. 319–36.

Conrad, Joseph. *The Nigger of the Narcissus.* New York: Doubleday, 1924.

Cook, Blanche Wiesen. " 'Women Alone Stir My Imagination': Lesbianism and the Cultural Tradition." *Signs. Journal of Women in Culture and Society* 4 (1979): 718–39.

Cox, Crystal D. " 'She Looks Quite Capable of Having Deceived': Critical Avenues and Answers in Virginia Woolf's 'Memoirs of a Novelist.' " Barrett and Cramer, *Re:Reading* 162–7.

Cramer, Patricia. "Notes from Underground: Lesbian Ritual in the Writings of Virginia Woolf." Hussey and Neverow, *Miscellanies* 177–88.

———. " 'Pearls and the Porpoise': *The Years*—A Lesbian Memoir." Barrett and Cramer 222–40.

Cuddy-Keane, Melba. "The Rhetoric of Feminist Conversation: Virginia Woolf and the Trope of the Twist." Mezei 137–61.

———. "Virginia Woolf and the Varieties of Historicist Experience." *Virginia Woolf and the Essay.* Ed. Beth Carole Rosenberg and Jeanne Dubino. Basingstoke: Macmillan, 1997. 59–77.

———. "Virginia Woolf, Sound Technologies, and the New Aurality." Caughie 69–96.

Dahl, Christopher C. "Virginia Woolf's *Moments of Being* and Autobiographical Tradition in the Stephen Family." *Journal of Modern Literature* 10.2 (1983): 175–96.

Daiches, David. *Virginia Woolf.* New York: New Directions, 1942.

Davenport, Tony. "The Life of a Monday or Tuesday." *Virginia Woolf: New Critical Essays.* Ed. Patricia Clements and Isobel Grundy. London: Vision and Barnes & Noble, 1983. 157–75.

De Araujo, Victor. " 'A Haunted House': The Shattered Glass." In Baldwin 121–29.

DeSalvo, Louise. "Lighting the Cave: The Relationship between Vita Sackville-West and Virginia Woolf." *Signs. Journal of Women in Culture and Society.* 8 (1982): 195–214.

———. "Shakespeare's *Other* Sister." *New Feminist Essays on Virginia Woolf.* Ed. Jane Marcus. Lincoln: University Nebraska Press, 1981. 61–81.

———. *Virginia Woolf's Final Voyage. A Novel in the Making.* London: Macmillan, 1980.

DeSalvo, Louise and Mitchell H. Leaska, eds. *The Letters of Vita Sackville-West to Virginia Woolf.* London: Virago, 1992.

Desmond, Raymond. *The History of Kew.* London: Harvill, 1995.

Dick, Susan, ed. *The Complete Shorter Fiction of Virginia Woolf.* Second Edition New York: Harcourt Brace & Co., 1989.

———. " 'I am Not Trying to Tell a Story': Three Short Fictions by Virginia Woolf." *Virginia Woolf: Critical Assessments II.* Ed. Eleanor McNees. East Sussex: Helm Information Ltd, 1994. 31–46.

———. " 'I am not trying to tell a story': Three Short Fictions by Virginia Woolf." *English Studies in Canada* 15.2 (1989): 162–77.

Eagleton, Mary. "Gender and Genre." Hanson, *Re-reading* 55–68.

Ejxenbaum, B. M. "O. Henry and the Theory of the Short Story." May, *New* 81–80.

Eliot, T. S. "Hamlet." *Selected Prose of T.S. Eliot.* Ed. Frank Kermode. NewYork: Harvest Books, 1975.

———. "The Metaphysical Poets." *Criticism: The Major Texts.* Ed. Walter Jackson Bate. New York: Harcourt, Brace & World, Inc., 1952. 529–534.

———. "Tradition and the Individual Talent." *The Critical Tradition: Classic Texts and Contemporary Trends*, 2nd Edition. Ed. David H. Richter. Boston: Bedford Books, 1998. 498–503.

Engler, Bernd. "Imagining Her-story: Virginia Woolf's 'The Journal of Mistress Joan Martyn' as Historiographical Metafiction." *Journal of the Short Story in English* 20 (1993): 9–26.

Felski, Rita. *The Gender of Modernity.* Cambridge: Harvard University Press, 1995.

Ferguson, Suzanne. "Defining the Short Story: Impressionism and Form." May, *New* 218–30.

———. "Defining the Short Story: Impressionism and Form." Hoffman and Murphy, 287–300.

———. "The Rise of the Short Story in the Hierarchy of Genres." Lohafer and Clarey, 176–92.

Fisher, Philip. *Making and Effacing Art: Modern American Art in a Culture of Museums.* New York: Oxford University Press, 1991.

Fleishman, Avrom. "Forms of the Woolfian Short Story." *Virginia Woolf: Revaluation and Continuity*, Ed. Ralph Freedman. Berkeley: University of California Press, 1980, 44–70.

Flint, Kate. Introduction. Virginia Woolf, *Flush.* London, Oxford: Oxford University Press, 1998.

———. "Revising *Jacob's Room*: Virginia Woolf, Women, and Language." *Review of English Studies* 42 (167): 361–79.

———. *The Woman Reader 1837–1914*. Oxford: Oxford University Press, 1993.

Flora, Joseph M. ed. *The English Short Story 1880–1945*. Boston: Twayne, 1985.

Flynn, Elizabeth. "Gender and Reading." *Gender and Reading: Essays on Readers, Texts, and Contexts*. Ed. Elizabeth Flynn and Patrocinio P. Schweickart. Baltimore: Johns Hopkins University Press, 1986. 267–88.

Fox, Alice. "Virginia Liked Elizabeth." *Virginia Woolf: A Feminist Slant*. Ed. Jane Marcus. Lincoln: University of Nebraska Press, 1983. 37–51.

Friedberg, Anne. *Window Shopping: Cinema and the Postmodern*. Berkeley: University of California Press, 1993.

Friedman, Norman. "Recent Short Story Theories: Problems in Definition." Lohafer and Clarey, 13–31.

———. "What Makes a Short Story Short?" Hoffman and Murphy, 100–115.

Friedman, Susan Stanford. "Lyric Subversion of Narrative in Women's Writing: Virginia Woolf and the Tyranny of Plot." In *Reading Narrative: Form, Ethics, Ideology*. Ed. James Phelan. Columbus: Ohio State University Press, 1989. 162–85.

———. *Mappings: Feminism and the Cultural Geographies of Encounter*. Princeton: Princeton University Press, 1998.

———. "Spatialization, Narrative Theory, and Virginia Woolf's *The Voyage Out*." Mezei, 109–36.

Froula, Christine. "Rewriting Genesis: Gender and Culture in Twentieth-Century Texts." *Tulsa Studies in Women's Literature* 7.2 (1988): 197–220.

———. "War, Civilization, and the Conscience of Modernity: Views from *Jacob's Room*." *Virginia Woolf Texts and Contexts: Selected Papers from the Fifth Annual Virginia Woolf Conference*. Ed. Eileen Barrett and Beth Rigel Daugherty. New York: Pace University Press, 1996. 280–95.

Fry, Roger. *The Artist and Psycho-analysis. A Roger Fry Reader*. Ed. Christopher Reed. Chicago: University of Chicago Press, 1996. 351–65.

———. "The Artist's Vision." *Vision and Design*. New York: Oxford University Press, 1981. 33–38.

———. "An Essay in Aesthetics." *Vision and Design*. New York: Oxford University Press, 1981. 12–27.

———. *The Letters of Roger Fry*. Ed. Denys Sutton. London: Chatto and Windus, 1972.

———. "Post Impressionism." *A Roger Fry Reader*. Ed. Christopher Reed. Chicago: University of Chicago Press, 1996. 99–110.

———. "The Post-Impressionists." *A Roger Fry Reader*. Ed. Christopher Reed. Chicago: University of Chicago Press, 1996. 81–85.

———. *Vision and Design*. New York: Oxford University Press, 1981.

Gillespie, Diane F., ed. *The Multiple Muses of Virginia Woolf*. Columbia, MO: University of Missouri Press, 1993.

———. *The Sisters' Arts: The Writing and Painting of Virginia Woolf and Vanessa Bell*. New York: Syracuse University Press, 1988.

Glendinning, Victoria. *Vita: A Biography of Vita Sackville-West*. New York: Alfred A. Knopf, 1983.

Gordon, Lyndall. *Virginia Woolf: A Writer's Life*. Oxford: Oxford University Press, 1986.

Graham, John W. "The Drafts of Virginia Woolf's 'The Searchlight.'" *Twentieth Century Literature* 22 (December 1976): 379–93.

Guiguet, Jean. *Virginia Woolf and Her Works*. Trans. Jean Stewart. London: Hogarth, 1965.

———. *Virginia Woolf and Her Works*. Trans. Jean Stewart. New York: Harcourt/Harvest, 1976.

Gullason, Thomas A. "The Short Story: An Underrated Art." May, *Short Story Theories* 13–31.

Hafley, James. "On One of Virginia Woolf's Short Stories." *Modern Fiction Studies* 2 (1956): 13–16.

Handley, William. "War and the Politics of Narration in *Jacob's Room*." *Virginia Woolf and War: Fiction, Reality, and Myth*. Ed. Mark Hussey. New York: Syracuse University Press, 1991. 110–33.

Hankins, Leslie Kathleen. "Virginia Woolf and Walter Benjamin Selling Out(Siders)." Caughie, *Virginia Woolf in the Age* 3–36.

Hanson, Clare, ed. *Re-reading the Short Story*. New York: St. Martin's Press, 1989.

———. *Short Stories and Short Fictions*, 1880–1980. London: Macmillan, 1985.

———. "'Things Out of Words': Towards a Poetics of Short Fiction." Hanson, *Re-reading the Short Story* 22–33.

Hardy, Sarah. "The Short Story: Approaches to the Problem." *Style* 27 (1993): 325–26.

Hardy, Thomas. *Collected Poems of Thomas Hardy*. London: Macmillan, 1970.

Harris, Wendell V. "Vision and Form: The English Novel and the Emergence of the Story." May, *New Short Story Theories* 181–91.

Haule, James M. "'Le Temps passe' and the Original Typescript: an Early Version of the 'Time Passes' Section of *To the Lighthouse*." *Twentieth Century Literature* 29 (1983): 267–311.

———. "*To The Lighthouse* and the Great War: The Evidence of Virginia Woolf's Revisions of 'Time Passes'." *Virginia Woolf and War: Fiction, Reality and Myth*. Ed. Mark Hussey. Syracuse: Syracuse University Press, 1991. 164–71.

Head, Dominic. *The Modernist Short Story: A Study in Theory and Practice*. Cambridge: Cambridge University Press, 1992.

Henry, Holly. *Virginia Woolf and the Discourse of Science: The Aesthetics of Astronomy*. Cambridge: Cambridge University Press, 2003.

Hildick, Wallace. *Word for Word*. London: Faber, 1965.

Hoffman, Michael J. and Patrick D. Murphy, eds. *Essentials of the Theory of Fiction*. 2nd Edition. Durham: Duke University Press, 1996.

Hoffmann, Charles G. "Fact and Fantasy in *Orlando*: Virginia Woolf's Manuscript Revisions of *The Years*." *PMLA* 84 (1969): 435–44.

———. "From Lunch to Dinner: Virginia Woolf's Apprenticeship." *Texas Studies in Literature and Language* 10 (1969): 609–27.

———. "From Short Story to Novel: The Manuscript Revisions of Virginia Woolf's *Mrs. Dalloway*." *Modern Fiction Studies* 14.2 (1968): 171–86.

———. "Virginia Woolf's Manuscript Revisions of *The Years*." *PMLA* 84 (1969): 78–89.

Hulcoop, John F. "McNichol's Mrs. Dalloway: Second Thoughts." *Virginia Woolf Miscellany* 3 (Spring 1975): 3–4, 7.

Humm, Maggie. "Visual Modernism: Virginia Woolf's 'Portraits' and Photography." *Woolf Studies Annual* 8. New York: Pace University Press, 2002. 93–106.

Hussey, Mark. "How Should One Read a Screen?" Caughie, *Virginia Woolf in the Age* 249–65.

Hussey, Mark and Vara Neverow-Turk, eds. *Virginia Woolf Miscellanies: Proceedings from the First Annual Conference on Virginia Woolf.* New York: Pace University Press, 1992.

Huyssen, Andreas. *After the Great Divide: Modernism, Mass Culture, Postmodernism.* Bloomington: Indiana University Press, 1986.

James, Henry. *Novels and Tales of Henry James.* New York Edition, Vol. X. New York: Scribner's, 1908.

———. *The Portrait of a Lady.* Ed. Geoffrey Moore. London: Penguin, 1984.

Jouve, Nicole Ward. "Too Short for a Book?" Hanson, *Re-reading the Short Story* 34–44.

Kaplan, Carla. *The Erotics of Talk: Women's Writing and Feminist Paradigms.* New York and London: Oxford University Press, 1996.

Kemp, Sandra. Introduction. *Selected Short Stories: Virginia Woolf.* Ed. Sandra Kemp. London: Penguin, 1993. ix–xxxii.

Kirkpatrick, B. J. and Stuart N. Clarke. *A Bibliography of Virginia Woolf.* 4th Edition. Oxford: Clarendon Press, 1997.

Kurtz, Marilyn. *Virginia Woolf: Reflections and Reverberations.* New York: Peter Lang, 1990.

Lackey, Michael. "Woolf and the Necessity of Atheism." *Virginia Woolf Miscellany* 53 (Spring 1999): 3.

Lanser, Susan Sniader. *Fictions of Authority: Women Writers and Narrative Voice.* Ithaca and London: Cornell University Press, 1992.

Lassner, Phyllis. " 'The Milk of Our Mother's Kindness Has Ceased to Flow': Virginia Woolf, Stevie Smith and the Representation of the Jew." *Between Race and Culture: Representations of "the Jew" in English and American Literature.* Ed. Bryan Cheyette. Stanford: Stanford University Press, 1996. 129–44.

Laurence, Patricia. *Lily Briscoe's Chinese Eyes: Bloomsbury, Modernism, and China.* Columbia: University of South Carolina Press, 2003.

Lawrence, Karen. "Gender and Narrative Voice in *Jacob's Room* and *Portrait of the Artist as a Young Man.*" *James Joyce: The Centennial Celebration.* Ed. Morris Beja et al. Chicago: University of Chicago Press, 1986. 31–38.

Ledger, Sally. *The New Woman: Fiction and Feminism at the Fin-de-Siecle.* Manchester: Manchester University Press, 1997.

Lee, Hermione. "*To the Lighthouse*: Introduction." *Virginia Woolf: Introductions to the Major Works.* Ed. Julia Briggs. London: Virago, 1994. 157–86.

———. *Virginia Woolf.* London: Chatto and Windus, 1996.

Lessing, Doris. "Foreword." *Carlyle's House and Other Sketches.* Ed. David Bradshaw. London: Hesperus Press Limited, 2003. vii–xii.

Levenbach, Karen L. *Virginia Woolf and the Great War.* Syracuse, New York: Syracuse University Press, 1999.

Levy, Heather. " 'Julia Kissed Her. Julia Possessed Her': Considering Class and Lesbian Desire in Virginia Woolf's Shorter Fiction." Hussey and Neverow, 83–90.

Lilienfeld, Jane. "Mastering the Mind: Voice in Virginia Woolf's Short Fiction." Discovering Virginia Woolf's Short Fiction. M/MLA Convention. Regal Riverfront Hotel, St. Louis. November 5, 1998.

Little, Judy. "Feminizing the Subject: Dialogic Narration in *Jacob's Room*." *Literary Interpretation Theory* 3:4 (1992): 241–51.

Lohafer, Susan. *Coming to Terms with the Short Story*. Baton Rouge: Louisiana State University Press, 1983.

———. "Introduction." Lounsberry et al., *The Tales We Tell*, ix–xii.

———. "Introduction to Part I." Lohafer and Clarey, 3–12.

———. "Introduction to Part III." Lohafer and Clarey, 109–14.

———. "Introduction to Part IV." Lohafer and Clarey, 171–75.

Lohafer, Susan and Jo Ellyn Clarey, eds. *Short Story Theory at a Crossroads*. Baton Rouge: Louisiana State University Press, 1989.

Lounsberry, Barbara and Susan Lohafer, Mary Rohrberger, Stephen Pett, and R. C. Feddersen, eds. *The Tales We Tell: Perspectives on the Short Story*. Westport, CT: Greenwood, 1998.

Luscher, Robert M. "The Short Story Sequence: An Open Book." Hoffman and Murphy, 148–67.

MacCarthy, Desmond. *Manet and the Post-Impressionists*. London: Ballantyne, 1910. Exhibition Catalog.

Majumdar, Robin and Allen McLaurin, eds. *Virginia Woolf: The Critical Heritage*. London and New York: Garland, 1997.

Mansfield, Katherine. *The Selected Letters of Katherine Mansfield*. Vols. 1–4. Ed. Vincent O'Sullivan and Margaret Scott. Oxford: Clarendon, 1984–94.

———. "A Short Story." In *Novels and Novelists*. Ed. John Middleton Murry. London: Constable, 1930. 36–38.

Mao, Douglas. *Solid Objects: Modernism and the Test of Production*. Princeton: Princeton University Press, 1998.

Marcus, Jane, ed. *New Feminist Essays on Virginia Woolf*. Lincoln: University of Nebraska Press, 1981.

———. *Virginia Woolf and the Languages of Patriarchy*. Bloomington: Indiana University Press, 1987.

Marcus, Laura. *Autobiographical Discourses*. Manchester: Manchester University Press, 1994.

Marder, Herbert. *Feminism and Art: A Study of Virginia Woolf*. Chicago: University of Chicago Press, 1968.

Matthews, Brander. "The Philosophy of the Short-Story." May, *New* 73–80.

May, Charles E. "Chekhov and the Modern Short Story." *The New Short Story Theories*. Ed. Charles E. May. Athens: Ohio University Press, 1994. 199–217.

———, ed. *The New Short Story Theories*. Athens: Ohio University Press, 1994.

———. "Reality in the Modern Short Story." *Style* 27.3 (Fall 1993): 369–380.

———. *The Short Story: The Reality of Artifice*. New York, Twayne, 1995.

———. *Short Story Theories*. Athens: Ohio University Press, 1976.

McLaughlin, Ann L. "An Uneasy Sisterhood: Virginia Woolf and Katherine Mansfield." *Virginia Woolf: A Feminist Slant*. Ed. Jane Marcus. Lincoln: University of Nebraska Press, 1983. 152–61.

McNees, Eleanor, ed. *Virginia Woolf: Critical Assessments*. Vols. 1–4. Sussex: Helm Information, 1994.

McNichol, Stella. "A Reply." *Virginia Woolf Miscellany* 9 (Winter 1977): 3.

Mepham, James. *Virginia Woolf*. London: Bristol Classical Press, 1992.

Meyerowitz, Selma. "What Is to Console Us? The Politics of Deception in Woolf's Short Stories." Marcus, *New Feminist* 238–52.

Mezei, Kathy, ed. *Ambiguous Discourse: Feminist Narratology and British Women Writers*. Chapel Hill and London: The University of North Carolina Press, 1996.

Miller, C. Ruth. *Virginia Woolf: The Frames of Art and Life*. London: Macmillan, 1988.

Miller, Jane Eldridge. *Rebel Women: Feminism, Modernism and the Edwardian Novel*. London: Virago, 1994.

Minow-Pinkney, Makiko. "Virginia Woolf and the Age of Motor Cars." Caughie 159–82.

Munt, Sally, Introduction. *New Lesbian Criticism: Literary and Cultural Readings*. Ed. Sally Munt. New York: Columbia University Press, ix–xxii.

Naylor, Gillian, ed. *Bloomsbury: The Artists, Authors and Designers by Themselves*. London: Pyramid, 1990.

Neverow-Turk, Vara and Mark Hussey, eds. *Virginia Woolf: Themes and Variations*. New York: Pace University Press, 1993.

North, Michael. *The Dialect of Modernism: Race, Language, and Twentieth-Century Literature*. New York: Oxford University Press, 1994.

Oakland, John. "Virginia Woolf's Kew Gardens." *English Studies: A Journal of English Language and Literature* 68 (1987): 264–73.

O'Connor, Frank. *The Lonely Voice: A Study of the Short Story*. 1963. rpt. New York: Harper, 1985.

Olano, Pamela. "'Women Alone Stir My Imagination': Reading Virginia Woolf as a Lesbian." Neverow-Turk and Hussey, 158–70.

Pasco, Allan H. "On Defining Short Stories." May, *New* 114–30.

Peach, Linden. *Virginia Woolf*. London: Macmillan, 2000.

Pearce, Susan. *Museums, Objects, and Collections: A Cultural Study*. Washington, D.C.: Smithsonian Institution Press, 1992.

Phelan, James. *Reading People; Reading Plots: Character, Progression, and the Interpretation of Narrative*. Chicago: University of Chicago Press, 1989.

Poovey, Mary. *Uneven Developments: The Ideological Work of Gender in Mid-Victorian England*. Chicago: University of Chicago Press, 1988.

Prince, Gerald. "The Long and Short of It." *Style* 27 (1993): 327–31.

Rabinowitz, Peter. *Before Reading: Narrative Conventions and the Politics of Interpretation*. Ithaca: Cornell University Press, 1987.

Radin, Grace. *Virginia Woolf's "The Years": The Evolution of a Novel*. Knoxville: University of Tennessee Press, 1981.

Raitt, Suzanne. "Fakes and Femininity: Vita Sackville-West and her Mother." *New Feminist Discourses*. Ed. Isobel Armstrong. London: Routledge, 1992. 113–18.

Rappaport, Erika Diane. *Shopping for Pleasure: Women in the Making of London's West End*. Princeton: Princeton University Press, 2000.

Reed, Christopher, ed. *A Roger Fry Reader*. Chicago: University of Chicago Press, 1996.

Reid, Ian. *The Short Story*. London: Methuen, 1977.

———. "Destabilizing Frames for Story." Lohafer and Clancy, 299–310.

Reid, Panthea. *Art and Affection: A Life of Virginia Woolf*. New York: Oxford University Press, 1996.

Rice, Thomas Jackson. *Virginia Woolf: A Guide to Research*. New York and London: Garland, 1984.

Rich, Adrienne. "Compulsory Heterosexuality and Lesbian Existence." *Adrienne Rich's Complete Poetry and Prose*. Ed. Barbara Charlesworth Gelpi and Albert Gelpi. New York: Norton, 1993. 203–24.

Richards, Thomas. *The Commodity Culture of Victorian England: Advertising and Spectacle* 1851–1914. Stanford: Stanford University Press, 1990.

Richter, Harvena. *Virginia Woolf: The Inward Voyage*. Princeton: Princeton University Press, 1970.

Roe, Sue and Susan Sellers, eds. *The Cambridge Companion to Virginia Woolf*. Cambridge: Cambridge University Press, 2000.

Roof, Judith. "The Match in the Crocus: Representations of Lesbian Sexuality." *Discontented Discourses: Feminism/Textual Intervention/Psychoanalysis*. Ed. Marleen S. Barr and Richard Feldstein. Urbana: University of Illinois Press, 1989. 100–16.

Rosenbaum, S. P. "The Philosophical Realism of Virginia Woolf." *English Literature and British Philosophy: A Collection of Essays*. Chicago: University of Chicago Press, 1971. 316–56.

Rosenberg, Beth Carole. *Virginia Woolf and Samuel Johnson: Common Readers*. London: Macmillan, 1995.

Sanders, Valerie. "'Fathers' Daughters: Three Victorian Anti-Feminist Autobiographers." *Mortal Pages, Literary Lives*. Ed. Vincent Newey and Philip Shaw. London: Scolar Press, 1996. 153–71.

Seeley, Tracy. "Virginia Woolf's Poetics of Space: 'The Lady in the Looking-Glass: A Reflection.'" *Woolf Studies Annual* 2 (1996): 89–116.

Seger, Bob. "Against the Wind." Bob Seger & the Silver Bullet Band. *Nine Tonight*. Rec. 19 June 1980. LP. Capitol, 1981.

Shaw, Valerie. *The Short Story: A Critical Introduction*. London and New York: Longmans, 1993.

Showalter, Elaine. Introduction. *Mrs Dalloway*. By Virginia Woolf. London: Penguin, 1992. xi–xlviii.

Silver, Brenda. "Textual Criticism as Feminist Practice: Or, Who's Afraid of Virginia Woolf Part II." In *Representing Modernist Texts: Editing as Interpretation*. Ed. George Bornstein. Ann Arbor: University of Michigan Press, 1991. 192–222.

Smith, Angela. *Katherine Mansfield and Virginia Woolf: A Public of Two*. Oxford: Clarendon Press, 1999.

Squier, Susan. *Virginia Woolf and London: The Sexual Politics of the City*. Chapel Hill: University of North Carolina Press, 1985.

Staveley, Alice. "'Kew will do': Cultivating Fictions of Kew Gardens." *Virginia Woolf and the Arts: Selected Papers from the Sixth Annual Conference on Virginia Woolf*. Ed. Diane F. Gillespie and Leslie K. Hankins. New York: Pace University Press, 1997. 57–66.

———. "Voicing Virginia: The *Monday or Tuesday* Years." *Virginia Woolf: Texts and Contexts: Selected Papers from the Fifth Annual Conference on Virginia Woolf.* Ed. Beth Rigel Daugherty and Eileen Barrett. New York: Pace University Press, 1996. 262–67.

Stevick, Philip, ed. *Anti-Story.* New York: Free Press, 1971.

Stewart, Susan. *On Longing: Narratives of the Miniature, the Gigantic, the Souvenir, the Collection.* Durham: Duke University Press, 1993.

Stimpson, Catherine. *Where the Meanings Are: Feminism and Cultural Space.* 1981. New York: Routledge, 1988.

Strachey, Lytton. *Eminent Victorians.* 1918. New York: Harcourt, Brace, Jovanovich, nd.

Stone, Wilfred. *The Short Story: An Introduction.* Second edition. New York: McGraw-Hill, 1983.

Tratner, Michael. *Deficits and Desires: Economics and Sexuality in Twentieth-Century Literature.* Stanford: Stanford University Press, 2001.

Tremper, Ellen. *"Who Lived at Alfoxton?": Virginia Woolf and English Romanticism.* Lewisburg: Bucknell University Press, 1998.

VanStavern, Jan. "Excavating the Domestic Front in 'Phyllis and Rosamond' and 'The Journal of Mistress Joan Martyn.' " *Virginia Woolf: Emerging Perspectives. Selected Papers from the Third Annual Conference on Virginia Woolf.* Ed. Mark Hussey and Vara Neverow. New York: Pace University Press, 1994. 252–59.

Warhol, Robyn R. "Guilty Cravings: What Feminist Narratology Can Do for Cultural Studies." *Narratologies: New Perspective on Narrative Analysis.* Ed. David Herman. Columbus: Ohio University Press, 1999. 340–55.

Watson, Robert A. " 'Solid Objects' as Allegory." Baldwin 117–21.

Wicke, Jennifer. *Advertising Fictions: Literature, Advertisements, and Social Reading.* New York: Columbia University Press, 1988.

———. "Mrs. Dalloway Goes to Market: Woolf, Keynes, and Modern Markets." *Novel* 28 (Fall 1994): 5–23.

Willis, J.H., Jr. *Leonard and Virginia Woolf as Publishers: The Hogarth Press, 1917–41.* Charlottesville: University of Virginia Press, 1992.

Winchester, Simon. *Krakatoa.* New York: HarperCollins Publishers, 2003.

Winston, Janet. "Reading Influences: Homoeroticism and Mentoring in Katherine Mansfield's 'Carnation' and Virginia Woolf's 'Moments of Being: "Slater's Pins Have No Points".' " Barrett and Cramer, *Lesbian Readings* 57–77.

Wolff, Janet. *Feminine Sentences: Essays on Women and Culture.* Berkeley: University of California Press, 1991.

Woolf, Leonard. *An Autobiography.* 2 vols. Oxford: Oxford University Press, 1980.

———. *Downhill All the Way: An Autobiography of the Years 1911–1918.* New York: Harcourt Brace Jovanovich, 1967.

———. *Three Jews.* London: Hogarth Press, 1917; rpt. *Virginia Woolf Bulletin* 5 (September 2000).

———. *The Wise Virgins.* 1914. New York: Harcourt Brace Jovanovich, 1979.

Woolf, Virginia. *Between the Acts.* Ed. Susan Dick and Mary S. Millar. Oxford: Blackwell, 2002.

Woolf, Virginia. *Between the Acts*. San Diego: Harcourt/Harvest, 1941.

———. *Between The Acts*. Oxford: Oxford University Press, 1992.

———. *Books and Portraits*. Ed. Mary Lyon, New York: Harcourt Brace Jovanovich, 1977.

———. *Carlyle's House and Other Sketches*. Ed. David Bradshaw. London: Hesperus Press Limited, 2003.

———. *Collected Essays*. Ed. Leonard Woolf. London: Hogarth Press, 1967; 1996.

———. *The Complete Shorter Fiction of Virginia Woolf.* Ed. Susan Dick. New York: Harcourt Brace & Co, 1989.

———. *The Complete Shorter Fiction of Virginia Woolf.* Ed. Susan Dick. London: The Hogarth Press, 1989.

———. *The Common Reader, First Series*. 1925. London: Hogarth Press, 1975.

———. *The Death of the Moth*. London: Hogarth Press, 1942.

———. *The Death of the Moth and Other Essays*. 1942. New York: Harcourt Brace Jovanovich, 1970.

———. *The Diary of Virginia Woolf.* 5 vols. Ed. Anne Olivier Bell and Andrew McNeillie. New York: Harcourt Brace Jovanovich, 1977–84.

———. *The Essays of Virginia Woolf.* Vols. 1–4. Ed. Andrew McNeillie. London: Hogarth, 1986–94.

———. *The Essays of Virginia Woolf.* Vols. 1–3. Ed. Andrew McNeillie. New York: Harcourt Brace Jovanovich, 1986–88.

———. *Flush: A Biography*. Oxford: Oxford University Press, 1998.

———. "Friendship's Gallery." Ed. Ellen Hawkes. *Twentieth Century Literature* 25 (1979): 275–302.

———. *Granite and Rainbow: Essays*. New York: Harcourt Brace & Company, 1958.

———. *A Haunted House and Other Short Stories*. Ed. Leonard Woolf. London: Hogarth Press, 1944.

———. *A Haunted House and Other Short Stories*. New York: Harcourt Brace, 1949.

———. *A Haunted House and Other Short Stories*. 1944. Ed. Leonard Woolf. New York: Harcourt/Harvest, 1972.

———. *"The Hours": The British Museum Manuscript of* Mrs. Dalloway. Ed. Helen M. Wussow. New York: Pace University Press, 1996.

———. *Jacob's Room*. Ed. Edward L. Bishop. Oxford: Blackwell, 2004.

———. *Kew Gardens*. London: Hogarth, 1927.

———. *The Letters of Virginia Woolf.* 6 vols. Ed. Nigel Nicolson and Joanne Trautmann. New York: Harcourt Brace Jovanovich, 1975–80.

———. *The London Scene: Five Essays by Virginia Woolf.* London: Hogarth, 1982.

———. MAJOR AUTHORS on CD-ROM. Ed. Mark Hussey. Woodbridge, CT: Primary Source Media, 1997.

———. *Melymbrosia: An Early Version of "The Voyage Out."* Ed. Louise DeSalvo. New York: New York Public Library, 1982.

———. "Memories of a Working Women's Guild" (Introductory Letter). *Life as We Have Know It*. Ed. Margaret Llewellyn Davies. London: Hogarth, 1993. xv–xxxix.

———. *Moments of Being*. New York: Harcourt Brace Jovanovich, 1976.

———. *Moments of Being*. Ed. Jeanne Schulkind. London: Hogarth Press, 1985.

————. *Moments of Being.* Ed. Jeanne Schulkind. Introduced and revised by Hermione Lee. London: Pimlico, 2002.

————. *Monday or Tuesday.* London: Hogarth Press, 1921.

————. Monks House Papers. University of Sussex Library.

————. *Mrs. Dalloway.* 1925. London: Penguin, 1992.

————. *Mrs. Dalloway.* 1925. New York: HBJ/Harvest, 1990.

————. "Mrs Dalloway in Bond Street." Unpublished holograph, M106 19 in the Berg Collection.

————. *Mrs. Dalloway's Party: A Short Story Sequence.* Ed. Stella McNichol. London: Hogarth, 1973.

————. *The Mrs. Dalloway Reader.* Ed. Francine Prose. Orlando: Harcourt, 2003.

————. *Night and Day.* Ed. J. H. Stape. Oxford: Blackwell 1994.

————. *Nurse Lugton's Golden Thimble.* Illustrated by Duncan Grant. London: Hogarth Press, 1966.

————. "On Not Knowing Greek." *The Common Reader, First Series.* New York: Harcourt Brace Jovanovich, 1925. 24–39.

————. *Orlando: A Biography.* New York: Harcourt Brace Jovanovich, 1928.

————. *Orlando.* Ed. J. H. Stape. Oxford: Blackwell, 1998.

————. *The Pargiters: The Novel-Essay Portion of "The Years."* Ed. Mitchell A. Leaska. New York: Harcourt/Harvest, 1978.

————. *The Pargiters: The Novel-Essay Portion of "The Years."* Ed. Mitchell A. Leaska London: Hogarth, 1978.

————. *A Passionate Apprentice: The Early Journals, 1897–1909.* Ed. Mitchell A. Leaska. New York: Harcourt Brace Jovanovich, 1990.

————. *A Passionate Apprentice.* Ed. Mitchell Leaska. Toronto: Lester & Orpen Dennys, 1990.

————. [Phyllis and Rosamond] holograph. MH23. Monks House Papers. University of Sussex. Sussex, England.

————. *Pointz Hall: The Earlier and Later Typescripts of "Between the Acts."* Ed. Mitchell A. Leaska. New York: University Publications, 1983.

————. *Roger Fry: A Biography.* London: The Hogarth Press, 1940.

————. *Roger Fry: A Biography.* 1940. New York: Harcourt Brace Jovanovich, 1976.

————. A *Room of One's Own and Three Guineas.* London: Penguin, 1993.

————. A *Room of One's Own and Three Guineas.* Oxford: Oxford University Press, 1992.

————. *To the Lighthouse.* 1927. London: Penguin, 1992.

————. *To The Lighthouse.* 1927. Oxford: Oxford University Press, 1992.

————. *To the Lighthouse.* 1927. Foreword by Eudora Welty. New York: HBJ/Harvest, 1989.

————. *To the Lighthouse: The Original Holograph Draft.* Ed. Susan Dick. Toronto: University of Toronto Press, 1982.

————. Unpublished letters. Hogarth Press Archives, folder 569. Reading University Library. Reading University, England.

————. *The Virginia Woolf Manuscripts: From the Henry W. and Albert A. Berg Collection at The New York Public Library.* Microfilm. 21 reels. Woodbridge, CT: Research Publications, 1993.

Woolf, Virginia. *The Virginia Woolf Manuscripts: From the Monks House Papers at the University of Sussex and Additional Manuscripts at the British Library, London.* Microfilm. 6 reels. Brighton, Sussex (UK): Harvester Press Microform, 1985.

———. *Virginia Woolf's* Jacob's Room: *The Holograph Draft.* Ed. Edward L. Bishop. New York: Pace University Press, 1998.

———. *The Voyage Out.* New York: Harcourt Brace Jovanovich, 1920.

———. *The Voyage Out.* 1915. Oxford: Oxford University Press, 1992.

———. *The Waves.* New York: Harcourt Brace Jovanovich, 1931.

———. *The Waves.* 1931. Oxford: Oxford University Press, 1992.

———. *The Waves: The Two Holograph Drafts.* Ed. John W. Graham. Toronto: University of Toronto Press, 1976.

———. *The Widow and the Parrot* 1982. Illustrated by Julian Bell. Afterword by Quentin Bell. New York: Harcourt Brace, 1988.

———. *Women & Fiction, The Manuscript Versions of* A Room of One's Own. Ed. S. P. Rosenbaum. London: Shakespeare Head Press, 1992.

Wordsworth, William. *The Fenwick Notes of William Wordsworth.* Ed. Jared Curtis. London: Bristol Classical Press, 1993.

———. *The Prelude. The Major Works.* Oxford: Oxford University Press, 2000.

Wright, Austin M. "On Defining the Short Story: The Genre Question." Lohafer and Clarey, 46–53.

Wussow, Helen M. Introduction. *"The Hours": The British Museum Manuscript of Mrs. Dalloway.* By Virginia Woolf. Transcribed and edited by Helen M. Wussow. New York: Pace University Press, 1996. ix–xxx.

Zwerdling, Alex. *Virginia Woolf and the Real World.* Berkeley: University of California Press, 1986.

Index

poetry, 22, 62 n. 14, 150, 152,
    157–60, 163, 173 n. 3, 176
  as opposed to prose, 152
  Romantic, 153
  see also lyricism
  see also Woolf, Virginia, "lyrical"
    stories
point of view, 7, 22, 38, 74, 88, 105,
    111, 117–18, 144–5, 149, 151,
    164, 167, 172, 180–1
  see also narration
  see also narrative
  see also perspective
politics, 13, 13 n. 3, 18, 26, 40, 47,
    52, 58–9, 62 n. 13, 85–7, 92,
    143–4, 179
Poovey, Mary, 40
popular fiction, 2, 44, 95, 146, 179, 184
  see also culture, mass
Post-Impressionism, 12, 93, 121 n. 2,
    161–5, 173 n. 9, 178
Pound, Ezra, 181
Prose, Francine, 123 n. 11
Proust, Marcel, 21
psychological concerns, 4, 18, 23,
    25–6, 28, 37, 66, 128, 151, 182

Rabinowitz, Peter, 173 n. 12
Radin, Grace, 122 n. 5
Raitt, Suzanne, 183
Rappaport, Erika Diane, 97 n. 10
reader, the, xx, 1, 2, 5, 6–13, 21, 24,
    26–36, 41–9, 52, 58–9, 60 n. 7,
    62 n. 17, 63–80, 86–7, 90–1,
    95–6, 105–6, 108–9, 111, 113,
    117–19, 122 n. 5, 122 n. 11,
    128, 130–1, 133, 136, 146,
    148, 151, 155 n. 12, 158–9,
    163–72, 173 n. 10, 173 n. 11,
    173 n. 12, 182
  see also Woolf, Virginia, reception of
    Woolf's work
reality, xvi, 6, 8, 11–12, 17–20, 22,
    24, 26–7, 34, 37, 46–7, 51, 68,

    70, 116, 140–1, 143, 162,
    170, 176
Reid, Ian, 64, 138 n. 2
Reid, Panthea, 85, 173 n. 9
Reiman, Donald, 103
religion, 18, 26, 31–2, 79, 97 n. 7,
    137, 182
  see also myth
Renoir, Auguste, 162
Resnais, Alain
  Last Year at Marienbad, 22
revision, 2, 131
  see also manuscripts
  see also Woolf, Virginia, drafts
  see also Woolf, Virginia, holograph
    manuscripts
  see also Woolf, Virginia, and revision
  see also Woolf, Virginia, typescripts
rhetoric, 37, 41, 43, 48, 50–1, 56–8,
    60 n. 9, 97 n. 3, 173 n. 10
Rhone River, 21
rhythm, 22, 43, 67, 73, 161, 176
  iambic, 21
Rice, Thomas Jackson, 60 n. 5
Rich, Adrienne, 10, 69
  and "compulsory heterosexuality," 10
Richards, Thomas, 81
Richardson, Dorothy, 3
Richmond, 58
Richter, Harvena, 13 n. 1
Rodmell Women's Institute, 180
Roe, Sue, 121 n. 2
Romanticism, xii, 4, 30, 57, 67,
    153, 188
Roof, Judith, 79
Rosenbaum, S. P., 140–1, 153 n. 1
Rosenberg, Beth Carole, 173 n. 10
Rossetti, Christina, 127
Rossetti, Dante Gabriel, 61 n. 10,
    173 n. 6
Rousseau, Jean-Jacques, 129
Royal Botanic Gardens, 50
Royal Navy, 180
Ruskin, John, 127

works—*continued*
House and Other Short Stories, xx,
105, 121 n. 4, 123 n. 11; "Heard
on the Downs: the Genesis
Myth," 57; *The Hours*, 111; "How
Should One Read a Book?," 6;
"Impassioned Prose," 158; "In the
Orchard," xvii, 11, 145–7; "The
Introduction," 8, 20, 23, 105–16,
122 n. 4, 122 n. 10, 123 n. 30,
11, 123 n. 13 *Jacob's Room*, xvii,
9, 39–40, 43, 53, 59 n. 1, 112,
125 n. 15, 177, 180, 186; "The
Journal of Mistress Joan Martyn,"
11, 126, 130–6; *Kew Gardens*, 1;
"Kew Gardens," xvi, 3, 4, 9,
11–12, 13 n. 2, 21–2, 38, 39–62,
62 n. 14, 67, 75–8, 80 n. 4,
126–7, 145–7, 157; "The Lady in
the Looking-Glass: A Reflection,"
xviii, 9–10, 12, 22, 25, 33–6, 84,
88–91, 121 n. 3, 176–8, 189;
"Laetitia Pilkington," 136;
"Lappin and Lapinova," xix,
20–1, 148, 150–1, 175; "The
Leaning Tower," 1; "The
Legacy,"xix, xx, 69, 71–2; *The
Letters of Virginia Woolf*, xv–xx, 3,
41, 44, 54, 56, 63, 74–5, 78, 95,
102–3, 112–14, 126, 128–9,
133, 135, 160; "Life and the
Novelist," 95; "Life on a
Battleship," xix, 12; "Lives of the
Obscure," 136; "The London
Docks," 97 n. 3; "London in
War," 141; *The London Scene*, 97
n. 3; "The Man Who Loved His
Kind," 74, 105–8, 110, 113,
115–16, 122 n. 4, 123 n. 11, 123
n. 13; "The Mark on the Wall,"
xx n. 1, 3, 11, 19–20, 38, 58, 60
n. 5, 60 n. 8, 90, 95, 112, 124
n. 15, 126, 140–6, 153, 154 n. 3,
157, 177; "Memoirs of a

Novelist," xv, xvi, 3, 11, 12, 41,
47–8, 60 n. 4, 68–9, 126, 135,
136–7, 138 n. 8; "Modern
Fiction," 2, 5, 12, 146, 162; "The
Modern Novel," 31; "Modern
Novels," 31; *Moments of Being*, xx
n. 2, 59 n. 4, 138 n. 5, 144, 172,
176, 184, 188, 191 n. 7;
"Moments of Being," xviii, xx, 10
17, 21, 38, 63, 76, 78; *Monday or
Tuesday*, xvi, xvii, xx, 1, 12, 38–9,
112, 122 n. 11 158–9, 163–5,
173 n. 2, 174 n. 14, 175;
"Monday or Tuesday," xvi, 8, 11,
12, 18, 21–2, 157, 164–5, 168,
171–2, 174 n. 14; Monks House
Papers, 126, 154 n. 4; "Mr.
Bennett and Mrs. Brown," xi, 2,
186; *Mrs. Dalloway*, xvii, 10, 65,
73, 75, 78–9, 82, 84, 91–5, 98
n. 11, 101, 103–19, 122 n. 4,
122 n. 7, 123 n. 11, 123 n. 12,
124 n. 16, 175; "Mrs Dalloway in
Bond Street," xvii, 10, 12, 72, 83,
84, 91–3, 123 n. 11, 124 n. 15,
175; *Mrs. Dalloway's Party*, 38,
121 n. 4, 123 n. 11; *The
Mrs. Dalloway Reader*, 123 n. 11;
"The Mysterious Case of
Miss V.," 66–8, 77; "The Narrow
Bridge of Art," 147, 152, 172;
"The New Biography," 128,
136–8; "The New Dress," xvii,
xviii, 105–13, 116, 122 n. 4, 122
n. 10, 123 n. 11, 123 n. 12, 123
n. 13; *Night and Day*, xv, xvi, 39,
112; "Notes for Stories & c.,"
104, 106, 118, 122 n. 6; "Notes
for Writing," 104; "Nurse
Lugton's Curtain," 11, 148–9,
151; "On Not Knowing Greek,"
158, 173 n. 2; "On Re-Reading
Novels," 157, 164; *Orlando*, xviii,
75, 129, 138 n. 3, 138 n. 8, 173